LOVE Y♡U Now

NEW YORK TIMES BESTSELLING AUTHOR

JULIA KENT

Editors: Elisa Reed, Maria Connor

Cover design: Qamber Designs

Love You Now

by Julia Kent

Ana DaSilva is looking for a palate cleanser. A one-night stand. A reboot.

Instead, she gets fireworks, sparks, chemistry, and the perfect guy. No one wants to meet Mr. Right when he should just be Mr. Rebound, but this Mr. Right is just so *right*.

Until he goes from Mr. Right to Mr. Never, because when she learns she's pregnant three days after that wonderful night with Dennis, she realizes her sleazy drug-dealing ex not only left her with the legal mess she knew about, he gave her a life-long present.

One that means ignoring Dennis's texts and phone calls, no matter how much she wants to answer.

Dennis Luview wants to escape his pain. Coming back to his hometown of Luview, Maine–the cheesy tourist trap where every day is Valentine's Day–means facing a past he left behind twenty-four years ago. Yes, his family is loving, and sure, he has deep roots in the small-town community where people step up for each other.

But the naïve eighteen-year-old who left to serve his country is now a retired special ops vet with a heavy entourage of ghosts and PTSD. No woman deserves all the baggage he's lugging around.

Including Ana, who clearly wants nothing to do with him, no matter how intense their one haunting encounter really was.

It's one thing to have ghosts and quite another to be ghosted.

Which is why, six months after that hot night, he's stunned to run into her at a festival in his hometown, her ripe, pregnant belly swelling under her cotton dress.

A public confrontation turns into a very private reunion. As Dennis pursues Ana, she opens up, but is he crazy to want her—and what turns out to be another man's baby—to settle down and find stability and love?

Or is he deluding himself that the happiness an instant family could offer would heal the scars of the terrible past?

If you're looking for a secret(ish) baby, one-night stand, strangers-to-lovers romance set in a town where every day is Valentine's Day, featuring a veteran with PTSD who volunteers at an animal-rescue sanctuary and a therapist who keeps picking the wrong men (until now), then settle in with a cup of coffee and a maple bacon doughnut and catch up on the Love You, Maine series that features the Luview family.

One-night stand
    Strangers to lovers
    Secret(ish) baby
    ... and a sugar glider named Magic

Chapter One

Dennis

The kitten's plaintive cry stopped him dead in his tracks.

And made him groan.

Dennis Luview was a just-retired Special Forces fighting machine, an Army veteran who couldn't talk about his work even if he wanted to–and he *didn't* want to–but there was one defining weakness that cut through his elite combat skills, his experience in taking out terrorists, and his stone-cold soldier's mind:

Strays.

When the service door at the end of the hallway to the kitchen snicked shut, he realized the kitty must be outside, in the alley.

In January.

In Boston, Massachusetts, where the poor thing would be a frozen catsicle in no time flat.

Looking ahead, he teetered. The hotel's carpet had a dizzying pattern that forced him to stop in place, firmly plant his feet on the ground, and get his bearings. After thirteen straight hours of travel from Germany, he'd checked in at his hotel, taken a much-needed shower, shaved, and dressed in what he assumed passed for normal, informal, hotel-bar attire.

He was now a freshly minted civilian on his way to have a few drinks, cobble together dinner from bar food, do pretty much anything except–

Deal with a stray cat in distress.

"Haven't even had a single damn drink yet," he muttered, then pivoted to go down the hall. Garlic wafted through the air like a temptress, basil joining in to make his stomach growl.

He'd landed at Logan Airport too late to pick up the new truck he'd ordered and drive up to his hometown of Luview, "Love You", Maine–the tourist trap where every day was Valentine's Day. And it was just as well.

A man needed a night of transition before facing all that sickening happiness.

As he approached the hotel's exit, he was keenly aware of his surroundings, his back vulnerable to attack. A door to the left led to the kitchen, the one straight ahead letting in sour notes of dumpsters and furtively smoked cigarettes.

Dennis knew his way around an alley. Spent more than enough years working in them.

Pressing the door bar, he opened it and–

"Mew."

He froze. Blessed–or cursed–with extraordinary hearing, he knew he'd been right. The sound was too soft. Too weak.

But where was the kitten?

"Sweetie," said a woman's voice, muted as if she were buried under the mound of black trash bags that reeked to high heaven. "Come on. I have a special treat for you."

She spoke like she was talking to a preschooler.

His shoulders dropped.

Whew. Not a stray. Not his job.

"Come on, kitty. Let me help you. You look so lost."

Ugh. Yes, a stray.

Not your job, he chided himself. *Go away and leave it. Don't get tangled in someone else's mess.*

"*Pffft!*"

Standing on tiptoes, he looked across the top of the over-stuffed dumpster and saw the tiny tabby, faced away from him, giving quite the butthole show. The kitten was barely off mother's milk, so small that he could fit it in his shirt pocket.

"How did you get here?" the hidden woman asked the cat, as if it would answer. Her voice was tinny, with an echo that made Dennis stare harder.

Responsibility was Dennis's strong point and his greatest weakness. This mystery woman he couldn't see had the situation under control. No need to interfere. The cat would be fine; she obviously cared.

In fact, it was probably hers, and he'd just complicate things, so he should turn around and—

"I can't help you if you don't let me!" the woman said, her voice beginning to shake, as if she were about to cry. The sound of plastic being shuffled around filled the air, and it dawned on him that she must be *in* the dumpster. "I just want to feed you and make you warm and safe!"

Besides stray animals in need of rescue, there was one other thing Dennis couldn't handle.

And that was a crying woman.

Checking the ground, he found a small bucket full of sand and cigarette butts and used it to prop the heavy metal door open. Experience taught him that these big exterior doors often locked from the inside. No need to start his retirement from rescuing people being the *object* of a rescue.

There wasn't much of a moon tonight, but floodlights gave everything a gritty glare.

His jacket, an afterthought when he'd left his hotel room

to head down to the bar for dinner, was turning out to be a saving grace. Pulling his arms out of the sleeves, he readied it.

"What's your cat's name?" he called out, jacket in hands, spread wide to protect from kitty scratches.

"AIIIEEEE!" the woman shrieked, a sudden thump on metal followed by a major curse word. The kitten, scared half to death, shot backwards, giving Dennis a chance to reach up and grab it in his makeshift blanket, sparing him from shredded forearms.

"Ow! Who is that?"

With a firm hold on the frantic kitty in his arms, he peered over the edge of the dumpster, breathing through his mouth to manage the odor. On tiptoes, he looked down to find her inside, obscured by darkness, but not for long.

Because he got a gorgeous view of her ass as she started to climb out.

Then slipped.

"Ow!" she shrieked again, her hand coming back up to grip a small bar near a sliding plastic door on the other side.

"You need help?"

"NO!"

Snowflakes began to float down on them, lazy and new. He still couldn't see her face, but her huffing and puffing included a few more curse words.

Salty woman. He liked that.

"You know," he joked, "my brother found his wife in a metal charity-donation box. When he hears this, he'll think I'm trying to one-up him."

The woman paused with one leg out the plastic door, the other still inside the dumpster, her shapely figure making him smile.

Then she was through.

"Is there a deep-seated psychological problem in your

family that manifests with men seeking out women in unsafe situations involving discarded items and abandoned debris?"

As he tried to process *that*, she tore around the corner of the dumpster, holding her hand on the top of her head, glaring at Dennis like he was there to mug her.

When he was younger, he'd have been offended. Now?

Now he just snorted.

Wrestling the bundle of claws in his hands was easier than managing that glare.

"What are you doing to that poor kitten?"

"Calming her down."

As the woman entered the light, he felt something other than his jaw clench. Glossy brown hair, long and straight, fell on either side of a fine, elegant neck. Below her strong bangs were bright red lips and eyes that were open and warm.

Skeptical, though.

Of him.

"See?" Under the jacket, the kitten was slowing down, Dennis using one hand to pet it through the fabric. "If you'd been successful, she'd have shredded you."

"Is it your cat?"

"Huh? No."

"Then how do you know it's a she?"

"I don't."

Silence rested between them, the only noise emanating from the kitchen. A little further away, whooshing sounds came from the busy highway, heavy trucks occasionally vibrating like minor chords of modern music.

The quiet they shared should have been awkward.

It wasn't.

"What are you going to do with her?" the woman finally asked, brushing her hair behind her ears. Gold hoops, small but striking, hung from her lobes. Those warm eyes were a rich, dark brown, with long eyelashes and bands of white around the irises. A fierce, probing look rounded out his partner in cat recovery.

If Dennis were in the mood to date, she'd be his type.

But tonight was off limits. He needed tonight to find his bearings before going home.

And completely changing his life.

"Don't know." Pulling the bundle close to his chest, he felt the kitten relax. Intuition made him open the fabric a bit, hoping the little thing didn't pee all over his coat in a panic.

One sniff made it clear that hadn't happened.

Yet.

The tiniest of pink noses poked out from an inverted-V opening in the cloth.

The woman broke off a corner of what looked like a piece of cheese and reached out to the kitten, who took it eagerly, then disappeared back into the cave of Dennis's jacket.

"What were *you* planning to do with her?" Dennis asked as he felt the cat chewing, knowing that taking it out now might still mean a clawfest.

He had no interest in showing up back home with rake marks all over him. Oh, the jokes his brothers would make about his first night as a free man...

"I wasn't planning at all. I came down the hallway looking for a bathroom. I heard the poor thing mewling and came outside, but then the door snapped shut on me and I was trapped out here in this nasty alley." She smiled at him, demeanor changing, her eyes darting to the propped ashtray bucket. "You were smarter than I was."

"Training," he said, regretting the word the second it was out of his mouth.

"Training? You work here?"

There were lots of ways Dennis could answer that question. The easiest would be to lie, give her the cat, and disappear.

Something about her made him never want to lie.

"No."

Her hand went to the top of his coat, caressing the cat through it. The back of her hand was filthy. Surprisingly, her clothes were fine, without a single spot on them.

But those hands reminded him of the Army. Hard work. Dirty work. The kind that gets stuff done but goes unacknowledged.

"Looks like you weren't afraid to dig in and find her," he commented. The woman's hand lifted up, fast.

"Oh, sorry! My hands are disgusting and I just touched your jacket!"

"I'm sure the kitten's done worse to it by now."

She looked up. *Way* up, because Dennis must have been a solid foot taller.

"What's your name?" she asked.

"Dennis."

"Hi, Dennis. I'm Ana."

She pronounced it AH-na, but had no discernible accent.

"Nice to meet you, Ana. What should we name this little bugger?"

She giggled, holding her hands gingerly before her, looking around. "I don't know you well enough to be naming animals we find together. I think that's Step Four in dating." Her hand went to her mouth to cover it, as if shutting herself up, but then she grimaced in disgust as she realized what she had done, touching her lips.

Big, loud laughter rumbled out of his chest, of a kind he hadn't heard from himself in years.

It scared the cat, who struggled in his arms.

"We're terrifying the poor thing," she said.

"You brought up dating," he replied with a wink. "Not me."

Maybe tonight wasn't off limits for the *right* woman.

7

"Excuse me? I did not... oh!" She laughed, the sound contented and self-assured. "You're right. I did say the D word. Sorry. My bad."

Before Dennis could respond, the metal door was pushed wide open, slamming hard against the brick wall, and a kid no older than ten stood on the threshold, breathless and upset.

"My kitty! Has anyone seen my kitty?"

Dennis's ears began to ring.

Damn it.

The kitten jumped out of his arms and ran straight for the kid, whose face lit up like exploding ordnance.

"PILLOW!" he screamed, voice cracking, the kitten snuggling up against the boy's shoulder as Dennis's heart rate skyrocketed. Grateful young eyes met his.

"Thank you, mister! You found him!"

"Him," Ana said with a laugh, then gave Dennis a concerned look.

Every molecule in his body was ringing. He couldn't tear his eyes away from that kid.

"Are you okay? What's going on?" Ana asked, her hand going to his forearm, which was covered by the long sleeve of his Henley shirt. Striking red fingernails made the hunter green knit seem festive.

Christmas-like, even.

It was the first week of January, and they were in an alley in Boston, but Dennis didn't feel the cold. Transported to the opposite extreme, he was in sand and heat, a place where the hot wind stole a piece of your soul every time it decided to blow.

"Kieran!" A mother's shrill voice pierced the air. "Did you lose that kitty again?"

"I didn't lose him! He ran away."

A very harried woman in a white kitchen uniform, splattered with an assortment of red and orange-colored foods, came to a sudden stop when she saw Dennis and Ana.

"Oh! My goodness. I am *so* sorry. Are you guests here at the hotel? Did my son rope you into helping him?"

The fear in her voice cut through Dennis's triggered state, the world narrowing slightly.

"No," Ana said calmly, pressing her hand harder against Dennis's skin, as if she knew it grounded him. "Your son didn't ask. I heard the kitten mewing when I was trying to find a bathroom, and then I found it in the dumpster."

"Poor Pillow! In the dumpster? That's where *I* found him!"

Kieran's mom, who wore a name tag that said Lainey on it, pressed her lips together and took what appeared to be a patience-gathering breath. Whether it worked or not wasn't easy to discern, but Dennis joined her.

The ringing in his ears did not lessen.

"Maybe he was just trying to find something to eat," Ana said, her charm turning up as she talked to the boy. Then she frowned, apparently thinking of something new. "You said you found him in the dumpster?"

"Uh huh." Kieran eyed the pile of trash bags, shivering in the cold Boston night. "A few hours ago. It was empty then. If we didn't find him when Mom's shift started, he could have gotten buried in there alive! Or frozen!"

Buried.

Alive.

Kid.

Dennis's skin suddenly felt covered in bugs, his eyes unable to focus, ears doing their best to double as fire alarms. Ana nudged him, looking up, studying him.

"You need a drink," she said, turning him back into the hotel.

He was in no condition to argue.

"And I need to wash my hands," she added. "Ewww."

"Here," the mother said, opening the door to the kitchen. Dennis watched as Ana went straight to a small hand washing station right next to the door, her messy hands and forearms clean within a minute as she scrubbed with determination, all smiles when Lainey spoke to her.

"Sir?" the little boy said, looking up at Dennis with a worshipful gaze. "Thank you."

"Welcome."

"Me and Pillow are best friends. Mom's letting me keep him."

"Nice."

"I would do anything for Pillow. *Anything*."

Ana and Lainey reappeared, both of them struggling to center themselves but for different reasons.

Ana plucked his jacket from his hands and shook it lightly, sniffing it.

"You're in luck," she said brightly. "Pillow didn't desecrate it."

She wrapped it around her own shoulders, shivering.

"Hmmm," was all he could manage, but it was more than a moment ago, and that helped.

"Bye! Thanks!" Kieran called as Ana guided Dennis over to the door leading to the service hall and then to the main thoroughfare. A right turn there would take them to the bar.

"Ma'am? Sir?"

The pleading tone made his throat tighten. They both turned around to find Lainey standing in front of the now-closed exit door, her face an uncomfortable mash-up of emotion, hand on Kieran's head.

Possessive.

Motherly.

"Um, please don't tell management? He's a good boy. Comes straight here from school now—we don't have the money for him to go to the after-school program since the budget cuts for the Boys and Girls Club, and sometimes I have to work nights like this. We don't normally find strays, and this one is distracting him."

Dennis cleared his throat and stopped her.

"Won't say a word."

Her shoulders dropped with relief.

"Thank you! What room are you in? If you order room service, I'll add something to it."

Dennis waved her off, his tongue thick, his eyes dry.

"Take care of Pillow."

"Thank you!" Kieran said as someone hollered in the kitchen, Lainey skittering back in through the swinging door.

Every lightbulb sang to him.

Each line in the rug's pattern became three dimensional.

And Ana's hand on his forearm was the only thing keeping him in this world.

"You can tell me," she said softly, standing on tiptoes, her body warm as she moved closer.

"Tell?"

"You're quiet. Too quiet. And frozen."

"It was cold out there. Of course I'm frozen."

Gently, she offered him his jacket back. He took it, folding it over his arm where her hand had just been. Ribs unlocking, they let him take in a deep breath, the image of Kieran superimposed over a very different boy clearing from his headspace.

One step. Then a second. Soon, he walked with purpose toward the hotel lobby, Ana at his side.

She turned with him. They both stopped and looked at each other.

"Have a drink with me?" he asked, the words coming out of him as if some unseen hand reached in and typed them out for his tongue to speak.

"You don't have to do that."

"Of course I don't *have* to."

"Dennis, I need to ask you something."

"Sure."

"Are you... a bodyguard? Security of some kind?"

"Why?"

"You seem out of place."

"I'm always out of place."

"Add the word *babe* to that line and you're a smooth operator."

The clink of silverware on plates, the murmur of private conversation, and happy laughter were the background for his own surprised chuckle.

"Are you feeding me pick-up lines?"

"The last thing I want tonight is to be picked up, Dennis." Ana was smiling, but with a twisted look that said she had a story to tell, too. "But I'll take you up on that drink. You buy the first round, I'll buy the second."

"That's quite a commitment for a woman I found in a dumpster."

"I wasn't really *in* the dumpster. More like *on* the dumpster."

"You have a tender heart."

"Says the man who cuddled a feral kitten in his jacket."

"Never said I wasn't a pushover for strays."

From the way she jolted, he knew he'd touched a nerve.

Chest rising and falling faster with each breath, she worked hard to stay even-keeled. Dennis recognized her response.

This woman was trained to stay focused and calm.

"Is that why you're asking me for a drink? Because *I'm* a stray?" she finally asked, voice tight.

"How the hell did you get from the kitten in the garbage to *that* conclusion? Who hurt you so badly that you got *that* out of my comment, Ana?"

The look on her face made it clear he wasn't just touching a nerve.

He was tap dancing on it while pouring roofing tacks on top.

"Nice meeting you, Dennis," she said, chin up, hand out to shake.

Dismissed.

He was being *dismissed*.

Fingers pressing into hers, he was taken with how soft her skin was. His eyes combed over her. Plenty of women were available back on base, and his work had put him in more than enough situations that involved opportunities, but something about Ana made his body respond.

"Can we reboot?" he asked, holding her hand for longer than was socially acceptable for a kiss-off handshake.

"Reboot?"

"Start over. Start fresh. I meant it when I offered you that drink. I could use some company."

"Plenty of company in a hotel bar," she said with a snicker, her meaning obvious.

She wasn't going to sleep with anyone tonight.

Good.

Dennis wasn't looking for a quickie. Easy lays were just that—easy romps that meant nothing the next morning and more often than not, left him with an emotional hangover.

Not that he'd had a long string of them, but he'd had his share.

Ana interested him. Something deeper and more intuitive rested in those warm brown eyes.

"Not the kind I'm interested in," he finally said as he released her warm hand, his thumb remembering the pulse of her wrist.

"And what kind is that?"

"The kind who goes out of her way to rescue a little kitty who needs some help."

"You're looking for a little kitty, are you?" Sly and bold, the innuendo made his blood rush.

"You are unpredictable."

"Hah!" The laugh was unexpected, brash and unfiltered. "Nope. I'm the opposite. Criticized mercilessly for it, too."

"You've been told you're too predictable?"

"Yes. And that's *boooring*."

"Who's been saying that?"

"Someone I don't want to talk about."

His inner radar pinged again.

Rebound.

Ana was on the *rebound*.

"We don't have to talk about your ex in order to share a drink." He eyed her, purposely obvious about it, until she began to smile.

"What?"

"You're a mule."

"Excuse me?"

"Moscow mule."

"You're trying to guess my drink?"

"I'm very good at it."

"Not this time. Dead wrong."

"Then what?"

"Caipirinha." The way the syllables flowed off her tongue was beautiful, mesmerizing and sweet.

"You're Brazilian?"

"Second generation."

"Não falo Portugues muito bem," he replied.

A mishmash of confused reactions covered her face, Dennis's explanation–in Portuguese–that "I don't speak Portuguese very well" bemusing her.

The squeaky wheel of a room service cart caught his ear,

and he and Ana both took a step to the right as a uniformed service worker walked by, well within earshot.

"How can you say you don't speak Portuguese very well in such a perfect accent?"

"It's basically the only phrase I know, other than 'Me ajude, meu amigo levou um tiro' and 'Não, obrigada, não preciso de uma boa hoje à noite.'"

"That's 'Help, my friend has been shot' and 'No, thanks, I don't need a good... screw... tonight.'"

"Except it's not the word screw."

She began to sputter.

"You live a colorful life."

So she spoke Portuguese, or at least understood it. His intrigue meter clicked up another notch.

"Make it even more interesting and have that caipirinha with me?" Head spinning, he was wooing her, compelled by a warm, intense feeling that he couldn't shake.

Didn't want to shake.

In the bar, live piano music began, a jazz melody that added to the glow inside him. If being around her made him feel like this–even without a beer–what would an hour or two of her undivided attention do?

"I don't have drinks with strange men in bars," she said, but one corner of her mouth curled up, making it clear he was an exception.

Better act like one, then.

"Why don't we up the ante and make it dinner, then?"

"I get the sense you up a lot of antes, Dennis. So what *do* you do for a living?"

"Before I answer that question, you need to answer mine. I didn't hear a firm yes in there."

"You like things firm, too?"

And that was when he knew.

Knew that tonight, there were no limits.

Chapter Two

Ana

What was she saying?

WHAT WAS SHE SAYING?

You like things firm, too? Did she really make that double entendre?

Walking down that hallway, she'd been lost in her quest for a bathroom before heading to the hotel restaurant for a sad little "Party of One" display. Her plan didn't include getting filthy in a dumpster, outmaneuvered by a teeny little kitten.

Then *he* arrived.

Dennis was the size of an action movie star, with shockingly smart eyes and a closed-off demeanor that belied his sweet, tender manner with that little kitty.

He was nothing–*nothing*–like her type.

Then again, dating her type had gotten her into her current mess: dumped, absolutely suckered, and being interviewed by the DEA.

"What am I supposed to say in response to that?" Dennis teased as Ana went to war with herself, convinced her instincts regarding men weren't just bad.

They were so flamingly awful, she should be banned from dating.

"I–I don't know!" she giggled, too caught up in her own thoughts to keep the banter going. "I'm definitely not at my best tonight."

"I think you're fine."

"You don't know me."

"We're practically besties. Completed our first mission just now."

"Mission?" Aha. Her radar was right. Military dude.

"Rescue mission. Subject found unharmed and returned home safely. Mission complete."

"You're military."

"Retired."

"You? Retired? How recently?"

"Very. Today. Just got home."

"You live *here?*" Pointedly looking around the hotel, she made it clear she was joking.

Dennis laughed, gesturing toward the bar.

"If you're going to interrogate me, I have to insist it happen over food and drink."

"Is that in the Geneva Convention?"

"Am I your prisoner?" His eyes dropped to her mouth. "Or are you mine?"

"*I'm* not in the military."

"Neither am I. Anymore." He peered at her. "Police?"

"No."

"What do you do for a living?"

Slowly–as if one of her feet was reluctant to follow him, the other eager–they made their way toward the bar. It was a sprawling, open complex that was more lobby than restaurant.

A shimmering feeling deep in her belly made its way toward her skin, spreading slowly. Its delicious pace made her feel half in one world, half in another, the new one glorious and welcoming, full of delights to explore.

Hold up there, Ana, she cautioned herself. *Don't let this sweep you away.*

"What do you think I do?" she asked, surprised by her own coyness. Once he found out, he'd chill toward her, right?

If he didn't, it would be a red flag. She should have realized that sooner with Harris, her ex.

The fact that he'd leaned *in* when she said the words had been a screaming clue to run away.

"I think you rescue people."

"Because you saw me rescuing a cat?"

"Because of how you touched my arm when I was having... trouble."

She knew *trouble* wasn't what he started to say.

Flashback was more like it.

"You noticed."

"I did. Thank you."

"Military, huh? How many deployments?"

"Twenty years' worth."

"No one has two decades of nonstop deployment," she said, laughing as they approached the host's stand, but Dennis's face didn't spread into the smile she expected.

While he wrestled with his answer, he turned his attention to the hostess, a sweet young thing who looked young enough to carry a Cinderella license.

"Table, or bar?"

Conversation pits were laid out in circles of varying sizes, the cavernous area feeling more like a futuristic movie set than the flagship property of a hotel chain.

"Table," Dennis answered with so much assurance, she stopped pondering the question the second he decided.

The hostess led them to a small round one, far away from the bar, with a curved, upholstered banquette. Menus were set down and they slid into their seats.

He gestured to the left side for her, placing himself where he could see all the exits. This guy wasn't a player. He was trained for a line of work that didn't lend itself to discussion.

Hmmm.

"Two caipirinhas, please," he said to the hostess, who smiled and nodded before leaving.

"As I said before, your pronunciation is perfect."

"I know enough to get in trouble."

"You were deployed in... Brazil? Portugal?" She said it with healthy skepticism on purpose, to make it clear she knew that was unlikely.

"Not deployed. Spent a little time in Brazil, though."

"I get the sense you've spent a little time in a lot of places."

"I get around."

"But now you're retired? Settling down?"

"Something like that." He leaned back, giving her a chance to see how he moved his body when they weren't in a cold alley. Comfortable yet also on edge, he was a study in contrasts.

Big military guy cuddling a stray kitten...

"You still haven't answered my questions, but you've asked me plenty, so I know what you do for a living, Ana."

"You're ready to guess?"

"Not a guess. I'm certain."

"Really? If you're right, I'm buying."

"And if I'm wrong?"

Just then, a server appeared, dressed in black pants and a dark purple collared shirt. Her hair was shaved on one half of her head, the other styled in layers with purple highlights.

"Hi, there. Don't get too many of these," she said, setting

the drinks before them. "Can I get you some appetizers? Water?"

"Do you have a charcuterie board?" Dennis asked politely, looking to Ana for confirmation.

She liked how he checked in with her. Didn't take over, but he also clearly knew what he liked.

"We do. Large or small?"

"We'll be here a while. Let's get the large. And a bottle of sparkling water. Ana?"

"Sounds great."

She meant it, too. It was as if he'd profiled her, known in advance what she liked.

A tendril of fear shot through her. What if he wasn't what he seemed? Retired military, just happened to come across her while she was rescuing a kitten. Buttering her up and asking her out for drinks.

Then knowing exactly what she liked?

After the mess with her ex, Harris, over the last month, what if he were some kind of undercover operator?

Or worse...

A fed?

When the server left, Dennis leaned forward and picked up his drink, watching her with renewed interest. He took a sip, eyes sharp and processing what his taste buds brought to his neurons.

"Mmm." He swallowed. "A bit sugary for me, but I like it. I can imagine drinking this on a beach."

"You like beaches?" she asked.

"The ocean, yes. Sand, not so much."

Ana eyed her drink. She knew he hadn't touched it, but her paranoia was coming on fast, and she had to check herself.

He sensed it, looking at her.

"You okay?"

"Sure."

"That's not very convincing."

Changing the subject wasn't a tool only he could use.

"So what do you think I do for a living, Dennis?"

"You're a psychologist."

"Whoa!"

"Told you. Wasn't guessing." He winked at her. "But I'm paying for dinner. My treat."

"That's not how our bet goes!"

"I'm just happy to be right."

"I thought you were already certain."

"I was, but there's always a margin of error."

"What made you think I'm a psychologist?"

"You sensed what was wrong with me. Used grounding techniques. Very subtle."

Ana just blinked and reached for her drink. Given the direction of their conversation, she was going to need it.

"If we're confiding, I have to ask: Why are you really here?"

"Huh?"

"Is this about Harris?"

Reading people was her superpower. Since toddlerhood, her mom always said, Ana could sense a person's innermost self. If little Ana didn't like someone, eventually the truth about that person would come out.

And the reaction on Dennis's face when she mentioned Harris made it clear he had no idea what—or who—she was talking about.

"Whatever this Harris guy has done," Dennis said slowly, "it's got you rattled. No, I have nothing to do with him. Why would you ask?"

"It's a long story."

He spread his arms out along the back of the curved banquette and grinned at her, broad chest flexing under his knit shirt. The guy was big. Strong and masculine, the epitome of what Hollywood considered tough.

And the opposite of every man she'd ever been with.

"I don't check out until noon, and my only other friend at this hotel is Pillow."

That made her laugh, but wouldn't someone undercover do that, too? Relax the mark, get her loose so she talks?

"Tell me about Harris," Dennis persisted. "Sounds like a jerk."

"Worse than a jerk. And I chose to be with him, which means I'm stupid for picking a jerk."

"Past tense means he's your ex."

"Yes."

"Bad breakup?"

"He fled the country about a month ago under drug smuggling charges."

"And left you to be interrogated and your life nearly ruined by the DEA."

"You know way too much not to be some kind of under-cover person," she groaned, hating herself for falling for the stray kitty act. Her voice hardened. "Who are you? Did Marlo and Guy send you? I already told them Harris is in Morocco, and I told the feds everything I know. We didn't share bank accounts, so–"

"Hold on there." Dennis cut her off, his big hand on her wrist. Warm and heavy, it felt like the touch went straight to her heart. Pained but intrigued eyes met hers. "Back up a bit. You really do have one hell of a break-up story to tell."

"Not to a private investigator paid by Harris's parents. If he even has parents. Or an undercover DEA agent. Or – does he owe you money? Because – "

Never in her life had she heard a laugh like the one that came out of this man.

Rolling deep in the back of his throat, it began as a

chuckle, turned into a chortle, then blasted the air like a foghorn. He laughed until he grabbed his ribs on his right side and began gasping.

"Can't. Breathe. Oh. No. Not. Under. Cover. Ana. Ahahahahaha."

Faced with a man with a hundred pounds and a foot of height on her turning into a puddle of giggling goo, all she could think to do next was drink.

"Swear," he said as he finally came up for air, reaching for a cocktail napkin to wipe his eyes. "I swear I'm not undercover. And I'm not here to kidnap you or pump you for information or... any of that."

"You know a lot about drug smuggling." The kidnapping comment made her knees go weak.

"That's what Harris did?"

"Oh, please. You already know."

"I swear I'm not who you think I am."

"Hmmm." She wanted to believe him.

"I know a little, but from the other side. Military side."

"What did you do?"

"Can't talk about it. I just retired."

"Officer?"

"Colonel."

Her face couldn't hide that she was impressed, but if he was lying...

"Want to see my discharge papers? My ID?" He winked at her. "They're up in my room, with my etchings."

She was being silly.

"No. If you were here to hurt me, you could have done it in the alley."

"I would never, ever hurt you," he said, suddenly serious.

"I'm doing it again. Some psychotherapist," she said aloud, her eyes rolling so hard, she could feel them etching the word *stupid* into her skull. "I can't even enforce my own boundaries."

"Boundaries?"

"I'm oversharing. Paranoid. And I really shouldn't be drinking this." Holding the drink aloft, she made a point of drinking about a fourth of it, the kick of alcohol in the cool, sweet citrus making her feel a bit wild.

"Are you trying to scare me off?" He crossed his arms over that big chest. "Won't work."

"I'm sorry, Dennis. Today is not my best day."

"Is any day really our best day?"

"That's a very philosophical question."

"Nah. More like rhetorical."

"You don't believe in best days?"

"Any day I wake up is a best day."

"I *really* want to know what you did in the military."

"And I really want to hear the whole story about your ex."

"Seems like we have a lot of stories to share," Ana said, her stomach fluttering with attraction. The paranoia was slipping away. There was nothing a private investigator could get out of her that wasn't already known by law enforcement, and besides, there was something about Dennis that made her believe him.

Trust him.

Her stepfather's voice shattered her mood: *You always trust too easily. Look where that got you with Harris.* She visualized stuffing a giant marshmallow in his face and he was muted.

"You go first."

"Mine is easy. I met Harris when we both rescued a kitten from a dumpster behind a hotel restaurant kitchen."

Dennis paused mid sip, and Ana felt a little thrill of success. The guy was clearly struggling not to do a spit take.

"Really? What a coincidence."

"It was love at first sight." The joke was meant to be light-hearted and playful, but he went serious at her words.

So soulful. The butterflies in her stomach fluttered harder as he captured her gaze.

"And what did Harris do for a living?"

"What did he *say* he did, or what did he *really* do?"

"You can tell me anything you want, Ana."

"He *said* he sold high-end residential real estate along the New York-to-Portland corridor for wealthy international clients."

"And he actually…"

"Dealt drugs. A lot of them."

"Bet he laundered money, too. Lots of Russian house hunters?"

"How did you guess?"

Dennis just smiled.

And drained his glass.

"Am I really that naive? Does everyone know something I don't? Harris seemed like a nice guy when I met him. Plenty of nice people sell real estate to wealthy buyers."

"'Nice' people launder money and deal drugs, too."

On the other side of the restaurant, the piano player began a Billy Joel song, but at a slow speed, giving it a mournful, resonant tone.

"Harris was nice. Until he wasn't."

Dennis looked at her, sharp and dangerous, his eyes boring into her.

"Don't tell me he hurt you."

Not really a question, not exactly a threat, the simple sentence turned her libido into a shockwave, attraction for this mysterious man going into hyperdrive.

Harris had turned her into a tool, and she'd gone along so innocently, a con's sucker to the max. Processing it with a friend who was a therapist over the last month had been key to finding her confidence again.

Barely. She needed time. Lots more time. The trauma from Harris's deception wasn't going to slip away easily.

"No, he didn't *hurt* hurt me. And thank goodness for my stepfather, who protected me financially."

"Banker?"

"Tax lawyer."

"Even better."

"Harris and I were together for a few months. Wild commissions would come in and he'd be flush. Worked long hours, his schedule was never the same. He blamed it on his clientele, who viewed time zones as archaic."

"Because the rules didn't apply to him."

"I see you know him."

Just then, the server appeared with a bottle of sparkling water and a charcuterie board that made Ana groan in advance, knowing her pants would need to be unbuttoned after eating half of that.

Then again, at the rate this date-not-date was going, she might be unbuttoning her pants later for a very different reason.

"Amazing," Dennis told the approval-seeking server, who placed two empty glasses next to the water bottle.

"Another round?" she asked him, pointing.

"Another?" he deferred to Ana.

"Bourbon, neat. Maker's. Double." Her need to tell the story was greater than her desire to maintain firm boundaries.

"I'll have the same," Dennis said smoothly, cutting a wedge of brie as the server left.

"Matching me drink for drink?"

One eyebrow cocked as he paused, a cracker in his hand. The way his eyes roamed up and down her body made her wonder how it would feel to roam her hands over those big, tight muscles, to be caged between those thick arms, under him in bed, his powerful thighs pumping.

"I could drink you under the table, through the floor, into the lobby, and down the sidewalk into a sewer grate."

"I'm not a lightweight!"

"Compared to me, you are." He took a bite and smiled at her as he chewed, then reached for the water bottle and poured them each a glass.

"I'm not getting drunk tonight just to prove a point."

"Good. Because neither am I."

"I'm getting drunk tonight because I've had a terrible day."

"Yet another thing we have in common, Ana."

"Tell me about your terrible day."

He scrunched up his face as if it weren't worth talking about. For two beats, she thought he'd gone silent, but he sighed and replied, "I'm not sure who I am right now."

"You just discovered that today?"

"Over the last few months."

"Literally? As in, you were adopted as a child and only recently found out?"

He stared at her.

"Man, you're dark and intense, Ana. Why would you even say that?"

"Because it's one possible interpretation of what you're saying."

"You ever work with a patient who had that happen to them? For real?"

"Maybe."

"Can't tell me? Confidentiality and all that?"

"Maybe."

"This is going to be fun."

"Why?"

"Because normally *I'm* the cagey one."

"How do you know? You just said you don't know who you are."

Laughter, sonorous and deep, was his answer.

"I'm fine on that. My childhood was great, parents love me, good relationship with my siblings, blah blah."

"Not blah blah. Good for you."

"I had nothing to do with it. Tell my parents good for them."

"You love them?"

"Hell, yes."

She reached for a deglet noor date and a slice of manchego.

"Wonderful."

"But they live a really specific kind of life. Small town in Maine. Really rural."

"You're moving back home?"

"I am."

"From..?"

"All over, but in the last ten years, mostly the Middle East. Some time in Germany and Ukraine."

"Big life."

"Big life, now small life."

"This is your choice? You weren't kicked out?"

"One hundred percent my choice. I loved my job. Left home at eighteen. Earned a bachelor's and master's degree in the Army. Then I spent the better part of a decade and a half doing work I couldn't talk about–*can't* talk about."

"Sounds evasive."

"See? We're twinsies."

Maybe the alcohol was loosening her up. More likely, though, it was the conversation.

"Not twins, Dennis. You had a loving childhood. Parents who love you."

"You don't?"

"I have my mom. My dad died when I was thirteen."

"What about your mom?"

"She's fine and alive."

"Sorry about your dad. How did he die?"

"Plane crash."

"Oof. Small aircraft?"

"How'd you guess?"

"Most people say the flight number when they talk about big commercial plane crashes. Not so with small planes."

"He was a wealth manager. One of his ten-figure clients invited him for a golf week at Cape Kidnappers in New Zealand."

"The Bannister crash?"

"How do you know that?"

His face went blank.

"I just do. It was in the news. I was home on leave then and my mom was sort of obsessed with the coverage. I remember how the reporters called it the eight-billion-dollar crash. Combined net worth of everyone on board. Freak lightning, right?"

"Yes. Completely random. And my mom was supposed to go, but didn't."

"Good thing."

"Well... she didn't because she was having an affair with my grandmother's tax attorney."

"Ouch. And that man is now your stepfather?"

Sharp. He was paying attention.

"Why am I telling you this?"

"Because I was actually a psychologist in the Army and people tell me I'm a good listener."

Her laugh felt like a pressure cooker getting some relief.

"Liar."

"Good instincts. But I'm right, aren't I? She married the attorney, didn't she?"

"Yes."

"And you don't like him."

"We're... cordial. Polite. I've always felt like he doesn't like me."

"Who couldn't like you, Ana?"

"Apparently, my stepfather." Laughing, she gave him an odd smile. "He's been my stepfather for almost two decades. It's fine. Just... distant."

She reached into her purse and pulled out a credit card, handing it to him.

"What's this for? I said dinner's on me."

"I owe you for this impromptu therapy session, Doctor..?"

"Love. Call me Dr. Love."

"Original and not at all cheesy."

Before he could reply, his phone buzzed. He reached for it. Read the text.

And began to laugh.

Chapter Three

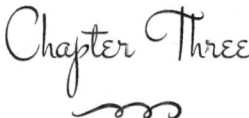

Dennis

Dennis loved his mother. He really did.

But not when he got texts like *Check the weather in the morning sweetie because a snowstorm might hit and we don't want you to do a Colleen.*

Yes, what had happened to his sister was cause for concern, but–

Because you haven't driven on snow in years and you're out of practice.

That.

That's the part that made him grit his teeth.

"Something wrong?"

"My mom. Texting me." He rubbed the bridge of his nose. "Warning me to be careful in case it snows."

"Careful?" His eyes caught the impression of her lips on the edge of her glass, the red lipstick lacy along the rim.

"On the road."

"Where are you driving?"

"My hometown in Maine. And you?"

"Mass. Newburyport. What part of Maine?"

Hoo boy.

Dennis hated this question.

In fact, in some ways, it's why he left his hometown twenty-four years ago and until now, hadn't been back for more than a short R&R.

Because Dennis hated—with the passion of a thousand glittering hearts, ten thousand baby Cupids, and one horny moose—where he was from.

Not the people. People were great.

Not the weather. Snow was awesome.

The problem was the kitsch.

Dennis hated the lovesick tourist trap with his last name attached to it.

"Northwest."

"Long drive ahead of you?"

"Tomorrow. Yeah."

"Retiring and going back home? Do you have a job lined up?"

"Family business, actually. My dad was disappointed that none of my siblings wanted it. I'll step in and he can slow down."

"What kind of business?"

"Trees."

"Trees?"

"Yeah."

"Growing them or cutting them down?"

"Cutting. Climbing. Treating."

"You're leaving the Army to be a tree guy?"

"Yep."

"Are you one of those people who can climb a tree with just the harnesses? Like a human cherry picker?"

"It's more like cherry pickers are mechanical arborists, actually."

"Wow. I could never do that."

"Why not?"

"I'm terrified of heights." She looked up and watched the moving glass elevators nervously. "I practically needed a Xanax to check into my room on the twenty-third floor."

"That bad?"

"Yeah. Got dizzy and a little flushed on the way up."

"You look good with some pink in your cheeks."

His comment added more.

Bzzz

Dennis looked at the screen.

Please reply so I know you're alive, Deanna Luview texted, a familiar line from her.

He took a picture of a slice of prosciutto on the charcuterie board and sent it to her, typing, *Sorry. Donner party already got me.*

Almost instantly, she replied:

DENNIS!

And then:

Who is the woman in the red shirt with the beautiful nails?

He looked at the picture again. Damn. Part of Ana was in the shot.

Suppressing a groan, he closed his eyes and tried to think of a clever response that would get his mom off his back.

"What's wrong? Something at home?"

"My mother is interfering in my life."

"Join the club," Ana groaned. "My mom still feels like she has to make up for what happened to Dad when I was a teen, so she constantly hovers. I have a therapist's license but she would cut my meat for me at dinner if I let her."

He refrained from making a joke about sharing the same mother.

A ragged sigh escaped him as he stared at Deanna's text. Rude to text with her during a date, of all things, he wanted to power off and ignore his mom.

But if he did that, she'd double down.

It was only now dawning on him that coming home meant he'd have his mother, who meant well and loved all her kids to pieces, butting into his life all the time.

Talking about that aspect of his retirement was off limits with his siblings, even Colleen. While she was the one he was closest to, he knew he'd cross a line if he admitted that their warm, caring mother had been an obstacle in his decision to come back to Luview and help ease their father's burden with running the tree company.

"Struggling to come up with a good reply?" Ana asked, watching him with amused eyes.

"Yes. Help me out here."

"What's your goal?"

"Goal?"

"Do you want to get her off your back? Mess with her head a little? Please her?"

His groan felt like an earthquake.

"I just want the interference to stop."

"She does this all the time?"

"Actually, no. It's just that I've almost always been out of contact in the field when she did it."

"You mean you'd come back into communications contact and find a giant pile of texts asking about you?"

"Exactly."

"Which meant you could batch your feelings and reactions."

"Right," he said slowly, amazed that she put it into words. Dennis had never had a phrase he could use to describe it before. "Batching. That's very insightful."

"It's my training."

"It's more than your training."

"Why do you say everything as if it's a settled fact?"

"What do you mean?"

"You're very confident in your declarations about me, and yet you don't know me."

"Doesn't mean I'm wrong."

"See? That's what I mean!"

"Are you calling me arrogant?"

"No. It's not that. Not at all." Clearly wrestling with her words, she reached forward and plucked a tiny bunch of grapes from the board. "You don't say these things to establish dominance, or to preen."

He nearly sprayed her with his drink.

"Right?" She laughed. "You and 'preen' don't belong in the same sentence."

"Insight. Again. You have a fluidity about you, Ana. I like it."

"Fluidity?"

"Adaptability? Flexibility? Something more. You're intuitive, but you're also compassionate. Maybe I'm just not used to being around someone so caring and attuned to people from a position of helping them to be grounded."

Her eyes flared again, this time with surprise.

"What other position would someone take?"

"You can be highly attuned to the people around you from a position of fear. Or violence."

"Hypervigilance."

"Yes, but the kind of hypervigilance where you have to focus on a specific goal. And it's fatal if you don't."

"You have seen some *stuff*, haven't you?" She pushed her drink aside, making a face and filling her mouth with the food in her hand instead.

"I'd use a worse word than *stuff*, but yes."

As she nodded, he watched how her hands moved, the way

she breathed, how all the parts of Ana were synchronized. The woman wasn't cool as a cucumber, and certainly didn't give off vibes of being a calibrated operative.

She was the real deal.

And the tops of her breasts were sprinkled with crumbs now.

Bzzz

He looked at his phone.

You don't have to answer, his mom wrote. *I'll just find out when you come home tomorrow!*

Whatever sound emerged from him was bad enough to make Ana laugh boisterously, her lovely throat bobbing as she swallowed.

"Oh, my. They have a special way of making us feel completely out of control with a single sentence, don't they?"

"Sure do."

K, was all he wrote back, knowing it would drive Deanna nuts.

Reaching for his double bourbon, he drank it down fast, savoring the heat that ran down his throat and exploded in his chest.

"What's *your* mom like?" he asked her.

With a very loud snort, she began snickering, licking her lips with a cute little tongue maneuver that made him wonder how she kissed.

"My mother is fine. Busy with her life. Very independent."

"What does she do?"

"She's a hospice nurse."

"Mad props to her. Takes some serious backbone and lots of empathy to do that kind of work."

"Yes. She started doing it as a volunteer–the hospice part, not the nursing–when my dad was still alive. Busy executive's wife doing volunteer work. Most of her friends were on charity boards, but Mom liked the actual work with the families and patients. She had a biology degree already, so she slowly took nursing classes. All her friends thought she was bizarre."

"And your dad?"

"He encouraged her. Loved it. She was in her final semester when he died."

"Ouch."

"Yeah." Ana spread some olive tapenade on a piece of bread, taking a bite. He knew what she was doing.

Stopping herself from sharing more.

"My mom works with my dad. Helps run the company," he offered, getting the sense that sharing a piece of himself would put her more at ease.

The way her face relaxed told him he was right.

Warming up and getting loose, he felt the alcohol kick in, though he didn't want more. Didn't *need* more. Around them, the restaurant was beginning to fill, small groups and couples chattering animatedly, the occasional single at a table on a phone or reading a book.

Without Ana, he'd have been one of those singles, watching one of the televisions over the bar. A Bruins game was on, closed captioning letting patrons follow without sound.

Ana finished her mouthful and took a sip of her water, then asked, "Is the whole family involved?"

"No. Mom, Dad, and my brother Kell."

"How many siblings do you have?"

"Three. I'm the oldest. Then my sister, who is a nurse. Brother who is a cop. Baby brother who works with my dad."

"Big family!"

"What about you?"

She shook her head, her smile going wistful. "Only child. I always wished I had brothers and sisters."

"Stepsiblings?"

"Nope. Just me."

"Pressure."

"What's that?"

"A lot of pressure. All your parents' hopes and dreams in one kid."

"I–I never thought of it that way," she said, stumbling over her words, giving him a look that said she'd underestimated him.

He shrugged. "You don't strike me as someone who caves in to other people's demands."

"I don't?"

"You seem to know yourself well."

If a smile could truly light up a room, Dennis would need sunglasses right now.

"Thank you. I believe that's the nicest compliment I've ever received."

"You're very welcome."

Four musicians–they appeared to be a jazz quartet–began setting up around the piano player, who shifted to a slow song. Dennis recognized it as a show tune but couldn't name it.

"I know that's a Broadway song, but I can't place it."

"Sondheim," Ana murmured.

The melody swelled into a chorus, Dennis's heart rate picking up as they both sat poised, pattern-matching.

Together.

"Ahh! No one is alone!"

"What?" he asked, startled. What did she mean?

"The song! Sondheim–it's called 'No One Is Alone'–I remembered!"

He clinked the rim of his glass against hers in congratulation.

If they'd been here three weeks ago, the air would have been filled with Christmas songs, the place decorated for the holidays. He took a handful of marcona almonds. As he munched, he felt his body relax, more than it had in years.

Until he saw a little kid in his peripheral vision.

The girl had long, dark brown hair in braids on either side of her head. Clutching a teddy bear, she followed a harried woman pulling a large suitcase with a smaller one balanced on top, the whole contraption bungee-corded together. A man wearing a wool topcoat over a suit was with her, carrying an infant in one of those front-pack carriers. The two were clearly frazzled and snapping at each other.

Reminded Dennis of carrying a forty-pound backpack on his front. Weighed more and was way less fun than a baby.

Corners of her mouth turned down, the girl looked up at her parents with sad eyes.

His hands began to shake.

Ana's gaze followed his, and although he wasn't looking directly at the child, she knew.

Knew something was wrong.

"Do you know them?" she asked politely, but he could tell she was holding back. Someone so perceptive would see the pattern soon.

Two different kids.

Two destabilizing reactions.

"No," he said, using her own technique to forestall talking, lifting a piece of cheese from a stack on the wooden board and putting it in his mouth. A burst of fruit hit his taste buds, maybe some fig jam somewhere in there.

The parents continued marching toward the elevators, the woman putting her hand on the little girl's back, guiding her.

Ana smiled sweetly. "You have kids?"

"Me?"

"No. I was asking the olives." She gestured to the bowl. "Yes, you."

"No. God, no."

"Don't want them?"

"Uh...."

"That was a pretty intense response."

"I just meant no. No kids. No wife, no picket fence, none of that. The life I live doesn't really allow for it." He frowned, rethinking his words. "Lived. The life I *lived*."

"Past tense hard to get used to?"

"It's more like getting used to a whole new vocabulary."

"Or maybe you're regretting your choice?"

He closed his eyes and willed intrusive images away.

"No regrets."

"Was it an epiphany?"

"Huh?"

"An epiphany. You know." She used her hands to mimic fireworks. "Poof! Instant life change. Mindset change. You just suddenly knew you needed to go down a different path."

"Something like that."

"But not that, exactly?"

"Right."

"But you said leaving the military was your choice?"

His gut tightened at the question.

"Honorable in every way." Cynicism was hard to hold back, but he did his best. "Retired with full benefits."

"Something haunts you, though."

"In my line of work? If it didn't, that would be a problem."

"Don't worry, Dennis. I already figured out you're not a psychopath."

"Oh, yeah? You sure?"

"Yes." Her brow knitted. "Maybe. I'm questioning my radar these days."

"Because of your ex?"

"Mmm hmm."

"He's an idiot."

"You don't even know him."

"Anyone who hurt you would have to be."

The way she stared at him turned his world upside down. Heart, too. He felt the perpetual knot of control that pervaded every moment of his existence loosen just a little, just enough to sense how she connected to him.

Accustomed to being the one in charge, responsible for everything when it went wrong and taken for granted when it went right, he was completely blindsided by this plane of existence.

A space where he could breathe her in and she really saw him.

Reading a woman's signals wasn't new, and Ana was sending plenty of interested vibes his way. Would she spend the night with him if he asked? He got the feeling that a direct approach would scare her off, and besides, he didn't want just a one-night stand.

Not with her.

Ana was the kind of woman you savored. One brief taste with all the walls up would feel like a pale imitation of what could be.

He wanted so much more.

"Dennis?"

"Yes?"

"Are you going to hurt me?"

Having the wind knocked out of him was common on his missions, a physical state that sucked and hurt, but it was time limited. Pain limited, too. Like so many blows, he knew it would pass.

But never in his life had a woman done it with one simple question.

"Hell, no," he rasped, taking in a long, deep breath until he found his bearings again.

Who was this woman?

And why did those pretty brown eyes seem to see directly into his soul?

"Good," she said, popping a grape in her mouth, smiling. After she swallowed, she added, "Because I think we're both carrying around a lot of hurt right now. How about we find a way to let some of it go?"

"How would we do that?"

As if on cue, the jazz quartet began playing "It Had to Be You," the first notes making them both smile. No singer accompanied the band, the soft drum beat and piano coming through. Couples began floating to the dance floor, an even split of folks with gray hair and younger couples their age.

"Do you dance?" he asked with a smile he didn't know he still had.

"Me? You mean, like that?" Pointing to the group of eight or so couples, all milling close to the band, she seemed completely taken aback.

In command, he made a decision. Standing and looking down at her, he held out his hand. Those minky lashes framed wide, curious eyes, her cheeks pinker than when they first sat down.

"Come on, Ana. Let's drop some of that hurt on the dance floor."

With a laugh that was pure warmth for the cold corners of his heart, she stood and looked at the dancers, biting the side of her lip nervously.

"I'm more of a line dancer. You know. Macarena. Electric Slide."

"You've never gone to a middle school or high school dance? Been a bridesmaid? Danced with your dad?" He winced, hating himself for that last one. "Sorry. Insert boot in mouth."

"That would hurt."

She took his outstretched hand, their touch electrifying. It wasn't just him—she felt it, too.

Whatever this was, whatever it might be, it was enough in this moment. That's all Dennis had, and it was all he could focus on.

Leading her to the dance floor, he put one hand on her waist, her soft curves so tempting to explore, but he was a gentleman.

Trying to be, at least.

Both her hands went to his shoulders and he couldn't help but chuckle.

"Here," he murmured in her ear, taking the moment to inhale her scent. Something cinnamon and sugar was in the air around her skin, and he had a flash of his hometown bakery, all warm and cozy.

All smiles and love.

His hand took one of hers, leaving the other on his shoulder, and he began to lead.

Ignoring the beating his toes were taking, he used a simple box step, but she stumbled.

"Sorry! I'm so sorry!"

"For what?"

"I'm hurting you!"

"It takes a lot more than that to hurt me. You're learning."

"I–"

"Just soften. Follow. Let your body go with me."

"How do you know how to dance like this?" As her joints relaxed and she leaned into him, they began to flow together a bit more.

"Just do."

"The Army made you learn?"

"*Shhh*, Ana. Just have fun." He smiled down at her and her eyes met his.

"You are nothing but surprises," she said, one eyebrow going high.

"Is that a good or bad thing?"

"I think I need to get to know you better to answer that."

"Ah," he said, pulling her closer. "A good thing."

Chapter Four

Ana

Whirlwinds were *not* a good thing.

Ana liked a steady life. Ups and downs were part of any existence, of course, but she preferred an emotional range of experience that had a relatively low high point and a reasonably high low. No sharp ups and downs.

Gentle slopes were more her speed.

Even keeled was her jam.

This was anything *but*.

Less than two hours ago, she was walking down a hotel hallway, looking for a bathroom.

And now?

Now she was in his big, strong arms, being glided so smoothly across a dance floor, her body responding to the music and Dennis and *oh*, how she wanted him.

Wanted more.

Wanted it all.

Harris had put her through the wringer for the last month, leaving her with a constant stomach ache, several panic attacks, and an ever-present feeling of shame at being duped. Without her stepfather's legal advice, she'd be in so much more trouble, and she hated needing Rick's help.

The worst of it, though, was the discarding.

Harris threw her away like someone threw that kitten away.

Which did make her a stray, in a sense.

"You went quiet."

"Enjoying the dance."

"Are you?" Dennis's finger slid under her chin, gently pushing it up so their eyes connected. "So am I."

"You're very tall."

"Maybe you're very short."

"I think we're both just *very*."

"Something else we have in common. At least we're being *very* together."

The song wound down, couples disconnected, polite applause making her body move on autopilot. The reluctance she felt stepping out of his embrace reminded her of free-spirited, childlike moments on swings and amusement park rides, when you just didn't want the fun to end.

But it had to, eventually.

Dennis watched her while they both clapped, then walked back to their seats as the band took a break. She reached for her bourbon but her stomach—and her head—said no.

Drinking too much right now would be a bad, bad idea because she could turn into a bad, bad girl if she weren't careful. Never the type for one-night stands, she found herself so magnetically drawn to him that she was becoming unrecognizable to herself.

Where was even-keeled Ana? Careful, purposeful, steady-state Ana, who always found her equilibrium?

After her father died in such a huge, public way, life had been nothing but terrifying overwhelm in every direction. Too much attention or too little. Too much energy in the wrong places. Her mother had put on a brave face and done her duty in public, but behind the scenes she'd been depressed. Sedated.

Drunk, too.

A lot.

Thirteen-year-old Ana hadn't understood the full extent of it until Rick had started appearing at their house way more than any tax attorney should. Even then, Ana just thought he was being helpful.

Overhearing her mother and her aunt fighting about her mom's affair and guilt over it was a turning point. That night, teenage Ana had firmly decided she would never be like her mother, pulled in all directions by emotion.

Oh, no.

Ana would live in a constant state of emotional moderation.

And for the most part, she did.

Except for this moment.

As Dennis's baby-blue eyes consumed her, all she wanted was to be consumed. To dive in. Fall deep.

Be swept away.

"Excuse me," Dennis said, arm raised, flagging down the server. His words shook her out of her head, a gasp of air filling lungs that were holding tight, waiting.

Waiting for her to come back down to earth.

A tangy Provençal olive gave her something to focus on, and as Dennis ordered more water, he looked at her full bourbon.

"You okay?"

"Hmm?"

"Lightweight after all," he proclaimed, nodding at her drink, then at her.

"Guess so," she said slowly, smiling. "You're welcome to have it. I haven't touched it."

"Nah, I'm good. But thank you. I want my wits about me."

"That sounds so old fashioned."

"I guess it is. Something my mother says all the time."

"Sounds like you're close to her."

"Close enough. I guess. Weekly FaceTime calls. See my family once or twice a year. Pretty typical relationship."

"Weekly FaceTime calls? While deployed? I don't think I see my own mother and stepfather weekly, and they live fairly close by."

"Meaning you don't pressure them, or they don't visit you?"

She smiled. "The latter."

"So, all the expectations and none of the reciprocity? Seems unfair."

How did he hit the nail on the head so clearly, so easily?

"You *do* sound like a therapist."

That made him laugh harder than she'd heard all night. "I know my limits and my strengths. Definitely not a strength."

"You have extraordinary clarity."

"For other people's issues. Not my own."

You really could be a therapist, then, she thought but didn't say.

The band began another familiar show tune, this one from *Damn Yankees*, done in a slow jazz style that made Ana sink back against the cushions. Dennis scooted closer to her, clearly more comfortable in their shared space after that dance. His fingers brushed her wrist as he captured her gaze.

As if she could turn away.

"You really are lovely," he said, admiring her openly with a confidence that only fed her own boldness.

"And you really are direct."

Her purse buzzed, the forgotten phone startling her, and she tilted slightly closer to him as she fumbled to find it.

"If that's *your* mother warning you to drive carefully in the snow, I'll eat this charcuterie board. The actual wooden board," he said with a chuckle.

Though she'd like to see that stunt, it wasn't her mom. This was Brie, her bestie.

How was the conference? I can't believe you spent two whole days talking about nothing but trauma and neurofeedback, she wrote, followed by a shocked emoji.

Funny how she and Dennis hadn't even talked about why *she* was here in the hotel. It wasn't because he was full of himself; the time would come when he remembered to ask.

Brie was right, though. For the last two days, she'd thought about nothing but the sessions on trauma. Continuing education credits for her license were a necessity, and conferences like this one, which had ended right before she'd gone on her quest for a bathroom before dinner, were part of the way she met her requirements.

But that wasn't the primary reason she went. She went because learning how to connect with trauma survivors was crucial in her line of work.

It's good. I'm kind of busy right now, she typed back as Dennis gave her a come-hither look that turned her panties into a puddle.

Busy watching more baking shows? Or some serial killer documentary? You're never busy in the evenings at conferences.

Kind of am this time, Ana wrote back, knowing she was swimming in dangerous waters.

More shocked emojis greeted her, followed by Brie's response in all caps.

OMIGOD WHO IS HE??

"Based on your reactions as you type, this is either your best friend or your other best friend."

"Best friend. Brie."

He looked at the cheese section of the board on the table. "You have a friend named after a cheese?"

"Her parents literally own a fromagerie."

"Please tell me they didn't name one of their kids Camembert."

"Cam's a really nice guy!" she answered, deadpan.

He snorted. "Let me guess. The twins, Wensleydale and Manchego, are so sweet!"

"No, of course not," Ana said as she debated how to respond to Brie's screaming response. "But her sister, Fontina, is a very sharp accountant."

"Brie, Camembert, and Fontina? You're pulling my leg."

"Fine. Don't believe me. You'll just have to meet her one day."

"Meet her, huh?"

The implications of her comment hit her, spreading warmth throughout her body. This was a chance encounter that wasn't supposed to be more than a drink together.

Dennis added food, then a dance, and now they were getting to know each other with an ease that she not only had never felt before, but didn't know could exist between two strangers.

Suddenly, she wanted him to meet Brie.

And not just to prove that her bestie's parents really were *that* warped.

Ana turned her phone toward Dennis so he could see the exchange. As he chuckled reading the last line, he leaned closer, his lips nearly brushing her ear.

"Who *am* I, Ana? How are you going to answer that?"

Her shiver was pure lust, entering each cell of her body at the same time, a controlled invasion designed to take over. Every part of her wanted him, knowing she shouldn't.

Strangers weren't her style.

Instant attraction wasn't real for her, too heady and emotionally charged. Give her a nice work acquaintance. Maybe a friend's cousin. Someone you slowly warm up to and get to know, where the emotions play nicely together and follow the rules.

Harris, for all his flaws, stayed within her comfort range until the last few days of their relationship.

Instead of answering Dennis's question, she looked back at him, her moderate, polished self standing back as the rest of her came roaring forth.

He leaned forward, his intent clear, and she'd been aching for this moment.

When anticipation became reality.

She met his mouth with a kiss as he came closer, their joining mutual and oh, so delicious. That he initiated the kiss didn't surprise her. The attraction was impossible to ignore.

That she kissed him back so hard, her arms stretching to wrap around such a big, muscled man, certainly did.

This was no ordinary first kiss.

This was scorched earth.

No other kiss would ever measure up. The heat of his tongue against hers made her melt, his mouth seeming to understand who she was.

Their phones buzzed at the same time.

They both took them out, pressed the power buttons, and turned them off.

His arms wrapped around her as the music continued, the beat driving her hips closer to his. With every breath, their unspoken arousal flowed faster. One palm caressing her back, he tipped her chin up to meet him, the kiss charged but still restrained.

They were in public, after all.

But not for long.

Her decision was quick, decisive, like leaping from a great height into a swimming hole. Trusting herself took courage.

Old rules didn't apply when his mouth beckoned.

Each kiss held an invitation, a temptation, a chance to toss away the old and try the new.

New felt good.

New tasted even better.

"That was nice," Dennis murmured as the music wound down and her ears cleared, hearing all the slices of conversations, the distant mutterings, laughter at the bar–and realizing how exposed they were.

So open.

So carefree.

So *bold*.

"Just nice?" she asked, the question less about qualitative value and more an entry point. Feeling him out seemed redundant, because it was clear he was interested.

But in *what*, exactly?

"A good start."

"A beginning of sorts?"

"If I thought you'd say yes, Ana, I'd ask you to come back to my hotel room and finish what we're starting here."

"What makes you think I'd say no?"

The way he laughed, a gentle huff through his nose, made a piece of her heart melt a little more.

"Most women would say yes or no to that. Instead, you open the question wide and give it nuance."

"What's wrong with nuance?"

"Never said there was anything wrong with it."

"From what I've seen, you are a crystal-clear man, Dennis. Why don't you try the direct approach?"

Inching closer, his inhale like the rush of a conch against her ear, Dennis smiled, his grin broadening, genuine happiness filling his features in a way that made her feel pride.

Pride that she could elicit that from him.

"Come to bed with me, Ana. I love the feel of you in my arms on the dance floor. Your kiss tastes so good, I want to taste all of you. My room or yours?"

Pure energy shot through her, most of it between her legs, coalescing into a throb. Fire lit up her skin, his caress as he cupped her jaw and kissed her again so anchoring.

And so damn hot.

Few moments in life call for complete abandon, but for Ana DaSilva, this was one of them.

Without question.

Without hesitation.

And without regrets.

"Your room," she whispered against his mouth, her hand moving to his rock-hard thigh. The sheer size of him made her marvel. Never in her life had she so much as kissed a man so big.

And now, she was about to do much, *much* more.

Dennis waved down the server, who brought the check, Dennis running the tab to his room before Ana could object.

"You can get breakfast," he rasped against her ear before biting the lobe, and she nearly moaned.

"Deal," she gasped as they slid out from their seats, his arm around her shoulders, hers around his waist. Guiding them to the elevator bank, he reached for the buttons and pressed the number 19.

"Oof," she said. "You got a better floor."

"I did?"

"I'm on the twenty-third."

"There are better and worse floors?"

"When you're afraid of heights, yes."

"Ah," he said, giving her a protective squeeze. "Don't worry."

"If I could stop worrying, it wouldn't be a fear."

Six. Five. Four. The numbers ran down on the red-lighted panel until the elevator arrived, packed with people, a mix of frazzled parents with kids, nightclubbers, and older folks clearly headed for dinner.

Overstuffed with people in winter coats, wearing gloves, hats in hand, the elevator seemed bigger when she and Dennis, along with five or six other passengers, stepped aboard.

The ride up felt tense, fraught with lust and impatience. It seemed the elevator stopped at every floor. The doors slid open each time with an aching slowness to reveal a hotel guest who had pushed the button to go down, then frowned and stepped back when Dennis pointed up.

Anticipation was building in her blood, and she found herself helpless to fight her growing desire for him. Sweaty, naked, tangled in each other's bodies–that's what she wanted next.

Her two drinks, the second one half abandoned, couldn't take the blame for her choice.

Awakenings came in many forms, and Ana was reveling in what she was about to do.

Her decision.

Her need.

Her *leap*.

Finally, the doors opened on the nineteenth floor and Dennis took her hand, cutting through the small crowd on the elevator like a warm knife through butter. He walked with a slow, deliberate pace that she admired.

The man knew what he wanted, and he was in no rush to get it.

Because he knew he was absolutely, positively getting it.

As he waved his smartphone over the metal plate on the door, the *click-click* of the lock opening from the app made her stomach flip, tingles shooting through her.

Brie was going to die when she found out.

And cheer her on, too.

Before the door had even closed, Dennis was kissing her, lifting her off the ground with two big hands that filled themselves with her ass. When her feet left the floor, it was like he defied gravity itself. Reflexively, she wrapped her legs around his hips, his erection pressing against her sensitive skin, the urge to move against him so great.

His mouth claimed hers and she was wordless, all tongues and pressure and groans, as he took her to the bed.

Cocooned between his arms, his mouth on her neck, kissing along her collarbone, she felt the broad expanse of his back under his knit shirt. His heat was impossible to ignore.

He was a sun, a furnace, a fireball.

"You're so beautiful," he murmured against her skin as his hand found her breast, thumb turning her into a gasp, her nipple hardening in a second.

"You're so big," she whispered, the words honest and true, and he chuckled a deep sound of appreciation.

"You're supposed to wait until after we're naked to say that," he joked, the words catching her off guard, making her laugh as well. Then he resumed kissing her, fingers unbuttoning her shirt like a bomb specialist disarming a device.

He was smooth. Sharp. Skilled.

Watch out for Rebound Man, Brie's voice intruded. *Don't confuse him with Mr. Right.*

The thought made her hesitate. Dennis picked up on it instantly, pausing, his arms suddenly more cuddle than kink.

"What's wrong?"

"Nothing."

"Ana."

"I–a thought."

"You're still thinking? Then I'm failing you." His hand went between her legs, but stopped at her upper thigh. "Unless the thought is no? Because I'll absolutely stop."

"No!"

He pulled away, holding his palms up to show her his respect.

"No, I meant *no!*"

"I hear you, sweetheart." As he rolled away, she began panting with need, heart in freefall, straight down into a crater above the throbbing between her legs.

"No, the thought *isn't* no! Yes! It's an enthusiastic yes!" Reaching for him, she smiled. "Get back here and kiss me again."

"*Whew.*" His hand went back to her thigh, mouth on hers, the kiss full of smiles on both their parts, her hands in his thick, sandy-blond hair, then tracing down his neck to his shoulders, where the hem of his green knit shirt made her wonder how he looked out of it.

She was about to find out.

"And you're even hotter when you do that," she said against his mouth.

"Do what?"

"Consent check. Making sure I'm still all in."

"Isn't that just called being a decent human being?"

Brie was never, ever going to believe this.

"You're perfect," she blurted out, hand sliding under the hem of his shirt and finding one, two, three, four ridges.

Eight-pack, as she suspected. Her fingers played it like piano keys, a sonata of skin.

"I'm absolutely *not* perfect. If you're looking for perfect, you've hit anti-matter. Sorry."

"Right. You're Mr. Rebound."

Dennis gave her a piercing look.

"Mr. *What?*"

"Rebound."

"Ahh. Which means I'm the first since your sleazy ex?"

"Yes. You're not supposed to be perfect."

"According to whom?" The question came with a kiss between her breasts.

"According to... I don't remember." The way he touched her, hand moving slowly up her rib cage, cupping each breast, the kisses lush and full–it *was* perfect.

"There we go. Let go of the thoughts and expectations. Tonight we don't have to live by any rules except the ones we make for ourselves."

"Really?"

"Really. Go ahead. Give me a rule."

"Keep doing that," she gasped as his fingers found a spot between her legs.

"This?"

"Mm hmm." Her assent was punctuated by a moan so raw, she was embarrassed.

"Make that sound again," he whispered against her ear. "I love how you moan. Love to make you moan even more."

And for the next few hours, Ana did indeed make that sound.

Again, and again, and *again*.

Until she fell asleep in his arms, sated beyond belief, wondering if it was possible for one man to be Mr. Right, Mr. Rebound, *and* Mr. Perfect.

Because if so, she may have found him.

In a dumpster.

Chapter Five

Dennis

He smelled her.

Then he smelled *them*. The scent of all they'd done last night. Going for it last night had been the right move.

Being right felt so good.

Because she had tasted good. Delightful, in fact.

And this morning, he'd have more. Breakfast in bed meant something completely different on this–to use her word–*perfect* morning.

Eyes closed, Dennis reveled in the cool sheets slipping against his skin as he rolled over, led by his nose.

And another body part considerably further south.

Last night had been a feeding frenzy. No other way to describe it. The last time Dennis had made love with a beautiful woman was so long ago, he was pretty sure it was a different decade.

But now, now...

Empty cotton was all he found.

Again, and again, and *again* as he patted the sheet.

Eyes open now, he realized he was alone.

And her side of the bed was cold.

"Ana?" he called out, hoping she was just in the bathroom.

Silence.

"Hello?"

More silence.

With a mouth like the Sahara, he climbed out of bed, walked into the bathroom naked, and although he already knew the answer, looked for her.

In vain.

Found a glass. Filled it. Drank it. Repeated that, wiping a line of water that dribbled out of the corner of his mouth, down his chest and belly, a few drops ending at his navel.

"*Damn* it," he said to his reflection, his hands going to his head, fingers digging into his scalp.

One-night stand.

She'd fooled him.

After three rounds of mind-blowing sex, she'd cuddled up to him, their bodies practically bonded together by sweat, juices, and a kindred-spirit energy that gave him not only the best lay of his life, but the best night's sleep he'd had since before basic training.

Ana was magic.

And when you witness magic, you're never the same again.

Scanning the room as he walked back to the bedroom, his gaze caught a note propped up against the television screen.

Neat, old-fashioned cursive made him fall for her a little bit more.

Dear Dennis,

. . .

Thank you for last night. You really are perfect. You started the night by saving a cat and you ended it by rocking my world. My world, though, needs to be steady right now. Nice and steady. So I hope you can remember our time together as a precious moment of magic as we stand on the edges of two different lives, our pasts about to be archived, our futures yet to be written.

I can't let you be my Mr. Rebound, so I need to let you go, so you can be someone else's Mr. Perfect.

All my best, always,
Ana

He let out a string of profanity that wouldn't make any of his Army brothers blush, but would have required a deposit of $7.25 in his mother's swear jar.

Ana couldn't do this.

Last night had been too special. Too aligned. Too–

Just... *too.*

A kind of kismet he'd never felt before. Sure, the sex had been phenomenal, Ana not shy about telling him what she wanted, where to touch, tease, lick, and–on one occasion–bite.

And the easy way she had of opening him up pulled him toward her, overriding his closed-off nature.

I can't let you be my Mr. Rebound, so I need to let you go, so you can be someone else's Mr. Perfect.

Screw that. What if *she* was *his* Ms. Perfect?

Fumbling for his phone, he finally found it in his discarded pants, the six-digit unlock code an impediment he had no patience for.

Then he paused.

Because his stupid self hadn't thought last night to get her phone number.

"Dumbass," he muttered. "What do you know about her? Ana. Ana on the twenty-third floor. Ana who lives in Newburyport. Ana who smells like cinnamon muffins and tastes like pineapple and limes. Slam dunk for finding her."

Banging his head lightly against the wall did not, surprisingly, jar any additional ideas loose.

The phone in his hand buzzed. With a rush of hope, he looked at it, but–

Nope.

His mother.

What's your ETA? she asked. *Kell's shoveling the path to your cabin. We'll start a fire in the stove when you text that you're on your way.*

Shoveling. Fire. All the advance planning that his mother juggled in her head made his start to hurt.

A look at the clock told him it was 9:03. That was super late for him.

Tap tap tap

The knock on the door made him lurch, halfway there before he realized he was still naked. Finding his pants again, he stuffed his legs into them.

"Hang on!"

Surely, she'd changed her mind. Reconsidered. Realized how special they were together

Come *back*.

Cold feet happened, right? After what they'd shared last night, he understood she'd be a bit skittish, unaccustomed to sleeping with someone a few hours after meeting. Same with him, minus the nervousness.

He knew.

Just *knew* they had a spark, the kind worth following to see where the illumination took them.

As he reached for the door handle, he ran his fingers through his hair, her scent imprinted on him.

Disappointment greeted him on the threshold.

Disappointment, and... bacon?

"Room service, sir," a guy in a white shirt and black pants said, carefully avoiding eye contact. He held a tray.

"I didn't order room service."

"A woman ordered it for you. She said, and I quote, 'breakfast is on her.'"

Oh, geez.

Dennis had no emotional blueprint for this situation. Zero training. No framework. Blindsided, he just gaped at the guy, feeling his blood pressure rise.

"Would you like me to put the tray on the bed or on the desk?"

Dennis let out a small growl.

"I'll just set it down right here, sir," the server said nervously, "and let you enjoy your breakfast. Dial 4 for the kitchen if you have questions. Bye!"

As the guy lit out of there, Dennis took in a deep breath and quietly muttered profanity.

What was she doing? Disappearing in the middle of the night, which was no small feat. He'd slept like crap for decades; every tiny sound woke him up.

Yet... not this time.

The one time it would have been beneficial.

Some kind of trance had come over him, her smile bewitching, her charms so powerful. No, he didn't believe in that kind of magic, but Ana did cast some sort of love spell over him.

One he wanted more of.

Glaring at the tray, he bent down with a grunt and picked it up, the bacon too good to ignore. As he set the tray on the bed with its mussed sheets, his gut tightened.

She should be right there, under those covers, his mouth on her skin, her hands in his hair.

Bacon was a poor substitute for morning sex, but it would have to do.

As he poured himself coffee from the carafe and started making his way through the breakfast—pancakes, bacon, fruit salad, scrambled eggs, and toast—he eyed the pancakes and smiled.

In Love You, Maine, everything was heart shaped. These were probably the last round pancakes he'd be seeing for a while.

"Oh, Ana," he muttered, swallowing his sorrow with a dose of hot coffee. The scald felt good, as if a little pain and a shot of caffeine could mend his bruised heart.

Not broken. Not even battered. Just... a little tender.

Closing his eyes, he let the memory of last night wash over him, knowing that he had no real choice. If he stuffed his emotions, they'd just leak out. Anger wasn't appropriate here, and grief seemed melodramatic.

Her rejection sucked, plain and simple.

"Lick your wounds, soldier," he said with a sigh as he popped a sweet strawberry into his mouth.

Sure, he wanted more. Another date would have been nice. Newburyport was where she lived, and if memory served correctly, that meant she was about two hours south of his hometown.

Doable, but she didn't want to do *him*.

Again, anyway.

Hydration and caffeine were helping a little, although not as much as a kiss from her.

Instead, he got a kiss *off*.

"Hold on," he said, arguing out loud with himself. Ever since he was a kid, he'd done this. Thinking the words wasn't the same—they needed to be spoken to be real, considered, evaluated.

Validated.

"Maybe I should be flattered. Someone like her doesn't go around screwing just any guy. She ran out because she panicked, she didn't know what to do."

Putting another piece of bacon in his mouth, he mulled that over.

"But she's a therapist. Aren't they supposed to be super emotionally healthy? Or are they just human and flawed like the rest of us?"

"Oh, shut up," he told himself. Plowing through the rest of the food, he tried not to think.

A plan. He needed a plan. The clock now read 9:33 and he needed to shower, pack, and check out. All he had was a small rolling carry-on and a backpack. Movers had shipped the rest of his stuff straight home.

Home.

A few years back, his brother Luke had proposed that the whole family buy the old camp they'd attended as kids. Luke had been recently widowed, and Dennis knew the idea came from pain.

Luke's pain of losing his childhood sweetheart, the mother of their child.

Amber's death had left Luke all alone with a four-year-old, Harriet, a true sweetie. If he had any regret about living abroad, it was that he hadn't gotten to know her.

But now he would.

Because he had a new home now, one of the cabins at the old camp, and it would be the first time he had his own permanent place.

Apartments and barracks and extended hotel stays added up to *home* for him for all of his adult life, until today.

Today was the first day of the rest of his civilian life.

His phone buzzed. Probably his mother.

But to his surprise, it was Rafe, his closest friend.

You up? was all it said.

Eating room service in a hotel before driving home, Dennis replied.

Room service? You went soft on day one?

Rafe was still in the Army, shocked more than anyone else by Dennis's retirement, yet also the person who understood it the most. A die-hard soldier through and through, his friend would never leave.

Or, as he often said, he'd leave, alright.

Leave the Army in a body bag.

Rafe hadn't witnessed the incident six months ago, so he couldn't evaluate Dennis's choice. Best friends were best friends, though–through and through.

Having Rafe check in on him felt good, but also bizarre.

What's that? he typed back. *I can't hear you above the sounds of bacon being chomped and my fluffy down pillow being plumped.*

You'll get plenty plump eating bacon. You really ready to go home to Lovetown?

"Luview," Dennis muttered to himself.

Hell, no, Dennis texted back. *My mom is sending me texts warning me about driving on snow. She's treating me like I'm ten.*

You drove at ten? Badass.

Shut up, Rafe.

Don't make fun of your ma. She's a nice one, Rafe chided him. When his parents had visited him in Germany a few years ago, they'd met Rafe. Insisted on taking them out to dinner at a biergarten. His dad picked up the tab.

Both of them were colonels. Dennis probably made more than his parents.

Still, even Rafe knew not to argue with Dean Luview.

Who said she isn't nice? She is. She's also nosy. Overbearing. Hovering.

That's called love, Dennis. You know. An emotion you lack.

I have plenty of love in me.

Only thing I've ever seen you love is every stray animal that comes across your path. Bet you picked one up last night.

"Oh, man," he muttered as he stabbed eggs onto his fork and ate them quickly. Tempted to tell Rafe about Ana, Dennis held back, knowing that was a genie he couldn't shove back in the bottle once it was out.

Rafe would tease him mercilessly. Grill him endlessly for details. Probably search databases to find every detail about Ana.

And then team up with Dennis's mother to make him find her.

Rafe was an old-fashioned romantic. The guy could pick off a sharpshooter from 700 feet with a clean shot, but he also read Nicholas Sparks novels for fun, and thought *50 First Dates* was the best movie ever.

A study in contrasts, he was Dennis's best friend through thick and thin. Which meant Dennis wasn't going to say a word just yet. Once your best buddy knew about a woman, it was fodder for teasing.

Forever.

Found a cat in a dumpster last night, Dennis confessed, which he knew would make Rafe whoop with laughter.

In response, he got a string of laughing emojis.

Only you, man. Only you would pick up a cat and not some nice—

His next word started with P and was a euphemism for cat.

Maybe I did that, too, Dennis shot back, hitting Send before he realized what his temper was doing.

His phone instantly rang.

Not Rafe.

Mom.

"Hi, Mom."

"Dennis!" When Deanna Luview was happy, she gushed, like a geyser of love. "I can't believe this is really happening! I get my boy home!"

"Been home plenty of times before, Mom."

"Not for *forever*!"

He sighed. "Are you calling to tell me that for the seventeenth time, or is there something else important to tell me?"

"It's always important! We're so excited. Harriet made this beautiful banner to hang on your porch. It says Welcome Home, Uncle Dennis."

"Original."

"Hey!"

"Sorry. Let me guess. It's covered in glitter?"

"Of course. And Kylie made you her special unicorn muffins!"

"*Edible* glitter."

"Yes! How'd you know?"

He didn't have the heart to explain that Colleen poked fun at Kylie's glitter obsession, so he just replied with, "Lucky guess."

"It's so sweet living here, Denny." The old nickname made him feel two feet shorter and a hundred and twenty pounds lighter. "Everyone has coffee together in the mornings. We run to the store for each other. Harriet gets so much attention. Even the animals benefit."

That made his heart sing.

"Mel is going to be so happy to have you helping her, too!"

Once all his retirement paperwork was in process, Dennis had reached out to Mel Chassi, the woman who ran the animal sanctuary in Luview, Maine. Her ex-husband was

Darren Duarte, the local veterinarian, and the family was interwoven with the town.

"Glad to work with her," he said. "Strictly volunteer. My time learning the tree business is my highest priority, Mom."

"Dad and I are just so thrilled! You cannot fathom how happy you've made him. I mean, Kell's been working with him since he came back from D.C., but..."

"I know. We've talked about this before. Kell wants to focus on his poison ivy business."

"And we'll have lots of family dinners. Kell, Moore, and Luke can help you renovate your cabin. It's going to be so much fun!"

"Mom. I'm sold. You don't have to convince me."

She laughed. "Some part of me thinks I do."

"I'm checking out soon. Headed to the dealership straight away. Be home around two, maybe closer to three if there's a lot of traffic."

"Your truck is ready?"

"That's what the dealer says." He smirked, though she couldn't see it. "And don't worry, Mom. It has brand new tires. I won't slide off the road."

"Don't joke about it! Colleen nearly died."

"I know. Her accident was terrible. Doesn't mean I'll get into one, too."

"But you've been living without snow for so long?"

"I see plenty of snow, Mom. I just don't talk about it."

"You mean you *can't* talk about it."

"Same thing."

"Well, young man, that's all over. Working with us at Luview Tree Service means talking about all the work, all the time. No secrets!"

"Governments aren't going to topple because I tell you about a termite infestation in an oak tree on the common,

Mom. Or tree roots invading the sewer pipe to the coffee shop."

"The world might end if that happened! What would poor Rachel do if she couldn't get her daily Love Bomb!"

"What's a Love Bomb?"

The question triggered a sharp inhale.

"It's a coffee drink Rachel practically invented, and Reef put it on the menu."

Every time someone in his family mentioned a Luview local, his brain short circuited for a moment while he mentally morphed people to their current age.

In Dennis's mind, Reef Matthews was a dinky little kid in an oversized Little League shirt, regardless of the fact that he'd seen the pierced and tatted-up dude a few years ago on a trip home.

"I'll have to try it," Dennis said slowly as he finished his second cup of coffee.

Ana's breakfast treat.

He'd much rather taste *her*.

"Rachel will make you."

While he knew Rachel Hart had moved to Luview some time ago, in his mind, she was brand new to the family. All sorts of new realities would hit when he got home.

In just a few hours.

"Sounds great, Mom, but I really need to get packing."

"Having breakfast with that woman from the picture last night?"

Although he knew her intention was good, the question was a gut punch.

"Uh, no. That was just some woman in the background."

"Oh." Deanna's disappointment was clear. "Well, maybe you'll find love right here in your hometown."

"Mom."

"What? A mother can't hope for her son to settle down and be happy?"

"Mom."

"Don't take that tone with me!"

They laughed together before he hung up.

And stabbed the rest of the food, shoveling it in until he was full.

The shower was hot, steamy, and exactly what he needed to transition between last night and his departure. Washing away all traces of Ana was both miserable and liberating.

She didn't want anything more than what they had last night.

That had to be enough.

Dressing in layers, he prepared himself for the drive north, a turtleneck under a merino wool sweater and socks from the same company, nice and warm. While much of his career had been spent in warmer climates, he was still a Mainer, born and bred.

Adapting to the snow wouldn't be hard.

Packing was a quick process and soon, he found himself scanning the room for any stragglers.

Nope. All his items were secured.

Time to check out.

Unable to help himself, he grabbed the pillow on Ana's side of the bed, taking in a deep breath, a trace of her perfume still there. Or at least, it was there in his imagination, elicited by hope.

As he tossed the pillow back on the bed, he squared his shoulders and laughed at himself as he pulled a bill from his wallet and left it as a housekeeping tip.

Maybe Ana *was* the transition.

A bridge of sorts between Colonel Dennis Luview and plain old Dennis, the tree guy in Love You, Maine.

Thinking of her that way felt better than viewing their night together through a lens of rejection.

No one else was in the hallway as he rolled his carry-on to the elevators, housekeeping carts standing outside open doors, women inside vacant rooms chattering about sheets and soaps.

Between two pairs of elevators at the end of the hall was a section that was like an observation deck, so you could watch the glass elevators run. Looking down, he had a moment of vertigo before he fully oriented. Glass capsules shuttling people in a vertical line made him ponder the engineers who designed it all.

Thousands of people pushed through space daily.

Plenty of them probably had bruised egos like him.

One of the elevators was way up, close to the top floor, and he watched it descend. As it began to slow at the floor just above his, he waited patiently. This one would be for him. Looked empty.

Like his bed this morning.

"Whatever," he muttered aloud to himself. "At least you had last night. More than you deserve, bud."

The rejection still stung, though. He'd thought there was more than just a good shag to what he had with Ana.

Guess not.

Then the elevator arrived and he realized that maybe, just maybe, life was giving him a second chance.

Because it wasn't empty, after all. It had an occupant.

One who was about to get his undivided, *perfect* attention.

Chapter Six

Ana

"OMIGOD, ANA! SERIOUSLY?"

Calling her best friend while she rode the elevator down to the lobby to check out had been a mistake. For years, this had been her routine: Call Brie to ride out her fear of heights.

Telling her about Dennis, though...

"I know! One-night stand..."

"You left him in bed? Snuck out after how many times?"

"Three. Well, for him. I think it was more like ten or so for me."

"TEN???" If Brie screamed any louder, the public address system would pick up her voice.

"I don't know. It was just–"

"Go back to his room."

"What?"

"*Go back to his room!*"

"I can't!"

"Of course you can."

"No, I can't! It would be horrifying!"

"Embarrassing, maybe, but not horrifying. Bet he's disappointed, Ana."

"I'm sure he's fine. Probably does this all the time."

"That's morning regrets talking."

"That's common sense kicking in. I never do things like this, Brie! What was I thinking?"

"You were thinking ten orgasms in one night, that's what you were thinking."

"I couldn't have known how good he was in bed before we slept together."

"You just knew. Intuition. You're a highly intuitive woman, Ana, right?"

"I'm really not."

"You certainly are about sex."

"Not *all* sex. If my intuition was that good, I never would have fallen for Harris."

"Okay, that was a mistake. But you're allowed to be wrong sometimes. No one's gut check is a hundred percent."

"Which is why I snuck out!"

The elevator began to slow at the twentieth floor and a rising sense of horror flooded her.

"No," she gasped. "Oh, no."

"What's wrong?"

"That intuition you said I have?"

"Yes?"

"It's dancing a funeral jig in my stomach right now."

"A funeral jig? That makes no sense, Ana."

"Gotta go. Talk later," she barely managed to say before ending the call, because she knew.

Knew.

DING!

The doors opened on the nineteenth floor, and there

stood Dennis, a full backpack over one shoulder, his hand on the retractable handle of a hard suitcase.

Their eyes met.

His expression hardened, one eye narrowing. Coupled with his slow, skeptical inhale, it was enough to make her feel really lousy, really quickly.

"So you're not dead," he muttered as he stepped in, eyes checking for the lobby button.

It was already lit, of course.

"I'm—uh." In her hand, her phone screen lit up, Brie obviously trying to reconnect. Turning it off, she shoved the damn thing in her purse.

"Or you're dead and haunting me." He cast a sidelong look her way. "*Perfect* me."

She winced. It hit the mark so hard because she deserved it. Embarrassment was too weak a word to describe what she felt right now.

"Not dead. Wishing for a giant sinkhole to swallow me whole right now, but not dead."

Dennis looked behind her, out the wall of glass that constituted this elevator.

"Not likely here."

Following his gaze, she realized her mistake immediately, but it was too late.

Her legs turned to rubber bands and she collapsed, Dennis grabbing her at the last second and breaking her fall.

"What's wrong? Is it the height? Vertigo?" His voice was emotional, filled with a concern she didn't deserve.

And he had one hell of a memory.

She nodded. "Glass. Fall. Help."

Kneeling next to her, his hand went to her wrist, then her neck.

"Your pulse is crazy high."

74

"Panic," she said as the familiar squeeze in her chest began. Pain radiated from her breastbone.

"You weren't kidding when you said you were afraid of heights."

She shook her head.

"Or is this just an elaborate ruse to get me to feel sympathy for you after you ghosted on me?"

Panting, she replied, "I'm not enough of a masochist to do this to myself over a one-night stand."

"Good thing we weren't just a one-night stand, then," he said, but his implication was clear.

She'd hurt him by sneaking away.

"I'm sorry," she gasped.

"Thanks for breakfast." His sarcasm was clear. "Last night, when I said I wanted to enjoy breakfast in bed? I didn't mean alone."

"You're angry."

"No. Just... hurt." His voice dropped on the word *hurt*, making her heart squeeze a bit.

"I hurt you."

"A little."

"And I'm the one... who needed reassurance last night... that you wouldn't hurt *me*." Her breathing was still ragged.

"Ironic, huh?"

An answer would have been the polite next step, but Ana's mouth opened and nothing came out. Her heart was pounding so hard, it felt like it was breaking her ribs with each beat, and white spots still filled her vision.

"Breathe," he said to her, getting right in her face, blue eyes penetrating hers. "Breathe."

"Can't."

"Yes, you can."

"Don't tell me what I can or can't do!"

"I see you're going to be fine."

She expected that to be sarcasm, but the way he said it–with a grin in his voice–made her laugh.

Which loosened her chest.

Which made it easier to breathe.

Which... made him right.

Until she looked over his shoulder as the elevator continued its death drop, and the world spun again.

"Sixth floor, Ana. Want me to stop the elevator?" Dennis stood, but her depth perception was off, altered by her panic, and suddenly, he was a giant.

"No!" About to black out, her fingertips tingled, the skin behind her knees turning electric, copper filling her mouth.

On his knees in seconds, he was with her again.

"Five. Four," he tracked, counting down the floors.

Of all the times *not* to be stopped by other hotel guests.

"Three–"

His voice cut off as the car suddenly lurched to a stop. Ana's scream was completely involuntary, her body shaking uncontrollably, and Dennis scooped her into his lap and cradled her as she trembled.

Hot breath ran across her forehead as he mumbled a curse.

"It's fine. We're fine," he assured her.

"We're trapped!"

"Are you claustrophobic, too?" he inquired gently.

"NO! Just a realist!" The thin burgundy carpet looked like old blood.

Dennis gently let go of her, stretching to reach up and push the emergency button. A long, loud ribbon of alarmed buzzing began, making matters worse.

But before he could wrap his arms around her again, it stopped.

Feedback cut through the air, adding to her near-delirious state. Dennis tightened his hold on her.

"HELLO?" someone shouted through a small speaker in the control panel.

"We're in here," Dennis called out. "Two adults."

"We're working on fixing this," the man replied. "Sorry for the inconvenience."

"This happen often?" Dennis asked, as if making small talk.

"No, sir. We have no idea what's going on, but no one here knows how to fix it. We called a repair person and they're on their way."

"How long?" Dennis barked back.

"At least ten minutes to arrive, and then they have to get to the control room."

"Ten minutes!" Ana gasped. "We're going to die! There isn't enough air in here!"

"We'll be fine," Dennis said in a soothing voice, brushing her bangs off her face. "There's plenty of airflow."

"You're being very nice to me," she said with a whimper. "I don't deserve it."

"You know you do."

"I feel like an ass."

"That's normally my line when I'm in a mess." He grinned at her. "Yet another thing we have in common."

The silence between them should have been tense, but it wasn't. Maybe because she was in his lap? Maybe because he really was as wonderful as she'd thought last night, but talked herself out of this morning?

"Dennis, can I—can I explain why I left this morning?"

"Yes. But not before you give me your phone number."

"My—number?"

"Mmm hmm." He pulled out his phone and gave her a raised-eyebrow look. "What is it?"

She recited the digits, and her phone buzzed in her purse.

"There. Now that the technicality is taken care of, go ahead and explain."

"Why do you want my number after what I did to you this morning?"

"Trust me, I've been asking myself that same question." He looked down at her with vulnerable eyes. "It hurt when you left like that, and the breakfast didn't help."

"It didn't? It was supposed to be a peace offering."

"Felt more like a kick in the teeth."

"Damn."

"Yeah." He frowned. "Did last night scare you off? Did *I* scare you away?"

"No. It wasn't that."

He sighed. "Please don't tell me the sex sucked."

Her own snort made her laugh, her heart like a gemstone being polished in a tumbler.

"Are you kidding me? It was—you were—phenomenal."

The guy was already big, but she could swear he puffed up even more at that.

"Then you left because it was *too* good."

"Sort of. I know it sounds bizarre, but—"

"I get it."

"You do?"

"I think so. I'm not you, so I can't know what you think and feel, but I do understand how meeting someone so... perfect might be frightening."

"Not frightening. More like destabilizing."

"If you're looking for stability, I am definitely not your man." His voice had an amused tone to it, but the undercurrent of truth was there, too.

"I *am* looking for stable. After Harris, I—well, I think I don't trust my own radar."

"Because he burned you so badly? You're taking the blame?"

"The responsibility, yes. I should have seen it coming."

"No one's that sharp. Even con men get conned, Ana. Being a sucker isn't always the mark's fault."

"You sound like the antithesis of my stepfather."

"He blames you for being too trusting?"

"Yes! How did you know?"

"A guess."

"Your guesses make me feel seen."

"You're seen, all right." Craning his neck, he looked over her head and his chin jutted slightly. "We have an audience."

"Audience?"

"A crowd is forming on the second floor, where the coffee shop and retail stores are. They're all watching us." His eyes roamed appreciatively over her body.

"Great. Not only am I humiliated by running into you, now I'm on public display."

"I don't want you to feel humiliated because of me. You didn't do anything wrong by leaving."

"I'm sorry."

"But I will say that waking up alone made me wonder what was wrong with me. Had I read you wrong? Done something I shouldn't have? It dredged up... a lot."

Her stomach lurched, and the words she was preparing for a reply disappeared as she worried she would be sick.

"You really are perfect," she whispered.

"Nah." He reached for her hand. "Your fingers are ice cold. Can you stand?"

"Stand?"

"Let's get some circulation going in you."

"I'm afraid I'll pass out."

"If you do, I'll catch you."

Slowly, he stood, lifting her with him. Her body slumped against his, knees like jelly, eyes closed.

"I can't open my eyes," she said into his chest. "If I do, it'll be worse."

"I'll be your eyes for you."

"You're being my everything for me."

"And that's okay, too. You need help. I'm here."

"I made a mistake." Opening her eyes, she looked up at him, her fingers on the neck of his sweater. "I wish I could take it back."

"Take what back?"

"Leaving your hotel room this morning."

"You're in luck, then."

"I am? How?"

"When I was in the Army, I worked on a secret project." He glanced around as if he were in a spy movie, voice lowering to a bare whisper. "So secret, I have to kill people who know about it."

"What does this have to do with my sneaking out on you this morning?"

"I am getting to the point."

"Is this your way of saying you're about to tell me the secret, then kill me? I am a captive, after all."

His arched eyebrow made her laugh as he said, "That project? It was a time machine."

"DENNIS!" She batted at his chest.

"All right, fine. It wasn't. But how about the next best thing?"

"What's that?"

"A do-over. A reboot. How about we pretend you didn't wake up next to me–Mr. Perfect–and decide to sneak out of my hotel room? How about we pretend you didn't call room service and order the guilt breakfast?

"Guilt breakfast!" She was now laughing so hard, her abs hurt.

"Tasted like bacon and regret. *Your* regret." His voice

dropped to a smoldering tone as he whispered, "I like the taste of *you* better."

A flash of their naked bodies in bed last night made every part of her want him. Leaving like that was cowardly, but she'd convinced herself it was for the best.

Now, though, she saw how wrong she'd been.

Forgiveness was an issue she helped her patients manage, and forgiving yourself was often harder than extending that grace to others. Dennis was clearly still interested in her, even as she struggled for composure in a broken elevator, facing one of her worst fears.

Let him like you, her inner voice whispered with compassion. *Second chances count for you, too. Take the reboot.*

"Can I, really?"

"Reboot? Of course." Sheer happiness radiated from his smile.

"Then I—"

Before she could finish, the elevator car dropped about five feet, sending her to her knees, the pain of the impact shooting sparks through her brain.

Shrieks she couldn't control pierced the air before Dennis knelt beside her, burying her in his embrace.

"*Shhh.* It's okay."

But it wasn't.

Because suddenly, the elevator car dropped again.

Even further.

Chapter Seven

Dennis

Her scream broke his heart.

And triggered a flashback.

Instantly, the elevator was filled with the whirl of helicopter blades, the piercing Doppler effect of bullets whizzing past his ears so crisp and real. Hot air filled his lungs with a suffocating pull, chest expanding with his sharp inhale. Dust crowded his nose, nostrils burning, as memory obliterated the present.

The hard stop from the elevator's brake system shocked him back into the moment, Ana sobbing in his arms, shaking as if her tendons were about to snap. None of this was tenable. A cold sweat broke out across his face and chest.

Too much.

It was all too much.

"Your heart—it's racing so fast!" She pulled her face away

from his neck, mascara streaking down her cheeks. His dysregulation seemed to yank her out of her own.

"I'm fine," he grunted, both of them knowing damn well he was lying.

"What's wrong?"

"Nothing." Speech was hard, his tongue moving slower than it should. Ears ringing, he felt like his lungs were out of sync with his mouth, which was working to funnel air into him.

"Flashback?"

All he could do was frown.

"Tell me. Tell me what happened."

"What?"

"What do you see? In your mind's eye?"

"I'm not your patient."

"Of course not. But you can tell me. You can share. There's nothing you can't say to me."

"Ana, twenty seconds ago you were shrieking like you were dying. Suddenly, you're tough?"

"Not tough. Still freaking out. But you need attention, too."

An acrid gunpowder smell burned in his nose.

"I'm good."

"Your jaw looks like it's about to break in half. Your shoulders are blocks of granite." Her hand was on his arm, rubbing his shoulder cap lightly.

"I work out. Thanks for noticing."

"Ah. I see. Deflection."

"Lady, if I didn't deflect, I'd have died long ago."

"I'm sure that's true for parts of you," she said softly, her doe eyes soft and smart, inviting him to be softer, too. "But it's not true any longer. You can change. You can let other parts of you step in."

"What parts are those?"

"The part that's retired and never has to be in combat again."

He laughed, his mouth opening so abruptly, it hurt along the jawline. He almost said, *You've never been in Luview on Valentine's Day, have you?* but the joke would fall flat.

And he didn't want to get into the whole "You're a Luview?" b.s. conversation he'd had hundreds of times in his life. Last thing he needed right now was more complication.

A loud crackling sound cut through their conversation from the speaker in the panel.

"Folks? Sorry about this—we're close to getting you to the lobby. One more floor to go. Can't pry open the doors because you're between the first and second floors, so we have to bring the car all the way down. Just a few more minutes. We're so sorry. You need anything?"

"Bottle of vodka and some fresh underwear!" Dennis shouted back, which made Ana laugh, anemic as it was. His voice boomed enough to bring his brain back to the now, so that he noticed the texture of the carpet beneath him and the soft curve of Ana's hip against his thigh.

Pressed against each other on the floor, they were not intimate, but also not tense.

"No promises, but we'll work on it!" the guy said from the speaker, laughing.

Situational awareness would help, he knew, so he stood. Looking down through the wall of glass, he was stunned to see that there were now forty or so people in the lobby, all watching the spectacle of their mishap.

Bending down, he offered Ana his hand. Her fingers were ice cold and she looked ill, but a wan smile greeted him as their eyes met. Pulling her up took no effort.

Neither did wrapping his arms around her and pivoting her so that she faced the doors.

"*Shhh*," he whispered into her ear. "You'll be fine once we're on the ground. And you don't need to take care of me."

"I know I don't need to. I *want* to. We can be equals, you know."

That wasn't a question. Her voice didn't rise at the end.

Ana was making a declaration, and he was here for it.

"Equals. You tell me your secrets, I confess mine?"

"Something like that."

"I'm not a spill-your-guts kind of guy. Takes time. A lot more time."

She chuckled against his chest.

"We have nothing but time right now."

"And an audience."

"They're still there?" she squeaked, peeling slowly away to look through the glass, then burying her face in his chest. "I can't look!"

"I'll look for you."

"When you tense up, what do you feel? Something triggers you, right?"

"Yeah," he finally relented. "Not sure exactly what it is, but yes."

"What do you experience?"

"It's like I'm back in Afghanistan. Or... other places I can't talk about. Heat. Dust. Crowded market."

"Something traumatic happened there?"

"More like daily life was trauma there."

"A constant bath of it?"

He couldn't believe they were trapped in a broken elevator while he comforted her during her acrophobia and she psycho-analyzed his combat flashbacks.

"It was... a lot."

"You strike me as someone who can handle a lot."

"I can. I could. Until I couldn't."

Her sigh against him made his nipple heat up as her warm breath filled his shirt.

"That's often how trauma works."

"I'm fine. Just need to adjust to being stateside. Soon I'll be in the woods, where the only sniper I need to worry about is a guy with bad aim and too much whiskey during deer-hunting season. Or a brain-damaged moose."

"A brain-damaged *what?*"

As he opened his mouth to begin explaining Randy the moose, the car jolted, dropping a few more feet. Ana tightened her grip on him, his hands around her shoulders, the scent of her hair so fresh.

So inviting.

Knees slightly bent, he made sure he was positioned to handle whatever kinetic force the broken elevator threw their way, but Ana trembled in his embrace. His hand caressed her between her shoulder blades, gentling her.

"It's okay. They're working on it. Just a glitch," he murmured against her ear.

"I know," she mumbled against his arm. "Still scary. Just because the rational part of me knows there's a solution coming eventually doesn't mean that the piece of me that lives in a constant state of mute terror isn't screaming right now."

"That's a remarkably accurate description of fear."

"Thank you."

"Was that a compliment?"

"You're the one who said it!"

"Then compliment it is." He pulled back so they could look at each other. "Is your fear of heights from your dad's plane crash?"

"Hah. Good insight, but no. It's because when I was six, I decided that if I put my mind to it, I could actually fly like a Powerpuff Girl."

"No."

"Yes!"

"I am going to assume you failed."

"Gravity puts a real damper on childhood imagination," she said with a fake pout that made something inside him unclench even further.

"Gravity can be so mean."

"Right? Laws of physics win: Gravity, one. Ana's arm, zero." She slid her right arm out of their embrace and pushed up the sleeve of her lightweight sweater, showing an old, faded scar. Then she pointed to another, right above her elbow.

"Ouch. Broken?"

"Dislocated elbow. Broken ulna. Broken humerus."

"Your arm became a bag of marbles in a sock."

"A magenta pink sock, bucko. I was so popular in first grade!"

"What did you jump off of?"

"A treehouse my dad had made for me."

"Your dad built you a treehouse? So did mine."

"No," she said, her mouth twisting into a wry smile. "He had it made for me."

"Ah. Gotcha. Not the handy type?"

"My father was handy with money. Everything else, not so much. He was really loving, but with big, grand gestures."

"And he died when you were thirteen?"

"Yes."

"I'm sorry."

"Thanks. It was so long ago, I'm—well, thanks."

"How old are you?" he asked, realizing she could be anywhere from mid-twenties to early forties. There was a timeless quality to her that he couldn't quite put a name to.

"Thirty-five. And you?"

"Forty-two." Something in him cringed. "I'm ancient."

"Anything but. My father was twelve years older than my mother."

"Really?"

"And Rick is fourteen years older."

"Rick?"

"My stepfather."

"Ah. My mom and dad are the same age."

"See? Plenty of ways for couples to match up."

"Are we a couple, Ana? Do you want to be?"

Before she could answer, he covered her lips with his fingers, needing to say more.

"You snuck out of the room this morning, and that's fine. I am not pressuring you. At all. It's just, there's something about you I can't shake. When I woke up and you weren't there, it was like... like I'd found a piece of myself I didn't know I was missing, and then I lost it again. Your absence threw me off, but I'm a big boy. I can handle rejection."

"I wasn't rejecting you." As she spoke, he lifted his fingers. "I was so stunned by my own behavior that I panicked."

"Your behavior was pretty damn awesome in my estimation."

"If you mean in bed," she responded softly, "you, too. And that's the problem."

"Being incredible in bed together is a *problem?*"

"I wasn't ready for you," she said hotly, as if Dennis were pushing her buttons on purpose, egging her on, baiting her into an argument.

Except he wasn't.

"That's okay, you know," he replied, suddenly serious. "You don't have to be."

"What?"

"You don't have to be. I would never push you into something you don't want. We can just stop here."

"I don't want that, either!"

"Then what *do* you want, Ana?" Quieter now, his words

felt like silk strands on the wind, the tips brushing her lips with a featherlight stroke. "What do you really, deeply want?"

"If I knew the answer to that, I wouldn't have left your room this morning."

"Do you mean you want more of this?" He gestured between the two of them.

"I think I'm getting in my own way because I can't believe this is real."

"*Ah.*" The proverbial light bulb switched on, casting light over their half embrace. "Now I understand."

"Do you?" As she tilted her head to study him, he noticed people below them holding up phones. So strange, this phenomenon. Why record complete strangers like that? Were they hoping the elevator would plunge to disaster? Planning to gain followers on some social media platform that didn't matter?

"Do I understand that being with you feels too good to be true? Yes. Absolutely." He let out a long breath. "My whole life changed overnight. I was expecting it to. From active duty to retirement. From living overseas to coming back home. I leave here and pick up my new truck from a dealership in Boston, and I'll drive it to a home I've never known. My parents, brother, and sister all sold their houses and we're living on a big piece of land together."

"That sounds amazing!"

"It is. But everything familiar will be gone. Not my hometown, but my childhood home. My brother and sister's homes. My baby brother moved out of his apartment and bought into the new property, too. All of my siblings have partners who have come into the family over the last few years. I've been the outsider by choice for more than two decades, and now I'll still be the outsider, but at home. *That* major life change I was expecting. You, though. You," he said with a chuckle, "are an upheaval that was definitely not on the radar."

"Bad timing for us both," she said in a low murmur.

"Is timing a good reason to give up on something so..."

"Perfect?" she answered with a hopeful expression.

He kissed her then, full and hard, the rich feeling of her lips against his so gratifying, so beautiful. Nothing about their embrace felt awkward or strange. On the contrary, she fit against his body as if they were molded for each other.

Serendipity had a funny way of occurring exactly when you least expected it–and when you needed it most.

A sound like thunder in the distance filled his ears as he lost himself in the kiss, her grasp desperate and eager, her body responsive in his hands.

Then a loud whistle pierced the muffled undertone and he realized what he was hearing–but didn't break the kiss.

Applause. From the audience.

Suddenly, the floor moved beneath them, his hands instinctively tightening around her, and the elevator car descended slowly to the lobby, coming to a gentle stop.

The *ding!* of the doors opening made Ana's muscles instantly go slack.

But her legs had another idea: to exit the elevator as fast as possible.

Four men in blue uniforms with company logos on the chests were standing in a line, all frowning. Their faces changed as they saw Ana, who sprinted off like an Olympian. Two of the guys stepped onto the elevator and grabbed their bags before Dennis could do it, so he followed Ana, who looked like a timid mouse being interrogated by bears.

"Give the lady space. *Lots* of space," he growled at the group, who swayed away from her instantly. Dennis slipped his arm around her waist, blocking them with his body, and she leaned into him. The fragile beat of her heart was like a hummingbird's.

The elevator fiasco had gone on for so long, too long for her nervous system to handle it all.

A man in a suit, wearing a hotel name tag on his lapel, approached them, a tablet computer in hand.

"My goodness! We are so, so sorry about that!"

She waved the man off. "I'm fine. I don't need any compensation. I just want to go home."

"But surely we can—"

"You heard her," Dennis said, fixing the man with an unblinking stare. "We're fine. Leave us alone now."

Dennis knew that when you confront someone so clearly, you have to be prepared for pushback.

He also knew this guy's job was to cover his corporate employer's butt in case of liability.

"Um, yes, sir. I—"

Their bags were next to them. The uniformed crew were now all over the elevator, touching and probing, an Out of Order sign already hanging crookedly over the button panel next to it. Dennis slung his backpack over his shoulder, then pulled his phone out of his pocket and checked the time.

Twelve eleven.

"We missed check out," he said as he reached for the handle of her bag, now pulling one in each hand. "Where are you going next?"

"Train station. I live in Newburyport, remember? I'll take the train to Gloucester and my mom will pick me up. She's expecting me."

Dennis absorbed that information.

"Your mom and stepfather live near you?"

"They live in Gloucester."

"Nice. You know, I'd offer you a ride if you can wait a bit. I have to go pick up my new truck at the dealership, but – "

"I – you're very sweet. Really. But can you accept that I need some time alone? To clear my head and regulate?"

"I can indeed."

They reached the big doors to the outside and stopped, each checking their coat, zipping up, preparing for the blast of cold air that winter always brought in Boston. Cabs were lined up at the curb, and his stomach dropped.

"That was a lot to go through, Ana. Are you sure you're okay?"

"Better than I would have been without you there," she said, squeezing his forearm with a casual, friendly touch that made him grin.

"Happy to help."

"What's your number?" she asked.

"It's in your phone. Remember?"

He realized her next question would be his last name, a ritual he despised with anyone in the United States.

Say the name *Luview* and everyone knew. Asked again. Teased and joked.

The longer he could delay it, the better.

To his surprise, she didn't ask, but instead said, "Text me back!"

Dennis sent the word Test, Ana replying with a single heart.

"I'll call you," he said, but her face was neutral. Was she holding back from being too attached? Hiding a waterfall of emotion?

Or had her sneaking out of his room this morning been a clue?

"Promise?" she asked, standing on tiptoes, giving his cheek a sweet kiss. "Don't guys always say that after a one-night stand?"

"This wasn't a one-night stand."

"It wasn't?"

"Can't be if we see each other again. And we will. Promise."

On impulse, he flipped his phone to camera mode and held it up, Ana instinctively moving closer to him, going for the selfie he was after. A flick of his thumb and the picture was taken, preserved with so many others that were important to him.

"Before you go," he said, pulling her aside, "I never asked you why you're here. In the hotel."

"A conference."

"On what?"

Smiling, she closed her eyes, squeezing them tight as if afraid to admit something.

"Trauma."

"Seriously?"

"Seriously."

"Man, you were super-prepared for me, then, weren't you?"

"Actually, no." Her smile dropped. "I'm not sure what to do with you."

Impulse got the better of him and he kissed her again, the tip of his nose brushing against the rim of her wool hat as he angled their lips, the chilly air making her cheek cool.

"Well, I know what to do with you. And I know that whatever this is between us, it's special."

"I feel the same way."

"Then let's follow up."

"That sounds very businesslike."

"Then let's have dinner? Is that better?"

"Perfect." She kissed him again, a light, sweet brush of her lips on his, the kind of kiss you give someone you know you'll see again. "I'm going to miss my train, so..."

"Goodbye, Ana. I'll reach out soon."

"Goodbye, Dennis. Thank you for being such a wonderful surprise."

"You deserve wonderful surprises, Ana. As many as life can possibly send you."

And with that, she disappeared down the street, Dennis turning in the opposite direction to get his new truck, drive to his new home, and start his new life.

The valet was hailing a taxi for him when he felt his phone buzz.

It was his mom.

About to leave? she asked.

Yes.

A giddy feeling, something young and raw, made him add, *And I have a story to tell about that woman in the picture.*

You do? she replied. *What a wonderful surprise!*

Yes, he wrote back. *Life is throwing nothing but surprises my way these days.*

Chapter Eight

Ana

Ana hated going to the doctor. Not irrationally, just not her favorite way to spend time.

Self-care meant good medical care, but there was something about the sterile feel of medical offices that made her uncomfortable.

Plus, they reminded her that she was mortal.

The strange waves of nausea and dizziness that had started at the hotel weren't fading. After the excitement of being with Dennis, she'd taken the train to Gloucester, uncharacteristically falling asleep for the final fifteen minutes. Her mother had commented on how "ragged" she looked.

A good night's sleep was all she needed, she'd thought.

Or maybe she caught some exotic subtropical illness from Dennis? If so, it was worth it.

Maybe.

But the fatigue and mild nausea wouldn't go away, so here

she was, ready to be done with this ridiculous bug. Reluctant to cancel any of her clients, she'd re-booked today's two appointments, clearing her schedule.

"Ana?" Peggy, the nurse practitioner Ana had been seeing for the last two years, poked her head into the waiting area. "Come on back." At this practice, pediatrics was separated from adult patients, but on the long walk back to the farthest exam room, Ana caught a peek of small children with runny noses playing with colorful bead toys.

She smiled reflexively.

In the exam room, Peggy began going through the preliminaries.

"Can you describe what's going on?"

"It started over the weekend. I was at a work conference, and when I started drinking and eating, I lost my appetite."

"Any specific stressors in your life?"

Ana worked to explain how run down she felt, the ball of lead in her stomach not helping matters. Somatic stress was certainly a possibility, as she knew professionally.

But this felt different.

Then Peggy asked the question Ana hated most.

"Could you be pregnant?"

"No," Ana said sadly.

"Haven't had sex in more than six weeks?"

"Oh—well, yes, I have. But I can't be pregnant."

"You used protection?"

"Yes. Condoms."

"Anything else?"

"No. But with my gynecological history, I doubt—"

"Let's run a urine test just in case." Peggy smiled. "Standard procedure."

About to argue, Ana stopped herself. Harris had been adamant about not wanting kids, and Dennis, well... she'd just slept with him three days ago. She couldn't possibly...

Peggy pointed to a small bathroom down the hall.

"We have dip strips in there. Just follow the directions on the laminated poster on the wall."

"I do it myself?"

"Sure. It helps."

"Helps?"

"Patients can have their first reaction in private."

"Ah. Gotcha." Sadness washed over her. When she was seventeen and went for her first gynecological exam, the doctor had stopped the exam rather abruptly. Telling her to dress, he left the room and within minutes, came back in with her mother.

The doctor explained what he saw: a unicornuate uterus.

A rare condition, the abnormality meant that Ana had only one ovary, one fallopian tube, and half a uterus. Her mother had freaked out, but the doctor had stayed calm. The finding made other issues make sense, especially Ana's irregular periods.

The chances she could successfully conceive, carry, and deliver a child were low, but there was hope.

Hope that Ana had deliberately stuffed into a box to deal with later.

In the bathroom, she located the urine strips, followed the clean-catch instructions, and set the test down to wait for the five minutes required. Bathrooms, by nature, weren't interesting, but this one seemed designed for pregnant folks.

A comfortable chair in the corner, a basket of magazines, and lots of general information about reproductive health.

Her phone buzzed as she waited.

Brie.

How are you feeling?

Like crap.

I'm sorry. Maybe that guy gave you something? The flu is going around.

Dennis didn't give me the flu.

Heard from him yet?

No. But it's not even been three days.

Maybe he's a stickler for the three-day rule. Doesn't want to seem desperate.

Dennis doesn't strike me as the type to follow someone else's arbitrary rule.

You really like this guy! Just text him!

I will when I feel better. How did the cake tasting go?

Brie was newly engaged. She met her fiancé, Martin, when they both attended sommelier training. Martin was a chef at one of Boston's most famous tapas restaurants, and the couple had plans to open their own farm-to-table restaurant and grocery store.

Someday.

The cake was fantastic. I had no idea vegan baking was so advanced, Brie replied. *Mom and Dad still can't believe I'm marrying a guy who will never take a bite of their cheese, but hey.*

He's still wonderful even if he doesn't eat dairy, Ana replied, startling when a knock on the door interrupted her texting.

"Ana? Everything okay?"

Peggy, calling through the bathroom door.

Right, pregnancy test. Time's up.

Dropping her phone in her bag, she picked up the little strip and looked.

Then looked again, disbelieving.

A very clear positive line was showing.

Heart tripping over itself as it tried to flee her chest, every system inside her skin suddenly went haywire.

"Faulty," she murmured. Opening the door, she held the test out to Peggy, who looked at it, eyebrows going up though her face remained neutral.

"Ana?" Peggy guided her back to the exam room like the pro that she was.

"Faulty. These tests must be expired or something. I can't be pregnant."

"You've had intercourse within the window of conception?"

"Sure, but..."

"That's why we do the screening," Peggy said in a calm, careful voice. Ana knew that tone all too well. She used it all the time with her own clients, in therapy sessions. "I'll add a pregnancy test to your blood work. You'll get confirmation either way by late tomorrow if we get the draw done in the next few hours. You can go downstairs to the lab," Peggy checked the clock, "as a walk-in. Worst case, you have to wait two days for an answer."

"You mean to get a negative. This could be lots of things. A cold. The flu. A weird virus that makes pregnancy tests come up with false positives. Right?"

"Well—no. But there are other causes of false positives."

"Really?" She practically squealed with joy. "Like what?"

"A recent pregnancy. An abortion."

Ana shook her head.

"Some medications—anti-anxiety meds, anti-convulsants. Parkinson's medications. Some diuretics. But your medical chart shows none of those."

"I'm not on any. But you're saying there are lots of explanations for false positives?"

"There are. Some medical conditions can explain it, too." Suddenly guarded, Peggy looked away.

"What kind of medical conditions?"

"Let's not borrow trouble."

"I'll just Google it the second I leave," she said with a little laugh.

"Something as simple as a urinary tract infection can trigger a false positive on a pregnancy test."

"Oh, thank goodness!"

"Do you have UTI symptoms?"

"No."

Biting her lower lip, Peggy finally cracked a little, giving her a more personal response. "If you *are* pregnant, how does that feel?"

Still laughing nervously, Ana felt a thin line of hysteria rising up in her, tangled with a hope she'd systematically killed off years ago.

"I can't be. And if I am, the father is, well..."

"Out of the picture?"

"So far out of the picture, he's in another country."

One without an extradition treaty, she almost added, but prudence seemed the best option here.

"Ah. I see. Let's not get ahead of ourselves. You can always retest on your way out. Or buy a test at a drug store. Some women try two different brands to check. Plus the blood test."

"I can't believe this."

"Why don't we finish up and get that lab work going? I think you'll feel better with those results."

In a daze, she did exactly as Peggy suggested, ignoring Brie's texts until she was down in the lab, waiting her turn behind an elderly gentleman who used a walker. As he made his way slowly into the phlebotomist's room, she finally looked at her phone.

And teared up.

If she was pregnant, it was Harris's. No doubt.

Which meant all hope of ever being with Dennis was now completely out the window.

No. Not true.

Assuming she was pregnant, there was no hope with Dennis.

But how could she be pregnant? The last time she and Harris had slept together was...

Damn. Long enough to be in the window of possibility. They'd used a condom. It hadn't broken.

This was unreal.

Mind racing, she handled random partial thoughts, memories, and gut reactions like they were being shot at her by a machine gun.

How many drinks had she had since Harris left?

One. Plus the half a caipirinha with Dennis. Drowning her sorrows after the mess with Harris had been about sugar, thankfully.

Not alcohol.

But geez. Even one and a half drinks made her feel a wave of guilt. Thank goodness she hadn't actually consumed that double bourbon she'd ordered.

Her periods were irregular because of the uterine issue, so when nothing had come two weeks ago, she hadn't blinked.

The test had to be faulty. *Had* to.

"DaSilva?" A woman in scrubs held a clipboard and looked at her.

Ana rose.

As long as she didn't actually look at the needle being inserted into her arm, or the blood filling the vials, she could handle the draw. And she did, with equanimity.

Because that's who she was.

Even. Calm. Measured.

Not this anxious bundle of nerves that had emerged since Harris dumped her so spectacularly.

Although *dumped* was a bit of a stretch, since the jerk hadn't technically broken up with her. He just ghosted, leaving her with federal officers at her front door, a ton of interrogations, and fortunately, a bulldog lawyer for a stepfather, who helped get them off her back.

Pregnant? *Really?*

As the phlebotomist taped a wad of gauze to the insertion site, Ana let out a small laugh, the woman smiling as well. Her name tag said Tracy.

"Don't have too many people laughing when they get poked."

"Just thinking about something funny."

"Good! Most of my patients are in a state of agony or anxiety. Nice to have some happiness for a change."

Ana was confirming her name and birthdate on all the vials of blood when a woozy feeling hit her, the air suddenly sharp and cold against the roof of her mouth, the chair she sat in hot and hard.

Baby.

The blood work was going to rule it in or out, but Ana was possibly pregnant.

Her phone buzzed in her purse.

Hello? Brie texted. *Remember our coffee date?*

Ana's head snapped up to find the giant wall clock she'd noticed when she walked in.

Damn it. She was fifteen minutes late.

Sorry, she typed, remembering that Brie was just two blocks away. *I had to get extra blood work.*

Something wrong?

The words stared at her, judging her, daring her to say it. Once she told Brie, she could never take it back.

Once she said *pregnant*, it made it real.

What if she wasn't, though? What if it was a fluke? Maybe she did have a UTI. Or maybe some medication she'd taken recently screwed up the test.

Then she'd create drama for no reason, and feel like a fool.

Would she, though? Really? If Ana were one of her own clients, she'd say that the support of a good friend in a time of fear outweighed possible foolish feelings later.

I'll tell you over coffee, Ana replied, her stomach going tight at the thought.

Decaf, a voice whispered in her head. If she really were pregnant, then she should stick to decaf.

Ana stood, ready to sink into the comfort of her best friend, deciding on the spot that she had to tell her. This was too big. Too important.

Too shocking.

"Honey? I know you're texting and busy, but you just wobbled a little in that chair. Are you okay? Need some apple juice? Crackers? I've been drawing blood for twenty-six years and I can spot a fainter from a mile away."

"Faint? No," Ana said, her voice fading as her ears began to buzz.

"Sit right here." Tracy's tone was firm and authoritative. "Put your head down and breathe in for a count of four, out for a count of four."

No argument from Ana; Tracy was right. She was dizzy and overwhelmed, and now was no time to try to push through it.

A text buzzed.

You seem off. Are you still at the doctor's?

Brie was the one who got Ana to start coming to this primary care practice.

Yes. Dizzy at blood draw, she finally confessed. *Lab tech helping me.*

OMW! Brie replied, triggering a sense of relief in Ana that surprised her. Panic was unusual for her, and having Brie here would let the piece of her that was freaking out stand down.

"My friend is coming," she told Tracy, who was rummaging in a small fridge. She turned around with an apple juice container in her hand, the kind hospitals served, with an aluminum foil top you peeled back.

"Here," Tracy said, opening the foil an inch and handing it to her. "Drink this. I'm glad you have a supportive friend."

"Brie is going to die if I'm really pregnant."

"I'm sure it won't actually kill her," Tracy said under her breath, which made Ana laugh weakly.

"No, it's just, I'm not supposed to be able to conceive."

"That makes it a double blessing!" But Tracy's mouth immediately jerked down, alarm in her eyes. "Or did I say the wrong thing?"

"It's okay. I'm just–this is a lot."

Tracy patted her hand. "Life is a lot, isn't it?"

Great. Ana was being comforted by a phlebotomist in a lab as she awaited the results of a blood test that would determine the course of her entire life. The therapist was being assessed and fed apple juice.

"Life is very complicated," Ana whispered, eyes filling with tears.

Closing her eyes, she took a long, deep inhale and let herself feel her feelings. Fear, shame, disbelief, disappointment, excitement–it all welled up, competing for space in her heart.

Pushing it down wouldn't make her feel less. It would just make the feelings come out in dysfunctional ways.

So she breathed. Felt. Cried.

And simply *was*.

"You sit here as long as you need," Tracy said. Ana heard a keyboard click. "I don't have another appointment for fifteen minutes, and the walk-ins can wait."

"Thank you."

"Have a sip of that apple juice. It could really help."

Harris came into her mind's eye, her imagination putting Dennis next to him, hulking and rageful, ready to tear her ex limb from limb. The fantasy was fabulous, but with tears dripping from the corners of her eyes, she realized that another feeling was growing.

Sorrow.

Dennis wasn't a possibility now.

Definitely not.

Two tentative taps at the door made her open her eyes, and a receptionist showed Brie in. Where Ana had long brown hair she kept pulled back in a ponytail or braid, Brie was blonde, her loose curls cut short. Curious, caring brown eyes met hers, and a whiff of Brie's ever-present lavender scent made her feel instantly better.

"What's wrong, Ana?"

"I'm feeling better now." She smiled shakily. "I think I just got woozy."

"That can happen," Tracy said with a smile.

Ana stood up again, walking carefully to the door. Steady now, she gave Tracy a grateful look.

"Thank you."

The response was a casual wave. "No problem. Thank you for not throwing up."

"Ew!"

"Happens more than you'd think." Tracy looked at Brie. "Give her lots of air and rest."

"Will do."

Walking through the lobby, Brie linked her arm in Ana's. "What was that about?"

"Can I tell you over coffee?"

"Are you up for it?"

Outside, the gray sky made Ana feel gloomier, a sense of dread overwhelming her.

"Yes. Warm coffee shop. Private corner."

"You're scaring me. What did you learn at the doctor?" Brie halted on the sidewalk, putting her hands on Ana's shoulders. "Tell me."

"I–"

"Is it cancer?"

"What? No!"

"Oh, thank God." Brie's mother, Morgan, had just finished chemo for stage 2b breast cancer.

"It's—I..." A hysterical laugh began, choked out by sobs.

"What the hell is going on, Ana? Are you—"

"Pregnant."

Brie's eyes nearly fell out of her head.

"Did you just say—"

"Pregnant. Urine test was positive, now I'm waiting for the blood test. Results tomorrow or the next day."

"How can you be pregnant?"

"It's—I don't know! It was a pee test—it might be wrong."

"Are you having any symptoms?"

"Maybe? I'm really tired. And nauseated."

"That could be lots of things."

"Right."

"But..." Brie drew out the word. "If you are, is it Harris's?"

"Who else have I slept with?"

Brie tilted her head. "Well..."

"Dennis? I slept with him three *days* ago. It's not him."

"Anyone other than Harris?"

"NO! Of course not. I would have told you."

The magnitude of the problem began to hit Brie, her face changing as Ana watched.

"Oh, no. Ana! Harris? *Harris* really is the father?"

"I—I guess?"

Brie began spewing a string of profanity that Ana wholeheartedly agreed with, especially the part involving various objects that Harris could shove where the sun didn't shine. Hearing her bestie scream "unlubricated fire hydrant" was jarring.

But a bit cathartic.

By the time they got to the coffee shop, Ana felt more

stable, so she grabbed a small cheese bagel and ordered a black coffee.

Decaf, just in case.

Brie gave her a judgmental look.

"Already? Decaf?"

"I know. Might as well be water, but what if? I already drank alcohol three days ago, and if I really am, you know…"

"Pregnant with Harris McSlimeball's baby?"

"Um, right. If I am, then the last thing this, um…"

The word *baby* didn't want to be in her mouth.

"Noodle."

"Excuse me?"

"Let's call it a noodle. Makes it easier to talk about."

The suggestion hung in the air like the steam rising up from the espresso machine as the barista made Brie's cappuccino.

"Okay. Fine. Noodle."

"You're being very good to your hypothetical noodle," Brie said with approval. "I wouldn't worry about a tiny bit of alcohol or caffeine, though. Noodles are hardy."

"Noodles require a lot of care! They're defenseless and need to be treated just right for optimal growth."

"Yes, but you can't be perfect. No noodle ever gets perfect parenting."

"My noodle will!"

"Not with Harris as the… noodlemaker."

"I am the noodlemaker, thank you very much. He just added the… secret ingredient."

A very puzzled barista was sliding their drinks toward them.

"You two work in a restaurant?"

Brie rolled her eyes and slid her credit card into the machine. Soon, Ana was nibbling her parmesan cheese bagel and sipping her brew, finally back on an even keel.

"That jerk," Brie muttered.

"I know."

"He needs to make this right."

"How?"

"He needs to help you! Be here!"

"He didn't do this to me."

"Of course he did!"

"No, I mean, it's not like he got me pregnant on purpose. Something must have gone wrong, if I even *am* pregnant. We still don't know for sure."

"You had a positive test. You're feeling nauseated and tired. Do your boobs hurt?"

"Huh?"

"Boobs." Brie looked down at her own. "Are they tender?"

"Sure, but that usually happens right before my period."

"Ana." Brie gave her a flat look.

"Oh, no," Ana moaned, taking a sip of coffee. "More proof."

"Did you call Harris?"

"WHAT? No! He wouldn't answer even if I tried."

"You need to try. He needs to know."

"So he can do what? Taunt me from Morocco?"

"I still can't believe he offered to have you join him there. I think that text was fake."

"I think he half meant it, but he also said I was on my own getting to Marrakesh."

"Such a gentleman. I am so furious at him. How can you be so calm?"

"Am I calm? I think I'm just in shock. I have a broken–""

"A broken heart." Brie patted her hand.

She'd almost said uterus. Brie didn't know about her abnormal uterus. Leave it to Harris to screw up the natural order of the universe. Now she'd be forced to reveal it and oh, right.

She also might be a *mother*.

Ana just blinked, unable to stop. Her right hand moved to her belly, fingertips brushing it.

"You need to call him."

"No way! Not until it's confirmed by the blood test. I really, really don't want to talk to him unless I have to."

"You shouldn't be afraid of him."

"I'm not."

"You're *something* of him."

"I'm ashamed."

"Why are *you* ashamed?"

"Because I didn't see what a sleaze he is. I should have spotted it."

"Just because you're a therapist doesn't mean you know everything about everyone."

Those words made Ana tear up. Brie was right, but she still felt so stupid.

"You should call him. Tell him," Brie repeated.

"No." Ana let out a long breath that she hoped would evacuate some anxiety. "I can't until I know it's true. Right now I have a pee test, feel a little sick, and that's it. If I call him now and it turns out I'm not pregnant, it's just stirring up trouble."

"True. I still want to find him and beat the hell out of him with a cheese pot."

"If I'm pregnant, it's not his fault. We used condoms. It just means one of them broke."

"He deserves the anger anyway."

Ana tapped Brie's cup with hers. "I'll drink to that."

For the next few minutes they drank and ate, Ana's stomach slowly unclenching, her mind clearing a bit. Being with Brie was always soothing, a deep layer inside able to unfurl and flatten, turn loose and serene. They'd been friends since their freshman year of college, Ana a psychology major, Brie in nutrition.

And here they were, almost two decades later, best buddies.

"Let's talk about something more pleasurable, like your wedding," Ana said, happy to change the subject.

"I can't believe it's happening."

"You're going to be so beautiful. That silk dress is stunning."

"Isn't it amazing that I can wear Grandma's dress? I love the neckline. Did I tell you that Mom found a tailor in Boston who uses scraps from other vintage dresses to update yours? But I don't think it needs much work, really just needs to be taken in a little at the hips."

As Brie chattered about her plans, Ana nodded, trying to focus. Being her maid of honor meant supporting her friend. Ana had been a bridesmaid twice, both in the two years after grad school, those brides now distant friends she followed on social media and visited with when they were in town or she was near where they lived.

Brie, though, was special. Her family's cheese shop was in Rockport, and Ana even helped out sometimes during holiday rushes. They paid her in product. It was a mutually beneficial arrangement.

As she listened to Brie talk about invitations and whether to invite distant cousins from Quebec, her phone buzzed.

I was told it's customary to wait three days to text someone so you don't seem desperate. It's been exactly 72 hours since I last saw you, so...

The words were impossible.

Blinking hard at her phone, she nearly shrieked when another text appeared, this one a photo.

The picture was of her and Dennis, the selfie he snapped before they'd parted.

"Ana? What's up?" Constitutionally curious, Brie looked at Ana's phone and made a low sound of approval.

"He is HOT, Ana! Is that the guy from the hotel?"

"Dennis," Ana whispered. "Oh, no." Setting the phone down, she rested her forehead on her palms, burying her fingers in her hair.

Brie picked the phone up and read his text aloud.

"Awww. He sounds awesome. When are you planning to see him again?"

Choking, Ana looked at her in disbelief.

"See him? *See him?* I'm pregnant with another man's baby!"

Brie cursed, still studying the picture. "Those arms! How do you look at those arms and not drool?"

"I don't. I wore a bib around him."

"Ana!"

"What am I going to do, Brie? If I'm pregnant, I can't be with Dennis!"

"But what if you're not?"

"Fine. Then yes. So what do I do about his text?"

"Ignore it until you get the blood test results?"

"That's another day or two."

"He waited three days to text you. Make him wait two more."

"It feels rude."

"Ana. Stop holding yourself to impossible standards when it comes to others' feelings."

"You know what I do for a living, right?"

Laughing, they stared at each other.

"So say something to the guy, then don't say any more until you get the test results. The second they come in, call me. I'll read them with you, and we'll manage Dennis and Harris from there."

"I feel so irresponsible! I could be pregnant by my ex, and I don't know what to say to the new, wonderful guy!"

"Not irresponsible. Human. Frankly, I'm impressed."

"You're impressed? With me? In this mess?"

"Yeah. I am. You took some really great leaps."

"I feel like I leapt and someone pulled away the safety net."

"It's all going to be fine," Brie soothed. She looked again at the selfie on the phone. "You look so happy with him."

"I was. How can someone you've known for less than twenty-four hours make you feel so complete?"

"Until I met Martin, it was inconceivable," Brie said.

Inconceivable.

That word arced through her mind like a firework, the shrill whistle of it exploding in her head. She burst into tears, crying so hard, she couldn't breathe, Brie squeezing her hand and trying to infuse her with a sense of calm.

Inconceivable?

No. Not anymore.

Chapter Nine

Dennis

The internet was a blessing and a curse.

Because it damn near turned him into a stalker.

Finding out where Ms. Ana DaSilva lived and worked was easy. *Too* easy. Didn't need to be a private investigator to access way too much of her personal information.

And her mother's. And her stepfather's.

Holding back from contacting her was the thin line of decency Dennis forced himself to stand behind.

She'd ghosted him back at the hotel, only talking to him when they were trapped in the elevator. Had he misread her signals a second time? The way she kissed him as the elevator bumped down to the first floor hadn't been fake.

No way.

Nothing about how her body responded to him said she was placating him to get away. The way she leaned against him. Looked him in the eye. Flirted with her elegant hands.

She'd made love with a tender eagerness and a hot streak that he could still hear, feel, and taste when he concentrated hard enough, in the fitful dark, body throbbing for her.

He hadn't misread their night together, not by a long shot.

So what had changed?

I was told it's customary to wait three days to text someone so you don't seem desperate. It's been exactly 72 hours since I last saw you, so...

Sending her that first text had left a smile on his face for hours, and he'd been elated when she'd finally replied back with:

You don't seem desperate. How are you?

Better now that I've connected with you. How's life? His simple reply was meant to be polite and keep the conversation going.

But then hours turned into a half a day, then a full day, and now here he was, two days after texting her, and...

Nothing.

A big, fat nothing.

"Hey." Kell tossed a toolbag into the back of the Luview Tree Service truck, then opened the passenger-side door and climbed in. Dennis looked up from his phone.

"Hey, what?"

"You look a million miles away," Kell said, peering at him. When Dennis left home and joined the Army, little Kellan was just that: *little*.

Ten years younger than Dennis, his brother was now about twenty pounds heavier, though it rested differently on his body. Military posture really was a thing, and Dennis had it.

Kell didn't.

Rafe called Dennis's build "super medium," and hated him for it.

"You have zero body fat, man," Rafe frequently bitched,

but his buddy managed the same hundred-pound loads Dennis carried on five-mile climbs, and matched him on his ten-mile runs.

Barely.

Kell wasn't fit in the same way Dennis was, but no way did Dennis want to get into an arm wrestling match with the Paul Bunyan impersonator his brother had grown into. Getting used to the beard was a struggle. Absorbing the change in the brother he remembered was turning out to be a paradigm shift.

Like everything in Luview, Maine.

"Just thinking."

"What's her name?"

"Huh?"

"You have a look on your face I've never seen before. Has to be about a woman."

"Why does everything have to be about a woman with you? Just because you're completely besotted with Rachel doesn't mean that the rest of us live our lives daydreaming about our partners."

Kell's eyes narrowed.

"So it *is* about a woman." He carried a big travel thermos printed with the words *Love You Coffee, where love is caffeinated*.

"Not talking about it." Dennis shook his head.

Kell finished taking a sip, pulling his upper lip in right after.

"I think it's great if you've already got someone. Make it easier on yourself."

"What's *that* supposed to mean?"

"You kidding me, bro?" Kell snorted. "You are a hot commodity on the Love You meat market."

"Meat market," he repeated. The words conjured an image

of Kendrill's Market for Dennis, nothing more, until he realized what Kell meant and groaned.

"Annabeth Khouri is already imagining the engraved wedding invitations."

"Oh, come on. You think I'm going to find someone to date *here?* That's Mom's dream. She probably has a china pattern picked out for some imaginary bride she thinks I'm going to find in Luview." Dennis sighed. "I knew this would happen if I came back."

"Mom would try to run your life?"

"That there would be expectations."

Kell snorted.

"Where do you get to live without other people's expectations? You want that, bro, go be a monk on a mountain."

"Don't tempt me."

Dennis checked his phone again. Still no text.

"She ghosted you?"

"Not talking about it."

"Sorry."

Dennis closed his eyes slowly, as if even his eyelids needed to show restraint.

"Where are we going?" He opened the GPS on his phone, though it wouldn't do much good on many of the back roads. Cell signals were the very definition of intermittent reinforcement here in the mountains of western Maine.

"Mel's."

"Mel Chassi?"

"Yep. Tree got hit by lightning, pretty close to her big barn. Happened about two years ago. We've been watching it for a while, and now it's got to come down."

Kell handed Dennis the work order. Half typed but with added notes in their mother's neat penmanship, it detailed the job. He looked at the price estimate.

"That's half what we'd normally charge," he grunted.

"Mel's animal sanctuary is a non-profit. Dad gives her a break."

"Dad's a softy."

"Yep. Just like you." Kell's grin made his beard spread, showing off teeth that were perfectly straight after two years of braces when he was a tween.

When Dennis joined the Army, those braces hadn't even been put on yet.

"Me?"

"You and Mel have a thing for animals."

"It's called compassion."

"I have compassion! I love Calamine."

"Your cat is bigger than most five-year-old humans."

"Better behaved than most of them, too. And don't say anything negative about Cally in earshot."

As if she were eavesdropping, Cally's orange head popped up from the backseat of the truck's cab.

"See?" Kell said with a laugh. "You hurt her feelings."

"It was a compliment! She's objectively huge." Growing up around Maine Coon cats meant Dennis had gone out into the world and found regular-sized cats weird.

And it wasn't just cats, either.

Like bowling. The first time he went bowling during post-boot camp Army training, he referred to what he saw as "big-ball bowling" and was howled out of existence, cursed with the nickname Big Balls for the next three weeks, until training ended.

All because he'd only seen candlepin bowling in his corner of Maine.

"So are you," Kell said, eyes appraising him. "I thought I was the biggest guy in the family."

"You're taller than me."

"By half an inch."

"Still counts."

"But we still both beat Luke. He's the puny one." Kell grinned.

"Luke is anything but puny," Dennis said drily, navigating the dirt and gravel camp road that took them down to the numbered state route. It was a steep hill, layers of snowstorms mashed into the dirt and stone, with a few ice patches in there for good measure. "Anyone who can defuse Lyle Morgenstern in person without a single blow has mad skills. And he's trained in hand-to-hand self-defense."

"So?"

"So am I. Which means we're both stronger than you in that arena."

"Is that how it is? We're going to rank the three of us in different ways?"

"No. You started it. I don't need to compare myself to you two. I already know I'm superior." He couldn't finish the sentence without smirking, knowing how ridiculous the words sounded.

The right turn out of the camp's entrance took them closer to town, though Mel Chassi's place wasn't downtown. As he drove, Dennis assembled a dossier in his head about Mel. Only back for a week now, this was happening increasingly often, a psychological tool to re-orient himself to his hometown.

While he'd been coming home once a year since he enlisted, and he knew the comings and goings of half the town because Deanna wouldn't stop delivering gossip, he still felt a temporal unreality about his new life.

Sure, Mel Chassi was now a grown woman, divorced from Darren, and had a son. But Dennis remembered her as a camp counselor, then director, and local horse-riding specialist.

"Want to grab something from Greta's before we head over to Mel's?" Kell asked.

"No."

"Come on."

"You asked whether *I* wanted to. If *you* want to, just say so."

"I want to go get a croissant at Greta's."

Dennis took the left fork ahead, instead of the right toward Mel's animal sanctuary. Kell shifted his weight in the front seat, brow knit together.

"I never thought of it that way," he said, scratching his hairline under the thick, red wool cap he wore.

"What way?"

"I wasn't asking permission. But it's how we ask for stuff like that."

"It's not direct. I'm used to direct communication."

"Do you expect everyone here to change to your style?"

"No. But that doesn't mean I won't point it out."

"You spent a lot of years in the Army. It'll take a long time to get out of those habits."

"Why would I want to change those habits? They're functional."

When they reached the outskirts of town, Dennis widened his eyes, then chuckled.

"This place. So much red, pink, and white."

"I'm so used to it, I don't notice." Kell frowned. "Rachel comments on it all the time, though. You'd think she'd adjust after living here for a few years, but so far, no."

"Hard to adjust to something so ludicrous."

Dennis paused at a stoplight, looking at the library, a big red-brick building with a heart-shaped sign. When he was a kid, their mom took them to story hour, then summer reading clubs, with an almost military regularity. Dennis enjoyed reading as much as the next person, but as an adult, he preferred non-fiction. History and biography.

Anything but *Jane's Intelligence* case studies.

"Is that why you get up at four every morning? Army

habit?" Kell asked as Dennis moved through the now-green light, finding a parking spot within ten seconds. Small-town life meant not fighting for the daily needs that were challenges in more urban and populated areas. Easy parking was taken for granted here in Luview, at least in the off season for tourists.

People complained if they had to walk a whole two blocks.

"How would you know when I wake up?"

"Cally scratches at the door when you leave your cabin at four-thirty."

"I've never seen her outside."

The spot he chose was directly across the street from Greta's, which was quiet right now.

"What do you do at four-thirty in the morning?"

"I go for a run."

"A run? Why?"

"Exercise. Conditioning."

"Chop wood if you want exercise!"

"I do that, too."

"How far do you run?"

"In this snow? Two miles."

"Hold on. *Snow?* You don't run on the roads?"

"Trails have about eighteen inches on them. Compact snow. I run on it."

"Did you buy snowshoes?"

"I don't wear snowshoes. I wear winter boots."

"That's not running! That's–"

"A phenomenal workout."

Dennis put the truck in park, turned off the engine, grabbed his hat and gloves, and climbed out, Kell following suit.

They barely had to look both ways to cross. Luview was quiet this time of day.

"*Punishment* is more like it." Kell made a derisive sound in the back of his throat.

"It's just conditioning."

"You do know you left the Army, right? No need to abuse yourself."

"It's not abuse. I enjoy it."

"The pleasure centers of your brain need to be rewired."

"Gonna take a long time. Twenty-plus years doing what I've done gets in deep. Plus, I've heard it's good for my mitochondria," he added as a joke.

Kell's glance didn't go unnoticed. Dennis knew his family all wanted to press him for details about his various missions, but he literally, legally, couldn't give them details. It had been hard for them to suppress all their questions about his location over the years, and for Deanna, who loved gossip and collected individual details about people like an archivist, it meant perpetual frustration.

He'd suspected part of the reason she was so happy he was moving back home was that she'd always know where he was.

With hearts cut into the shingling and trim, Love You Bakery, affectionately known simply as Greta's to the locals, was the stuff of brochures. Painted in the classic town colors, the three-story Victorian house held the café and bakery on the first and second floors, with a rental apartment on the third.

Approaching the front door, Dennis could smell maple and chocolate, coffee and bread. Mouth watering, he couldn't help but grin.

Kell wanted a croissant. Dennis knew they'd leave with enough carbs to last them a week.

"No! The warrior is truly home!" Greta Mitteracht called out as she shuffled from behind the register to plant a huge kiss on Dennis's cheek. Almost as round as she was tall, Greta was in her eighties now, but still had the fierce gaze of a woman who knew things.

"I don't know about the warrior part. I'm just here to climb trees and chop wood."

"And kick ass," Kell muttered under his breath, giving Dennis an eye roll.

"Deanna must be in heaven!" Greta's German accent was still present, even after decades of living in Maine. "All of her children, right there with her in that strange commune you all created."

"It's not a commune," Kell insisted. "We just decided to pool our money and live at the camp together."

"That is the definition of a commune."

"No, it's—"

"Are you here to argue with the lady or get some baked goods?" Dennis interrupted, shooting Kell a look. "Mel's waiting for us."

"Mel?" Greta asked as she walked behind the bakery display. "All those years rescuing people in the world, and now animals, too?"

"Rescuing people?"

Greta waved vaguely.

"I don't know what you did in the Army. So mysterious."

"I want a Morning Glory muffin and a maple scone. How's that for clearing up any mystery?" Looking at the display case, he groaned internally. Every muffin, cookie, and brownie was in the shape of a heart.

Every damn one.

Reaching into his back pocket, he nodded to Kell. "Order yours. I'll get it."

"Thanks! I'll take two croissants, Greta. Almond and chocolate." He turned to Dennis. "A man could get used to starting work days like this."

"It's a one-time deal. *Don't* get used to it."

"One time?" Greta protested. "Come in every day! And you get a ten percent discount."

"We do?" Kell's eyebrows shot up.

"Not you. Only him."

"Why?" Kell's voice went up with amusement.

"He is a veteran." Greta bagged their order and handed the white bag with the big red heart on it to Kell as Dennis slipped his credit card into the tiny reader on the counter. When he'd left home, Greta's still had the old metal cash register at the hostess station, the *ding!* of machinery signaling that the sale had been made.

Now he just inserted a piece of plastic with a chip in it, added a tip, and *bam!* Transaction complete.

More change in his hometown, even when so much was the same.

"You come in more often, Dennis. I'll save you a spot for Sunday brunch."

Kell's jaw dropped open.

"You never save tables on Sundays!"

"I can do whatever I want, Kellan Luview! This is my shop, and if I want to save a table for Dennis, I will!"

"I had no idea you played favorites like that, Greta." Kell winked at her. "How can I get the VIP treatment?"

Greta's jaw tightened, though Dennis could tell from her eyes that it was all in good fun.

"You are on my naughty list."

"Me? What? Why?"

"Rachel."

"What about Rachel?"

"She wants to move the electric trolley stop right in front of the shop."

"What's wrong with that? More foot traffic."

"And more *ding! ding! ding!* during my naptime!" Greta *harumphed*.

"I'll put in a good word for you." Kell winked again.

"I have tried already! She said that Love You Yoga needs quiet more than we do."

Low-grade panic began to form in Kell's eyes as he realized he was in a pickle. Dennis decided to rescue him.

Plus, the scent of his pastries made his stomach growl.

"Gotta go, Greta." He shook the bag. "Thanks! And I'll definitely take you up on the Sunday offer."

As he grabbed Kell's arm, his brother pivoted fast, grateful for the save.

"Thanks," Kell said with a loud sigh as they crossed the street. "That was about to get brutal."

"Rachel seems like a lightning rod in town."

"You don't know the half of it. She thinks she's helping the town to grow and thrive. Townies think she's intruding on the way things are and should be. I get stuck in the middle a lot."

"You realize *you* are a townie."

"Sure. But I'm an enlightened townie who likes progress. There aren't many of us."

Back in the truck, Kell opened the bag and handed Dennis his muffin with a napkin wrapped around it. Dennis pulled out of the parking spot and made a right turn to get back on track for Mel Chassi's place.

"How's it feel, being home?" Kell asked as he worked on his croissant.

"Fine."

"No, Dennis. How does it *feel?*"

"Why are you so focused on feelings?"

"I'm curious. I went to D.C. and lived there for a year. It felt super weird at first. You and I are the only ones in the family who went out into the world and lived somewhere else. Mom, Dad, Luke, and Colleen have never lived anywhere but here."

"Luke went to college."

"Yeah. In *Maine*."

"He spent a semester in Italy."

"Why don't you tell me about *your* feelings about being gone first?"

"I loved every damn minute of my time in D.C.," Kell said in a low, rumbling voice that made Dennis blink hard in surprise.

"But you came back."

"I did. The very end was awful. People can be really unkind. Scheming. Conniving."

"They are here, too, in the *love*-liest place on Earth, kid," Dennis grumbled. "Just in a different way."

"I know how to handle Nadine Khouri or Nancy Bilbee or Dane Morgenstern. Didn't know how to handle co-workers who stabbed me in the back while smiling at me."

"I heard it was your heart that got stabbed, and you ran back home."

"I don't need to rehash the past," Kell replied, voice tight, turning to his coffee to break the tension.

"Maybe my heart's feeling a little bruised right now." The words came out before Dennis realized he was going to say them.

If his stupid mouth was going to get him into trouble, stuffing the rest of his muffin in there was self-defense.

"What did she do?"

Dennis just chewed.

Kell waited him out.

Finally:

"It's what she's not doing that's killing me. Ignoring my texts."

"Ouch. Were you seeing her long?"

"No." With zero desire to elaborate, Dennis made the turn onto the dirt road that took them up to Mel's place, steering around a huge pothole in the middle of the road. Loads of people in their area had long driveways leading to remote homes in the woods, but as they drove on and on, Dennis began to notice just how remote her place was.

"You know," he said with a long sigh, scratching his beard along the right side of his face, "when Rachel and I were having trouble, it ripped my heart out. I couldn't sleep, couldn't focus, the whole bit. I was so sure I was right, suspecting her of being cruel to me in D.C." Kell let out a chuckle. "And now we're living together, engaged, and happy."

"You're also about to become Portia Starman's son-in-law. Have fun with that."

"We don't pick our in-laws."

"Actually, we do."

The road opened up to a big, wide field with electric fencing on the right. Still no sign of a barn or house anywhere, and they'd driven at least a mile.

"Driveway's up ahead, about a half mile," Kell said, pointing.

"This was just the road?"

"Sorta. Mel's is the only house on it."

"Gotcha." The fact that Dennis had never been to this animal sanctuary, yet Kell knew exactly where he was going, was becoming part of daily life. Unaccustomed to being the least informed person in any given group, he really disliked his ignorance.

Only time would improve the situation.

"And you're right. We do pick our in-laws, don't we? I guess I'm stuck with Portia and Stan for life."

"Rachel gets Mom and Dad. Quite a trade."

That just made Kell's eyes go out of focus and a bit glassy as he stared straight ahead.

Hah. Mission accomplished.

For the next few minutes, there was peace in the truck

cabin, until Dennis turned into Mel's driveway and had to slam on his brakes at the big gate.

Kell hopped out, popped the gate latch like he'd done it a thousand times, and opened the big metal entry. Dennis drove through, then Kell closed it behind the truck, giving Dennis a chance to look around.

In less than a minute, he saw two cows, an emu, an actual ostrich, a few llamas, a bunch of smaller creatures from dog size on down, and–

"Is that a camel?" he asked, pointing to a small courtyard near a barn, as Kell climbed in.

"Probably," Kell muttered as he shut the door. "You know how Bilbee's Tavern's phrase is 'If we don't have it, you shouldn't drink it'?"

"Yeah?"

"Mel's sanctuary's should be, 'If we don't have it, you can't save it.'"

"Aww."

Kell shot him a funny look. "Don't come home with a bunch of animals."

"Why not? I have my own place, finally. Maybe I'll get a dog. A cat. A camel."

"Harriet would love a camel," Kell deadpanned.

"Other than the spitting, they're great."

"Your definition of 'great' is very different from mine. I'm trying to imagine Rachel dodging camel spit."

"Even better reason to get one. The comedy would be worth it."

Calamine jumped up onto the top of the seat, right by Kell's head, as if jealous they were discussing other animals.

"Don't you worry, Cally," Kell crooned, petting her. "You're my one and only."

"Rachel know you talk to your cat like that?"

"Yes, and she loves it. Rachel understands that Cally is her sister wife."

Dennis laughed hard at that one. His little bro had a sense of humor, and something inside him relaxed a little.

It's only been a week, he told himself. *Let life unfurl at its own pace. Nothing's a rush.*

The adjustment counselor back on base had told him as much.

So why did he feel like he was slacking all the time?

"Pull up over by the barn," Kell instructed.

"There are three of them." A huge barn, faded gray by weather and time, was on the right side of an old yellow farmhouse. To the left were two smaller barns, one so new, Dennis thought he could smell the curing wood, the other a two-story, bare-bones beast. Lots of fencing, with subgroups set off from the others, made for a chaotic layout of pens, but he knew it was organized chaos.

The whole scene made him grin.

A three-legged dog, part Dalmatian, part something browner, looked up from a big chew toy and locked eyes with Dennis. For the first time since he'd come back to Luview, his shoulders really relaxed.

"OVER HERE!" A whistle cut through the air and Dennis and Kell turned to look at the source. A person in a red knit hat and black snow coveralls, holding a bucket of some kind of feed, waved them to the gray barn.

"Mel," Kell said as Dennis guided the truck very slowly toward her, stopping when she put up her palm.

They climbed out, and Mel gave Dennis a once-over. The crisp January air came into his lungs like he was sucking on a hookah in Tangiers.

"Dennis! Great to see you." Sharp eyes met his, more wrinkles than he remembered at the corners and underneath, but otherwise the same.

That description fit him as well.

"Know anything about camels?" Mel asked, looking pointedly at a beast.

Kell started laughing.

"What do you hope I know?"

Kell stopped laughing and gave them both a confused look.

"Got one who refuses to engage. Seems depressed. Can you take a look?"

"Only thing I've ever done with a camel is ride it. Never given one talk therapy."

At the words *talk therapy*, a memory of Ana slammed through him. How her neck tasted against his lips and tongue. The way her smile lit up the night as she rode him, her hands on his shoulders, breasts pert and–

"Don't need to psychoanalyze it. Just trying to understand why it won't eat."

"Why's it here?" he asked, his voice cracking a bit as he tried to stop living in his head in Sexland and came back to reality.

Cold reality. Snow began falling, light and fluffy.

"Because I brought her here?" Mel shrugged. "Her name is Sandy."

Kell groaned. Mel grinned.

"Okay," Dennis said, matching her shrug. "Thought we were coming here to take care of a tree."

"You are." Mel winked. "But if you're the same Dennis I knew years ago, you're a softy with strays."

"Oh, geez."

"And what's better than a guy with a soft spot for strays who has also spent a bunch of time in the desert?"

"I wasn't a camel jockey." He frowned. "Sandy wasn't used for racing, was she?"

"Camel racing?" Kell choked on his question.

"It's a thing," Mel confirmed, nodding, giving Dennis a look that said she was impressed. "I asked the same question when I got the call about her. She had a broken knee when we brought her here. Darren fixed it."

"How did a camel end up in Maine?" Kell asked, eyeing the barn. "Isn't it too cold here?"

"She's a Bactrian camel, and they're used to both heat and cold, but we have special heat lamps for her. Waiting for someone down south to have a spot for her. She's sweet as can be, but definitely depressed. I give her lots of affection," Mel explained.

Kell gave Dennis a look, then pointedly tipped his head toward the tree they were supposed to cut down. It was crooked, with the telltale lightning scar where the blast had sheared off a third of the tree.

Dennis just raised his eyebrows and followed Mel.

Animals brayed and chittered, quickly turning into background noise as he stomped through frozen mud and hit thinly scattered hay. Then Mel opened a door and a rush of heat told him this must be the place where Sandy was housed. When he stepped inside, Dennis burst out laughing.

A large plastic pool, the kind you put in your backyard for kids, was filled with sand.

"Look," Mel said in a defensive tone, "I meant it when I said I've tried everything."

"Please tell me that's not play sand from the toy section of a store."

"Hah. Of course not. I got Roy to give me some from the public works department."

When Mel opened the door, the camel hadn't even looked up.

Dennis frowned, squatting down, one knee pressed into the hay. Camels were tricky animals, he knew. They spat and could kick you easily, with joints that rotated in a circle. While they were friendly and extroverted, they were incredibly volatile as well.

His vigilance training kicked in.

"Could she be pregnant?" Dennis asked Mel, who shook her head.

"Nope. Darren confirmed."

"Fun exam."

"He did an ultrasound during surgery."

"Darren performed surgery on a camel?"

She waved her hand dismissively.

"He's seen it all. Comes with being a rural veterinarian."

"I'd think Darren would be more likely to work on a polar bear than a camel around here."

"If the polar ice caps keep melting, that might happen sooner than you think."

The camel had big, beautiful eyes, with brown fur that shed, the hair pulling into thick clumps like dreadlocks. The fur around her mouth was a lighter color, and it looked like she was puckered up for a big old kiss.

But those eyes. So sad.

"How long has it been since she's eaten?"

"About a month."

"A *month?*" Kell exclaimed, which made Dennis smile.

"Camels can last a few months without food. She drinking water?" he asked Mel, who shook her head.

"No, but she's fine there, too."

"So you just... *feel* like she's depressed?"

"I don't feel it. I *know* it."

Moving slowly and keeping his feet under him, Dennis assumed a low crouch, rolling back on his heels enough to get the balls of his feet free, in case he had to jump back quickly. Sandy could rise suddenly and pose a huge threat to them all.

Or she could hock a loogie in his eye.

"Hey there, girl," Dennis said softly.

Sandy blew out a breath through her nose, the snort hot and yeasty. Dennis began breathing through his mouth, but barely opened his lips. All you needed was one taste of camel spit and you were good for life.

After an incident in Qatar, he was all set.

Sandy blinked once, slowly, then closed her eyes. With a gentle hand, he touched her head with two fingers, stroking the fur.

She just breathed, the sound ragged but steady.

"You walking okay?" he asked her. Kell shifted his weight in Dennis's peripheral vision, leaning against the gate.

"Do you think she's just cold?" Mel asked quietly from behind him. "Darren says that's probably not it."

"Are you cold, girl?" he asked the camel, who didn't reply, but who seemed to relax enough that Dennis moved closer, petting her head, scratching a bit on her forehead.

"Maybe she's lonely. Are camels pack animals?" Kell asked.

Lonely.

The word was a gut punch, conjuring a feeling about Ana. No images in his mind. No words. Just a heavy, painful ache.

"They're pack animals, as in animals used to carry freight for humans," Mel answered. Sandy's fur was thick and filthy, and as Dennis continued petting her, he found the sensory experience liberating.

Life here in Maine was so... American. Organized and clean. Mechanized and constricting.

Or maybe he was just having adjustment problems?

Probably not that.

"I mean, do they travel in packs? Like dogs or wolves. Maybe she misses having a camel buddy?" Kell clarified.

"They're social," Dennis said softly, watching as Sandy closed her eyes and tipped her chin up, seeming to enjoy the head scratches. "Live in herds."

"Then get her a herd."

Mel started laughing. "I just take in the sick and wounded animals. I don't matchmake."

"Is she broody?" Dennis wondered aloud. "Maybe she wants a male?"

"Darren says she's old enough to have a calf."

Kell moved closer to Sandy, mimicking Dennis, and she opened her eyes and tensed.

"Stay back," Dennis said in a low, firm voice. "One human at a time,"

Kell's hands went up in a gesture of surrender.

"No problem." He backed up. "How long are they pregnant?"

"About thirteen months. A little less," Mel replied.

"How do you know all this stuff about random animals?" Kell asked her, just as she walked into Dennis's line of sight to the left.

"*Shhh*," Mel said, looking down.

"It's a reasonable question," Kell replied, sounding a bit put out.

"Wasn't talking to you," Mel muttered as something rat-like crawled up from her overalls pocket. Palming it, she make chittering noises at it with her tongue and teeth.

"Is that a rat?" Kell asked in a disgusted tone.

"No," Mel replied calmly. "Sugar glider."

She turned her wrist a bit, showing the tiny marsupial. No more than six inches long, it had a face like a lemur and a body like a flying squirrel.

"Who is this?" Dennis asked, stepping away from Sandy. It was time to give her some space, anyhow.

His mission had been accomplished.

"Careful with her hind leg there." Mel held the little creature out so Dennis could see.

The leg had obviously been damaged recently, the wound not even scabbed over.

"Did something eat her foot?"

"Yes. Completely. Would have been worse if her former owner hadn't discovered it. Kid had her as a pet and the family poodle decided to be a predator."

"Gross!" Kell yipped.

"Yeah. This one keeps chewing the bandage off. They don't make cones of shame for sugar gliders."

"What's her name?"

"Magic."

"Magic?"

"As in magic carpet. Ever seen one of these fly?"

"Sure. In Australia."

Kell let out a grumpy huff, as if Dennis was being annoying for having life experience.

"We need to get to that tree," Kell announced, turning and calling back his goodbye to Mel as he left.

"Awww," Dennis said, giving the little fella a tummy rub. "Is Magic a girl or a boy?"

Mel held the little guy up to Dennis and bluntly replied, "Male. See?"

"Gotcha."

Magic curled inward as Dennis's affectionate touch was clearly welcomed.

"You're really good with animals."

"Thanks."

"If you're ever bored, or just need an escape from your family compound, feel free to come volunteer."

"Bored, I don't know about. Plenty of work to keep me from bored. But that second part..."

They laughed together, Mel handing Magic off to him. The little beast slipped inside a pocket of Dennis's ski coat and curled up.

"That foot stump will get infected," Dennis said, worried.

"He needs lots of care." Mel gave him a look of consideration. "Ever fostered a sick animal?"

"Fostered?"

"Like a foster parent. Just with an animal."

"Are you asking me to take care of Magic until he's healed?"

"That would be great! Thanks for offering!" Mel said with a wide grin, walking over to Sandy to give the girl some warm pats.

"Hah. I'm not that easy to rope in." But looking down into his jacket pocket, his heart melted a little for the wee thing.

"I can handle Magic, but he seems to like you. And that stump needs antibiotic cream. The problem is, he's prey. I have too many animals here to keep him one hundred percent safe."

"What happens after he's healed?"

"An exotic-animal person might adopt him. Or I could keep him. Not sure."

"You think I'll keep him, don't you?"

"He is a sweetie."

"I was thinking I'd adopt a dog or a cat, Mel. Not a bat with fur that looks like a lemur."

"For a man who spent two decades exploring the world, you sure are small minded when it comes to pets. Expand your horizons a bit. Who wouldn't want something so warm and sweet up against them all the time?"

Mel winked at him.

It wasn't a come-on. They'd basically grown up together and he knew it was just a joke.

But his Ana craving came back with a vengeance.

"A cat can do the same."

"Looks like Magic picked you."

"Kell and I have to take down your tree. I'm not doing

that with a sugar glider in my pocket." He popped open the pocket, Magic's sweet little face looking up at him.

"Fine. I'll take him back." They exchanged the poor creature, Dennis's watchful eye on the raw stump. "Finish up the tree and come on in for coffee crumb cake."

"Haven't had that in decades."

"Great time to start again." Magic settled into her coveralls pocket, eyes on Dennis as if saying, *Pick me. Choose me. Love me.*

As Dennis stepped outside to find Kell unloading equipment, he paused at the truck, his phone buzzing in his pocket. Hope springs eternal, and not hearing from Ana all week felt like an eternity.

But no.

Not her.

Deanna.

Can you and Kell get two gallons of milk at Kendrill's before you come home?

Dennis had rescued dozens of kidnapping victims. Managed tense hostage situations. Even delivered blackmail and ransom money.

No one—no one in the whole, wide world—had the power to turn him into an errand boy.

Except his mother.

Sure, he texted back. *Starting the job at Mel's now.*

She replied with a thumbs up.

Unable to stop himself, he flipped over to his text stream with Ana.

Nothing.

Another day of nothing.

With a sigh, he realized that adjusting to hometown life was hard.

And adjusting to her silence was even harder.

Chapter Ten

Ana

Positive.

The test results stared at her, glowing from her phone screen.

POSITIVE, it said, in all caps, like it was *screaming*.

"Oh, honey," Brie said as Ana sagged against her, the ginger ale she just drank turning to acid in her stomach. The notification had come into her email, and when she'd logged into the lab's website, she'd clicked on the PDF and...

This.

She was *pregnant*.

Pregnant with Harris's baby.

"How is this my life?" she said in a whisper-scream, Brie giving her a sympathetic look, the weight of all the emotion behind that like a millstone around her neck.

"It's—well, it just *is*, isn't it?" Brie replied, clearly uncertain what to say. Hell, Ana was a trained therapist with a license that said she was supposed to know what to say to comfort someone, and even *she* had no idea how to react.

Then again, she wasn't her own patient.

Her phone rang. It was the doctor's office. Tempted to ignore it, she let it ring three times, Brie's eyes getting bigger with each ring, until finally she answered.

"Hello, is Ana there?"

"Hi, Peggy."

"Oh! Hi, there. Is this a good time to talk? Your pregnancy test results came in."

"I'm staring at them right now."

"I see. Are you in a good place?"

Ana knew what that meant.

"My best friend is right here with me."

"Excellent. Now, according to the HCG level, we're estimating you're six weeks or so along. We'd like for you to come in and talk."

Ana also knew what *that* meant.

"Of course," she said. "Can–can I call back later after I've looked at my schedule? Then I can pick a time for an appointment in the next few days?"

"Definitely. You have lots of decisions to make in the next few weeks, and emotions to process. I'm glad you have support."

Brie squeezed her hand.

An image of Dennis came to mind, making her heart hurt. Ignoring him while she waited for the results had felt like holding her breath for so long, the world disappeared.

And now, not only had the world as she knew it disappeared, so had any hope of ever being with him.

"I have lots of wonderful people in my life."

"Excellent. Call back for an appointment, then."

"I will. Thanks."

Ending the call took some of the immediate pressure off.

"I have to tell Harris," she moaned, and Brie made a growling noise at the mention of his name.

"I am so glad you didn't move in with that rat bastard."

"Hey. That's not nice."

"You're right. Rats don't deserve to be compared to him."

"He's the father." The word *father* felt strange in her mouth, like it was coated in bitter dust. Ana's hand went to her belly, shaking slightly. A little being, no bigger than a grain of rice, was in there.

Growing.

Having a unicornuate uterus wasn't something she had ever talked about with anyone other than her mother and her doctors. Even Brie didn't know. It was invisible, a medical condition that shaped her life but was easy to hide.

Being told years ago that she would struggle to conceive at all, and carrying a child to full term would be risky, if not impossible, had meant that she'd just floated through life, trying not to think about it, postponing any big internal processing.

She was thirty-five now, right on the threshold of major fertility and family planning, and she'd thought she'd deal with it next year.

With a long-term partner.

Nature had a different plan.

"You don't have to tell him," Brie said firmly. "He's out of the country. Plus, this is your..." Brie's eyes darted away, then back to Ana, "...your choice."

"Oh!" Ana's eyes filled with tears.

"You do have a choice," Brie continued. "And Harris has no say."

"It's not—not that."

Mind racing, she struggled to think what to say. Although she was adult enough to know that she didn't owe Brie an explanation, she also felt powerless suddenly. So many aspects of her life were thrown into tumult by the blood test, and a long list of actions and decisions was starting to pile up, pressing against the anxiety centers of her brain.

Like laying on the horn.

"What do you mean?" Brie pried gently.

"If I'm–" Ana cleared her throat, mind scrambling to comprehend her new reality. "Okay, I *am* pregnant. And that's a bit of a miracle."

"Miracle?"

"I've never talked about it with you before, but I have issues. Medical issues with my uterus."

"You do? Like, endometriosis?"

"Something different."

"You don't have to share." Brie caught Ana's hesitation instantly. "It's none of my business."

"You're my best friend, and my uterus, well... it *is* your business. Now, at least. Because I'm going to need you. Need your help."

"I'm here. No matter what. Always here."

Brie's hug felt so good, warm and comforting, accepting and unobtrusive. Having a friendship like theirs meant walking around with a sense of security, knowing that there was goodness and light at the core of her life.

"I know." Her hand went back to her belly, and Ana smiled. "I would never, ever pick Harris to have a child with after what he did, but this might be my only chance."

"Really?"

"I–I don't know. And it might not even stick."

"Stick?"

"I have a high chance of miscarrying. My uterus is misshapen."

"It is?"

Giving an anatomical lesson on her body's anomaly was not how Ana had planned for her day to go, but nothing seemed to be under her control when it came to Harris, so she took in a long breath and adapted on the fly.

"I have something called a unicornuate uterus. It's like having half a uterus. I only have one fallopian tube, too."

Brie looked at her, chin dropping in increments until she was staring up at Ana from under the fringe of her long, beautifully thick eyelashes.

"You have that and never told me?"

"I–"

"Never mind. No, no, Brie, stop!" Brie chided herself, then placed her hand on Ana's arm, eyes warm and caring. "But thank you for explaining now. Is that why your periods are always so erratic?"

"Yes. I only have one ovary."

"Wow."

"So conceiving like this is..."

"A surprise."

"A *huge* surprise. And..." Ana's voice trailed off, emotion rising like a thermometer as she struggled to stay calm. "And it might be my only chance!"

"You don't know that."

"I kind of do. I'm thirty-five. Just got dumped. I already had a less-than-fifty-percent chance of conceiving, and there's still a decent chance I'll miscarry. So," she said, suddenly certain. "So unless Harris drops some bombshell on me, I already know what I'm doing."

"Co-parenting with that asshole for eighteen years sounds like hell."

"I know. I've thought about that."

"A lot, I'll bet."

The way her friend looked at her made Ana believe in mind meld. All she could do was nod.

"Harris could make this very difficult, but I don't think he will. He fled the country. He's a jerk," Ana began, but Brie cut in.

"Enough of a jerk to never bother seeing his own child, ever? Oh, wait. Rhetorical question." She snorted. "He absolutely *is* that big of a jerk."

"Yeah," Ana said as she reached for her phone. "And now I have to leave yet another message he'll ignore."

"You're going to tell him he's about to become a father by leaving a voicemail? Savage."

"Not savage. Practical. He won't answer his phone, and he doesn't reply to texts or emails anymore. I have an obligation to let him know. Once he knows, we'll go from there."

"One step at a time."

"Right."

"I wish I could offer you a drink for fortitude."

"How about a hand?"

Clasping hands, they intertwined their fingers and Ana closed her eyes, soaking in her friend's love. Years of being a therapist meant she had plenty of experience in helping people to regulate their emotions, but that didn't make her a pro at managing her own.

Especially in a crisis like this.

"Look. We're here for you. The whole cheesy family."

"Thank you."

"I mean it."

"I know you do." Ana began to tear up. "And I'll take you up on it, all of it. Because Harris is going to make this hard. I need as much help as I can get."

"Screw Harris. But you know, it's going to be hard without him, too. You'll be a single mother."

A memory of Dennis, how he laughed as they held hands at the bar, made her tears pool deeper.

"I will. Everything's changed, just like that." She snapped her fingers with her free hand.

"It's going to be fine, Ana. You'll be an incredible mother."

Mother.

For so many years, she'd forced herself to set that idea aside, knowing the chances were twenty percent at best for natural conception and full-term pregnancy. Reproductive technology was her best bet, her specialists always said.

Ana had defied the odds. At least, for this stage.

Harris had some determined swimmers, escaping a condom like that.

"Mother. Right." With the edge of her palm, she wiped the tears that flowed freely now. "Guess I'm off the market, then."

"Huh?"

"No worries about dating. It's a relief."

But the taste of Dennis's kiss wouldn't leave her tongue.

Memory always seemed to invade at the worst of times, and this was one of them. She knew that inside, some part of her was screaming for him, while her more practical self was moving into protective mode.

The more practical self was winning, but the one who wanted Dennis would not go down without a fight.

"You're a catch, no matter what. And think about your boobs!"

"My... what?"

"Boobs! You know. Pregnant women have big racks."

"You think I'll have more guys interested in me for my pregnant boobs?"

The two burst into hysterical laughter, Ana's eyes still dropping tears as her belly shook with giggles.

"We're procrastinating," Ana finally said, steeling herself for the call.

"Have you decided what to say?"

"No. I'll wing it."

"He's blown you off every other time. Why would this be any different?"

Phone in hand, she hit Harris's contact and waited for the inevitable voicemail.

The recorded monotone of his intentionally boring voice came on.

"It's Harris. I'm not a slave to my phone. You know what to do."

Beep

But did she, really? Know what to do?

"Harris, it's Ana. You haven't answered any of my other messages, so I'll be blunt—"

Brie snatched the phone out of her hand and said loudly, "Ana has money that belongs to you. A lot. Call her, asshole. This isn't a joke."

Then she hung up.

"BRIE! I can't believe you did that!"

Brie just stared at Ana's phone with a look of resigned disgust.

"What are you doing now?" Ana asked.

"Waiting for the asshole to call back."

"He won't! I told you—"

But Brie was right.

Her phone rang. *Unknown Number,* the screen said.

Ana knew.

Knew it was him.

"Hello?" Brie said as Ana reached to take over.

"Put Ana on. What's this about?"

"Ana has a very valuable package for you." Then she put the phone on speaker and set it between them.

"Ana?"

"Hi, Harris."

"What is this about? Someone brought money for me?"

"No. Brie said that to get you to return my call."

"Damn it, Ana. I don't have time for this. I told you you could come to Morocco if you want–"

"But there is something critical I have to talk about with you."

"Let me guess. You need to process your feelings." His mocking laugh made Ana's stomach turn.

"No."

"Then what is it?"

"I'm pregnant."

"Excuse me?"

"I'm pregnant. It's your baby. I counted back the days and–"

"Of course it's my baby, Ana," he said harshly, but there was a quality to his voice that made her feel slimy. Gross.

Exposed.

"You don't sound surprised."

"I am. I am, actually. I'm surprised that it worked."

"What... worked?"

His laughter turned more sinister. Instant regret flooded through her veins. Calling him had been a mistake.

A big one.

"When I knew the feds were closing in, I figured I'd pull an Elizabeth Holmes."

"A what?"

"Theranos? Hello? Elizabeth Holmes?"

"I know who she is. She founded that lab company and was convicted of fraud."

"And she used her pregnancies for leniency during the trial."

Brie's eyes nearly popped out of her head as Harris's words slowly seeped in. If Brie was reacting like this, then Ana wasn't misinterpreting his words.

"You–you–" Brie sputtered.

"I poked a hole in the condom. A few, actually, just to

make sure," he said smoothly, as if informing Ana he'd accidentally given her caffeinated coffee instead of decaf, as if dispensing a trivial bit of information about a minor mistake.

"Hole? In the condom?" Ana said in a voice she didn't recognize.

"And it worked. Huh. My swimmers are strong. This shows it." Hubris had always been an issue with him, but this took the cake.

"You impregnated me without my consent!"

"Technically, I poked holes in the condom without your consent. Any intercourse has risks," he said dryly.

"You did this to me on purpose because you thought you might get sympathy in court?"

"Never needed it, though. I got out of the country before it was necessary."

"HARRIS!" she said, louder than her lungs seemed capable of producing. "You got me pregnant to manipulate a judge?"

"Sure. I guess. If you want to think of it like that."

"We're having a baby!"

"No," he said slowly. "*You* are. If you want it. Get an abortion if you don't."

Brie gripped Ana's hand with superhuman strength.

"I–I want to keep it."

"Whatever. Your choice. Are we done here? Is this your big reveal? You somehow think I'll get back together with you if you're having a baby?"

"I was informing you that you're going to be a father. We'll be connected as we raise this child."

"We? What's this 'we' shit?"

"It takes two to have a baby."

"You got my sperm. We're done."

"You–you don't want to be part of everything?"

"Hell, no. I don't plan to ever set foot in the U.S. again."

Brie made a clapping gesture that would have made Ana laugh if she weren't so miserable. So stung. So horrified.

Ana picked up the phone, as if touching it would make Harris's words make sense.

"It wouldn't bother you to have a child in the world who you never got to know?"

He made a dismissive sound. "No. I donated sperm in college for some extra money. I'm sure there are plenty of my spawn roaming around the Greater Boston area by now." He chuckled. "Remember that documentary we watched about the fertility doctor who used his own spooge to get hundreds of women pregnant? And some of them dated? Just watch out," he added.

Ana dropped the phone and sprinted for the bathroom, the sick rising up in her throat.

She barely made it, one hand holding her hair back.

As her body emptied her stomach, she heard Brie screaming at Harris, a shrieky, no-holds-barred affair that made Ana feel extremely cared for. Her bestie had a temper that could be triggered easily, but only by injustice.

Harris was a walking fleshbag of unfairness.

He poked a hole in the condom? He did this on purpose, not to raise a child together but to use the baby as some kind of sympathy chip in court?

And if he'd done this six weeks ago, he knew a long time ago that he was in trouble.

Probably from the start of their relationship.

How had she missed this breathtakingly enormous level of sociopathy?

She was a therapist! She should know better.

And now she was pregnant by such an odious man.

Waves of nausea, followed by spasms throughout her belly, forced her to focus on the present, the burning bile, her body rejecting what she'd just experienced. Only after she pressed her hot cheek on the cool side of the toilet and started to breathe slowly did she notice Brie behind her, in the doorway.

"I hung up on him. Prick. He really is that cold."

"He wasn't always," Ana said weakly.

"I'm not judging your taste in men. I'm judging his lack of a conscience."

"I feel so stupid. What did he say before you hung up?"

"That he doesn't care what you do. Leave him alone."

Alone.

Never had a word felt so profoundly freeing and so utterly terrifying at the same time.

Bzzzz

Ana's phone buzzed in Brie's hand. They both looked at it like it was a vampire rising up from the dead.

"He didn't have a change of heart," Brie said fiercely. "You know that."

"I know."

"Because that POS doesn't have one," her friend added, then looked at the screen. "It's, uh, your mom."

"Oh, no."

"Sorry. I'll ignore it."

Her mom. The thought of telling her mom she was pregnant made her heart race, but she smiled at the same time, because this meant her mother would become a grandmother.

Maybe.

Being an only child had always carried its own burden. Her unicornuate uterus had dashed her own hopes of motherhood but, to her credit, her mom had never said a word about how it affected her.

And then there was Rick.

The text loomed large in the space where she breathed right now, Harris's shocking mistreatment still stinging. How much more could she take? If her mother had a negative response, Ana would crumble.

She was resilient. Trained. Strong–but even the strong break eventually.

"Marian is going to be stunned when she finds out," Brie said, as if reading her thoughts.

"Stunned as in good, or stunned as in bad?"

"I don't know. I think she'll be thrilled, but her first reaction might be a little..."

"Operational?"

They laughed. Marian DaSilva Gianetti was a woman of action. A planner. A fixer. When presented with a problem, she created a point-by-point template for optimizing everything.

Those qualities made her an outstanding hospice nurse. Empathy came after organization, when everything was aligned, and being present was all that was left.

Her first go-to would be making sure Ana would be safe.

Which meant her mother would immediately involve Rick.

"Marian and Rick are formidable," Brie said, nodding slowly. "But this might be like a band-aid. Need to just rip it off and get it over with."

"I still can't believe Harris did that. Said that. He–he–" Overwhelming anxiety rippled across her skin. Processing what Harris had done was going to take countless hours with her own therapist.

"Yes, and–"

Ana's phone rang–her mother. She quickly glanced at the text before deciding whether to answer the call.

How did the doctor's appointment go? her mom had written.

Right. She'd told her about feeling under the weather. Mom was just following up.

What she thought might be the flu was turning out to be something very, very different.

With a sigh, she accepted the call and pressed the phone to her ear.

"Hi, Mom."

"Ana! What's wrong?" Marian might be a bit in her own world much of the time, but she could read her daughter like a book.

"I'm–well..."

"Bad news from the doctor? What is it?"

"It's not so much bad news. In fact, it could be good news."

"That makes no sense!" her mother exclaimed. "No one gets equivocal news from a doctor. Don't soften it for me, honey, just say it. I'm a nurse."

"I..."

"Whatever it is," her mom said softly, voice suddenly shaky, "we're here for you. Rick and I."

Muddying the emotional moment with a mention of her stepfather took a bit of the sweetness out of it.

But just a bit.

"I–I never thought I'd say these words to you, Mom, but, well... I'm pregnant."

An enormous sob, one that had been crouched deep in her gut, released itself, turning her into a ball of grief. Somehow, saying the words made her feel thirteen again, watching her mother take the phone call that changed their lives forever.

This felt that big and, somehow, that sad.

"Ana? Did you say *pregnant?*"

Ana nodded, then realized she was on the phone. Brie took the phone and switched it to speaker mode.

"Hi, Marian, it's Brie. I'm here with Ana. She's crying right now, and so am I. Yes, she's pregnant."

"Oh, my goodness! Brie! Are you–what is–pregnant? *Pregnant?*"

"Yes."

"Who is the–is Harris..?" Her mother's question ended with a slow hissing sound. It was an expletive.

One of the chambers of Ana's heart turned to a cloud of pure shame.

"It's Harris, Mom. Harris–"

"DID THIS TO HER!" Brie shouted. "That asshole poked holes in the condom!"

Ana looked at Brie in astonishment as her friend clapped her hand over her own mouth.

With a calmness that felt more clinical than personal, she said into the phone, "Yes, Mom. This is Harris's baby."

"And he knows? Wait. Of course he knows. You–he told you he sabotaged your birth control?"

"I don't have the energy to explain right now, Mom," Ana said, struggling to control her sobbing. Brie was banging her fist against her head in an act of abject self-punishment. Later, Ana would talk through Brie's blurting out of private information, but right now, she just needed to get through the call.

"I can't believe he would do this! On purpose! But Ana– oh, Ana, this is a miracle!"

Brie hunched over and gave Ana a red-rimmed look.

Sorry, she mouthed.

"I guess?"

"Of course it is! Is this why you've been feeling sick?"

"Probably. I have nausea and dizziness."

"So did I when I was pregnant with you. For fifteen weeks!"

Ana's stomach roiled at the thought.

"Not helpful, Mom."

"I'm–I'm so happy for you! I know that sounds strange, and I want to strangle Harris, but your chances of getting pregnant are so slim. You..." Her mom's voice halted, as if cut in two by a knife. "Oh. But you–how far along are you?"

"Probably six weeks, based on HCG levels. Not sure, though, because of my complications."

"So it's early."

Here came her mother's extreme pragmatism. She knew what Marian wasn't asking.

"Yes. It is. And I've decided to proceed."

"Oh!" The whoop of joy that came through the phone made Ana smile, scared parts of her relaxing. "I'm going to be a grandmother! Assuming, of course, that your body lets you keep the pregnancy."

Brie's jaw dropped in horror. Ana took it in stride.

"Yes, Mom. I have a long way to go."

"And Harris? Is that festering pus bubble in a beached whale's anus planning to step up and do the right thing?"

"AHAHAHAHAHA!" Brie barked out. "As if!"

"Rick! We need your help," her mother called. "I'm putting you on speaker."

Before Ana could even take a breath, her stepfather's voice chimed in.

"What's up?"

"Harris got Ana pregnant by poking a hole in the condom and now he doesn't want to help raise the baby."

"Worse!" Brie chimed in. Ana shook her head hard, signaling her to say no more.

"Worse?" Rick snapped into the phone. "Hold on. What the hell did you just say?"

"Harris got Ana pregnant by poking a hole in the condom and now he doesn't want to help raise the baby," her mother repeated, this time slowly.

"That's... a lot, Ana."

"No kidding," she muttered.

"First of all, you're pregnant?" His voice softened.

"Yes."

"Congratulations."

Never a warm and fuzzy kind of man, his sweet tone made her feel more connected to him than usual.

"Thank you. And to answer your questions, yes, I'm keeping it, and no, Harris won't help raise it."

"What did Brie mean by 'worse'?"

"Harris sabotaged our birth control because he knew the feds were closing in and he thought a jury or judge would be sympathetic to a father-to-be."

Rick's extraordinarily florid profanity flew through the phone like a geyser explosion.

"Ana!" Marian gasped. "I thought you meant he did it because you were dumping him and he wanted to force a connection between you."

"That would be better for my ego, Mom, but no."

"I never liked him," Rick stated, the words staccato and angry. "And I don't like this. He needs to TPR."

"TPR?" Brie asked.

"Terminate parental rights," Ana explained, knowing the term from her experience as a therapist. "I can ask him."

"Ana," Rick said, his voice grave. "You never told him about the trust, right?"

Brie's eyebrows shot up. She knew about the trust, but why was Rick bringing it up?

When Ana's father had died, an enormous life insurance payout, plus his own family's trust, all became hers. The income from the trust, managed by a bank in Boston, allowed her to live comfortably and keep a part-time private practice.

"No."

"Are you sure?"

"Yes."

"If he ever found out, he might try to use this baby to get his hands on it."

Ana didn't even bother to try arguing that Harris wouldn't.

He totally would.

"Rick," her mother said, "now isn't the time for details like this. Ana needs to–"

"Now is exactly the time for this! We need to get that rat bastard to terminate his rights."

"How will we convince him to do that?"

"Leave it to me. I always hated that slimy sonofabitch. This will be a pleasure."

"I just texted you his number," Brie said to Rick. "How *are* you planning to do this?"

"Bribery." Rick's single-word answer made Ana wish for a sinkhole.

"I really don't need this. I can handle Harris myself. And there's time to–"

"Honey," her mom said quietly. "This is what Rick is best at."

"You're a tax attorney, Rick. Not family law," Ana pointed out.

Marian ignored her. "And he's right. It's not just about the money. It's about Harris's character. He's done this to you without consent. He could come back at any time and try to manipulate you via the baby. Let Rick, or some associates he can consult with, strike while the iron is hot and cut that sick little piece of dirt off so he never has power over you again."

Ana knew that accepting Rick's help was smart, and she didn't have the stomach to handle any of this herself right now.

"Fine. Sure. Thank you," she said.

"No problem, kiddo. I mean it when I say it'll be a pleasure. Protecting you and the baby is job one," Rick said, again in a tone that seemed so alien.

So... supportive.

Surprise was written all over Brie's face, and Ana felt the same. A pleasant warm sensation spread across her skin. Rick was a tough-as-nails lawyer, what people outside the legal profession called a bulldog and what those inside it called, well... names not used in polite company.

Rick had a soft underbelly, apparently. It made her wonder what else she didn't know about him.

"Great." Ana heard the sound of palms rubbing against each other, like someone relishing a task. "I'll get on this right now."

"Ana? Honey? I have a board meeting in five minutes. Let me stop by later tonight and we can talk more?"

"Sure, Mom."

"I love you," Marian said, the words conveying so much more than they did even a day ago.

"I know, Mom. I know. I love you, too."

"Tell the baby we're good people. Worth sticking around for."

Dennis.

His name shot through her heart like Cupid's arrow, sorrow and beauty all mixing together in an unformed feeling.

"We are, aren't we?" Ana choked out, then ended the conversation as Brie held her hand. Once she set down the phone, Ana broke their grasp and shoved her hands into her hair.

"That went better than expected," Brie said.

It was true.

"Rick was a surprise."

"Who knew the human equivalent of a steel porcupine could be so gooey?" Brie cracked. Her words weren't far from the mark.

Ana picked up her phone again and opened the message stream with Dennis, a new round of tears blurring her eyes.

I was told it's customary to wait three days to text someone so you don't seem desperate. It's been exactly 72 hours since I last saw you, so...

Brie looked at the screen and gave Ana a look filled with such pity, it made her feel hollow.

"You really like him."

"I did."

"You do."

"Doesn't matter now, does it? I'm pregnant with another man's baby. Remember what you said yesterday? Inconceivable."

"What?"

"You said until you met Martin, falling for someone in under twenty-four hours was inconceivable." The pain of regret and loss filled her chest. "Turns out there's a whole different kind of *conceivable* happening in the mess that is my love life."

"You can explain it to Dennis."

"I want to. You have no idea how badly. It's killing me not to."

"Then do it!"

"And get rejected again? What Harris did to me hurt. A lot. And now you add in the sabotaged birth control. When did my life become a bad telenovela plot?"

"It's not..." But Brie's protest was unconvincing.

"I should text him the truth. Be an adult. Open and unapologetic. But I can't. I feel like the worst therapist ever." A numb shock started seeping into her skin. Harris' violation was soaking in on a cellular level.

"You're not *your* therapist. You're not your own patient. What you're feeling is human. And you owe Dennis nothing. No text, no explanation. You can ghost on him."

"I feel like I already have."

"Nothing here is black and white. You can always reach out to him later and explain the situation. If he's as special as you say, he'll understand."

"I feel frozen. Numb."

"What would you tell a patient in the same situation?"

"No patient would ever have such a surreal mess."

"Oh, come on. I'm sure you're not the only woman in history to have sex with a guy fleeing the feds for drug charges, who pokes holes in a condom and escapes the country, then you have your first-ever one-night stand with a hot retired military officer, find out you're pregnant from the ex, and–oh. Wait. Hmmm."

"You're not helping," Ana said with a hitched sob that turned into a hiccup that made her sound like a drunk parrot.

"But I did make you laugh. Laughter is the best medicine."

"I am so tired. So, so tired."

"How can I help? Should I go? Or do you want to see the flowers we've chosen for the wedding?"

"Distract me!"

And with that, Ana spent the next hour looking at shades of red, pink, and white that were all beautiful and in no way distinct from each other, while letting her limbic system return to a calm baseline.

Or a reasonable fascimile of calm.

Her entire world had changed with one single word, a word that she needed to embrace with her whole heart:

Positive.

Chapter Eleven

Dennis

It felt good to go down so hard.

The crack of the ax against the wood made a sound that cut through his emotions. Chopping wood was a time-honored tradition in the Luview family. He'd split more cords before he was ten than most men chop in a lifetime.

But lately, it had become an obsession.

Weeks had gone by since he'd sent that text to Ana, and nothing. Not one damned thing. No reply, no "Sorry, not interested," just the painful blankness of rejection underneath his careful little joke.

Turned out *he* was the joke.

And none of this was funny.

Sweat warmed his underarms, his core fired by the strenuous activity, until he stripped off his down vest and chopped in his long-sleeved t-shirt, jeans, boots, and red wool cap.

Handknitted by his mother, various hats littered the coat rack, waiting to be plucked for errands.

And chores.

The old camp had a century's worth of chores to be done, which was just fine and dandy as far as Dennis was concerned. The more he had to do with his hands, the less he had to think about Ana.

And what he'd done to her with his hands....

"Damn it," he muttered as he centered the next chunk of wood, arms arching in that just-right way that told him he was tipping over into a new exertion phase. The morning run in the snow had been a prelude to this.

"Son! You're making the rest of us look bad." His father appeared, wearing a lined flannel shirt under a thick down vest, a flannel hat with flaps, and carrying an enormous thermos of coffee. Leaning against a tree, he took a slow sip and just watched.

"You want me to stop?"

"You wouldn't if I tried. Don't you get tired?"

"That's the goal."

Neither spoke for a moment, and then:

"You chop like a man who's taking out his pain on the wood."

"Better than taking it out on Luke."

Dean's grin made Dennis remember why he'd decided to come back here, until he recalled the real reason.

And his hands began to shake.

The high-pitched shrieking began, taking over his ears, and his eyes didn't know where to look. Sharp smoke filled his nose, his breath suffocated by heat and confusion. Suddenly, he was staring at a mangy cat, dust stirred up from gunfire, a child's big, soulful eyes begging him.

Begging him not to let it happen.

"Den?" His dad wasn't touching him, thank goodness,

but he was close, hand reaching for him, fingers leading. "You okay? You rocked a little there."

"Fine," Dennis replied through a mouthful of sand. Screams tore through his memory, the sight of the boy's back, the explosion and the–

"Sit down." Through the ringing in his ears, his father's voice took a commanding tone that Dennis followed, knocking the chunk of wood off the stump he chopped on. His ass went cold the second he sat on the frozen wood, but the chill helped ground him.

All he could do was hold his head in his hands and grunt. Tongue like wet cardboard, ears clanging, he had to ride this out.

Tried to breathe.

Tried to get his heart, lungs, and blood to work together the way they were supposed to, but they hadn't gotten the synchronicity memo, instead deciding to work, sure–but not aligned. He felt like each breath chased his heart, his heart chased his blood, and where they were supposed to be in rhythm, they were jumbled.

Which made him feel even more screwed up.

"Whatever's going on, Denny, I'm here."

Denny.

It was one thing to hear it from his mother's mouth, but from Dean Luview, it told him he was in bad shape.

Really bad shape.

And damned if he didn't have to fight back tears.

"Just... crap."

"We all have crap, son, but I suspect yours is different than anyone else's here. I wondered if we'd ever get a sense of why you chose to come home. You don't have to say a word. I've seen vets going through flashbacks. You look like you're seeing ghosts and feeling like you're responsible for them."

If his mother was the one who noticed everything, his

father was the one who assigned meaning–deep meaning–to what he saw.

"You're smart, Dad," he finally gasped. "Why'd you stay in this podunk town?"

"Why'd you come back to it?"

"The brownies at the bakery are good. And it's cheap to live here. I can live like a king on my pension."

"I stayed for love," his dad said back in the same joking tone, but his smile softened, a wistful, loving gleam in his eyes. "And she was worth it. *Is* worth it."

In his mind's eye, Dennis saw Ana's face, pushing away the terror brought forth by the flashback and filling him with both hope and sadness. Dean sensed the shift and offered his thermos.

"Have some coffee."

"I'm fine."

"You're not fine, and a sip will help shake you out of it. I can tell something's changed already."

Bzzz

Before he could reach for the coffee, his phone buzzed, then did it again immediately after. Dean shook his head.

"We had a perfectly fine life before those things came along."

"Women?"

His dad nearly shot coffee out of his nose. "Ah, I was referring to smartphones."

Dennis reached into his vest for the object in question.

"Yeah. They're a source of frustration, too."

"Constant interruption. How's a person supposed to think if they're always on?"

As Dennis looked at his messages, he felt hope spring up inside.

And then the spring sprung.

Not Ana.

Mel Chassi.

Hey Dennis, any chance you can come over here and give me a hand? I have a problem with Magic.

Problem? What kind of problem could she possibly have with an itty-bitty sugar glider?

Is he sick?

I'll explain when you get here. You'd really be a help.

Sure. Just chopping wood now. Happy to come over, he typed back, then looked at Dean.

"Mel. Needs help with an animal."

"Does she, now?"

"What's that supposed to mean?"

"You've spent some time at her place. You two...?"

"Friends. Just friends. What is wrong with everyone in this town? All you think about is love."

"It's kind of a thing here."

"It's sickening. Always was, always will be."

"You really hate it that much?"

Shrugging into his vest, he moved the ax, aligning the wood so he left the situation cleaner than when he found it.

"We live in paradise here, Dad. Gorgeous, unfettered nature. Nice people, neighborly and caring. The permanent residents, at least. The lovesick crap is like covering a gold nugget with glitter paint and claiming it's more valuable that way."

"You're serious. You really don't like the love part of town."

"I told you that when I was a kid!" Dennis paused and thought for a moment. "Or more like early teen years. When I was little, I didn't know any better. This place is very good at indoctrinating us young."

"You sound like a conspiracy theorist."

"No conspiracy. That requires unilateral agreement and commitment to a mission, and there's no way the people running this town could ever come together like that. Nadine Khouri and Anne Petrinelli can't even agree on an approved font list for commercial signage," he said with a snort.

"Sounds like you've been listening to Rachel complain about her job."

"How can I avoid it? She blabbers on at morning coffee."

"You have a lot of complaints." The words were said in a kind tone, but they made Dennis bristle.

"Because I don't want a fake idea of love constantly shoved in my face means I'm complaining?" He paused. "Damn right, then. I'm complaining."

"Dennis, that's not what I meant."

"Then say what you mean! What is it with people being mealy mouthed?"

A minute ago, he'd felt like a little kid. Now he felt like the grown man he was, dealing with a fellow adult who wasn't being clear.

The stunned look on his dad's face made Dennis hold his gaze, face impassive, the question hanging between them.

Over and over, Dean opened his mouth to say something, then stopped. Tilted his head, pressed his lips together, then stopped. It gave Dennis the time to look at his father.

Really look at him.

Time had weathered Dean Luview like it seasoned a tree.

And like an old tree, Dean had deep roots that made it impossible to shake.

"I think you're ready for love and mad that it's not happening the way you want it to."

It felt like his dad had tossed an oak round right at his chest. Half his breath left his body without making a sound.

"Damn it," he growled, turning away. "I expect this shit from Mom. Not from you."

"This has nothing to do with your mother."

"Sure it does. She told you about Ana, didn't she?"

"Ana? Who is Ana?"

Ugh. Major mistake there. For a guy who'd brokered secrets most of his work life, he sure was bad at keeping them now.

"Ana is a woman I met right before coming home." Before Dean could ask, Dennis put his palm out. "We're not together."

"Sounds like you want to be."

"I am not talking about this." His truck keys were in his vest, fortunately, and as he walked away from his dad, he waved and shouted, "I'm a grown man!"

He heard his father mutter something that sounded like *Sure are*, but it didn't matter.

What mattered was finding a way to kill time.

Kill his desire.

Climbing into the truck, he got the engine going and pulled out onto the long road to the main numbered route. Going to Mel's was an easy drive.

An easy escape.

Aimless wasn't a word he'd ever use to describe himself, which meant that feeling this way was doubly painful. Retiring from the army was going to be a tough transition, he knew. Lots of guys in special ops talked about how they left but came back after a year, or even half a year, working for private companies as contractors on missions. The kind of work Dennis and his team did wasn't just a job.

It was in your blood.

Except blood was exactly why he'd left the service and come home.

Young blood.

Young, trusting–

No. He wasn't going to think about that.

He was going to think about trees.

Trees didn't bleed. Cut off a limb and they stayed silent.

Remove dead wood and you got new growth the next spring. Clear a fallen branch or tree from a roadway and you helped people.

Trim the rot and open up space.

Being home, though, involved people. Too many people. Yes, they were *his* people, but that didn't matter as much as he thought it would when he made the decision to retire, filing his paperwork with as little comment as possible.

The Army wasn't known for pushing paper fast, and during the transition, his guys had gone easy on him. Rafe, his best friend, got it instantly. BD (short for Bulldog) told him he was going soft anyhow, poking his non-existent love handles as a joke.

Tommy had just glared for days on end before dropping the sulk and treating him like normal.

And then there was Curtis. Curtis had been in that alley with him.

Curtis was out, too.

Except he left in a body bag.

The problem with living in rural Maine was that you had to drive long distances to get anywhere, and the mind could turn on you.

"Music," he muttered aloud, glancing at the dash to select a station before reflex made him slam on the brakes when something flew in front of him.

And it wasn't a bird.

Moose at a dead run are fast flyers, and this was a bull moose, big and determined, blowing through the three-foot ice-crusted berm like it was a pile of feathers, hooves on asphalt then–*bam*–back in the snow bank on the other side.

He raced out of sight through the thick woods as if the hip-deep snow were nothing but powder.

Compared to this, Dennis's daily snow runs were like a kid on coffee-can stilts.

Whatever the moose was after, it was life threatening. Heart pumping out of his chest, Dennis looked over to his right, to where the moose had stopped. A ghastly sound in the woods made his hair stand up on the back of his neck.

"Get out of here," he muttered to himself. Hitting the moose while driving sixty miles an hour would have been bad, but now–whatever was in the woods wasn't a threat to him.

And when the moose moved, he instantly understood.

The snarl sounded like a coyote, then the hideous, high-pitched yipping of a pack of them began. That moose was in protection mode.

All Dennis could do was lay on the horn, hard, then resume his journey. Man interfered more than enough with nature.

And Dennis wasn't stupid.

By the time he reached Mel's animal sanctuary, his nerves were back in place, heartbeat steady, but he'd had plenty of time to think about what he didn't know.

Which was enough to keep him busy for the rest of his life.

Outside the main barn, Mel stood holding onto a leash. At the other end was a tiny dog that looked like it lost a genetic fight with a rat.

"Hey," he said.

"Hey yourself. Thanks for coming,"

Dennis planted his hands on his hips and looked at the ratlike dog. It reminded him of a living Muppet.

"Is that why you wanted me to come over?"

"Ornery?" she asked.

"Uh... I guess I can be?"

"Ha. No. That's his name." She tugged the leash twice, lightly. "Ornery."

"What is it? Looks like a rat, a Chihuahua, and a Muppet had a threesome."

Mel just blinked at him. A lot. Then she looked at Ornery and laughed.

"That's the perfect description, isn't it? We have no idea what Ornery's made of. Someone found him in a ditch near Deke's, so he's here healing up."

"Okay."

"I need help with Magic."

"So the rumors are true."

"Huh?"

"You really are a witch." He winked. She laughed.

And then her breasts moved.

Dennis knew well not to look at her rack, but it was difficult when a small creature's head popped out from between her–

"Magic!" she exclaimed. Dennis shifted his gaze so that he watched the rack attack via peripheral vision. Two enormous eyes in a tiny little head stared at him. Mel reached down into her cleavage and pulled the little sugar glider out. White medical tape covered the poor thing's rear right leg.

No bigger than the palm of his hand, the little creature was so fragile. It pulled on tenderness strings around Dennis's heart that he didn't know he possessed.

"I wasn't kidding when I asked you to be his foster daddy."

Dennis groaned.

"Someone needs to watch Magic for about a week. He needs to heal up enough so that the other animals don't come after him."

"Just keep him in a cage."

"A cage?" Mel's tone told him that he had said the wrong thing. "You can't keep him in a cage! He's too social and he's injured. The poor thing needs to be close to a safe mammal."

"And *I'm* that safe mammal?" he said in a resigned tone because he already knew the answer.

Magic batted at his fingertip as he reached out. The poor guy was accustomed to jumping from tree limbs, its legs attached to webbing that turned it into a little magic carpet. But instead, Mel had to carefully transfer the sugar glider into his hands.

Magic looked up at Dennis with trusting eyes, as if to say, *You'd better not screw up.* And then he nestled himself right at the thumb crook of Dennis's right hand.

"See, he loves you already," Mel said. "He remembers you. He kept whispering, 'I want Dennis' in my ear."

"If you hear the animals talking to you, Mel, you need to get out more."

She just snorted.

"You tricked me into coming here. You knew I couldn't say no to those pitiful little Puss 'n Boots eyes."

"Yep."

"Have you no shame?"

"Come on, Dennis. Please? You're the best person I could think of for this."

"I'm the *only* person you could think of for this."

"You're strong. Gentle. Caring–"

"I'm already doing it. You don't need to lay it on thick. What do I feed him?"

"I'll text you instructions. I just need you to keep him alive for the next week."

"You want me to carry him around with me everywhere I go?"

She shrugged. "That's what I've been doing."

Politeness prevented him from pointing out that she possessed a body part he lacked that would allow the creature to nestle in somewhere warm.

As if Mel read his mind, she grinned and said, "You might want to start wearing vests and shirts with front pockets, or hoodies with pouches. Magic loves the girls." Mel looked down at her breasts. "You're going to have to find your own version of that."

Suddenly retirement wasn't looking so great.

"Got a question for you, Mel." Magic rested lightly in his hands.

"Sure."

"Does Randy ever take off at a run for no apparent reason in town?"

He didn't have to mention he meant the moose. Mel got it instantly.

"Randy? No," she said, thinking it through. "When he got hit by that car, it broke one of his legs. He can walk, but he's not a runner. Why?"

"I just almost hit a moose on my way over here. The thing shot right across the state route and into the woods."

"Huh," was all she said.

"Not many predators out there for moose," he said. His uncle Ted was the head of the agriculture department for the state of Maine. If there was anything the Luview children had been taught, it was how to manage themselves in the woods. When you cut down trees for a living and trim them along the side of the road, you see all kinds of wildlife.

"Can't be a wolf," Mel said. "Haven't been any in Maine for over a hundred years."

"Yeah, but you know all the rumors about coywolves."

"Sure. They caught one up by the Canadian border a few years ago. Genetic testing showed it was eighty-five percent wolf, but other than that, I can't think of too many things that could take out a bull moose. What about a bear?" she asked.

Dennis shook his head.

"Didn't see any. And it sounded like wolves."

"The only other thing I can think of," she mused, "is a wolverine, but that's a long shot, right? And they don't sound like wolves."

The crook of Dennis's arm started to ache, so he pulled Magic in close to him, looking down at his vest and long-sleeved shirt. Mel could tell he was struggling and said, "Stick him in your pocket."

"He'll be okay in there?" Dennis asked, transferring the creature into his left hand so he could clean out his right pocket. As he was stuffing his truck keys and his phone into his front pants pocket, Mel's phone buzzed. Holding up one finger, she took the call.

Dennis cradled little Magic in his hand. Sure enough, the sugar glider settled inside his vest pocket, leaving Dennis to wonder what his mom and dad were going to think when he came to dinner tonight with a guest at the dining table.

And his niece, Harriet? He was going to be her favorite uncle, instantly.

Hmmm. Maybe there was an upside to this animal foster daddy gig...

"A lemur? Webcam house? And a–an anaconda? How did the poor lemur escape being eaten by the anaconda? And what would a bunch of sex workers in a webcam house want a lemur for–oh, don't answer that!" Mel shouted toward the end, leaving Dennis to toe the mud and try to make himself useful. Could he muck stalls with Magic in his pocket?

Only one way to find out.

By the time Mel's call was over, she looked extremely pissed, but her eyes widened as she took in the llama section he'd mucked while she was on the phone.

"You're a doll," she murmured. Three stalls cleaned up.

"I'd rather muck stalls than handle a call like you just did."

Her cheeks went pink.

"People think rural life is quiet and sleepy. It's anything but. Webcam sex worker house near Fryeburg. A lemur and an anaconda."

"What were they... never mind." Like Mel, he shut off the questions he had no business—and no stomach—to ask.

"I just care for the little beasties. Not the human ones."

"Magic stayed put the entire time," he informed her. "Had to crook my elbow a bit to avoid friction on him, but otherwise fine."

"I knew you were the right person to ask."

"What if I had never retired?" he joked.

"I'd probably turn to Skylar."

"Who?"

"Skylar Lewiston? You know, works at Love You Coffee?"

He shook his head.

"Can't place the name."

"You really did leave town, didn't you?"

"I visited." Dennis took the question as an invitation to talk, leaning against a post, careful to use his hip so Magic had plenty of room. "But yeah, I left."

"I heard Greta fawned all over you the other day."

"Do people really gossip this much? I just went to Greta's for a pastry."

"People in this town gossip about anything, Dennis. You could miss a spot shaving and someone would have a detailed analysis within thirty minutes about how you were rushing to escape Annabeth Khouri's house because you two are having a secret affair."

"Damn. All that from a few missed whiskers." He rubbed his chin.

"And pretty soon, you're shacking up with Annabeth and she's planning which engagement ring you're buying her at Moore Mottin's store."

He reared back. "That's a very specific joking scenario you've just spun."

"Be warned. Annabeth's on the prowl. You're the only Luview brother left."

"Excuse me? There are plenty of us in town."

"Not from the core family. Dean's the only boy who kept the name going."

"You think Annabeth wants to–"

"Marry a Luview? Hell, yes!"

"She–that's ridiculous."

"You really don't know, do you?"

"Know?"

"The minute Deanna showed up at Kendrill's Market talking to Ed in the meat section about how you were retiring and coming home, one big game of telephone began. Before your mother was loading her groceries in her trunk, Annabeth was getting a mani-pedi to prepare for your arrival."

"That makes no sense."

"Doesn't have to make sense. We're in Love You, Maine, where people don't always make sense."

"I agree with you on that."

From any other woman, Mel's warning would feel like she was testing the waters. Dennis knew from his mother that plenty of single women would have him on their radar. His mom explicitly recommended he take his time in the "dating pool," as if he were on a new season of *The Bachelor: Love You, Maine*.

All this kind of talk did was make him want Ana more.

But Ana didn't want him, and that was that.

Wriggling in his pocket made him remember the sugar glider, whose nose poked out.

"He needs some freedom," Mel reminded him.

"Don't we all."

"I meant to eliminate, unless you want your pocket turned into a toilet."

"Keeping it real, Mel. Keeping it real."

Bubbly laughter, girlish and sweet, poured from her. Mel

was weathered and jaded, so the sound made him feel like he'd cracked open something good.

"If I have a role in this community, Dennis, it's just that: keeping it real."

Her phone buzzed again.

"Damn. Now I have to create a habitat for a lemur *and* an anaconda."

"Kell's an expert in lemurs," Dennis said with a snicker, unable to keep a straight face.

Mel rolled her eyes. "Lemur *costumes*, maybe."

She nudged a small box.

"Take that. You can carry him in it until you figure out a safe space. Dean and Deanna must have an old aquarium somewhere, right?"

Dennis set Magic down in the box. The poor little guy limped and looked up at him, as if to beg for more cuddling.

"Who can resist a face like that?" Dennis said with a laugh.

"That's what Annabeth Khouri says anytime she sees you."

If she weren't like a sister to him, Dennis would think Mel was sharpening some claws of her own.

"This entire town is too lovesick," he groused. "I expect this from my mother. Not you."

"Just warning you, Dennis. Annabeth is... determined."

"You can't force love, no matter how determined you are. Doesn't work that way."

"Someone has a mushy side."

"It's a fact."

"You ever been in love?"

"What?"

"You heard me. You ever been in love?"

"Why would you ask me that? Aren't you in a rush to go to Fryeburg and rescue some animals?"

Mel scratched her chin, eyes narrowing as if she were trying to read him.

"You've never married. Never brought anyone home for Dean and Deanna to meet. Never lived with anyone. Last person anyone in town remembers you dating was Tricia Houle, and she left town a few weeks after you did and never returned."

"She got into Penn, Mel. Met a math professor there and got married."

"Point being, you aren't exactly known for romantic relationships. Not public ones, at least." Her squint changed, as if she were rethinking that.

"I do fine."

"You deserve it, you know?"

"Deserve bachelorhood?"

She let out a barky laugh. "No. Love."

"Now you sound like my mom, and I don't need a second one. You want me to start prying in your business? Ask why you and Darren divorced when you seem to get along so well?"

The way she stiffened told him he'd hit a nerve. Good. She was banging on plenty of his like she had mallets on a calypso drum, so...

Her hand wave was dismissive, but she gave him a tight smile. "I deserved that. Sorry to be like the rest of them."

"No problem."

"You've got wounds, though."

"Don't we all?"

"Yours are a little raw."

"Now you're my psychiatrist?"

"All right. I hear you loud and clear. Going back to minding my own business."

"Thank you. Can I ask a favor?"

"Sure."

"Teach my mother that phrase?"

"Which one?"

"'Going back to minding my own business.'"

Mel laughed, her wheeze loud and infectious, and Dennis joined in. When she could finally speak, her eyes were red from tears.

Planting her hand on his shoulder, she looked at him and said, "Some favors are too big to ask. Impossible task, my friend. Impossible task."

Bzzz

His phone said Mom.

"Speak of the devil," he muttered, looking at her text.

Can you swing by Kendrill's on your way home and get some milk, rosemary, and a garlic bulb?

Followed by nine hearts.

"She's doing it again. I'm an errand boy now," he muttered as he typed back the letter *K*.

"Of course you are. What did you think would happen living in that family commune?"

"Compound. Not commune."

"Whatever. You're a better soul than I am. If I had to live with my siblings and parents, within three months, no one would be speaking to each other."

"It's not like that," he said, smiling. "At all."

"I know. Your family is special."

"It is."

"So special, Annabeth wants to join it."

"Mel," he said, backing up toward his truck. "You promised."

"I never promised not to tease you."

"BYE, MEL!" he shouted as he started up the truck, moving carefully so he didn't smash Magic. "HAPPY TO DO YOU THIS FAVOR! HAVE FUN WITH THE LEMUR AND SNAKE!"

Laughing, she was back in the barn before he was driving away.

When he reached the main road and turned toward town, he looked down at his jacket and sighed.

Then thought about the stray kitten in the dumpster at the hotel.

Softy. He was a softy when it came to animals. That was true emotion. Love and caring.

Not the red, pink, and white that threw up all over downtown and pretended to be Love.

As he crossed into the downtown district, the distinct *ding! ding!* of a trolley bell confused him, his memory flashing to San Francisco or Old Orchard Beach.

But no. He was home.

Waiting at a stoplight, he turned and saw the electric trolley Rachel was so proud of stopped at a covered station, just big enough to hold about ten people. Eager children held their parents' hands as they boarded, the small crowd bundled in thick winter clothing, a little girl dropping a pink mitten on the ground. Across the street, a bottle of Pepto-Bismol doubling as a police car made him smile.

The person in the front seat wasn't his brother. He didn't recognize the officer, who looked like a walking red pen in his standard-issue police uniform, with the red, well... everything.

Except black belt and shoes.

Man, he'd forgotten how bizarre Luview, Maine, really was.

Basic training had sucked as a barely eighteen-year-old, but it had *really* sucked when his fellow recruits found out where he was from. The teasing had been nothing but torment, though it toughened him.

All the circular baked goods in the mess hall had taken some getting used to, too.

Beep!

Caught up in his thoughts, he didn't notice the traffic light change, so he pressed the accelerator and made his way to the small parking lot behind the market. A chain of stores along this part of downtown meant that street parking was at a premium, though the trolley really cut down on tourists parking along the main drag.

He grabbed a spot at the far edge of the lot and went in, Magic tucked in his pocket.

With luck, no one would notice.

"Milk, garlic, rosemary," he muttered to himself as the automatic doors opened and he walked in through the rear entrance, which meant passing the meat department. Bending over for a basket, he hadn't even grasped the handles when he heard:

"Hey there, Dennis."

Looking up, he locked eyes with Ed Khouri, head butcher and Annabeth's father.

"Hey, Ed."

"Enjoying being back home?"

Stifling a groan, Dennis gave him the polite smile he was relearning and said, "Yep."

Perhaps going laconic would give him more peace.

Ed just nodded, but showed no signs of ending the conversation, so Dennis gave him a wave and walked toward the dairy section. Bracing himself, he spotted two more people he recognized—Dotty Chen, the town librarian, and Ford Adams, one of the mechanics at Deke's.

Dairy and produce, then he was out of here.

Head down, he grabbed a gallon of milk from the display case and turned toward produce.

Hold up. Did his mom want fresh rosemary? Or the kind in a jar?

Reaching in his pocket, he asked the question in a text, then headed for the garlic.

"Dennis!" a female voice squealed from behind him. Not one he recognized, either.

Turning around, he came face to face with Sheila Bilbee, his cousin Blake's wife.

A hug, like it or not, came before words. Angling his shoulder, he tried to protect Magic.

"Sheila. Good to see you. Watching out for Magic in my pocket."

Her body froze. "Excuse me?"

He winced, wondering how that sounded to her.

"Magic. He's a sugar glider." Stepping back, he gently pried the little creature out of his hiding spot, mostly to show Sheila he wasn't being vulgar.

"Oh, my goodness!"

"His name is Magic."

"Oh! So that's what you meant." Her face went pink. "Why are you walking around town with your pocket full of... *that*?"

He pointed to the bandage on Magic's leg.

"Helping Mel out."

"Awwwwwwww," she said in that tone women get when they see baby goats wearing sweaters.

Dennis just shrugged.

"Blake is so happy you're home. He always says you're his favorite cousin. Come to the restaurant!"

"I will. Promise. This time of year, though..." He nodded toward Main Street. "Getting crowded."

"People are coming earlier and earlier," she agreed. "We used to start filling up on February first. Now we're booked solid starting in January."

"A full month before Valentine's Day?"

"Yep." She grinned, clearly thrilled by their success.

Blake was two years older than Dennis, someone who helped him navigate the strangeness of high school when

Dennis appeared on the hockey team as a competent, but not particularly skilled, defenseman. By the end of his freshman year, he was a three-sport athlete, playing football in the fall, hockey in the winter, and competing in shot put in the spring.

All that activity bulked him up, fast.

"You coming to Bilbee's tonight?" she asked. "We're closed on Mondays, so we decided to go hang out with everyone."

Luke and Colleen had cornered him this morning and made it clear he was expected to attend, so he just nodded.

She beamed. "Great!" Her phone buzzed, face falling as she read the text. "I'm late! See you tonight."

As she walked away, he reoriented himself, his own phone buzzing.

Fresh is wonderful, was all his mother said.

I thought you had an herb garden in the greenhouse, he replied.

Jester ate the whole thing last week. Remember? When Darren swung by because we were worried he also ate some vermiculite?

Golden retrievers were great, and Jester was a wonderful companion, but he certainly added some excitement to their sleepy little compound.

Right. Want me to get you a rosemary tree? he responded, his finger hitting Send as a wave of perfume assaulted him.

Then a hand appeared on his forearm.

"Dennis."

He looked up.

The woman before him was dressed to the nines, with perfectly coiffed hair and makeup that looked like someone had used 3D modeling software to get every pixel perfect. But when she smiled and her ruby-red lips parted, her top front tooth was the tiniest bit crooked.

The look in her eye was unmistakable: She was on the prowl.

"Annabeth," he said simply, looking back at the meat counter, wondering if Ed had texted her.

"You look ah-*maze*-ing," she gushed as she came in for a hug, her height close to his in high-heeled boots that were about as practical in the Maine winter as a mesh mask in a flu ward.

Considering he'd spent the morning chopping wood, followed by mucking the stalls at Mel's animal sanctuary, Dennis did not, in fact, feel like he was ah-*maze*-ing.

He was likely quite ripe.

"Thank you. You, too." He pulled back, careful to protect Magic. Her eyes dropped to his pocket, then widened.

"Is your jacket... moving?"

Stifling a sigh, he reached for the critter and showed it to her.

"You're carrying a flying squirrel in your pocket?" Her tone was decidedly less gushy and cute.

"He's hurt." Dennis rotated Magic to show the bandage. "Helping Mel out."

Annabeth's smile didn't reach her eyes.

"How sweet." She leaned in. "How are you adjusting to life back home, where you belong?"

One part of coming back to Luview that he'd forgotten: the sheer level of judgment some people had baked into their personalities.

"Just fine."

"Grocery shopping?"

"No. Looking for bomb supplies," he said, deadpan.

She faltered, then laughed.

"You always were a joker."

They'd grown up together, but he'd never dated her. Never been close. Why the sudden pretense of familiarity?

He looked over her shoulder, spotted the herb section, and walked over to the rosemary. Tiny trees, three in total, were wrapped in cellophane. He put one in his basket.

"Deanna's making chicken for dinner?"

"I... guess?"

"She makes such a good smoked chicken. That rosemary and olive oil infusion she does is–" Annabeth used her fingers to do a chef's kiss, drawing his attention to her lips, eyes on him the entire time.

"Mom's a great cook." Being boring was his best option here. If he said even the tiniest thing that gave her a hook, it would only make this worse.

"Oh! Dennis!" Sheila suddenly appeared. "I forgot to ask. Dean has a blowtorch Deanna's lending us. Ours died, and you can't make crème brûlée without one. Can you bring it tonight?"

Annabeth's eyes narrowed like a lion spotting an injured gazelle.

"Sure," he said as Sheila waved thanks and disappeared.

"Tonight?" Annabeth asked, eyes pinging from the door Sheila departed through to Dennis.

Just then, Magic began writhing in his pocket, claws scraping hard against him. Dropping his basket, he fumbled to get the poor thing out, horrifying Annabeth in the process.

Which was an unintended bonus.

"What's up, bud?" he asked the little guy, who chose that moment to rise up, looking at Annabeth.

And then Magic did what sugar gliders do.

He leaped.

Legs splaying in midair, Magic looked like a rectangle of stretchy fur, but the injured leg pulled in, changing his shape into a lopsided quadrilateral. As he flew toward Annabeth, she screamed and backed up, her ass hitting the edge of an enormous avocado pyramid.

The rumble of hundreds of ovoid objects registered in Dennis's brain, but his full attention was on Annabeth, who was dodging poor Magic. Suddenly, the poor creature had nowhere to land.

Avocados spilled down like a landslide. Dennis jumped in front of Annabeth, his arm grazing her breasts as he struggled to give Magic a hand.

"WHAT ARE YOU DOING?" she shrieked, but he ignored the words, focused wholly on his mission: to catch the confused creature before it nosedived onto the hard linoleum.

Dodging Annabeth to his left, he felt her weight shift, those heels too high for stability. Her hip checked a sweet onion display and an avalanche of Vidalias joined the avocados.

Less than two seconds passed before his fingers connected with Magic's paws and he hit the ground hard, his hip and shoulder absorbing the majority of the impact.

But the produce landslide continued, an onion bouncing right between his eyes.

Turning away, he saw Annabeth pirouette, striking a basket of tomatoes on the vine, three or four bunches going airborne as a wave of avocados rolled off his back.

Staying put seemed advisable until the fray had settled. Annabeth righted herself, clinging to the edge of the wooden vegetable receptacle, one ankle shaky.

Laughter, muttering, and confused movement around him turned into a din as he looked at Magic, who was safely in his hands.

All he got was a wide-eyed, confused look right back.

"Me, too, buddy. Me, too."

In reply, Magic peed all over the palm of his hand.

"SO GROSS!" Annabeth screeched as her father appeared, shaking his head as he surveyed the mess on the floor between the two of them.

"You okay?" Dennis called out to her, but she was beyond polite talk.

"Dad! Do something!" she demanded of Ed, who took in the mess, then shuffled over to one of the displays.

"DAD?"

He returned holding a lime and a garlic bulb. Looking Dennis dead in the eye, he tossed both on the floor next to him.

"There," Ed said calmly. "Now you can make guacamole."

Chapter Twelve

Ana

"So that's it?" she asked Rick, who sat on the other side of his desk, laptop folded, reading glasses perched on the fine, long bone of his nose. He reminded her of her department chair in graduate school, when she explained she would be opening her own practice after graduating and getting her license.

Strategically neutral.

"That's the beginning."

"Harris really terminated his parental rights so easily?" She struggled to keep the shaking out of her voice.

"He has voluntarily surrendered. We have a legal document he has signed. He could try to contest it in the future, but I don't think he will, given the felony charge against him."

"What does a felony charge have to do with parental rights?" Ana fought the rising anxiety in her stomach. Now at eleven weeks, she was just starting to get some relief from the morning sickness.

This conversation brought the nausea roaring back.

"If he were ever convicted of a violent felony, you would have a strong case to terminate his rights."

"I thought you said he just surrendered them."

Rick sighed, removing the glasses. "Honey, I'm a tax lawyer. Not family law. I called in some favors from some friends. But I do know one thing: Guys like Harris are bad news, and he'll never set foot in the U.S. again with those charges against him. It's hard to terminate parental rights before a baby is born, and much harder if the parent in question is unwilling. By getting him to sign a surrender, and knowing he has felony charges waiting for him if he comes back to the States, I think you're in good shape. You don't have to put him on the birth certificate."

Her body flooded with an icy surge.

"What?"

"It's—it's your prerogative.

"That would make everything easier."

"Unless he comes back and wants a paternity test."

"But you just said—"

Rick held up his palm.

"I know what I said. And trust me, the bastard isn't coming back." He reached for a small glass on a cork coaster, the amber liquid familiar. Rick wasn't a big drinker, but he typically had a double shot of bourbon, neat, during a stressful case.

Pure, cold steel was in her stepfather's voice, a hidden agenda wrapped up in his baritone fury.

"Did you—did you threaten him?"

A harsh laugh was his answer. He finished his drink in one gulp, the ice clinking like an exclamation point, then lowered the glass, cradling it in his palm.

"I'm not stupid. He's not worth losing my law license over."

"Then... what?"

"He asked for money."

A groan the size of her regret over ever being involved with him came from deep inside.

"Of course he did."

"Let's just say I wasn't exactly shocked." Rick frowned. "You really never told him about your trust fund?"

"I told you I didn't."

"Why not?"

Conversations like this weren't typical with Rick. In fact, they were nonexistent.

"I don't know. Mom says maybe it was my intuition."

Rick's mouth went flat at that. "That's a way of saying you never truly trusted him."

"Turns out I was right."

"Sure were. Good thing you kept the money private."

"What did he ask for?"

"Bitcoin."

Ana's eyebrows shot up. "How many?"

"About enough to equal a million dollars."

"Please tell me you did not give him that kind of money!"

"Hell, no. A small fraction of that."

"Such an asshole."

"We established that a long time ago."

"How much did he take in exchange for giving up his... our... child?"

As he stood, Rick looked away. "You're an adult. This is all in the file." He tapped a manila folder. "And in the secure online vault. I know you have your own mind and will do whatever you want regardless, but I'm going to give you some unsolicited advice."

"Sure! Why not?" Ana said sarcastically. "Mrs. Montini next door has been doing it since she found out I was pregnant. I'm not supposed to eat apple seeds or black jelly beans."

"My advice is a little less specific." He gave her a gentle smile. It was almost fatherly. "Don't read the file. Don't think about Harris. Don't waste a single speck of your time or energy on him now. I took care of him."

A tiny chill shot up her spine. "Took... care?"

"Hah. Not like that. Just... I took out the trash, okay? And when the baby's born, we have other legal maneuvers we can use to shut Harris out even more, and make this rock solid."

"Like what?"

"Like if you meet a man and he wants to adopt the child. Or, uh..." he frowned. "A woman."

"A woman?"

"If you ever have a *partner*," Rick said pointedly, "who wants to be the other parent, that would make it easy to complete the termination of parental rights."

"Oh! Now I understand."

"Good. As far as I'm concerned, Ana, your baby has no father. Maybe you could think of it that way, too."

Relief was what she was supposed to feel, but a big bolus of grief, full and dark, rose up in her chest.

"Right."

"But he—she—will have a grandfather." The corners of his eyes turned warmer. "And the best grandmother ever."

"Mom is really excited."

"She's very fixated on getting you to twenty-six weeks."

"Age of viability. I know. Fifteen to go."

"You'll make it."

"Thank you. Let's hope. Harris being out of the picture legally really reduces my stress. Not that I'm planning to run out and find a guy who wants to be with a woman like me."

"Any man would be lucky to have a woman like you. Stop that nonsense."

Ah. That was the Rick she was used to.

"I'm not being self-deprecating, just stating a fact. Most

men truly aren't interested in dating an already-pregnant woman."

"Don't rule out a future with a partner who loves and accepts your child." He looked down, blinking rapidly, his shoulders loosening. "Look, Ana, I know we haven't exactly been close since I married your mom."

Oh. Wow.

This was a conversation she'd imagined a million different times, in a trillion different ways. One she'd talked about openly with her own therapists, and with her supervising therapist in graduate school and beyond. Losing her father in the very sudden, very public way she had at thirteen had been bad enough.

Having her mother marry Rick and learning they'd been having an affair, and that Rick was the reason her mother hadn't been on that plane trip, was even more complicated.

Now here she was, two decades later, and Rick was becoming emotionally vulnerable?

Her gut clenched, even as her wise mind and therapist training kept her grounded.

"That's a fair way of saying it," she responded, her tone kind and as moderate as possible.

"And I know that there is a complex history behind us," he added, his neck turning red, eyes widening as he avoided contact. Watching people struggle with their emotions, guiding them, was what she did for a living.

But she was helpless now, facing her own stepfather.

"There is," was all she could say, sticking to simple validation that didn't betray any of her own complex emotions.

"And we've never really talked about any of it."

There it was.

Rick just pointed to the elephant in the room.

"No. We haven't."

He let out a soft chuckle. "I must admit, I'm at a disadvantage here on two counts."

"What do you mean?"

"First, I'm terrible at talking about my emotions. And second, you're a therapist."

"I might be a therapist, but I'm really just a confused thirteen-year-old right now, Rick."

Shocked eyes met hers. "Really?"

"Really."

"Huh."

"We haven't talked about it. None of it. Not how it felt to realize you were with Mom that night."

He winced. She felt like she was ripping a band-aid off her heart, but it also felt good. Really good.

"Not how I had to pretend I didn't know. Not how it felt to be tolerated."

"Tolerated?" His voice dropped, air rushing through him. "By me?"

"Yes."

"That's—I never meant to make you feel that way."

"I know."

"No, Ana—I never felt that way about you. Not at all. I'm—I'm sorry I gave you that impression." He came around the desk and leaned against it, facing her. Rick was a compact man, a triathlete, driven and competitive. His face was clean shaven, hair just a little long and quite gray around the ears, but otherwise thick and dark. "Frankly, I think I was ashamed."

"Of sleeping with your friend's wife behind his back?"

He shook then, like a wet dog, but regained his composure instantly, the involuntary tremor so fast, she almost didn't see it.

"Yes. And for being the reason your mother wasn't on that plane."

"I'm *grateful* she wasn't on that plane!"

"Yes, of course, but...." He cleared his throat.

"Right. Complicated."

He looked pointedly at his empty glass.

"Ana, I brought this all up because I want to make it crystal clear that I am prepared to be this baby's grandfather, one hundred percent. I never had kids of my own. Only you, and that's been–"

"Complicated," they said in unison.

Then they chuckled in unison, too.

His face dropped, flat and serious. "If you'll let me, I'm all in. Harris is an ass, and I'm sure he hasn't told his parents, if they even exist."

"I have no idea where I'd find them."

"We tried. No luck."

"We?"

"Private investigators we hired."

"Oh. Whoa. You really did a lot here. I never met them. He didn't talk about them. I mean, it's not like we were together for years, but still, I feel so stupid."

"Stop feeling stupid."

"Maybe I should see a therapist for it."

That made him erupt into laughter, the nervous kind, a sound she'd never heard him make before. The idea that she made him anxious was simultaneously empowering and unsettling.

She instantly felt very, very mature.

"You know, Rick," she said as he wound down, taking some deep breaths, "we're adults. You're my stepfather, but of course you're not my father. I've always thought of you as Mom's husband. Not so much a father figure for me."

His expression became pained.

She held up a palm. "I don't mean that in a negative sense. But with this whole Harris mess, you've really helped me. I'm thankful. And maybe we can use this baby's arrival as a chance to reboot?"

His breath came out in a whoosh, emotion overflowing in his eyes. "I'd like that very much, Ana."

Her phone buzzed in her purse. She ignored it.

To her astonishment, Rick opened his arms like he was coming in for a hug. Ana could, quite literally, count on one hand the times he'd ever hugged her:

Their wedding.

Her high school graduation.

Her undergraduate graduation.

Her master's degree graduation.

And... now.

He smelled like expensive aftershave and fine cotton, a crisp scent that made her think of fresh money, so new that it threatened to cause papercuts if you handled it the wrong way. The hug was respectful, no bear hug or big, boisterous sighing. Just a gentle hug that bridged two decades of so much unspoken. Unacknowledged.

Unable to be said.

And much remained in the silence, but for now, this was good. This was soulful.

This was a start.

Ana surprised herself by not tearing up, her heart full, her nose in the cloth of Rick's business shirt.

He murmured against her ear, "I love you, kiddo. And that waste of skin can't hurt you anymore. Won't let it happen."

Her jolt was a reaction to Rick's fierceness, the words incongruous compared to his vulnerable outpouring of emotion, still controlled but far more than she'd ever seen.

This was how he showed love, she supposed. Through fierce protectiveness.

"Thank you. I love you, too."

The words were true. She wouldn't say them if she didn't feel them.

But they were also new. Brand new, because she'd never heard them from Rick.

As they pulled away, he sniffed, just once but enough for her to realize *he'd* teared up. Her smile felt real, so genuine that it stretched across time.

Healing came in unexpected moments.

"Well," he said, wiping one eye, looking away but smiling. "Didn't expect *that*."

"Feelings are unpredictable."

"Which is why I like tax law better."

Their shared laugh covered the buzzing from her phone, though the sound came through towards the end.

"Need to answer that? We're done here." He frowned. "I mean, in terms of Harris and the legalities."

"I probably should." She looked at her phone and saw the time. "Oh! I'm late for Brie!"

"Go," he said, sniffing again. "I don't want to keep you from whatever bride thing she's cooked up for you next."

"It's a Zoom call with her great-aunt. The one who's hosting the wedding."

"Hosting? At her house?"

"Not quite. I'll explain later."

"For a wedding that's eighteen months away, there sure is a lot of planning going on."

"That's how these things work."

"I wouldn't know. Your mom is the only person I've ever married, and we kept it small and simple." Eyes flashing with something close to shame, Rick looked away. Ana knew exactly why they kept their wedding small and simple.

And oh, so secret.

Because news coverage would have been too much.

"Bye," Ana said, ready for closure, Rick waving as she

closed the door. By the time she got in her car and pulled out of the law firm's parking lot, she was replaying everything she'd just experienced.

Always, *always*, she'd felt like a third wheel in her own family, at least since her father had died. Secrets seemed to surround Rick and her mother, but she hadn't understood the strange tension between them until she'd learned the exact nature of their affair.

And then she'd followed their lead and said nothing.

Brie was at her family's cheese shop in Rockport. The drive there was a cleansing time, as she recalled conversations, stitched together patterns, and realized that love was all that really mattered. Her love for her mother, her love for Rick, Rick's love for her, and everyone's love for the baby growing inside her.

"Stick around, baby," she murmured. At a stoplight, she fished around in her purse for the ginger candy she needed. Dry and sweet, her tongue eagerly worked it to get some saliva flowing, the first swallow helping to quell her low-grade nausea.

A chunk of Ewephoria cheese would help, too.

Hohenadel's Fromagerie was situated in a small plaza of three shops. On the right was a locally owned donut shop, complete with drive-thru, then the cheese shop in the middle, and a coffee shop to the left.

Sadly, their coffee sucked. Life was so unfair.

As she parked, she looked at the new awning Brie's father had installed, kelly-green canvas with their name on it and illustrations of various cheeses on either side of the words. It was clear.

They sold cheese.

Entering the store was always a delight because it felt like being greeted at your favorite bar.

"Ana!" Hugh Hohenadel called out from behind the

counter, his green apron over the belly he called his very own wheel.

"Hi there, Second Dad," she joked. His hug was as boisterous and messy as Rick's had been respectful and tentative.

"Fourth Child," he joked back, looking at her belly. "Still need Ewephoria?"

She nodded eagerly.

Leave it to Hugh to have figured out that this single cheese, a blend of sheep's milk and goat's milk, imported from the Netherlands, could reduce her nausea. Just one slice.

He came around the corner, holding it in a piece of paper. She took a nibble and sighed.

"Ginger and cheese. Weird combo, but it works."

"Forget about weird. If it works, it works, and that's all that matters. How's my first grandchild coming along?"

"Don't say that in front of Brie," she stage whispered as her friend came out from the back room. "She'll get jealous."

"Are you kidding? You're taking all the pressure off me! Now I don't have to produce a baby so soon," Brie said, though her face changed when she looked at Ana. "What's wrong?"

"What do you mean?"

"You look... different. Subdued."

"How about contemplative?"

"Spit it out."

Ana guarded her cheese. "Never!"

"Hah. You know what I mean."

The bell at the door tinkled. Hugh looked away from her and called out to the incoming customer, "Hey, Joel! Got some new Camembert for you!"

Brie pulled Ana aside. "Tell me. You met with Rick just now. Was he a jerk?"

"No. The opposite, actually. Everything's taken care of with Harris."

"He really gave up parental rights?"

"He signed whatever Rick asked him to sign. It's complicated, and might involve more legal stuff later, but Rick says the basics are in place."

"That's great!"

"It is. And... he hugged me."

"Rick *hugged* you?" Brie squealed, catching Hugh's attention, his thick gray eyebrows shooting up.

"Did the doctor tell him he has three months to live?" Hugh called out.

"Dad!"

"What? He's the least emotional guy I ever met. Like a robot, that one."

Brie made a face. "He's not... wrong."

"I know. He said he wants me to know he never had a child, other than me. And this grandchild—he'll be the best grandfather possible. Then he hugged me and told me he loves me."

Brie's hands flew to the sides of her face.

"Holy smokes!"

"I know."

Brie leaned in and whispered, "Maybe Dad's right and Rick is secretly dying."

"No," Ana laughed. "I think he's going through some emotional shifts. Good ones. It's nice."

"I'm happy for you. Who knew a baby caused by Harris being a massive dick could trigger so many good things?"

"I agree with you. I think. That's a lot to parse."

As her mood lifted and her stomach stopped twisting, she felt a warmth spreading through her. Brie was right.

So much good was coming.

Her hand fluttered to her belly, then pulled away.

Stay, baby, she thought to herself. *Stay.*

"Ready for our Zoom?" Brie asked.

"Can't wait."

"I wish we could drive up there, but the snow's bad right now, and the town is mobbed in February."

Ana grinned. "I can't believe you're really doing this. Getting married!"

"We are. Only eighteen months to plan. And now Auntie has offered to host!"

"It's awesome! Can she manage Zoom? She must be practically a hundred years old!"

"Not quite. In her nineties, though. And still involved in her store."

"Wow."

The bell at the door jingled again as Joel left with his Camembert and whatever else Hugh convinced him to buy. Hugh wiped his big hands on his apron and said, "You guys ready?"

"We're all on the call?" Ana inquired.

"Sure! You know she loves you," Brie said.

"We've visited her almost my whole life. You guys were so wonderful to bring me on family vacations."

"Not at all," Hugh corrected her. "I couldn't leave my bonus child behind!" His face soured. "Your parents brought you when you were younger, right up until the..." he paused, clearing his throat. "The plane crash. Then Rick didn't want to come."

Hugh's face made it clear what he thought of Rick.

"That's when we started bringing you with us."

"I wish you and Rick got along better," Ana admitted as they headed into the back of the shop, Hugh reaching for his go-cup of crappy coffee from the place next door.

Hugh and her stepfather were polite to each other. Barely.

Because Hugh and her father had been close friends, close enough for their families to vacation together for years.

"I wish for many things, too, Ana," Hugh said softly as

they passed by the back office and entered a large room with a cathedral ceiling that acted as a small event space. A big flat-screen television was on one wall, and Hugh began manipulating a computer behind a serving bar, setting his cup on its top surface.

"How do you drink that horrible swill?" Brie asked him, making a face.

"Like this." He took a sip and grinned at her.

As they shuddered, he punched some keys.

Suddenly, the three of them were huge heads on screen, all together.

"Aha. Now, the question... will Auntie remember how to log in?" Pulling his phone from an apron pocket, he began tapping.

"She's how old now? Ninety... what?" Brie asked.

Hugh squinted, thinking. "Ninety... I don't remember. Older than dirt. Born in 1930something."

"Dad!" Brie exclaimed, jokingly punching his shoulder. "Don't be mean."

Suddenly, the screen split in two, a regal woman appearing. Perfectly put together, her long, white hair was pinned up in a French twist, bright red lipstick on pursed lips that opened like rose blossoms as she looked at Brie.

"My dearies! Ana! Brie! And Hugh–do you wait on customers like *that*?" Her tone turned from joyful to scolding.

"Like what?"

"Without a collared shirt! Brie, your mother lets him do that?" she asked, apparently scandalized.

"Auntie, he was unloading a delivery truck," Brie lied, eyes twinkling.

"Well, in my day, my husband dressed properly, even to unload." She sniffed. "Donald was a cultured man, able to shift between negotiating a contract and cleaning a floor without missing a beat." Her second sniff made Hugh's jaw clench. "But enough about that. Have you considered my offer?"

"Yes!" Brie said with glee. "We'd love to get married at your shop!"

"You'll be the first," the old woman declared. "Boyce is convinced this is the wave of the future."

"I thought Boyce was retiring?" Hugh asked kindly. She was his wife's aunt, but he'd always treated her like his own.

"Boyce? Retire?" Merry blue eyes laughed at the idea. "He's been saying that for years. Came close a few years ago, when we nearly sold the shop, but now he's taking a different tack: expansion."

"Adding a reception hall to the chocolate shop is genius!" Brie enthused. "You'll book so many weddings there!"

"I hope so," Great-aunt Lucinda said with a broad smile, the wrinkles around her eyes pulling back to show spirit and delight. "And I am so happy to have you marry here. Every summer, you've come to visit, and it's always been such a highlight."

Ana smiled back and turned to Brie.

"Getting married in the *love*-liest place on earth was our fantasy when we were kids. I am so happy it's happening for you."

"You know what they say about Luview, Maine," Aunt Lucinda declared. "It's the town where everyone has a heart on!"

Hugh, who was mid-sip, sprayed the screen of the laptop. The camera escaped damage, thankfully.

"My goodness, Hugh! Control yourself!"

But Brie and Ana stepped off-camera because they, too, were unable to control themselves. As they laughed and laughed, suddenly, it hit Ana:

In eighteen months, her best friend would get her dream

wedding, married at the Love You Chocolate shop in Love You, Maine.

And Ana would be there by her side.

With a one-year-old.

Dreams really did come true.

Even if the journey had a few detours.

Chapter Thirteen

Dennis

Bilbee's Tavern was the last place he should bring a sugar glider, but his mom put him in a double bind.

"You go out with your brothers and sister and have some fun or I will personally call Annabeth and set you up on a date."

"I've been blackmailed by professionals, Mom, and they were far better than you."

"That right there is the key difference."

"Huh?"

"*Mom*. I'm your mother. Not a professional. Now shoo." She had literally waved a kitchen towel at him like he was a fly she needed to evacuate.

As he drove slowly through town, he let out a long, grumbly sigh. All his regular parking spots were taken, the sidewalks thick with tourists. It was the week before Valentine's Day and all the gullible, shallow people who thought the love-themed crap in town was fun were here.

In abundance.

"Okay, that's harsh," he said aloud. "They're just gullible. Not necessarily shallow."

And they were annoying him because he couldn't find a place to park, eyes scanning for–

Aha! Tail lights. The big SUV pulled out just as Dennis approached, as if God himself heard Dennis's curmudgeonly complaint and provided assistance. The spot was in front of Love You Chocolate, all the way across the downtown area from Bilbee's, but beggars couldn't choose.

Or something like that.

Parking his truck, he made sure Magic was safe in the pouch of his Army-green hoodie and pulled his coat on over it, the creature curled up nice and sweet in there. Luview was hopping tonight, and Bilbee's would be packed.

Steeling himself for the onslaught of people, he began walking along the sidewalk, deep in his thoughts, when he heard someone call his name.

A shaky voice, more frail than he'd ever heard it.

"Miss Lucinda?" he asked, turning to find her standing in the doorway of her store, clutching her unzipped coat to her chest.

"Come on! Come in!" she said, waving her arm.

You didn't defy an order from Miss Lucinda.

Stepping fast, he walked over and entered the store, the lush aroma of chocolate assaulting him, salivary glands activated. Working at Love You Chocolate had been his first real job at age fourteen, other than chopping wood for his dad.

And Lucinda Armistead was like a grandmother to him.

"I understand you have developed an unnatural affinity for carrying a rat on your person?" she said, upfront and direct as always. Time had shrunk her. The imperious woman who scared the hell out of him as a teen was just a little old lady.

Regal and composed, sure.

But her time on Earth, living and breathing, was winding down.

"Not a rat," Dennis said with a chuckle, surprised to hear himself reply from a position of certainty and stability. Maybe he really had grown up. Cupping Magic in his hand, he pulled the little beastie out to show her. "A sugar glider."

Unimpressed, her face was a sheet of granite. "Normal people don't walk around with a rat in their sweatshirt, Dennis."

"Since when have I ever claimed to be normal, Miss Lucinda? He's injured and needs a little extra foster care."

Her penciled-in eyebrows shot up.

"Why didn't you say so in the first place? I see Mel Chassi has gotten to you."

"Just helping her out."

"You always were a tender boy, Dennis. But then you left and lost so much of that tenderness."

"Can't be tender in the Army. They'd chew me up, spit me out, and let me roast in the sand until I desiccated."

"Then it's good you've moved back home to stay. Gives you access to your full humanity."

He just blinked. The old woman could pull out some zingers.

"I hear you're breaking ground on a new addition," he said, making small talk. The room felt like a chocolate womb, though the chatter of employees in the storage room and cooler at the rear of the store cut through their private conversation. The shop must have just closed for the day, which meant everything needed to be restocked.

How many thousands of pounds–*tons!*–of chocolate passed through these doors? he wondered.

"We are. It will start February 20th, right after the big day." By that, she meant Valentine's Day. "It was Rachel Hart's idea, you know."

"I heard it was Boyce's."

"Hah. Rachel just made Boyce *think* it was his idea." She winked, eyes glittering.

"Won't a reception hall add to the traffic here?" he asked, musing.

Her back stiffened. Oops.

"Plenty of other businesses expand."

"Didn't mean it that way, Miss Lucinda."

"You are the only child in this town who is allowed to call me that," she said with a soft smile.

"And you are the only person, other than my mother, who refers to me as a child."

"Then we are special to each other, Dennis," she replied, those red-lipsticked lips stretching across old teeth, crooked on the bottom, straight on top, and impressively intact for a woman in her nineties. "I'm not supposed to have favorite employees, but you definitely stood out over the years."

He wandered over to the wall where the famous picture–famous by his family's standards–hung on the wall, behind a display of a 25-pound chocolate heart. In the photo, he was fourteen and dressed in a red velvet heart costume, holding a platter of chocolate samples.

To his right was a laughing man, bright white teeth showing as he tipped his head back, dark hair messy. The man had his arm around a little girl, who was doing her best to hold up a big chocolate heart like the one on display. Hair in two perfect French braids, her eyes were crossed, tongue peeking out, as she fixed all her might and concentration on that giant chocolate heart.

"Still hanging here?" he asked Lucinda, who chuckled.

"Of course! It made *The Boston Globe*. Remember?"

"I do. And the man wouldn't give his name to Bert Boutin."

"Good old Bert. A true newspaperman," Lucinda declared. "God rest his soul. But the picture was still so wonderful, Bert sent it to *The Globe*. How long ago was that, Dennis?"

"If I was fourteen, it would have been twenty-eight years ago."

"Time flies," she said gently. "I was just about to turn, let's see... sixty-four. A spring chicken."

Uncertain whether it was impolite to laugh, Dennis kept his mouth shut and moved on from the picture. His mother had a copy of it in a photo album at home.

It was the last time he ever wore a love-themed costume. That picture may have been amusing, and a well-composed shot, but it led to too much teasing.

Teasing that *hurt*.

Teasing that made him turn on the love theme of his hometown. Blaming the touristy element in Luview, he'd turned bitter and disaffected, though puberty had plenty to do with it, too.

Nostalgia meant he could look at the picture now and laugh. In the image, his tray was held high above the laughing man whom Dennis had tried to pass, but some of the chocolate hearts had rained down on the man, caught in suspended drop.

The picture really was iconic.

"You were walking past when I saw you. I presume you're off to Bilbee's?" Lucinda's sniff made it clear she disapproved.

"I am. Mom's making me."

"You are a very strong, fit man in his early forties, Dennis. A retired Army colonel. I suspect no one *makes* you do anything."

"Do you make Boyce do stuff?"

She reconsidered with pursed lips, then smiled.

"You have a point."

"And... I have to admit, it's time to stop hiding." Why he was confessing anything to her was a mystery. Maybe he was cracking. Who knew?

"Hiding?"

"I'm here, right? Back in Luview forever. Spent my entire adulthood somewhere else, and now I've come back."

"It's changed."

"Yes, ma'am, it has."

"But let me guess. People treat you the same."

"Mom sure does."

"That's her prerogative."

Lucinda waved her hand and he laughed.

"It's not so much that people treat me like I'm eighteen. It's more that they treat me like I never left. It's hard to explain."

"I'd imagine it is. Luview is the kind of place where you're either an insider or you're not. And you're both."

"Hadn't thought of it that way."

"Listen to a very old woman, Dennis. Every feeling you have right now is fleeting. You won't feel it for very long. Let yourself experience it."

"You sound very Zen."

"I am a proper Christian woman, young man," she said seriously. "Nothing I said contradicts that."

"No, ma'am."

"People worry too much. Worry about what others think of them. Worry about making the wrong choices. Worry about losing chances. Worry about *taking* chances. Do you know what all that worry adds up to at the end of your life?"

"What?"

"Waste. Garbage. Trash."

"I'm not worried, Miss Lucinda. I'm just not eager to deal with a bunch of people who stick their noses into my life."

Astonishment wasn't an emotion he'd ever seen on her face, until now.

"Why, Dennis Luview!" she said with a whoop of laughter that made decades fade away. "Why on earth would you move back *here* if you didn't want people in your business?"

His phone buzzed in his pocket as his face turned hot with embarrassment.

"Your turn to make a good point."

"I believe," she said, laughter winding down, "that is the *only* point tonight. If you don't want anyone interfering in your life, why go to Bilbee's?"

"Because the pain of not going and being chewed out by my mom for being a recluse is worse than having a bunch of people intrude in my private life."

"Life is nothing but compromises, isn't it?" She winked, then returned to her default.

Being serious.

"Why move back here if you don't want the interconnectedness of small-town life? Especially when your family is so prominent?"

He shrugged, buying time, unwilling to tell the truth.

Uncertain he even knew the truth.

"I missed the slower pace of life. And Dad's not getting any younger."

"None of us are."

"I meant in terms of the tree business. He needs help. Kell's been great, but he needs more freedom to pursue his own business."

"You mean walking around town looking like an astronaut."

"Yep."

"That boy always was odd."

"Can't argue with that."

"Dean must be happy, regardless, to have you home."

"And now I can slowly take over, keep the tradition going."

"My Boyce has been a godsend for me in this family business. Dean and Deanna must view you likewise."

He grinned, and his phone buzzed again.

"You go answer that. And have fun at that place of ill repute."

"Wouldn't be Bilbee's without being a little bit vulgar."

She sniffed. "You and I differ on our definition of a little bit."

"Come on, Miss Lucinda. You know you love Rider's new Greek salad with those lemon potatoes."

"How did you know that?"

His turn to wink. "Small town, remember? Everyone knows everyone else's business."

And with that, he left her laughing, which was quite the achievement.

The walk to Bilbee's wasn't as quiet as normal, as throngs of tourists filled the town. When he was very young, the annual Valentine's Day energy revved him up, the town becoming an altar at which lovesick people worshipped.

Now though, in truth, it was painful. Loneliness was hard enough when he worked in the field, but at least there he had his team, and the belief that he wouldn't be lonely when he finally retired and settled down.

And then there was Ana.

So much for that.

It had been more than a month since he'd texted her. Still no reply. As much as he wanted to text again, pride stopped him.

Decency, too. He knew when to respect a boundary.

At the same time, he knew their chemistry was off the charts. Right?

Self-doubt like this wasn't typical of him, but when it came to her...

Unable to stop himself, he reached for his phone and looked at the selfie he'd snapped of the two of them. Spur of the moment, it wasn't the best shot, but it was all he had.

That, and her handwritten note she'd left in the hotel room. It was in his wallet, getting worn from too much handling.

He had to move on. His mom was right. Being stuck sucked.

A squeal, happy and light, came from a small crowd in front of Love You Jewelers, Moore Mottin's family business. Now that Moore and Colleen were a thing, Dennis viewed the store differently. Little Moore had grown up, for sure. He had a teenager now and, more importantly, he had Colleen's heart.

Never in a million years would he have predicted that Luke's lifelong best friend and his little sister would get together, but hearts didn't care what people thought.

They just chose.

As he got closer, he saw the reason for the ruckus. A man on one knee, looking up at a crying woman, her hand on his shoulder, a black velvet box opened, the diamond ring glittering in the streetlights. Sidestepping the small crowd sniffling and laughing around them, he reached inside his hoodie to secure Magic.

No need to ruin a perfect romantic moment with a flying squirrel attaching itself to the fiancée's head.

An unseasonably warm stretch last week had melted the piles of snow, the sidewalks clear and dry. A thin layer of the white stuff was ever present this far north in winter, but there wasn't as much as usual. Rachel had been thrilled about this turn of events, chattering happily this morning over coffee about how it made everything in town more accessible.

Dennis was still getting used to her.

Head down, he walked the rest of the way to Bilbee's, hoping not to run into someone who wanted to "catch up." While he appreciated the care and attention, he just didn't like being an object of curiosity.

Then again, maybe he shouldn't wear a sugar glider if he wanted fewer eyeballs on him.

"Dennis!" An arm waved wildly across the street, attached to his sister, who was bundled up in a calf-length black coat that could double as a sleeping bag. "Here!"

"I know where Bilbee's is!" he shouted back as he checked the street and walked safely along the crosswalk.

"I meant, here *we* are!" Colleen laughed, threading her arm through Moore's.

As Dennis approached, his memory banks fast-forwarded through time. It always happened when he came home for a visit, but now that he lived here, it was a never-ending process when he encountered people.

Even his own family, sometimes.

Reaching the two of them, he followed as they entered the old tavern, which smelled exactly the same as when he was a kid, and yet so different.

Sour beer, woodsmoke, and–garlic?

Thyme? *Cumin?*

The low wooden beams of the ceiling extended all the way back to the kitchen pass-through, giving the room a cozy quality.

"DENNIS!" his cousin Rider shouted from behind the bar. "Look who the dog dragged in."

Colleen took in a breath, looking angry, before Moore patted her arm.

"Let's just assume I'm the dog so you don't have to argue with him."

Wow. Moore really did know his sister well.

"Hey, Rider." Dennis looked around. "Nice and busy."

Rider's grin made his eye patch lift a little, the scars close to his missing eye deeper and twisted in contrast to the lighter lines along his cheek and brow.

"Week before V-Day always is, but you've got a big table in the back. If you came to play darts or pool, though, you're screwed."

"I came to hang out, man."

"And drink, I assume. What's your poison?"

He thought of Ana.

"Can you make a caipirinha?" he asked. Colleen overheard, snapping around to give Dennis a shocked look.

"A what?" she asked.

Rider grinned, the smile transforming his gruff, hard exterior into something joyful. "Now there's a man who knows how to explore the world. Hell, yeah, I do. Nice to use up some of my cachaça."

"You are speaking in a foreign language," Colleen said, giving him a bemused look.

"Portuguese. Brazilian, specifically," he replied. "Cachaça is a liquor made from sugar cane. And a caipirinha is like a mojito, minus the mint. Kind of like a lime mojito."

"When did you get all fancy? You normally like beer."

"I'm retired. I can do whatever I damn well want."

That got a laugh out of Moore, who had ordered two beers for himself and Colleen. Rider went off to the bottles and taps to fill their order.

"I cannot imagine being retired."

"He's not retired like old people retire. He's retired from the Army. Gets that nice pension. Now he'll spend the rest of his life doing tree work. Living like a mountain man.

Grunt grunt." She literally grunted the words, making Moore laugh.

Dennis, too.

"You've got me figured out, sis."

"Not really. You have loads of surprises in you. Did you start drinking these lime mojito things–what's it called?"

"Caipirinha."

"Cai-peer-een-ya?"

"Close enough."

"You started drinking them in Brazil?"

"No." He couldn't stop the smile. "Someone introduced me to them."

"Someone, as in, the lady in red?" Colleen asked as Rider brought their drinks over.

Moore gave him a nod that Dennis wasn't going to allow. Reaching into his back pocket, he opened his wallet and slid a credit card across the bar.

"Here, Rider. Start me an account. This one's on me."

Moore's dark eyebrows shot up.

"Not talking about it," Dennis emphasized to his sister, who stuck her tongue out as Moore opened his mouth to say something.

"But–"

Dennis cut Moore off before he could say a word.

"On me." He looked at Rider. "Our whole table is."

Rider let out a low, impressed whistle.

"Being a retired colonel pays."

"Just this once," Dennis said with a wink, but Rider's face had turned to an astonished scrunch, eyes dropping to Dennis's midsection.

"Is your hoodie... wiggling?"

Colleen let out a groan.

"You brought that thing here?"

"I bring it everywhere!"

"It's so annoying."

"Please tell me we're not talking about Dennis's joystick," Rider said as he lowered the tray the drinks had been on, each holding their respective order.

"I'm helping Mel out," Dennis started to explain.

"That does not make this sound better."

Slowly, Dennis reached into his pouch and pulled Magic out for public viewing.

Rider's mouth went tight. "You cannot have that thing in here. Health codes."

"*Shhh*," Dennis said. Magic's sweet eyes looked at Rider with what appeared to be love. "No one needs to know."

"Then put it back where it belongs! And so help me, if it gets loose and takes over the kitchen, I will charge you for the extermination bill and the health department fines, Dennis."

"I won't let him loose."

"Mel said the same thing about her capybara and let me tell you, those things are lightning fast. Took two days to get it out of the wall after it found a loose vent." If the eyepatch lifted when Rider smiled, it dug into his cheeks when his face scrunched up in disgust.

"I swear, man. Magic won't get loose."

"What'll you swear on?" Rider's eyebrow arched over his eye patch. It had two big scars in it where no hair grew anymore.

"I took a solemn oath to defend our country, Rider. That's not good enough?"

"So did Lyle Morgenstern."

Bringing up the town troublemaker and comparing the two of them didn't sit right with Dennis.

"Low blow."

Rider waved him off with a bar towel.

"Just don't let me have to call an exterminator."

Wandering to the back, Dennis pivoted as he made his way

through the crowd, Colleen behind him, Moore at the end. The big, scarred wood table where their group was located had assorted appetizer plates all over it, and four very familiar faces grinning at them.

Kell and Rachel sat to the left, Kylie and Luke to the right, and Colleen and Moore took seats facing the back, giving Dennis nowhere to sit.

Because he always sat facing the exit.

Luke leaned close to Kylie, so Dennis grabbed a seat next to him, his left side more angled than he'd like, but that would have to do. He told himself this was Luview, Maine, for goodness sake. Nothing bad ever happened here.

Not that it mattered. His mind manufactured plenty of reasons to stay vigilant, regardless of where he was.

"How's Magic?" Kylie asked, peering at Dennis's pouch. A sweet blonde he barely remembered from childhood, Kylie and Luke had reconnected about four years ago. She'd been raised in Luview until she was fifteen, but Dennis was long gone by the time the scandal around her father's affair caused upheaval.

All he cared was that she was a fabulous stepmother to his niece. A damn fine baker, too.

"Magic's good."

"Can I hold him?" Kylie asked eagerly.

"You sound exactly like Harriet when you ask that!" Luke exclaimed, chuckling before taking a swig of his beer.

"Because Magic is so cutesy-wootsy!" she replied.

"You never call *me* cutesy-wootsy," Luke challenged, then winked.

"You're not an injured widdle baby."

As Moore and Colleen started howling, and Luke looked at his wife like she was from another planet, Dennis made a split-second decision.

"Here. He needs a change of pace."

Taking the sugar glider from his hands, Kylie's face melted with sweetness. Luke rolled his eyes.

"You're just making it worse for me," he grumbled.

Dennis sipped his drink, which made him remember how kissing Ana tasted, which made him drink faster.

"How so, bro?"

"Harriet wants one. Bad."

"Wants a sugar glider?"

"Yes."

"She can babysit for me. Prove she can take care of a pet."

"She does fine with Jester," Kylie interjected, coming to Harriet's defense. Dennis liked that. Team player.

Especially if it meant his baby bro didn't get what he wanted.

"I am sure Harriet would make a fine sugar glider owner. I'll hire her to babysit Magic for me. Pay her."

Luke groaned. "You have no idea what you've unleashed."

Rachel leaned across Kell to be heard, the volume rising in the tavern.

"Magic reminds me of Satan."

Dennis had to hold back a sputter.

"Satan?" Kylie asked, rubbing noses with Magic. "Who could ever call such a cutie Satan?"

"Me," said Rachel flatly.

"He's not a squirrel," Kell said to her slowly. It was clear there was a subtext Dennis didn't understand.

"Doesn't matter! Rodents aren't pets," Rachel declared, giving Kell major side-eye.

"That's right!" Luke agreed. "Rachel has a very good point." The two clinked glasses, toasting each other's common point.

"If sugar gliders can't be pets, why is Dennis walking around wearing one?"

"Hold on," Dennis interjected. "Magic isn't my pet. I'm just fostering him."

The whole group started laughing.

"I mean it!" He picked up his drink, suddenly relaxing, even in the midst of being ribbed. The teasing, though different, reminded him of being with his team. If you were the butt of a joke, it meant you were accepted. Included.

One of the gang.

"Once his leg heals," Kylie said, looking at Luke, "Magic isn't going away. Dennis is keeping him, and the poor thing needs a friend."

"If we get one of those... things, Jester will think it's a chew toy."

"Jester's not that mean!"

"He's a dog. Dogs are predators. Jester will think it's a rabbit and he'll eat it. You want to explain to Harriet why her beloved sugar glider got eaten by the friendliest dog on the planet?" Luke asked pointedly.

"Aha!" Kylie declared. "So we *can* get one!"

"When did I say that?"

As the two bickered, Dennis felt an elbow in his ribs.

"Pass the fries?" Colleen asked, pointing to a huge basket of string fries. "And the rings?"

"Sure. Want a giant turkey leg to go along with it?" But he did as requested, Moore grabbing the rings and immediately chomping down on one.

"What? We're hungry. Besides, we always do this," she answered pointedly.

"Do what?"

"Have appetizers for dinner."

"Most people have dinner for dinner."

"Not on Bilbee's nights. And who the heck are you? Mom?"

"Nah. Just teasing."

"It's good to have you home."

Maybe it was the alcohol. Maybe the warmth—they were sitting close to the woodstove that heated much of the place. Perhaps the chatter of happy people, chill and engaged, having fun as their only goal, made something in him stand down.

Whatever it was, he was shifting. Breathing more deeply.

Settling in.

"Whatcha drinking?" Kell asked from across the table, holding up his own empty pint glass.

"Caipirinha."

Rachel's face lit up.

"I am so impressed!"

"What?"

"Rider has cachaça?"

"If he didn't, I wouldn't be drinking this."

"I never thought to ask!" She smacked Kell's thigh. "That's my next drink."

"Cai peer *what?*" Kell asked, puzzled.

"Cai-peer-een-ya," Rachel tried to explain. And then:

"It's like a lime mojito," Dennis and Rachel said in unison. A comically confused expression filled her face as they caught each other's eye.

Then laughed together. Maybe he had more in common with his future sister-in-law than he thought.

Quickly, Dennis finished his drink, then turned to Luke.

"I was going to stick to one, but any chance someone else is going light tonight?"

"Me," Kylie said with a sad smile. She shook her soda glass.

"Everything okay?"

Rachel leaned in and whispered, "Do you have something to tell the class?"

"Stop it," Luke said gruffly. "Don't start rumors like that. My mother would set off fireworks if she thought we were pregnant."

Kylie blushed. "Just a medication for a cut that went wrong." She pulled up her right sleeve and showed a bandage.

"Is that from the greenhouse? When you scratched your arm on the way down the ladder?" Dennis asked, remembering the incident.

"Yep. Infected. I'm on antibiotics, and alcohol doesn't mix well with them for me. So you all have a designated driver for another week."

"Remember when you lived in the apartment upstairs?" Luke reminisced, pointing to the ceiling of the tavern.

She snuggled against him.

"I know. If I still had it, we wouldn't need a designated driver. We could all just stay there."

"I loved my apartment," Kell said with a sigh. "Then you rented it, Kylie. It's like it's part of the family."

"Apartments aren't people," Dennis pointed out. "But there's a thought. Is it for rent? Is anyone living there now?" Dennis asked, earning a glare from Colleen.

"Don't you even think about moving out. Mom would kill you."

"Who said I'm moving out?"

"You've been a grump for a while."

"Since when?"

The whole table snorted.

In an instant, he saw himself through their eyes, but more broadly, he saw all three couples through the lens of their loving relationships. They had what he wanted: love, stability, and predictability.

A life partner.

A soul mate.

Someone you could be yourself with.

Being ghosted had hurt his ego. Draining the final drops of his drink, he stood.

"Anyone up for another?"

"The tab is all on Dennis," Moore announced to everyone. Protests began, but he held up his palm.

"No argument," Dennis announced. "Don't get used to it, but tonight, this is how it is."

"Then we're getting fried lobster bites," Colleen called out. "Double order."

"Rachel, you want a caipirinha?" he asked.

"Of course! Thank you! And then I'm done," she assured Kell, who was rubbing his fingers along her shoulder, smiling at her like she was his soul.

"I'm good," Kell told Dennis. "Too much Valentine's Day prep." He glowered, the look half fake, half real. "Someone is leaving town and dumped a bunch of work on me."

"Someone is me," Dennis told the table. "I don't want to be here for the festival."

"Why not?" Rachel sounded incredulous. "It's so much better than it ever was before!"

"Better?" Dennis crossed his arms over his chest, goading her. "How so?"

"We have the trolley, so parking is easier. We have more permanent wood kiosks on the common, which makes the look of the outdoor festival cleaner. Selena added more speakers to the outdoor music system, and now we have more live local bands in rotation at the gazebo. Lucinda ordered ten new heart costumes from Anya."

"Who?"

"Anya. You know, Grady's great-grandma? Judy's grandma?"

He frowned. "That really old lady who tailored our prom tuxes?"

Rachel nodded.

"She was a hundred when I was in high school! How can she still be alive?"

"That woman is a wizard with zippers," Kell muttered

before shoving a crab rangoon in his mouth, Rachel giving him an amused smile. Her engagement ring glittered in the light when she gently patted his cheek, which made him roll his eyes.

"Students dressed in the new heart costumes will walk around the festival and downtown carrying chocolate hearts. Anyone wearing one of the town's new pins gets a free heart," Rachel continued.

"New pins?"

"We've been handing them out on the trolley. Just started today! Lucinda generously donated them to the business development office!"

"Do you have any?" Colleen asked. "I'll wear a pin if it means getting free chocolate!"

"I'll *buy* my chocolate," Dennis said, walking away from the table. The bar was crowded, but he found an empty spot to wait his turn.

Rider moved like a speed demon, taking orders and making drinks, moving in a flow state. In no hurry at all, Dennis just bided his time, admiring his cousin's efficiency. When someone is highly competent, their work can be a form of beauty.

Finally, he turned to Dennis.

"Another caipirinha?"

"Two. And two orders of fried lobster bites."

Rider laughed. "Colleen's working your tab, huh?"

"Little sisters. What can I say?"

"Yours is way better than mine," Rider said, a bitter laugh punctuating his words.

Last time Dennis had been in a bar was at the hotel in Boston. A woman in a red dress caught his eye now, her features very different from Ana's, but the taste of his drink and the flash of red in his peripheral vision made him sigh.

Hung up on a memory. How pathetic had he become?

"Hey there, big guy," crooned a woman behind him, a voice he knew full well.

Annabeth had struck again.

"Hi, Annabeth."

Just then, Magic stirred between them.

Literally.

The sugar glider's head popped up from his pouch, making Annabeth let out a tiny squeal and lean back.

"What the hell, Dennis?"

"He's still injured."

Doubt filled her beautifully painted eyes. Annabeth was an attractive woman, without question, though much of her appeal was hidden under her beauty regimen. It wasn't that he didn't like makeup.

It was that she seemed to think she needed a lot of it.

"You sure you didn't have a head injury when you were doing your big military stuff?" she asked, a giggle at the end more mocking than flirty.

The worm had turned.

"I did. Plenty of times. Why?"

His bluntness caught her off guard, insecurity flashing in those pretty eyes.

"Oh. Just joking. Really? On a mission? You got hurt?"

"Sure did."

"Do you have," she asked, eyes combing over him, "scars?"

"Yes."

"What kind of work did you do?"

"You know I can't go into specifics." Rider put the two caipirinhas on the counter, then nodded toward the kitchen, signaling that the lobster was coming shortly. Annabeth leaned against the bar with her hip and raised a hand to catch Rider's attention.

He pivoted and returned.

"Another cosmo?" he asked her.

"Whatever he's having." Her eyes caught Dennis's.

"Another caipirinha coming up."

"On me," he said reflexively.

Her fingers went to his forearm with a possessiveness that made his mouth turn to metal. Glancing back at their table, he could see his siblings and their partners had all turned in their seats and were openly watching what was transpiring between him and Annabeth.

A gust of cold from the front door opening caught his attention, Blake and Sheila walking in. Luke waved and let out a small whistle, catching their gaze.

"Oh, my goodness, thank you," Annabeth gushed. "I haven't had a handsome man buy me a drink in a long time."

"I doubt that."

The pressure of her fingers shifted against the cloth of his sweatshirt, triggering Magic to crawl out and perch along the crook of his elbow.

"Ugh!" Annabeth snatched her hand away.

"He didn't even touch you."

"Are you ever alone, Dennis?"

"Excuse me?"

"I'd love to see you without that little rat."

"I'm his foster daddy."

"Does he sleep with you, too?"

"Every night. He's the best bed partner I've ever had."

Titters and chuckling came from those around them.

"Annabeth." Joe Boutin appeared over her shoulder, baseball cap on backwards, thick red flannel clean and sharp. "Buy you a drink?"

Rider appeared just then, sliding hers along the bar, dropping two baskets of lobster bites next to them. "A little too late, Joe."

Joe worked down at the quarry, delivering rock in the region. About ten years younger, the guy was friendly enough, though Dennis barely remembered him from when he grew up here.

Joe's eyes widened as they caught Dennis's.

"Sorry, man. Didn't know you two–"

"We're not. My bad."

As Annabeth sputtered, Dennis made haste to withdraw, secretly grateful for Magic's comic relief. Now he just needed his little hitchhiker to stay put until he sat down again. Navigating through the crowd with two drinks and two baskets was hard enough.

Victory was his. Setting everything down meant he'd made it. Rachel gave him a smile, but the jackals that were his brothers and sister dug into the new appetizers like it was their Death Row meal.

Blake took a lobster bite, ate half in one chomp, and made a face like he was impressed.

"Was Annabeth hitting on you?" Kylie asked, giving him a very sly look.

"She was trying."

"So she failed?"

"Not interested."

Colleen cut him a look that said he had two seconds to shut her up.

"I have plenty on my mind. Romance will come later."

"So you *do* think about it?" Rachel asked, oh, so innocently, across the table.

Kell began sputtering.

"Did Deanna put you up to that?" Kylie asked with a laugh, giving Rachel a smile.

"Of course not! Just making conversation."

Going quiet, Dennis thought again about how much love the table held. He wanted his own version of what Colleen, Luke, and Kellan had.

His cousin Blake, too.

Not exactly what they had, but his own, unique sliver of it.

"Whatcha want, hon?" Blake asked his wife. "I heard Rider got his hands on some Merlot from that vineyard we visited in Napa last year."

"Yes!"

As his cousin wandered to the bar, Sheila and Rachel began talking about restaurant capacity during the businest week of the year, and something about validated parking as a promotion in March.

Yearning won out, and he reached for his phone, pulling up the meager text stream with Ana.

Nothing.

Nothing, still.

Maybe it was time to move on. Leaving town for Valentine's Day wasn't just about hating the commercialism in Luview.

It was also about dodging his feelings for Ana.

Then clamor reigned as Moore and Kell got into an argument about *Game of Thrones*. Dennis cupped one hand around Magic, plucked two lobster bites from the basket, and almost–*almost*–closed his eyes.

Being back home meant adjusting to the new version of him.

Which would emerge slowly, one drink, one conversation, one run-in, and definitely one lobster bite at a time.

Chapter Fourteen

Three and a half months later

Ana

The little girl in her quivered with joy every time she reached the Luview, Maine town line.

A big heart-shaped sign, brand new from what she could tell, greeted them. Solid red, it was huge, with the words *Welcome to Love You, Maine: Where Every Day Is Valentine's Day.*

"We're here!" she announced happily, Brie bouncing up and down in her seat as she drove.

Visiting Luview on Memorial Day weekend had seemed risky, but Brie assured her it wasn't an overly busy holiday in the tiny hamlet, and certainly nothing like Valentine's Day. Earlier in the week, they'd celebrated a major victory:

Ana's pregnancy had passed twenty-six weeks.

Her baby boy was just across the threshold of viability.

The high-risk OB/GYN in Boston gave her the okay for this trip. Prohibited from flying, she could travel by car, but only if she stopped regularly to stretch, hydrate, and maintain overall wellness.

Life was good.

And being in Love You, Maine made it even better.

Brie's great-aunt Lucinda had invited them to come visit. Ground had been broken on the addition to the Love You Chocolate store, and it was time to visit the florists, caterers, and assorted and sundry shops that provided goods and services to wedding parties.

Brie and Martin had a budget, of course. Lucinda had insisted that the hall rental was her gift to them, which was extremely generous and gracious. And Lucinda had informed Brie that she would get the "local" price on everything, because Lucinda had already called Love You Flowers, The Food Alchemist, Bilbee's Tavern, and other related businesses to make certain they knew that Brie Hohenadel was her grandniece.

"You hungry?" Brie asked as the houses turned red, white, and pink, a small CPA firm the first building she saw that fit the town's color scheme.

"When am I not?"

"Let's hit Greta's."

It made Ana feel like such a local, calling it that. Love You Bakery was an institution in town, filled with tourists on weekends, locals during the week and on Sundays, for brunch. She and Brie weren't even close to being townies, but she felt like more than just a tourist.

A flood of memories poured through her.

For years, her parents and Brie's parents had been friends,

and the annual trip to Maine in the summer had made Ana feel like she had siblings. Marian and Paulo, her dad, always made time for the four-day weekend up here in western Maine. As a child, the trip just ... was. It was part of life.

All those joint family trips ended abruptly when her father died.

A loud bell made them both turn to look at the trolley, painted in the town's colors, stopping at a small bus stop.

"What the heck?" Brie said. "I know I haven't been here for two years, but that's new!" Last summer, the Hohenadels had missed their traditional summer trek because of the cheese shop had moved. Thanksfully, Aunt Lucinda was made of steel and was still alive, kicking, and taking names.

"I'll bet it cuts down on traffic and parking."

"I love it!" Brie pulled into the parking lot behind the stop. "Let's ride it!"

Ana rubbed her belly. Ripe and round, it was harder than she expected. Pregnancy had been nothing but revelations, the gradual realization that so much of what she'd assumed about having a baby was wrong.

Bellies weren't soft. Wombs were tough.

Babies weren't weak. They had feet that kicked kidneys like soccer players.

Pregnant stomachs were bottomless. Especially for chocolate.

Pregnant bladders instantly shrank to the size of a tablespoon.

"Shouldn't we drive to Auntie's house?"

"Let's have some fun, Ana. Ride the trolley, then come back for our stuff. There's a big festival on the common right now."

"There's always a festival in Love You."

"So let's go enjoy it! We're early, anyhow. We can ride the

trolley, grab a loaded brownie at Greta's, take the trolley back, and still make it to Auntie's at about the same time she's expecting us."

Ana reached for her seatbelt, unclicked it, and grabbed her purse.

"Why didn't you lead with the words 'let's get a loaded brownie at Greta's'?"

Brie's smile was dazzlingly awesome as they walked quickly to the trolley stop, where a line had formed.

Ana couldn't remember the last time she'd ridden a trolley. Maybe in London, five years ago, when she'd gone there with her mother? Marian didn't normally carve out much time for fun, so the trip stood out. They'd bought a special pass for a hop-on, hop-off trolley/bus thing that had been so easy, and saved a lot of shoe leather and tourist blisters.

"The police car!" Ana exclaimed as they settled into seats, Brie twisting to look behind her. "And the red uniforms!" A tall man wearing a red uniform bisected by a black belt, his red hat in his hands, leaned against his patrol car and watched the trolley. He had sandy blond hair, cut short, and curious eyes. Something about him seemed a bit familiar, but she couldn't place the guy.

As the riders all finished onboarding, the bus driver announced:

"Welcome to Love You, Maine, where every day is Valentine's Day. You're riding a special all-electric trolley with zero emissions."

As she spoke, a giant red silk heart suddenly entered the bus. It had legs.

And carried a silver tray covered with foil-wrapped chocolate hearts.

"Catch!" said the heart, the person inside the costume laughing and tossing candy to the twenty or so trolley patrons, children squealing and adults letting out sounds of surprise. A few people took hits of chocolate straight to the head, but by the time the heart had delivered its gifts, everyone was in good cheer.

"And if you like what you're tasting, you can get more at Love You Chocolate," the driver announced, starting the motor.

"Is there a store called Love You Beer?" one of the men called out. "When do *they* hand out samples?"

The chocolate coated her mouth, making her smile sweeter than normal. Baby Bean shifted a bit inside her, the rolling more like a stretch, as if he were doing a yoga pose in there.

Upward Facing Liver.

"You look so happy," Brie commented as they gawked out the windows like kids. On impulse, Ana waved to the cop, who waved back.

Seeing this, two little boys pressed their faces against the window and waved energetically at the cop.

He waved even harder, smiling.

"How could I be anything but ecstatic? Free chocolate. A long weekend in Love You, Maine. Planning your wedding."

"And Baby Bean is sticking nicely."

"All of it." She squeezed Brie's elbow. "All of it makes me happy."

"Good. You deserve everything good in life."

"I already have it. I can't ask for much more."

Longing, swift and unexpected, filled her bones.

Because that wasn't quite true.

She did want something else.

A partner. A *life* partner. Someone to walk through all her days with. To cuddle up in bed at night. To tell her secrets and confess her fears. To—

"Here we are, folks," the trolley driver announced. "Go get

more chocolate!" The store's sign was a white awning with the words LOVE YOU CHOCOLATE in red, all of the O's in the shape of hearts.

"I really, really want more," Ana groaned. Trying to explain pregnancy cravings was like trying to describe an orgasm.

You *could*, but no one else would ever really understand.

"The trolley goes in a loop," Brie said. "If we stay aboard, it will take us right back to the car. Can you wait until then? You know Auntie will have tons of candy for us."

Three-quarters of the riders had climbed off by the time the trolley doors closed. Ana relaxed into the seat as much as she could, the bottom of her belly resting on her upper thighs.

"Fine. But I'm going to eat as much as I want without shame."

"Deal."

"Next stop, Love You Coffee!" the driver called out in a voice that only a trained tour operator could have. "Who needs their caffeine fix?"

"I only get one cup a day and I already had it," Ana moaned.

"Decaf, Ana. You can have decaf."

"That's true."

"Good thing you were never a coffee addict."

"I'm not, but I always had two cups a day. I never realized how much I loved that second cup."

"We can swing by the coffee shop after we see Auntie."

"Won't she be offended? She always offers such a lovely tea spread."

As they talked, Ana marveled at the quaint downtown, which looked like a Norman Rockwell painting done in three colors: red, pink, and white.

Every sign had a heart on it.

Love You Jewelers. Kendrill's Market. Love You Coffee. Love You Books.

Love You India made her stomach growl, a mental note made to go there for lunch tomorrow. They drove past the dry cleaner's, Labrecque's, and the radio station with WLUV shining in pink and white. Ana noticed that some shops followed the Love You naming conventions and some didn't.

Was it age, she wondered? The older stores kept their original names? She'd have to ask Lucinda.

At the far end of downtown, the trolley made a U-turn in front of Bilbee's Tavern.

"Auntie says they're up to no good in there. Shameful, vulgar people," Brie whispered in a stage voice.

"Then we have to go there," Ana purred back. It was an old joke. They'd eaten at the tavern plenty of times as kids with their parents, and as older teens had played pool and darts when they visited, though always to a sniff of disapproval from Lucinda.

Ana loved coming back to Luview. Brie visited far more often and always filled her in on changes, but what Ana enjoyed most about the town was how she measured herself in it. Viewing "Love You, Maine" through the eyes of a child, then an adolescent, and finally as an adult meant seeing different versions of herself in the town.

And now, she thought, rubbing her belly, her son would do the same.

She resolved to bring him here every summer, hoping Auntie would be here long enough for him to have a memory of her. While Lucinda wasn't a blood relative, she was well-loved by Ana, and that was more than enough.

Brie's phone buzzed. She read the text and smiled.

"Martin?"

"Yeah. Telling me he loves me and wants us to have fun."

"He's so sweet."

"Someone should marry him," Brie said, smile growing.

"I love that we've grown up together, and we're still sharing our lives." Emotion squeezed her throat, tears at the ready. Turning away, she looked out the window.

And froze.

A shiny new pickup was parked on the side of the road, right in front of the town common. The trolley came to a halt at a stop, and passengers got off. Ana looked out the window at the truck's driver, a huge, muscular man wearing a navy blue t-shirt, the cotton tight against his well-sculpted chest, his sandy hair neatly clipped. His face was in shadow so she couldn't get a full look, but something in her pinged.

"Dennis?" she whispered as a new group of people climbed on, suddenly blocking her view.

"What?" Brie asked.

Ana pointed. "I swear I just saw... no."

"Who?"

"Dennis."

"Who's Dennis?"

Ana sighed, shaking her head. "I'm being silly."

"You mean that guy you met? At the hotel in Boston?"

"Yeah." By the time the new passengers settled down, the man was gone. Ana searched the streets and the common. No luck.

"You think he's *here?* Of all places?"

"I know. Like I said, I'm being silly."

"I mean, that would be a seventy-four-million-to-one chance!"

"Did you calculate that based on specific data?" Ana asked, laughing, but the flush of hope wouldn't leave her chest. Heart pounding, skin suddenly blazing, she remembered how it felt to touch him, her hands on his strong body, how he moved with her, against her.

In her.

"Based on absolutely nothing in particular," Brie said breezily.

"I think I'm conjuring him."

"Where was he?"

The trolley jerked as it began to move.

"In front of that truck. Why?"

"We could leave a note on the windshield."

"Why would I do that?"

"To contact him."

"I have his number. Remember? *I* ghosted on *him*."

Brie's demeanor changed when she realized Ana was in emotional pain. "Oh, Ana. Go ahead and text him right now!"

"I've ignored him for nearly five months!"

"So?"

"It would be rude."

"It could be a great way to open things up again. 'Hey, I know I never replied, but I'm in Luview, Maine and I swear I just saw you on the street' is one hell of a line."

"He's moved on."

"How do you know?" Brie's eyebrows shot up as she looked Ana over. "It's clear you haven't. Why assume he has?"

"A guy like Dennis? Big and powerful and smart and cunning?"

"You seem to know a lot about his cunning skills." Brie winked.

Ana turned to pure fire.

"Stop that!" she hissed as they came to yet another trolley stop, this time in front of the famous Luview hot springs. A merchandise stand with beautiful hand towels came into Ana's gaze and she wished for one.

Because suddenly, she was sweating.

And wet elsewhere, too.

As Brie cackled, Ana tried to tame her hormones.

And failed.

Rushes of sexual desire were confined to her dreams these days, as she focused more on work, life, and the baby. Getting her fourteen patients situated and ready for her maternity leave was turning out to be trickier than she thought, and never before had she been so grateful for her trust fund. Years of massive guilt over it had turned to deep gratitude.

Her father was providing for his daughter and grandchild, years after his death.

"How perfect," Ana said with a sigh as she watched happy groups of people walk toward the rising steam, the water piping hot, the air a temperate sixty degrees.

"We can swim later."

"I'd love that, as long as it's not too hot." She rubbed her belly.

"You can always just stand in it. They say you'll fall in love like *that*–" Brie snapped her fingers, "–if you touch the water at the same time as your true love."

"You know that's just a silly legend to make tourists come here and spend money," Ana said kindly. Nothing about Love You, Maine bothered her. Cheesy and over the top, it all made her smile, even if it was fake.

"And it worked!"

Brie's words sounded like a declaration of victory, so Ana let her win. Yet another person in a heart costume boarded, and soon Ana was catching candy, delighting in the sweet goodness once more.

She needed to go to Love You Chocolate and buy a five-pound bag of these red foil hearts.

And eat them all, one at a time, while binge-watching *Abbott Elementary*.

"Mmmmm, I love it here," Brie said as the trolley began moving, their final stop bringing them right back where they'd started. For the next few minutes, Ana let herself relax, closing her eyes and taking deep breaths.

That man.

That man by the truck.

While she didn't get a good look at his face, he *felt* like Dennis, and that stirred so much inside her. Would she ever get past their single night together?

So many times since January, she'd been tempted to answer his text. So, so many. But after finding out she was pregnant, she'd felt such shame at the thought of replying and trying to—what? Have a relationship with a man she'd slept with one time, all while incubating another man's child?

Too much.

Even for a well-educated, emotionally regulated, professional woman, this was churning too much shame in the waters.

Now, though, she was more settled. The baby was growing. Harris was long gone. Whatever Rick had done, they hadn't heard a peep out of what Brie called "the baby daddy from hell." And Ana had spent plenty of time with her own therapist processing what Harris had done to her.

No matter what, the little boy she carried was very, very loved.

Regardless of what his sperm donor had done.

The trolley slowed in front of a crowd assembled at the stop. Shuffling out, Ana and Brie made their way into the sunshine, Ana's denim jacket doing its job on the cool spring day.

"Off to Auntie's," Brie said, unlocking the car.

"Not a moment too soon," Ana murmured.

As Brie laughed, her phone buzzed.

"Oh, there she is!"

"She texts? Wasn't she born during the Depression?"

"She does, in fact, text. Boyce got her an emergency phone

with huge numbers. This one says, 'Dear Brie, Please meet me at the store. Sincerely, Lucinda.'"

"So formal!"

"Every text is like this. All of them."

"That's adorable."

"I hope when I'm her age, I'm making some big technological *faux pas* and my grandniece and her friend think it's adorable."

"We'll be adorable in our nineties."

"We'll be pains in the ass in our nineties."

Ana squeezed Brie's arm and grinned.

"I can't wait."

"By the time we're in our nineties, we'll have VR chips in our brains. No one will know the difference between dementia and virtual reality," Ana went on as Brie backed out of the parking spot and headed for the road. Although Love You Chocolate was just a few blocks away, they had their luggage and five big scrapbooks full of wedding ideas Brie insisted on bringing.

"Will the VR affect our taste buds?" Brie asked, looking worried at the thought.

"Good question. I have no idea. We need to consult a VR developer. If only we knew one..."

Brie grinned. Her brother Cam worked as one.

"Can you imagine being an old lady now? When Lucinda was born, she didn't even have a radio in her home. They were too poor," Brie said. "Television hadn't been invented. No Internet. No cell phones."

"Right," Ana mused. "And then they lived down at Sabbathday Lake at the Shaker community."

"I know. Such a sad story. Her father died and left her mother with three children, and the Shakers took them in. Does she ever go back and visit? Or do they shun her?" Ana knew the basics, but had never wondered about whether Lucinda visited her old home.

"Well, the Shakers aren't like other religious communities. Children living there decide whether to stay or go when they turn eighteen. Auntie fell in love with Uncle Donald and left the Shakers forever." Brie sighed, then continued, "She hates the touristy aspect of the farm now. I think she visits when it's quiet. There are only a few Shakers left."

"For obvious reasons," Ana said, pointing to her belly. "This doesn't happen there."

"Right. Celibacy is required. Part of their religious teachings. Auntie was so sad to have to leave, but she fell in love with Uncle Donald and that was that."

"I think she did just fine." Brie pulled the car into the Love You Chocolate back parking lot, as instructed by Lucinda, and parked in an "Employees Only" spot. They walked up to the back door and rang a bell.

One minute later, Lucinda appeared, all smiles and hugs.

"My dears! How wonderful!" When she kissed Brie, she sniffed. "You have been eating my chocolate—where?"

Ana gaped. "How could you possibly know that?"

"I can smell a Love You Chocolate heart from a thousand feet away."

"Really? You've tested this?" Brie teased, and Auntie laughed in Ana's arms.

"Oh, Brie. Let us go!"

"Go where?" Ana asked.

Lucinda was carrying a small red purse, and she wore a white blouse under a red cardigan, white slacks, sensible white leather shoes, and a white sun hat with a red ribbon.

"We're off to the common, of course. A lovely festival. Plus, the store has a booth there, and I need to make certain the teenage workers are behaving."

"Doesn't Boyce run the store now? You retired."

"I let Boyce *think* he runs the store," Lucinda declared, striding toward the sidewalk as Ana and Brie hustled to keep up. "How was your drive?"

"Fine," Brie said, brushing her unruly hair out of her eyes as they waited at a crosswalk. A gentle breeze blew Ana's yellow cotton maternity dress, covered in red flowers on the fabric's print. Brie had reminded her to wear as much red as possible, but maternity fashion did not allow for unlimited choices.

Her Chuck Taylors were red with white laces.

"Just fine?"

"We stopped and rode the trolley," Brie confessed reluctantly.

"Hence the chocolate on your breath," Lucinda said with a chuckle. The light changed and they crossed the street.

In the middle of the road, Ana nearly halted, Brie bumping into her. That same man in the navy t-shirt was emerging from the flower shop, carrying a bouquet of red carnations. Black-framed sunglasses covered his eyes, and he stared straight ahead, unaware of her gaze.

Forcing herself to finish crossing, she reached the sidewalk and looked again.

He was gone.

"I am really stuck in fantasyland," she muttered to herself as Auntie reached a white wooden bench and stopped, taking a seat.

"DENNIS!" a man shouted, and her neck jerked so fast in the direction of the voice that she pulled something, pain shooting into her jaw.

One of the town police officers reached the man, the two chatting, the flowers transferred over.

"Ana?" Brie asked.

"Oh, it's nothing." She massaged her neck and returned her attention to where it belonged.

"Are you feeling well, my dear?" Lucinda asked.

"I am. Thank you."

"There is nothing more blessed than a good mother with a healthy baby. I am very happy for you." Her eyes floated to Ana's left hand. "Brie told me you were with child, but every time I asked about your husband, she changed the subject. Tell me about him."

Ana's eyes widened. She shot a trapped look at Brie, who raised one shoulder in an apologetic shrug.

"Ah, I'm not married."

Lucinda frowned. "I see. But the father...?"

"He, ah–he–"

"He knocked her up and left her high and dry!" Brie said with rage. "I didn't want to say anything without Ana here to give permission."

"Which I technically *didn't*," Ana muttered.

"Scoundrel! That's not a man. That's a piece of slime pretending to be human!" Lucinda's voice went from polite to livid in seconds.

"Whoa," Brie exclaimed. "That's savage."

"*He* is the savage. I hope your lawyer stepfather has gone after him on your behalf!" Auntie's mouth went tight with anger.

"He's tried. But the, ah, the father disappeared on me."

"WHAT? Who does such a horrible thing?"

The longer her pregnancy went on, the more Ana came to realize her bladder was but a fleeting way station for its contents. Standing, she looked around, giving Auntie an apologetic look.

"Restrooms?"

"Over there," Lucinda pointed to a small brick building.

"I'll fill her in on all the details about the–what should we call him?" Brie asked, mouthing the word *Sorry* to Ana.

"SCOUNDREL!" Lucinda bellowed. She shooed Ana off. "Go! You need to void."

Struggling to hold back a snicker, Ana made her way to the bathroom, scanning the crowd for signs of the man in the navy t-shirt. Heart pounding, she reached the bathroom and stood in the line, six women ahead of her.

Two women in the front were talking.

"I told him to stop carrying that silly little creature in his shirt pocket, but he insists Magic isn't healed yet," the older one said to the younger. Their features were close enough that they might be sisters, more likely mother and daughter.

"Mom."

Question answered.

"What?"

"He is going to live his life however he wants, and if that includes wearing a rodent like an accessory for the rest of his life, just let him."

"No grown man does what he's doing. Plus, it healed a long time ago. I think he's just wearing it everywhere because it keeps Annabeth Khouri away."

"Hmmm. Maybe I need my own sugar glider."

"Colleen!"

"Harriet really wants Magic, you know."

"I know. Luke's putting his foot down."

"What if we use Harriet to soften Dennis up?"

Dennis.

She just said *Dennis*.

Stop it, Ana, she told herself. Plenty of men were named Dennis. There was no way on earth he was really here, or those women were talking about him.

"How would we 'use' Harriet?"

"What if we–"

Just then, the older woman caught Ana's eye and smiled at

her, the toilet flushing in the background. Her eyes dropped to Ana's belly, and her expression changed.

"Pregnant woman! Let her cut to the front!" the woman called, all eyes suddenly on Ana, the line moving to the right, instantly clearing a path.

"No, no," Ana protested. "I'm fine."

"You're pregnant," the woman insisted, warm gray eyes making Ana feel instantly at home. She brushed her dark hair off her cheek. "Your bladder is the size of a red foil heart. Go ahead of us."

All of the women nodded.

"Thank you." Ana wondered why this kind woman seemed so familiar. Perhaps she was a local she'd seen before on her visits to Luview? "I appreciate it." As she cut the line, she felt guilty, but her bladder told her that was nonsense.

Finishing her business was a quick thing, and while she was washing her hands, the woman and her daughter walked by, on their way to the stalls.

"How far along are you?" the woman asked.

"Twenty-six weeks."

"Your first?"

"Yes."

"I have four. Have fun!"

Laughter filled the two-stall bathroom and Ana joined in, joy filling her as she dried her hands and walked back to Lucinda and Brie, who were now standing next to the small table where they'd paused.s

"That was quick!" Brie said.

"But long enough for Brie to tell me how horribly you've been treated, Ana. If I ever see the man who did this to you, I'll give him a piece of my mind–and my palm!"

Ana and Brie's mouths dropped.

"Auntie! You're a pacifist, remember?"

"Not for this. Ana, sweet dear," she said, pulling her in for a hug, "you have been brutally taken advantage of!"

Across Lucinda's shoulder, she made a *Help me!* face.

Brie's hands went up in a helpless gesture.

"I'll be fine, Auntie," she assured the old lady. "I have good friends, a wonderful mother and stepfather, and an excellent medical team."

"That does not invalidate the horrors that vile man committed against you!"

Geez. Brie was laying it on thick, huh?

"I thank you for your concern," Ana said, going into therapist mode. "Truly. But I have lots of support. I would prefer to focus on Brie and Martin's wedding, and enjoy this beautiful Memorial Day weekend with you."

Out of the corner of her eye, Ana watched the gray-eyed lady and her daughter—Colleen—walk over to the police officer in the red uniform, the same one the big, muscled man had been speaking with earlier. They smiled at each other and pointed to a cluster of trees near the Love You Chocolate kiosk on the common.

"Hmph," Lucinda said, straightening to her full height, backbone strong and tall. "Some men deserve to become geldings, that's all."

"AUNTIE!"

Lucinda just curled her upper lip in disgust, then linked one arm in Brie's, one in Ana's, and proceeded to the Love You Chocolate booth.

An adorable young girl with dark brown curls rushed past them, basically dragged by a gorgeous golden retriever on a leash.

"Harriet!" the police officer shouted, taking off at a jog to head off the duo. "Over here with Grandma and Colleen." He used his fingers to let out a commanding whistle and shouted, "JESTER!"

The dog instantly changed its course, soon at the cop's feet.

A blonde woman with a unicorn painted on her cheek, her hair glittering in the sun, walked quickly to the group.

"I want a gummy bear chocolate heart!" the little girl–Harriet, was it?–said to the blonde. She shoved her hand in her front pocket and pulled out a folded pack of cash, peeling several bills off. "I have my own money! I earned it chopping wood and babysitting Magic!"

Magic. Dennis. Colleen. Harriet.

Who were these people? Somehow, they were all connected to the kind woman with gray eyes, eyes that were so familiar.

The cop scanned the area, a sour expression on his face as a man the size of a lumberjack and a very fashionable woman walked toward them.

"Kell? You've been paying Harriet to chop wood?"

"What?" The bigger guy looked genuinely baffled. "Not me. Dennis."

Ana's entire body went liquid with desire again.

This was ridiculous. She had to stop having this reaction to a man's name. Sure, it wasn't super common, but there were plenty of men in the world with that name.

Lucinda guided them to the small line at the kiosk, carefully scrutinizing the counter. A teenager in a red polo shirt, the store's uniform (other than heart costumes), started to shake visibly.

"Uh, Mrs. Armistead?" His voice cracked right in half. "Can I help you–did we do something wrong–what's the matter?"

"Dawson, please close your mouth."

He snapped it shut.

"Nothing is wrong, other than the fact that the samples are all turned in the wrong direction, there is a dirty napkin on the left side of the table, stuck under an empty water bottle, and..."

Brie began selecting chocolates to buy as Lucinda gave the young man some guidance.

"YAY!" little Harriet squealed, their group maybe twenty feet away. Someone else had joined them, an older man who was now holding the hand of the kind gray-eyed woman from the bathroom, and behind him was–

Oh.

Oh.

Oh, my *goodness*.

"Brie," she said, her knees going weak, her body starting to tremble like that teen boy's hands. "It's–*help*."

"Help? What's wrong? Is it the baby?"

Sharp as a tack, Lucinda left the boy hanging and turned to her.

"Ana? What's wrong? Do you need to sit? Is something wrong with the baby?"

Time *changed*.

Each second skipped like a stone on water, like a hummingbird's wings, like there was all the time in the world yet every bit of it was gone.

She took a step backward. Then another, her belly going heavy, her heart completely confused in her chest, trying to decide whether to jump for joy..

...or flee screaming.

The group of people was moving closer, step by step, each one more final than the last.

Each one clearer than the last.

The big man in the navy t-shirt, wearing sunglasses he was now slowly removing as he looked at her like an assassin peering through a rifle sight was, indeed, Dennis.

Her Dennis.

Dennis from their one night stand.

"ANA!" Brie said loudly. "What's going on?"

At Brie's words, Dennis's sunglasses dropped to the ground, his legs faster than she ever imagined something so thick could be. He ran around his group, startling the lumberjack dude, making the fashionable woman wobble on her high heels.

"Hey!" the guy called out, but Dennis ran, coming to an abrupt halt, his eyes on her belly.

Her big, ripe belly, as round as the sun.

Then he looked at her eyes.

Her belly.

Her eyes.

"*Ana?*" His face reflected her own yearning, her desperate wish, her desire, her–

"Dennis, I can explain–"

The group was behind him now, Lucinda and Brie on either side of him. His face changed, rage boiling up in him.

The change was frightening.

And wholly deserved.

He pointed to her.

"What are you doing here?"

"Dennis. I can explain," she started again, repeating herself like an idiot, trying to find the words.

Failing miserably.

"Dennis?" The gray-eyed woman called out to him, giving Ana a nervous, questioning smile. "Do you know her? We met in the bathroom and–"

"Stop talking, Mom. *Now.*"

"But, Dennis, I–"

"Shut. Up."

"Dennis!" The man–his father?–stepped forward. "You've never spoken to your mother like that before." Concerned eyes met Ana's. "Who is this–"

Ignoring everyone, Dennis took one step closer. His chest

was rising and falling faster and faster, pain joining the rage in his eyes as he pointed to her belly and blasted her, the force of his words making her take a step back, Brie's grip on her tightening.

"You're *here?*" he bellowed, eyes going wild, no longer readable. "You? In my hometown?"

And then his head snapped back and he inhaled raggedly before shouting, "And you're pregnant with *my baby!*"

Chapter Fifteen

Dennis

Dennis had never felt so much rage and so much yearning at the same time, in the same body, all of it consuming his blood stream, pumping at a rate of a million gallons a minute.

Her belly.

Her gorgeous, lush, round, beautiful belly.

Pregnant? She was *pregnant* with his child? He was going to be a father? Ana's ghosting had hurt him in so many ways, but this took the cake.

Before he could utter another word, Lucinda Armistead got in his face, shouting, "Dennis Luview! Are you saying *you* are the father of this baby?"

"Luview!" Ana gasped, looking at him with those incredible, minky eyes eyes. "You're part of the *Luview* family?"

"BABY?" Deanna screeched. "I'm having another grand-baby? Dennis, is this really your baby?" His father pressed his hands on her shoulders, holding her in place. Deanna looked like she was full of helium and about to ascend to the heavens.

"I–"

Suddenly, the world hit a speed bump, a tiny but annoying tickle of pain rippling along his jaw. The force of the blow wasn't enough to make him move more than an inch to his right, but he caught an eyeful of his entire family standing in a cluster, all their mouths forming an O of surprise, his mother's hands flying to her face.

Miss Lucinda had just slapped him as hard as possible.

"YOU ARE THE SCOUNDREL?" she bellowed. "YOU, OF ALL PEOPLE? YOU SICK, DISGUSTING MAN! HOW DARE YOU!"

Her body tall like a wizard's, her face full of the kind of righteous indignation only a woman of deep morals can conjure, Lucinda's single slap had brought all movement around them to a dead halt.

Other than the arm of Nadine Khouri, Annabeth's mother and town gossip, who was slowly raising her smartphone, clearly recording this.

"Poor Annabeth," he heard her mutter.

"Miss Lucinda!" he grunted, eyebrows knitting in deep confusion as he looked at her, then Ana, and back. "Why did you just *hit* me?"

"You are very lucky I don't have my shears, Dennis!" She turned to his mother. "I know you raised him better, Deanna, but he is a–a scoundrel. A cad. A ne'er-do-well who has caused severe harm to this beautiful little dearie."

"Harm?" His dad's voice rang out, loud and firm, a tone Dennis felt in his spine.

Because it was the tone he got in his own voice when he went into protective mode.

"I never harmed Ana!" he protested, looking at her in

shock. Disbelief radiated through him. Why would she lie about such a thing?

Lucinda raised her arm as if to hit him again. The woman with Ana stepped forward quickly then, grabbing the old lady by the elbow.

"You're the police chief," he heard Kell say to Luke. "Shouldn't you do something?"

Luke just shrugged.

"You!" Lucinda pointed at Dennis with her free arm. "You poked a hole in the condom and got this woman pregnant on purpose so you could gain sympathy from law enforcement!"

Ana looked at Brie.

"You told her?"

"Sorry!" her friend said as Lucinda struggled to free herself, clearly intending to hit Dennis again.

"Where's Moore? I need him to go get popcorn," Colleen muttered to Kell.

"Off with Jordy at his high school, remember? Something about set design for the production of The Laramie Project."

"I was making a bad joke. Sort of." She looked around, eyes scanning the crowd. "Of all the times for them to be gone. Moore's going to hate missing *this*!"

Dennis overheard everything, felt everything, but couldn't move.

What the hell was Lucinda accusing him of?

And had someone actually *done that* to Ana?

Leading with her belly, Ana walked forward and inserted herself between Lucinda and Dennis.

"Auntie!" she began.

"You're Lucinda's niece?" Deanna gasped.

"Sort of," Ana said, then returned to Lucinda. "Dennis is *not* the father of this baby."

"Looks like I am," he insisted. "You're about five months

pregnant. That lines up with when we slept together in Boston."

"Popcorn *and* nachos," Colleen hissed to Kell, folding her arms and leaning against a tree. Kylie quietly took Harriet and Jester away, luring them back to the chocolate kiosk.

His mom stepped forward then, grabbing his arm.

"Dennis. That woman is at least six months pregnant." She eyeballed Ana's belly. "Six and a half?"

"Twenty-six weeks," Ana answered. "Good eye."

"I've had four kids of my own. Let me introduce myself properly. I'm Deanna Luview, the scoundrel's mother."

Patience already as thin as silk, Dennis was having none of this.

"You're sure, Ana? The baby isn't mine?"

Pain filled her face. "I wish it were." Clapping her hands over her mouth, she was nothing but those huge orbs.

And huge belly.

"I'm so sorry, Dennis. I, um... I found out I was pregnant three days after we met. I was too ashamed to tell you, and–"

"I see." A rush of emotion nearly knocked him off his feet. "Now it makes more sense."

Sad eyes met his.

"Yes. I should have been mature enough to have let you know. Ghosting wasn't fair to you."

"Thank you. And–wait." He studied her, then looked at Lucinda. "She said someone poked a hole in a condom so that he could... *what*?"

"It's a long story."

"I have plenty of time."

"I'd really rather not air my laundry in public," she replied.

"Can't close the barn doors now," Colleen piped up. "Those horses are long gone. They're somewhere near Montreal by now."

"Then Dennis is *not* the father?" Lucinda asked, her breathing slowing, anger dissipating.

"No."

"And you're one hundred percent certain of that?" he asked again, needing to hear it in different ways so his brain could process it all.

"Yes." She reached out and touched his hand, the connection sending electricity through him. Their eyes met. "Again, I'm so sorry. I just... knew that nothing would happen between us."

"You what?"

"If I replied to your text. It was too late, and too complicated."

"Why would you say that?" he gasped, voice going low with hurt.

She let out a strangled laugh, then looked around.

"I can see I've interrupted a family gathering of yours."

"*I'm* the one who interrupted by barging across the common to confront you. If anyone should apologize, it's me."

The way she peered at him took his breath away.

"Look," he said, squeezing her hand. "Can we please talk? Somewhere more private?"

She looked at her friend.

"I'm here for Brie. She's getting married, and we're planning the wedding. I can't really–"

"Oh, yes, you really *can!*" Brie jumped in. "You've been talking about Dennis since the day you met him. Go! Shoo! I'll handle Auntie, and–"

"*Handle?*" Lucinda said in a dark voice. "I do not need to be *handled.*"

"Um, I didn't mean it that way." Brie's voice shook. "I just–I thought we were coming here to plan my wedding and have a lovely long weekend in Love You, and suddenly you turn into a boxer and hit a guy the size of a wall, screaming the word *scoundrel* over and over!"

The friend had a pretty good grasp of things.

Dennis noticed Kell elbow Luke, who sighed, slowly putting on his hat. As he walked over, he held up his hands.

"Hey, now, Lucinda. Let's stop the violence."

"You're a Johnny-come-lately, aren't you, Lukey Loo?"

Lucinda was spitting fire.

"I, uh—"

"You dicker about and wait until my grandniece steps in and defuses everything, *then* you bother to get involved?" Lucinda sniffed with contempt. "I hardly understand why taxpayers should be funding your nonsense."

"So you *want* me to arrest you for battery?" Luke asked, looking like he would rather eat a live snake head first than do that.

"I want you to find the disgusting man who hurt my poor dearie!"

"Hurt?" Dennis growled, Ana's hand still touching him. Now he sounded like Dean.

Luke turned to Ana, eyeing her midsection. "I assume that whatever led to your pregnancy didn't happen here in Luview? In this town?"

She shook her head.

"Then it's out of my jurisdiction."

"A crime has been committed!" Lucinda continued.

Dennis's insides twisted. A crime? He didn't like what he was hearing. Was Ana pregnant from an assault?

"Maybe we *should* go talk," Ana finally said. "Alone."

"GO!" Brie urged, giving Lucinda a fearful eye. "While you can."

Unable to tolerate the chaos any longer, Dennis acted swiftly. Taking Ana's hand in his, he marched across the common, with her keeping pace.

His hand sang.

The last ten minutes were a whirlwind, so many emotions flying, so many perceptions all queued up. Instinct had dominated, though he had let Lucinda sucker slap him.

Rafe would be laughing his ass off if he knew, telling this story for years.

"Dennis?"

"Yes?"

"Can we slow down?" She looked back at the chocolate shop's kiosk. "And, um, maybe get some chocolate?"

"Chocolate. You want *chocolate* right now?" Keeping the incredulity out of his voice was impossible.

Her hands went to her swollen belly, thumbs and fingers in a loose heart shape over her navel.

A serene smile almost made him kiss her.

"We were about to get some. I have a craving. It's hard to explain, and I'm not going to try to justify it, but I'll be in better shape to talk about all this if you can let me indulge myself."

The thought of going back to where his family were collected, all of them speculating and casting side eye their way, was intolerable.

"You want Love You Chocolate chocolate?"

"I do. And... do you want a coffee?"

"Excuse me?"

"Maybe we could pop into Love You Coffee, get some chocolate and coffee there, then find a place to sit and talk? I'm sure Skylar or Reef can help us."

"You know Reef?" He didn't even try to hold back his surprise. "Who *are* you?"

"Ana DaSilva."

"I know who you are." He glowered. "Know your last name, too."

"You do?" She rubbed her stomach. "Because I had no idea until just now that you're a Luview. Wow."

His temples began to throb. This morning, he'd left home with the bed of his truck empty, intending to pick up some lumber over in Fixby Hills, at the sawmill. Stopping to hang out on the common with his family had been organized by his mom, her idea of a fun weekend thing.

He owed her now. Big time. He'd tried everything not to come here. And if he hadn't, he wouldn't have run into Ana.

Dennis knew how to fix this. He pulled out his phone and started texting.

An instant reply pleased him.

"What kind of coffee do you like?"

"Decaf."

"Decaf what?"

"You want my order?"

"I do."

"This is from Love You Coffee?"

"Yes, ma'am."

"I'd like a decaf latte with turmeric and cinnamon."

His fingers froze. "You drink that?"

"I do now."

"Okay, then. There." Sliding the phone in his back pocket, he patted his left chest pocket, momentary panic racing through him until he remembered Magic was safe at home in his little habitat.

A rarity, and a well-timed coincidence that made this all so much easier.

"Reef will have a pound of mixed chocolate hearts and our coffees ready for us at the back door," he explained, their pace slower as they walked to the main drag.

"You know everyone, don't you? You're a Luview. I cannot believe I never asked you for your last name when we met."

Each step felt surreal, her body so close to his, a reality he'd imagined and craved for so long.

What a bizarre way to meet again.

And he had so many questions.

"Who did this to you? And did he do it without your consent?"

"Consent. I don't hear that word from many people."

"You're hearing it from me now." Fighting to keep the anger out of his voice, he paused, peering down at her. "You keep dodging the question."

"I can see how it seems that way. I'd prefer to get our order first. It isn't the kind of conversation that works well with interruptions."

"Got it."

In silence, they walked the rest of the way to the alley behind Love You Coffee, where Dennis texted Reef. Within a minute, the pierced and tatted-up dude appeared with a small white paper bag and a tray with two coffees.

Reef was a hardass, a quality Dennis admired.

So the grin he wore on his face took Dennis by surprise.

"Sucker punched by a ninety-year-old woman, eh? Nobody had *that* on a betting grid at Greta's."

"Shut up."

"I heard you used that line on your mom, too. You're getting in trouble from Dean for sassing off to Deanna."

"Reef," he growled.

"Is that any way to treat a friend?" Reef transferred the goods to Dennis, then looked at Ana. "Hey, there. How's it going, Ana?"

"You seriously know each other?"

Reef gave Dennis a withering look.

"Lucinda's my great-aunt, too. Remember? Brie and I are third cousins or something. Ana's been here tons of times with

Brie. If you'd bothered living here for the last twenty or so years, you'd know that."

With a slam, the door closed, and Reef returned to the store.

Dennis offered the bag to Ana, who immediately opened a cellophane pouch of red, silver, and pink foil hearts. She pulled out a red one and hurriedly unwrapped it, shoving the chocolate into her mouth, chewing while opening a second one quickly.

"You act like you've been shipwrecked and this is the first fish you could catch with your handmade spear, so you're taking a bite of it raw and alive," he said as he watched her dig in.

"That is a perfect description of a pregnancy craving."

The little moan she made as she ate the chocolate reminded him of their night in bed, making love. Never before had he competed with candy.

Right now, he was losing.

Holding the tray with the coffees, he pulled each cup from its cradle and tossed the tray in the recycling bin. The scene Lucinda caused back on the common was going to follow him throughout town, so he wanted to get them away from prying eyes.

And he sensed he was somehow losing Ana. Time was of the essence.

"You know," she said, in a voice he dreaded, "I–maybe I should just apologize again and take my leave. Lucinda and Brie are very kind to let me talk to you, but–"

"No!" He caught himself, realizing that came out too sharply. "No. Please. It's really good to see you."

To be this close to your amazing self, he almost added.

She looked at him full on.

"It's good to see you again, too."

"I know a place we can go." He nodded across the street.

"A little cove by the hot springs. It's too high above the water for people to swim there. Can we walk over and talk?"

"Sure."

A light wind picked up as they strolled to the crosswalk, her dress billowing, showing off the shape of her belly. Pregnant. Ana was *pregnant*. Never in all his imagined scenarios had he thought of this.

That she was refusing to reply to his text because she was pregnant with another man's baby.

No ring on her left hand, though.

"I take it you're not with the father?"

Ana snorted as they waited for the light to change, then opened another foil heart and ate it, rolling the wrapper into a tiny, tight ball.

"No. My ex is the one who... did this."

"The asshole you talked about in the bar?"

"One and the same."

"Harris."

She jerked in surprise.

"You remember his name?"

"Wanted by the DEA. Fled the country on drug smuggling charges. He–*he's* the baby's father?"

"Yes."

"And you're certain?"

Just then, the light changed, Ana jumping at the chance to run away from him.

Or so it seemed.

"Damn it. Sorry," he said, catching up. "Of course you know."

"I slept with Harris a month or so before we met. Last time was the day before he dumped me, okay?" she said through gritted teeth, in a low voice he strained to hear. Her pace was clipped and fast, the gait of a city dweller.

"Which direction?" she asked as they reached the edge of the woods around the hot springs.

"Here," he said, pointing to the back lot of Love You Chocolate. "It's around back of Lucinda's store."

"How do you know about it?" Smacking her forehead playfully, she added, "Because you're a Luview. Duh."

"Actually, it's because when I worked at Lucinda's store as a teen, I hung out there during my breaks."

"You worked there? I'm jealous."

"Jealous?"

The pivot to the right took them around the overstuffed parking lot. Love You Chocolate had its best month in February, but any busy weekend in town, especially three-day holiday weekends, brought out loads of candy fans.

"Brie got to work for a few weeks one summer. Auntie always said I could come, too, but my mom had me enrolled in language camp by then."

"What language?"

"Português, claro!"

"Português. Meu erro. Você é fluente?"

The skid of her Chuck Taylor soles on the pavement made a sound like a tiny shriek.

"You have got to be kidding me!"

"Whew. We're back to English. Because you were pushing the bounds of my fluency."

"You *really* have no accent, Dennis."

"Your father, right? Taught you his native language?"

"Yes." They resumed walking, Dennis pointing by holding one coffee aloft. Beyond a small clearing, there would be a cluster of fallen trees by the water, perfectly level for sitting on. "After he died, Mom sent me to language camp every summer until college so I'd retain it."

"She's not fluent?"

"She was good enough. No kid who is fluent likes hearing a non-fluent parent." Ana shuddered. "Her accent is abysmal."

"After your dad died, did she still speak it?"

"No. Then Rick moved in, and..."

"Will you speak Portuguese with the baby?"

"He will absolutely learn it."

"He?"

"Yes." When she smiled, a smear of chocolate showed on her lip. He wanted to kiss it off. "Baby Bean, the boy."

"And will you name him Paolo? After your father?"

Another abrupt halt from her, this time on dirt, as they had just reached the path.

"How do you know my father's name?"

"Let's sit down and have our coffee and chocolate. I'll explain."

By the time they sat down, Ana was on her fifth chocolate heart, which deeply amused Dennis. She was tucking the little red foil balls from the wrappers into her dress pocket.

Wide and worn of bark, the enormous tree trunk that acted as a bench was far too low for his long legs, but suited Ana perfectly. Knees nearly in his ears at first, he eventually stretched back, legs crossed at the ankles.

She gratefully took the coffee.

"Thank you. I owe you."

"For what?"

"The coffee. The chocolates." Instead of taking a sip of her drink, she ate another chocolate. The cove was so quiet, with barely any birdsong audible.

"Now tell me why you know about my father."

"When we met in Boston, you said he died in the Bannister crash. I looked it up. Figured you likely had the same last name. Looked *you* up."

"You know where I live?"

"Sure. Newburyport."

Her squint was half skepticism, half worry.

"You hired a private investigator?"

It felt good to laugh so hard.

"Ana. I have skills that far exceed a PI. It didn't take long to learn a great deal about you."

"Oh. And you never used that information?"

"To do what?"

"Try to find me?"

"Why would I do that? You didn't answer my text. I respect that. I'm a man who knows a boundary when I see it, and I don't cross them." Anger rose inside him. "Unlike your ex."

"Wow. And I had no idea who you were. Afterwards, I wished I'd gotten your last name. Can you imagine how different our bar conversation would have been?"

"Yep. Which is why I never mentioned it." A sour taste filled his mouth. "People get weird when they hear the Luview name."

Steadily, she made her way through more chocolate, alternating between candy and coffee.

"It must get tiring."

"It does."

"So you stay quiet."

"I do."

"I didn't reply to you, and you didn't chase me. Until we just ran into each other, I assumed we both were done."

He reached for her hand, taking the chance.

"I am anything but done."

"Really?" Hand going to her chest, her laugh was high and nervous. "Dennis, I'm about to be a single mother. Raising a child I conceived a month before we met. You're... not done?"

"Are you? Done with me?"

"I've had maybe twenty minutes to even begin to get over the shock of running into you on the common and watching

Auntie slap you. I'm a fast emotional processor, but this pace is beyond my abilities."

"Got it. Sorry for the hard press."

Laughter, loud and boisterous, rose like steam from the other side of the springs. Splashing and shouts made them both smile.

"This is awkward as hell," she observed.

"It doesn't have to be."

"I'm a trained, licensed therapist. It's my job to navigate emotional terrain with as much equanimity and grace as possible. And after our extraordinary night together, I was so joyful. So hopeful. Then I got sick."

"Sick?"

"Turned out that what I thought was a bad cold was... Baby Bean." She winced, then smiled. "He heard me talking about him and decided to stretch."

"He's moving around?"

"Yes."

Eyes on her round midsection, he took in the print of her dress, how the cloth folded underneath breasts far bigger than the last time he'd seen her. Then he studied her face. She glowed, but it wasn't just the maternal air of pregnancy. Ana had a goodness about her.

Which made what that prick had done doubly bad.

"Tell me more about what he did to you."

Watching her smile fade hurt him, but he had to know.

"He... Look, the sex was consensual. Fully."

"Okay."

"But when I called to tell him about the baby, he expressed surprise that 'it had worked.'"

"*What* had worked?"

She unwrapped two hearts and put both pieces in her mouth at the same time, chewing, a finger held up to buy time. After she swallowed, she looked down at the ground as if embarrassed.

"He told me he'd poked holes in the condom because he thought having a baby on the way would get him sympathy from a judge or jury."

"That fucking animal." Fists curling, Dennis imagied breaking the guy's face.

"I–I am so sorry, Dennis. I really, really shouldn't be telling you so much personal stuff."

"Never apologize."

"Something about you makes me let my guard down. Not that I have a big one. I've done plenty of work with therapists around my own issues. Including this one. Harris breached my trust."

"Harris did more than that." He wanted to drill down, interrogate her, learn more. So many questions.

"Yes."

"I want to help you."

"Help?"

"I know guys who know guys. I might be able to find him and force him to face justice."

"That sounds very illegal."

"The line between moral and legal is sometimes open to interpretation."

"That's not where I want to focus my attention and energy."

"I'm not sure what that means."

"Dennis." She finished her coffee and set the to-go cup on the bench, fishing around in the nearly empty bag of chocolates, taking one of the three remaining. "I can focus on what Harris did to me and how he turned me into a victim for his agenda. Or I can focus on the joy of passing twenty-six weeks of pregnancy with a child I wasn't supposed to be able to conceive and carry to viability." She sighed. "There I go again."

"What?"

"Telling you all my secrets."

He touched her hand again.

"I'm here to listen to every single one of them."

"Why are you being so nice to someone who blew you off like I did?"

"Why are you sitting here with me on a fallen log on a beautiful spring day, eating chocolates and pouring your heart out?"

Chapter Sixteen

Ana

His question made her realize she'd left only two candies in the entire bag.

"I can't believe I just did that."

"Opened up to me?"

The bag was so light in her hand.

"Uh, no. Ate the whole bag. Here." Palm out, she offered him the two remaining chocolates.

He curled her fingers around the hearts and held her hand, his own so thick and strong.

"Those are yours. It's been fun watching you eat them."

"Fun?"

"You take great pleasure from every bite."

"It's true! I had no idea food could taste so good until I was pregnant. And be so important. And specific."

"Cravings?"

She nodded, the flow of conversation between them so

easy. You'd never guess that half an hour ago, he was screaming at her. That Auntie would slap him. That his whole family would watch.

If one of her patients told her a story like this, they'd devote months to unpacking and processing it.

Instead, when it happened to her, she ate chocolate.

"You didn't answer my question."

"I know. Guilty."

"I don't care."

"Don't care that I haven't answered, or don't care about my answer?"

"I'm just happy to be with you, Ana. Thrilled you didn't run away." The way he closed his eyes and inhaled through his nose made her see his gravitas. His goodness.

And that he'd suffered from their disconnect, too.

Some part of her had clung to that hope, the hope that he really did want her, that he was confused, that he'd pursue her. In a sense, he had, researching her.

Maturity and professional training told her that such feelings were unfair to him, but that's how feelings worked: They weren't rational.

"I should run away. Apologize profusely and leave you alone. You have your own life here, Dennis." A wave of sadness washed over her. "How I treated you was unforgivable."

"Hold on there. That's harsh."

He was right. Why was she being so hard on herself?

Tears came then, fast and full, months of pain pouring out. He noticed, squeezing her hand, putting his arm around her, and pulling her head to his shoulder.

"Hey. *Hey*," he said, helplessness in his voice, his warm skin so comforting that it made her cry more.

"Hormones," she mumbled into his shirt, but this wasn't just the swell of estrogen and progesterone. Far more than that, it was five months of worry and confusion, shock and grief, all coming out as she sat on an old log in front of a steaming hot springs, the sun shining down on the man she'd given up on out of shame.

So much shame. Shame she knew better than to feel because of her training, which triggered even more shame.

"This is healthy," she said, mostly to herself. "A normal release of emotion."

As she sniffed, he chuckled gently.

"You don't have to therapize yourself."

"Therapize?"

"What do you call it when a therapist talks to herself?"

"Tuesday?"

That made him laugh harder, then tighten his grip around her shoulders. He felt so solid. So kind. So caring and so right. Why, why, *why*–of all times–did the mess with Harris have to happen just as Dennis came into her life?

How different everything could have been if only...

And yet, that *if only* was enormous. Because the reason she hadn't replied to Dennis was that she was pregnant with another man's baby.

A baby she viewed as something close to a miracle.

A baby who began to move inside her as the sugar rush kicked in.

Dennis's little jolt was endearing.

"Was that–did the baby move?"

"He did. My fault."

"Your fault?"

"Sugar rush."

"Whoa." He scooched away from her, though his arm still rested on her shoulders. His gaze dropped to her midsection. "Can I–may I feel him moving?"

"You mean touch my belly with your hands?"

"Yes."

"Thank you for asking permission. Yes, of course."

Being touched like this wasn't unique, but being touched like this by Dennis made every cell in her body ignite. Tender and sweet, he cradled her belly like it was a small watermelon, head cocked in concentration, his eyes widening as he grinned.

"I felt him move! Is he rolling?"

"I guess? I haven't reached the point where I can identify body parts yet, other than the head."

"Twenty-six weeks, huh? Fourteen to go."

The absence of his hands when he pulled away made her throat tighten. Wanting more of his touch had become a new craving. Just as she'd devoured a bag of chocolates, she wanted to lose herself in Dennis's closeness.

But his words couldn't go uncorrected.

"Ah, not quite. I won't make it to full term."

"What do you mean?"

How much to tell? No other man would get her to open up like this, but Dennis wasn't any other man. She sensed he felt the same about her. Who forgives being ghosted and falsely accused of various and sundry scoundrelous behaviors, then buys a woman chocolate and coffee and holds her belly?

Dennis Luview. That's who.

"I have a complication."

"Is the baby sick?" He blinked, brow furrowed. "Or are you?"

"Not exactly."

"Is this a private matter you don't want to discuss? I'll back off."

Reading people was his superpower, wasn't it?

Or one of them, at least. She sensed he had many.

"I don't normally spill my guts like this with men I've had one-night stands with, then ghosted on, then run into on a town common where my ninety-something adopted Auntie turns into an MMA fighter."

"Sounds like any average Wednesday in this town."

What else could she do but laugh?

If she'd found him attractive, interesting, easy to talk to back in Boston, now she was drawn to him in ways that defied reason.

Who was she? This wasn't typical, rational Ana.

This was a self only Dennis could unveil.

"I have a unicornuate uterus. It means it's shaped oddly, like half a uterus. And I have only one ovary, one fallopian tube."

His eyes bored into hers, narrowing as he took in her words.

"Which is why you kept the baby. Because your odds are so low."

The sound of her breath, sharp as she inhaled with surprise, was like a train shooting past.

"Um—yes."

"Which makes what he did to you all the more grossly unfair. You have to balance his assault on you with the gift it brings."

"Good grief, Dennis, could you just pause for a second and stop being so insightful? It's like listening to someone dissect me without anesthesia!" she hissed, feeling vivisected. This wasn't just overwhelm making her shake.

It was as if she had nowhere to hide, because Dennis knew and saw everything about her.

"Sorry," he muttered, looking away. "Sometimes I just can't help it."

Heart hammering away like a metronome gone out of control, she looked at the soothing water, willing herself to watch it.

"You see things most people don't."

"Not see—*feel*. Intuit. Gut instinct. Pick a term."

"Funny trait for a military guy."

"Perfect trait for the kind of work I did in the military. It's why I didn't come home in a body bag, like plenty of my team."

The whirlwind speed of this conversation, with all its emotional overtones and undercurrents, was too much. Head spinning, she stood, moving slowly, the change of position making her toes tingle.

"Ana. Forgive me. I'm not being kind to you." He stood as well, looking down at her with worried eyes as she looked up.

"I'm not someone to be pitied," she said, her words measured and calm.

"Pity?" One cheek went up as his mouth curled in confusion, his eye narrowing. "Where the hell did you get pity out of anything we've just said?"

"I know what Harris did to me."

Dennis's face hardened, rage flashing in his eyes.

"There's a term for it. Reproductive coercion," she said softly.

"Sounds about right. I'd call it assault."

"Others use the phrase reproductive rape."

"There was no consent for pregnancy."

"Dennis. Please. I've processed so much of this with my own psychologist. I don't–I don't need you to–"

"You've processed it. Good. I'm genuinely relieved and glad to hear that you have support. But this is all new to me. Seeing you, the baby, learning how the baby came about, learning how special it is for you to even be pregnant." His smile softened. "It's all clouding the best part."

"What do you mean?"

"Do you know how many times I've imagined seeing you again? Touching you? Kissing you? Talking and getting to know each other? That night at the hotel was special for me, Ana. Very special. I came home in a depressed state and left the hotel elated. Excited about life. Eager to text you and go out on a date. I followed that stupid three-day rule, and spent the last five months kicking myself."

"What?"

"When you didn't answer, I spent every waking moment coming up with scenarios to explain why. Plenty of them involved me waiting too long to text you."

"Oh, Dennis. I'm sorry. I'm sure none of them involved me already being pregnant with another man's baby."

"Got me there."

His hands moved to her shoulders, cupping them, his touch a contrast to the tingling in her feet. Flexing her calves, she moved enough to shift weight from hip to hip, her pregnant body always needing adjustment.

"I'm a direct guy, so let me be crystal clear: I'd like to get to know you better. Spend time together. *Date* you. Are you interested in me?"

His last sentence floated in the air like a giant banner being dragged through the skies by an airplane.

"What?" All she could do was look up at him, squinting into the sun.

"You blew me off before, but I'm guessing that's because you assumed I wouldn't want to date a woman who's pregnant with another man's baby."

"Yes. That's exactly why," she answered.

"No other reason?"

"That's a pretty big reason."

He moved to one side, so the sun wasn't directly behind him.

"Is that better?" he asked.

"Thank you." The man's attention to detail when it came to her comfort was endearing.

"No other reason, though, for not replying to my text?" This time, the question was asked in a quieter voice, his head moving closer as he leaned down to ask.

"No. No other reason. Just my embarrassment that I was–"

Strong, callused fingers pressed her lips.

"*Shhh*. A simple no is all I need to hear."

She nodded her head and he pulled his fingers away. A thin sheen of sweat formed along her hairline as her body heated up. At the rate this was going, she'd be steaming like the hot springs.

"Ana, may I kiss you right now?" Still pink from Auntie's smack, his clean-shaven cheek lifted with his smile. In resting face, he was imposing and even grim, but when he grinned, it was as if the world were alight with joy.

Instead of answering, she stood on tiptoe, the flex giving her calves much-needed movement, her lips getting something they needed even more.

A kiss from him.

The man she'd rejected for all the wrong reasons.

The man who was now before her, asking for a second chance that she should be the one begging for.

Their lips met and the world righted itself, his body so big and comfortable, it felt as if he were meant for her and she for him. The feel of his arms around her, their mouths saying hello in new and increasingly luscious ways, how the sun warmed them both–even the trees seemed to murmur yes.

Yes to everything.

Coincidences like this didn't just happen. Today felt planned by an unseen force that wanted them both to smile. To feel joy. To be free.

To connect.

Dennis held her close, his heart beating steady against her ribs, her arms stretched up, hands around his neck. She pulled up as tall as she could, and then–

"Ack!" she said against his mouth, dropping low so fast, he

scooped one arm around her increasingly wide waist and stopped her.

"What's wrong?"

"CRAMP!" Her calf had seized, turned into a concrete block.

Instantly, she was in the air, in his arms as he brought her back to the log, sitting with her in his lap, her ankle twisting and flailing, flexing and extending.

Anything to relieve the pain, which took her breath away.

That meant she had nothing in her lungs, because the kiss had dispensed with her breath, too, so poor Ana suffered in excruciating pain at the exact moment when joy and lust, not spasm and torture, should have dominated.

"Here," he said, thumbs digging hard into the thick center of her calf, muscles along the top of her foot screaming in agony. "You need blood in there. And a banana. Potassium."

"Cantaloupe and kiwi."

"Huh?"

"They actually have more potassium than bananas. That's just a marketing ploy."

The look on his face was priceless as he turned her calf into a loaf of kneaded dough.

"You are a hoot."

"A hoot? Auntie says that all the time."

"Maybe it's a Luview saying."

Biting her lower lip, she wiggled off his lap and, limping over to a nearby tree, hooked her heel against the base, toe pointed up at the branches as she stretched.

"I cannot believe how much this hurts!" she groaned, her body's painful grip making her clench her jaw.

"Happen a lot?"

"Only when I'm on tiptoe."

"Then I'll have to bend over more when we kiss again. Or just have you in my lap instead. I liked that."

"You liked having me wriggle in pain in your lap?" she joked, trying to take a deep breath.

"The wriggling part, yes. The pain, no. What can I do to help?"

"Water. Salt? Something like that might help." Suddenly, the cramp lessened enough that she could put almost her full weight on her foot again.

"I'll carry you back to—where? Where do you want me to bring you?"

"You're not carrying me to the common, or to Auntie's store. I can walk."

"I would, you know."

"I don't doubt it." Laughing through her nose, the sound turned into a giggle as the pain finally relented enough. "You want to date me, huh?"

"Absolutely."

"Cramps and all?"

"Cramps and all. First date, I'll bring a cantaloupe and kiwi bouquet." His eyes darted to the almost-empty bag of chocolate. "And more red foil hearts."

Opening her heart to what he was saying was so tempting. Dennis Luview wasn't a player. This guy wasn't about games or pretenses. Yet he wasn't an open book, either. Decidedly guarded, he was showing her quite a bit of his inner self, which made her feel honored.

And, if she were being honest with herself, a bit scared.

One step turned into a limp again, but he crossed the space before she took another. Just when she was about to put her hands on his shoulders, he dropped to the ground.

Warm palms encircled her calf, slowly moving in a pattern, pushing blood up, the smooth rise of his hands to her knees, then back, so soothing.

So sensual.

Sex had been the last thing on her mind these last couple

of months, a stretch of time she'd used to process her emotions in therapy and to focus entirely on helping the baby to stick around. Only this week, after passing the twenty-six week mark, had she begun to relax.

Single motherhood, though, had been her assumption. No relationships. No complications. She'd have more than enough complexity in her life with a high-risk third trimester and all that came with parenting a baby alone.

But Dennis was another matter altogether.

And here he was, heart on his sleeve, chocolate hearts held out in a promised future, asking for the next step.

How could she say no?

"I'd like that," she said, looking down at him as he looked up, his thighs looking fine against his jeans, hair falling over his brow.

"How long are you in town?"

"You want to go on a date this weekend?"

"No time like the present." He stood, hands going about her waist, the feeling so unfamiliar. No one had touched her intimately since she'd been pregnant, and it felt weird, even as it felt so right.

"We just got into town, and we're here to start planning Brie's wedding. We leave Tuesday morning."

"It's Friday. Any chance you have a free evening for me? Or a lunch? I'll even take a breakfast date. I get up at 4:30 a.m."

"You *what?*"

"I get up at—"

"I heard you. Why? Aren't you retired?"

"I like morning runs."

"You like torturing yourself."

"I genuinely enjoy them."

"I am happy to get up at eight and eat a muffin while watching you run."

"By eight, I've chopped a cord of wood and saved three small American cities."

"That's all? Slacker."

This time, his kiss was full and real, all upfront and all at once. No tentative exploration, no asking permission, this kiss was the kind that whispered promises that made you wet, pinkened your cheeks, and left you quivering with anticipation.

Her phone buzzed in her pocket.

They ignored it.

His phone buzzed in his back pocket.

They ignored it.

Ana didn't know that a kiss could transport you to a place so private, so peaceful, so whole, and so right.

They may have started their relationship with the most clichéd of meetings–the one-night stand–but they were going to continue it with a real first date.

Right after this kiss.

The kiss she wished would never end.

Bzzz

Both of their phones buzzed yet again, Dennis's groan against her mouth making her laugh as they pulled apart.

"We're both being paged."

Ana pulled hers from her jacket pocket and looked at the time. More than an hour had passed.

She wanted more, *so* much more, with him.

Brie's text was simple: *At least you don't need to use birth control.*

Ana groaned aloud and Dennis gave her a look.

"Mine's worse than yours," he ventured.

"I doubt it."

He showed her his screen. A text from Deanna said: *Please bring Ana over for dinner if she's in town long enough. We love all grandbabies, no matter how they come into our lives!*

"Are you... blushing?" She looked at him in shock.

"Damn right I am. Meddling mother. What's yours say?"

After he shared his, she might as well.

Once he'd read Brie's words, they had a laugh, the shared vulnerability refreshing. When was the last time Ana could so boldly be herself with a man?

Gathering her in his arms, he pressed their foreheads together. When Ana looked down, her belly separated them. It was still a bump–a large one–but soon, it would be a basketball.

Soon, there would be pregnancy stress tests. A planned c-section. A possible emergency c-section if things went wrong. Complications defined her pregnancy and delivery, and bringing Dennis into her life meant he would have to accept the chaos, too.

That was a hard line for her.

"Look. I do have to go," he said apologetically. "I have to get some lumber in Fixby Hills, then we have a job we're doing over at Nordicbeth."

"The ski resort? In May?"

"There are trees along the alpine slide that need to be trimmed. Couldn't get to them last week because of storms, and the owners want it done now. How about tomorrow night? Dinner? We'll get out of town and I'll take you some-where that isn't dripping with fake love."

"What does that mean?"

He waved his hand, gesturing toward the other side of the hot springs, where the tourist information center was located. "You know. The *love*-liest place on earth." His tone was mock-ing. Derisive.

Downright negative.

"I love this town! *Love* it! Love You, Maine is my favorite place ever! Everything is so sweet here. So much heart, so endearing. When I was a teen, it was my dream to have a date here!"

"You're joking."

"I am completely sincere."

"My mother is going to love you," he muttered, then sighed. "Okay. Fine. We'll have a date here. Just–you have to understand that we're going to be constantly interrupted, right? I'm kind of an object of attention. Especially after what Lucinda just did."

"Oh." She paused, thinking it through. "Forget the whole date-in-town thing. We can improvise."

"You sure?"

"I am. And I don't even know if I'm free tomorrow night."

Bzzz

She looked at her phone.

If he asks you out, say yes. Auntie and I can plan my wedding without you while you go on a date with your freaking soul mate.

Ana winced as she read it.

"What's Brie saying now?"

There was vulnerable disclosure, and then there was *My best friend just crossed a huge line and no way am I sharing that.*

"She says I should go out with you if you ask, and she and Auntie can work around that."

"Great! You have a date with me tomorrow for breakfast, lunch, dinner, then on Sunday for–"

"Hold on there, cowboy. Dinner. Tomorrow."

"Perfect. Where are you staying? With Lucinda?"

She nodded, and Dennis touched his cheek.

"I'd better wear protective gear."

"She's going to feel terrible when her adrenaline wears off."

Bzzz

Brie again.

Auntie says if Dennis asks you out, he may pick you up here. She also wants to know if his favorite cake is still chocolate cherry bundt cake?

"Is your favorite cake still chocolate cherry bundt cake?" she asked Dennis, who did a double take.

"I guess? Haven't had it in years. Why?"

"Auntie wants to know. I think you're getting an apology cake."

"I should let old ladies slap me more often if it comes with my favorite dessert."

Ana risked another charley horse and stood on tiptoes, kissing him.

Because a man like this needed more kisses.

And frankly, so did she.

Chapter Seventeen

Dennis

Ana had insisted on walking herself back to Brie and Lucinda, leaving Dennis to hop in his truck and drive to Fixby Hills to get the lumber, then back to the camp, where his dad and Kell were waiting for him to head on over to Nordicbeth.

The taste of her was still on his lips, sugar-sweet and oh, so good.

What a day.

What a damned weird day.

The best day of his life, really, and it included a slap.

But that slap was apparently turning into an apology cake from Miss Lucinda, so if he played his cards right, he could have everyone back on his side *and* the woman of his dreams.

Could life get any better? If he were a whistling man, he'd be puckered up right now, making all the good sounds.

And tomorrow, if all went as planned, he'd have Ana in his arms, all puckered up and making even better sounds.

"Stop it," he muttered to himself as he came to a halt at the final stoplight on the edge of town.

Honk!

Behind him, a sea of pink filled his rearview mirror.

His brother, in a police cruiser.

A simple thumbs up got him another beep on the horn, then a text.

He looked at it. Luke, of course.

SCOUNDREL! was all it said.

Great. Just great.

He was headed home to meet up with his dad and Kell, where he would be teased to death. Poor Ana would never see him again. He'd be a no-show for their date because after his siblings finished with him, he'd be just a pile of humiliation and cotton, his clothes turned to burning shreds.

"Hah. They wish," he said aloud, waving at Luke as the light turned green. Luke followed him, which made him wonder what he was in for at home. Good thing he had to swing by Fixby Hills first.

A new text. Dad.

I grabbed the lumber. Just come home and we'll head out straight to Nordicbeth.

"Ugh," he muttered. It would be bad enough facing Kell and Dad, and likely Mom, too. They were probably all at home by now, Colleen with a bowl of popcorn the size of Kansas, Mom sitting with a pot of coffee and a cattle prod.

Had the last ninety minutes really happened?

Dreams never felt real, but this one *was*.

Skin buzzing, he let the happiness wash over him, months of torment melting away. Ana hadn't ghosted on him because she didn't like him.

She'd ghosted because of that sick, manipulative little dirtbag.

Mind racing, he thought of all the ways to find and punish that little piece of shit, but he would hold himself back.

For now.

Ana might have processed what happened and be at peace with it, but Dennis was anything *but*.

"Don't give him your energy, man," he said aloud, repeating one of Rafe's phrases. His buddy was smart and, like Dennis, a keen observer of humans, but less prone to rage at injustice. Not that Rafe didn't care. He did.

He just felt the unfairness with a little less sharpness. Rafe knew how to hold it at a distance to leave room for action.

Kissing Ana had felt like the world opened up to him, like his heart walked out from a dungeon into a fresh spring day after a sudden rain, the sun shining down on all the newly washed flowers, sending nothing but love throughout the land.

And he got to have more of her tomorrow.

The drive home also gave him a chance to think about what she'd said about loving Luview. Seriously? How could she like the cheesy town? All the excess he despised was what drew her to this place? Talk about opposites.

How could someone who fit into his heart so perfectly be so... *wrong*?

Everyone had at least one flaw. Ana certainly was showing him hers.

"Regroup." He shook his head hard, taking in deep breaths, fast and full, letting them out until he was empty. Nervous system resets were common in the field; he knew how to do it.

Ana had definitely triggered something in him.

Something *good*.

"She wants the full town treatment, man. Give it to her," he muttered as he drove the final miles back to the camp.

What would the perfect Love You, Maine date look like?

Red-foil chocolate hearts, of course.

A bouquet of red roses.

Dinner at a Love You restaurant. He'd have to see if Blake and Sheila had any tables available for tomorrow night at The Food Apothecary. Or did Ana like Indian food? Love You India didn't take reservations.

Worst case, there was Bilbee's. Although the thought of trying to have a romantic evening in that dump made him groan.

A walk around the hot springs, complete with touching the water at the same time.

"Gag me," he whispered, imagining his mother finding a nice red shirt he could borrow from Kell to round out the evening.

Maybe he should just get one of those heart costumes from Love You Chocolate and complete his humiliation.

Heart-shaped candy. Red roses. A great dinner on heart-shaped plates. The hot springs.

Done. He knew what to do next.

Turning onto the camp's dirt road that led to their driveway, he squinted, pulling the visor down as he drove. Sunshine on a weekend was lovely, and it made him think of gorgeous Ana in her sunshine-yellow dress, red flowers and adorable sneakers making him smile.

His heart swelled to three times its normal size.

As he parked, Luke pulled in next to him and climbed out of his cruiser, wearing that stupid red uniform.

"Hey there, Officer Ketchup Bottle."

Luke's mouth went flat. "*Scoundrel* is going to be a great nickname for you, Den."

"That was all cleared up on the common."

Luke's laughter turned to something braying, like a donkey, as Colleen came out from her cottage carrying an actual popcorn bowl.

"You think this mess has been cleared up?" Luke hooted. Ignoring him, Dennis walked into the big lodge. His home here was still rough, and the kitchen had yet to be outfitted properly. The commercial kitchen in the lodge was where almost everyone ate these days, anyway.

He needed caffeine. Now.

"DENNIS!" His mom was standing at the counter, chopping what definitely smelled like garlic.

Enough garlic to keep the entire camp vampire free.

"Yeah?" Unfortunately, the coffee pot was empty, so he quickly threw in a filter, some grounds, and water.

"Oh, goody. Coffee! I could use a nice cup. Let's sit outside and enjoy it. You can catch me up."

"Catch you up?"

Colleen appeared in the doorway, hip leaning on the frame, munching away. The big green plastic bowl she ate from was the one their mother always used for card game night.

"Yes, catch us up, dear brother!" she said in a mocking tone. "It's good to see the golden child fall so hard. And so publicly!"

"You think *I'm* the golden child?" Thank goodness Colleen gave him a deflection point.

"You're the one who got away! The only one Mom couldn't have nearby. Denny could do no wrong!"

"Denny did plenty wrong," he muttered, wishing he had a time machine so he could accelerate the coffee's brewing.

"Like knock up that woman."

"That woman has a name. Ana."

"Ah-na," Colleen said with unnecessary precision, "is the woman in red? The one Mom goes on and on about?"

"Mom. Stop."

"What?" Deanna moved to the large wash basin, washing her hands with foaming soap, then turning around to look at him as she dried them on a towel. "I told Colleen about your woman in red. Can you blame me?"

"Yes."

"So are you the baby daddy, or not?"

"Not. That was made very clear on the common today. Nobody needs to turn this into some nugget of hot gossip."

"Nugget? It's a boulder! An iceberg! A meteor!" Colleen said with great gusto.

"What? Why?"

"Why?" Deanna echoed as Luke appeared, mercifully changed into jeans and a t-shirt. Having a brother who walked around looking like a red wizard didn't set well with him.

"Yeah. Why?"

"Because you're so taciturn."

"And weird," Colleen added. "Don't forget the weird part."

"My business is *my* business."

All three of them laughed. His temper was starting to rise.

"Got a problem there, Scoundrel," Luke said as he crossed in front of Dennis and—damn him—took the first cup of coffee before it finished brewing. "Nadine Khouri was filming that."

"Yeah? So?"

"Problem is, Nadine didn't film *all* of it."

"Good for her. Maybe she realized it was a private conversation and not fit for public consumption."

His family was apparently part owl. Every single one of them hooted.

Loudly.

"Not exactly," Luke clarified. "She stopped at the part where Lucinda was beating you. Now she's showing it to everyone and they all think you poked a hole in the condom and got Ana pregnant on purpose."

His mother's face went somber. "Did that really happen? Some asshole really did that to her?"

Deanna Luview was not one to swear, so the impact of that curse word was huge. Luke's jaw dropped. Colleen stopped chewing.

And Dennis's body filled with gratitude.

"Yes. And it's private. No one else's business. Miss Lucinda should never have shouted that on the common."

"She thought you had done it, honey. She was horrified. So was I, for a split second."

"Why would you be horrified, Mom? Why would you ever entertain, for even a second, the idea that I would do something so shitty?"

"Uncle Denny!"

Everyone turned to find Harriet standing behind them, her face scrunched up in righteous indignation, Magic in her hands.

"You have to pay the swear box!"

Dennis's shoulders dropped in embarrassment as he fished in his front pocket for a dollar bill. "You're right. But Gamma said asshole, so she has to pay, too."

"TWO DOLLARS!" Harriet shouted to him, then turned her ire on her grandmother. "Gamma? Really? You can't say that word!"

"I said it about a really bad man, Harriet."

"Daddy takes care of bad people all day for his job and he doesn't come home and say those words."

"Not around you, kid," Dennis murmured near Luke, dropping two bucks in the clear acrylic container with the words SWEAR BOX written in a ten-year-old's handwriting.

It was pretty full.

"Okay. Good. Now—do you have my five dollars? Magic is healthy and good. I fed him and played with him and his leg is really coming along!"

Dennis found his wallet and gave her a five.

"Thank you. You're a great sugar glider babysitter."

"Can I do it again?"

"Babysit Magic?" The little beastie jumped onto Dennis's hand, then scrambled up his arm into his shirt pocket. "Sure."

"I'm saving up for something." She seemed suddenly nervous. "So, like, how much can I babysit him?"

"How much are you trying to earn?"

"Another thirty-five dollars."

He pretended that was a lot of money. Bending down, he got very serious, hand on her shoulder. Magic peeked out from his pocket.

"How about tomorrow night? Can you babysit him for, say, four or five hours?"

Magic decided that was too long to wait, leaping from Dennis's pocket to Harriet's head. Like a pro, she lifted her hand, the sugar glider folding himself between her fingers.

"See? I know how to take care of him!" she crowed.

Behind him, footsteps announced the arrival of his dad and brother.

"Whatcha doing tomorrow night?" Dean asked, leaning in to give Deanna a kiss.

"I have plans."

"A date?" his mom immediately asked. The sound of his sister's jaw loudly crunching more popcorn made him sigh.

"Plans."

"It's Ana, isn't it?" Deanna pursued. Dennis ignored everyone, grabbing a travel thermos and filling it with coffee.

"Equipment loaded?" he asked Dean, who nodded.

"We need water," Kell said, looking at Dennis with a grin. "Can you manage that, *Scoundrel*?"

Not wanting to give over any more of his money to the swear box, he let loose in his head but bit his tongue.

Then he decided to take control.

"Look. Everyone. I came back home for good. That doesn't mean I can't change my mind." His mom made a sound so high, it was like a deer whistle. Only he could hear it, but it was the sound of panic.

"I'm used to way more personal privacy than I get here. And the situation with Ana is complicated."

"She's pregnant with another man's child?" Kell asked in that way he had, where the question came from curiosity and not judgment.

"Yes."

"And you still want to date her?"

"Yes."

"When is she due?"

"In three and a half months."

"So if this lasts, you'll be dating a woman with a newborn."

"Assuming I'm that lucky, yes."

"Dennis," his mom interrupted, nodding her head for the gang to go outside. Bright sunshine made him squint a little, the fresh air deepening his resolve. He knew what he wanted.

And when he knew that, he always went for it. All in. One hundred percent.

No reservations, no second thoughts.

"Yeah?"

"You have that look."

"What look?"

Harriet set Magic down and played with him, their sweet interaction making him smile. He hadn't been here for her babyhood. Missed half her childhood already. What would it be like to be around a child from the day they were born?

Or... to help raise that child? Parent that child?

Be a father?

"The biological father isn't in the picture at all?"

"He shouldn't be. It's been taken care of."

"Sounds ominous," Luke said, his law enforcement background showing.

"That's Ana's story to tell. Not mine," Dennis said gruffly, protectiveness swelling in him.

"So there would be room for you to be this baby's father?" his mom asked, probing gently.

All eyes were on him now, except for Harriet, who was distracted by Magic. His parents, Luke, Kell, and Colleen all watched as he struggled to explain how he knew.

Just... *knew.*

Describing the indescribable was a form of madness.

How do you explain an instinct?

You don't.

"I don't expect any of you to understand this. I *do* expect you to respect my choices," he began.

It was Colleen who interrupted him, setting the popcorn bowl on a metal table and touching his arm.

"Dennis. Stop. You don't owe anyone a single word of explanation."

"I know that."

"What just happened on the common was a colossal mess. Huge gossip. Greta's must be buzzing right now, and Nadine is showing people only half the story. Be prepared for a lot of anger. People now think you intentionally knocked up Lucinda Armistead's grandniece and angered her so much that she slapped you in public. *That* is one compelling story, and it'll take a lot of work to set the story straight."

"I know. Which makes tomorrow night even harder."

"You mean your date?"

"Yeah."

"That's easy," Colleen said. "Just take her out of town."

"It's more complicated than that."

"Like... how?"

"She loves the town. *Loves* it. Has dreamed of having a romantic date in Love You, Maine ever since she was a teenager." He intentionally said the words *Love You, Maine* in a mocking tone, which he knew would piss off his mother.

"That is adorable! I like her more than I like you right now, Mr. Scoundrel," his mom replied, making him laugh.

"I don't give a rat's ass what people in town think of me. Ana and I talked it all through and we're going out on a date. The rest is just static."

"You've always been good at that, son." Dean came out of the kitchen carrying water bottles. "Finding what you want and tuning out the world."

"Served me well for more than twenty years."

"I think it's serving you even better now," his dad replied, adding a wink.

"I'm still stuck on the whole pregnant thing," Luke said as he took a sip of coffee, looking over at his cottage as if expecting Kylie to come out. She was off in Indiana, visiting her mother and attending a friend's wedding. Luke and Harriet couldn't go because of a problem with taking time off and a conflict with a Girl Scouts' camping trip.

Deanna had delivered her to the Manchester airport very early this morning, and now the rest of them had to deal with Brooding Luke for five days.

"What you are or are not stuck on doesn't matter to me," Dennis said, giving his dad an impatient nod.

"It really doesn't bother you?" Luke pushed.

"Should it?"

"It would bother most people," Kell said softly.

Dennis stopped mid-step, turning on his heel.

"If you met Rachel under the same circumstances, or Kylie," he said, giving Luke a pointed stare, "what would you do?"

"Aw, man," Kell said, swiping his hand through his dark hair. "That's not fair."

"Point taken," Luke replied in a clipped voice.

"Except," Kell noted, "we knew Rachel and Kylie before we reconnected with them."

"I knew Ana before today."

"For one night."

"That's all I needed."

"Really?" Dean, Deanna, Luke, and Kell all asked, loud enough to tear Harriet's attention away from her lovefest with Magic.

"Yeah. Really."

"Then it's settled," Dean said emphatically, giving Luke and Kell the glares they so richly deserved. Thanks to his dad, Dennis didn't have to do it. "Dennis lives his life however he wants, and we butt out of his life."

"A grandbaby!" Deanna said under her breath, making Dennis grit his teeth and practically bite his tongue not to respond.

It was easier just to head over to the big Luview Tree Service truck and climb in the driver's seat, hand reaching up to be thrown the keys.

"Hey!" Kell shouted, jogging behind him. "Who said you get to drive?"

"Me."

"I hate riding in the back."

"Then we can ride three in the front."

"That's even worse!"

"Kellan. Quit whining. You sound like the same age you were when I joined the Army."

"It's still not fair."

"You two!" Dean boomed. "I'll settle this." Opening the rear side door, he climbed into the back and stretched out in an exaggerated way. "I get the whole backseat to myself. Anyone have ear plugs?"

"For the chainsaws?"

"So I don't have to hear you two bicker. It's like going to a

Love Committee meeting with Anne Petrinelli on a tear about the Love You India sign."

Dennis and Kell groaned.

"We're not *that* bad," Kell replied, but he got in and shut the door, which was all Dennis wanted.

"You're worse," their dad said, then sat up and buckled in.

"We have two decades of bitching to get out of our systems with him," Kell pointed out. "There's a lot of pent-up need."

"If anyone has a lot of pent-up need, it's me," Dennis said, regretting the joke instantly.

"Not touching that with a ten-foot pole," Dean muttered, covering his face with a baseball cap and resting his head on the back of the seat.

Cranking up the radio, Dennis blasted WLUV, which they barely got out here. The signal would fade completely in ten minutes or so, but before that happened, they burned their ears listening to Rick Astley.

"You seriously rickrolled us, Dennis," Kell said in disgust, flipping off the switch before plugging in a USB port and his phone.

The B-69s came on.

"What in the hell is this?" Dean sat up straight. "This can't be the B-52s!"

"Better," Kell said with a grin. "A band that does covers of other bands in the B-52s style."

"This is so cool!"

"Dad thinks you're *cool*, Kellan."

"Shut up, Dennis."

Yeah.

He was home, all right.

Right back in the thick of things.

Chapter Eighteen

Ana

"How does the cake look, dear? He'll be here in ten minutes. I would bet that Dennis Luview is a prompt man. If he said he would be here at five, he will. I want to make sure the cake is appealing."

For the umpteenth time, Aunt Lucinda asked Ana her opinion of the chocolate cherry bundt cake, which looked like something Ana wanted to destroy singlehandedly with her bare hands, a pint of vanilla ice cream, and a brand new streaming comedy series.

But no. The cake was for Dennis.

Fine.

"It's fine, Auntie."

"I hope it's not overdone. Does it look a bit dark here, along this slope?"

"It looks perfect." Ana fought the urge to wipe saliva off the corner of her mouth.

"I feel terrible."

"You already apologized."

"I did, but that was an egregious error on my part."

"It's understandable. No one ever told you my–Harris's–name, the, you know..."

"The *real* scoundrel's name."

"Exactly."

"When Dennis marched up to you like that, so angry, so furious, asking you why you were there and pregnant with his baby, I do believe every protective instinct in me kicked in." Lucinda massaged her biceps. "Who knew I still have that kind of power in my arm? That poor boy. He must be in so much pain. Do you think I could have dislocated his jaw?"

Holding back a laugh, all she could do was pat Auntie's killer arm.

"I think we'd know by now."

"Ana would have noticed when she was kissing him yesterday," Brie added, entering the room with a glass of mint tea and a mischievous look.

Auntie's eyebrows shot up so high, they were nearly chandeliers.

"Kiss? You *kissed* Dennis Luview yesterday?"

"I did."

"Well, that was forward of him."

"I was just as forward, Auntie. It takes two to kiss, you know."

"Well. My goodness. My Donald always took the lead in matters of..." She paused, then whispered, "...*the flesh*."

Brie caught Ana's eye over the bundt cake, biting her lips to hold back a giggle.

"What was he like, courting you?" Brie asked, the old-fashioned word giving Ana a thrill.

Dressing up when you were nearly twenty-seven weeks pregnant was a little bit like being told you could wear either a black trash bag or a white trash bag. Of course, there's such a thing as cute maternity clothes, but it's just not the same. And she'd packed for a fun, relaxing weekend with Brie's great-aunt, not for a romantic night out with a guy who mattered.

Dennis *mattered*.

Was he courting her? This first date certainly felt old-fashioned, but in all the right ways.

"My Donald was the main reason I left my home in Sabbathday Lake, you know. So long ago. Such a sweet man." Her eyes went out of focus, clearly thinking back decades, long before Ana and Brie were born, before their parents had ever existed, to a time Ana imagined was simpler.

Same problems. Just... simpler.

"I was just eighteen. So young. So foolish and naive. I know so much more now, but if I could live my life all over again, I'd change very little."

"What would you change?" Ana pried, ever so gently.

"I wouldn't have waited with Donald. I made the poor man wait a year. That's a year of my life I wasted. A year of happiness and growth we could have shared."

"Oh!" Brie's hands went over her heart. Salty tears filled Ana's nose and the back of her throat.

"Auntie," Ana said through thick emotions. "That is so beautiful."

"I struggled. Oh, how I struggled!" Auntie's hands flew in the air, then came together, clapping lightly. The smile that stretched her wrinkled face was luminous. "I didn't want to leave Mama and my brother and sister. Donald was patient, but he was persistent, too." She batted her eyelashes. "He knew who he wanted. And he was right. I wish I had let him be right sooner. He's been gone for so long, but oh, what I would give for just one more day with him. One more hour. One more minute."

The top of Ana's shirt was now soaked with tears.

DING!

The doorbell startled all three of them, Lucinda the most, her hands flying in the air again but decidedly less graceful this time.

"Oh, goodness. Listen to me rambling like an old woman." Pulling herself up to full height, she touched her hair, then looked at Ana with alarm. "Your top!"

Brie sniffled as she studied Ana.

"You cried so much, it's like you're wearing a tear bib."

"I don't have anything else to wear!" Ana groaned. Luck meant she'd packed a red maternity t-shirt, stretchy and lightweight. Nothing else would really do for this date.

"It'll dry off." Brie looked at the front door. "Let's go upstairs and use a hair dryer on it."

While Lucinda answered the door, Brie and Ana made their way to the bathroom, where Brie grabbed a small hair dryer and turned it on low, pointing it at Ana's cleavage.

"Are you nervous?" Brie asked as she fluffed Ana's shirt, the two of them finding a way to get the water to evaporate faster.

"No. Should I be?"

"I don't know. This is awfully fast."

Ana reached for toilet paper to wipe her eyes.

"Auntie's story is gutting me. Donald's been gone for so long. How do you have that kind of love and then live the rest of your years alone?"

"Loads of women do it."

"It's not fair!"

"No, it's not. But I guess it's better than never finding it at all?"

The murmur of voices downstairs made her hope that Lucinda's apology wasn't too awful for Dennis. The old woman was deeply moral and was being so hard on herself. All day, Auntie had been systematically calling every person she knew in town to correct her error, hoping to shut down the Luview gossip mill.

She'd even called Deanna Luview. Ana could only imagine how *that* conversation had gone.

"Good enough," Ana said, the wet spot now vanquished. In the mirror, her reflection showed puffy eyes, but that was to be expected. Her face was rounder than normal, her breasts big and voluptuous. Pregnancy certainly took an average set of boobs and turned them into something lush.

"You look great," Brie declared. "Go get 'em."

"I already got him."

"You know what I mean."

"I don't."

"You're going to sleep with him tonight, right?"

"Uh... not here! At Auntie's house!"

"What about at his place?"

"He lives in a cottage at an old camp, surrounded by his entire extended family."

"Are they in a cult or something?"

"No."

"That's weird."

"Says the woman who works for her parents' cheese shop, along with all her siblings."

"We don't work there full time, and it's a family business!"

"Dennis works for his parents' tree service. So does his brother Kell."

"I thought he was retired military."

"He is."

"This is so confusing."

"Not for me."

With that, she descended the stairs, hoping her tears hadn't left salt stains on her shirt.

Dennis looked up from where he sat in Lucinda's parlor, a

half-eaten slice of chocolate cherry bundt cake on a dessert plate in front of him. He smiled.

"You're wearing red."

She noted his similarly colored shirt.

"You, too."

"My mom made me."

"Does your mother dress you all the time?"

"Only when I take beautiful ladies out for dates in Luview. Which means... this time."

Auntie winked at Ana.

"Dennis and I have resolved our misunderstanding."

"Miss Lucinda," he said, looking at the cake, "slap me around all you want if it means you make more of this delicious apology."

"Oh, you," Auntie said, delighted. "I'll make that for you any time."

A charmer, he was. Ana laughed at the sight, finishing her slow walk to the sofa, debating whether to sit or not. Getting up was getting harder these days, and not so graceful.

She stood, waiting.

"Ana, have a slice! Please," Auntie said, waving for her and Brie to sit.

"Dinner backwards?" Dennis offered. "Cake first, then our dinner at the restaurant."

"Followed by another dessert?" she asked, patting her belly.

They all laughed while Auntie cut more slices and poured tea.

For the next ten minutes, they were a group in bliss. Chocolate and cherry teased Ana's mouth, the relaxed companionship of people she cared about so fulfilling.

Dennis finished his slice and looked at Lucinda.

"That was the best cake I've ever had, Miss Lucinda. Thank you."

"You're flattering me," she said with a sly smile.

"It's not just flattery if it's true." Dennis leaned down and pulled a bouquet of red roses from the other side of his chair. He stood and walked over to Ana, who looked up at him, mouth still full of cake.

"Mmm!" she said as Lucinda smiled at her, then him, with approval.

"You wanted the Love You, Maine treatment, and you're going to get the full experience. I'm even dressing the part," he said, plucking his shirt. "We're not eating at a fine dining establishment, though. Hope that's okay."

Ana swallowed and quickly washed down her cake with some tea.

"Of course!"

As if the roses weren't enough, Dennis bent down again and produced an enormous bag of red foil hearts from Lucinda's store.

"Oh, my goodness!"

"You have excellent taste in chocolate, my boy," Auntie declared. She reached for the flowers. "Ana, let me put these in water and arrange them in a vase. Flowers this nice deserve good treatment."

"Dennis!" Ana said, standing slowly and reaching up for a hug, wishing they didn't have an audience. "Thank you!"

"Martin needs to step up," Brie said out of the corner of her mouth, making Ana laugh.

"Flowers, candy, and so much more." He smiled at her, then made a fake frown. "But I drew the line at wearing the heart costume."

"Got to save something for the bedroom," Brie muttered. If Ana were closer, she'd kick her ankle.

"Nice seeing you again, too, Brie," Dennis said, in a voice that made it clear he'd heard her perfectly. He turned to Ana. "Shall we?"

"Can't wait. Where to next?"

They said their goodbyes and walked to the driveway, Ana ignoring the movement of curtains at the window as Auntie peeked out, watching them.

"Not bringing the bag of candy with you?" Dennis teased as he pressed his hand on the small of her back. Her top had a tie there that she'd tightened earlier, hoping in vain to look... slim?

Impossible.

This really was not an ordinary date. So why pretend it was?

"Hah! Then I'd have to share," she shot back, making him laugh, a sound she adored. Serious on the surface, Dennis definitely had a softer side, light and funny. He hid it from the world. Getting him to reveal it to her was an honor.

"We'll make sure we have dessert. Are you a Hobbit, by any chance?"

"Huh?"

"A Hobbit. We can have second dessert instead of second breakfast."

"Oh, I'd love to be a Hobbit, then!"

As expected, he was a gentleman in every way, opening the passenger's side door for her. His truck was a beast, so high that she couldn't climb up easily. Dennis dropped to one knee and made a step for her foot from his hands.

"Grab the bar on the door."

"I never knew going for a drive could be so hard," she joked. "Thanks for the help."

"I was just looking for an excuse to look up your dress."

"So much for my gentleman theory!" She looked down at her leggings. "And I'm wearing pants!"

Laughing as he walked around to the driver's side, Dennis jumped in and started the truck. "We have two options tonight. Indian food or pub fare."

"Yes."

"Yes to which one?"

Her pregnant stomach growled. "Just… yes."

His deep chuckle filled her heart even more.

"I like your direct approach to food. Are you this way when you're not single-handedly building an entire human being from scratch with your body?"

"No," she said honestly. "I mean, I like going out. Trying new foods. But pregnancy appetite is nothing like regular appetite."

"I haven't been to Love You India since I've been home. If we go to Bilbee's, my cousins will tease me and interrupt us constantly. I know Meera and Davi on just a casual level. We've traded hellos and that's it."

"And if we go to Bilbee's…"

"Let's just say I'm already stuck with the nickname Scoundrel. The chef will probably spell it out in french fries on a plate."

"Chicken tikka masala it is."

A grateful smile came from him, his eyes quick to go back to the road.

"How are you doing?" he asked.

"Me?"

"Yeah."

"I'm fine."

"Ana. We don't need that. I mean, how are you really doing?"

"Are you always this direct?"

"Yes."

"Okay, then. You want reality?"

"I asked for it."

"My underpants are doubling as butt floss right now, I need water, and since you mentioned Indian food, if I don't have a samosa in front of me in thirty minutes, I might turn into an outraged Auntie Lucinda and slap someone."

"We can't have any samosa battery going on, so let's hurry." He hit the accelerator.

"What about you?" she asked, enjoying the view. His forearms were bare below the short sleeves, muscles running in parallel waves, corded and tight.

"My underwear fits just fine."

"Oh, geez. Was that a little too real?"

"I was mostly asking how it's going, staying with Miss Lucinda, but you gave me your own version of direct."

"Oh!" She sighed, laughing a bit at the end. "I feel guilty. We came here for Brie's wedding and I became the center of attention."

"Oof. That's my fault."

"It's not about casting blame."

"I didn't say blame. I said *fault*. There's a difference."

"Most people don't realize there's a difference."

"As you know, I'm not–"

"–most people," they finished in unison, then fell silent.

Lucinda lived in an old colonial house about three minutes from town, and they reached downtown fairly quickly. Ana was anticipating the big Love You, Maine sign and let out a soft laugh when it came into view.

"Every time I see that sign, I get so excited."

"You do? Why?"

"Because it reminds me of my father–he always pointed it out to me."

"Your father?"

"Until he died, we came up here every year. Brie's parents and my parents were friends."

"And that's how you know Lucinda."

"Yep! Brie and her siblings called her Auntie, and she told me I should as well."

"You stopped coming when he died? When you were thirteen?"

"My mom and stepfather didn't continue coming. Brie's family brought me up once a year, in the summer."

"Nice."

"Yeah. Only-child syndrome. Coming here made me feel included."

"Your mom didn't just bring you and do the family thing? For continuity?"

"That's a twisty story. Mom was having an affair with my stepfather."

"Right. The reason she wasn't on the plane." He squeezed her hand as he turned into a small parking lot, finding a spot fairly close to the restaurant.

"Yes. And Hugh and Dad were close."

"Hugh is Brie's father?"

"Exactly."

"That *is* twisty."

"Sure is. Nothing like your family, right? Your parents look like they've been in love for decades. Like birds chirped and the sun sighed and Cupid shot them both with a chocolate arrow and they found true love instantly."

"Have you been spying on them since before you were born? Because yes to all of that."

"Must have been wonderful growing up."

"How so?"

"My mom and dad were in love when I was little. Dad worked constantly—the trips here were one of the only family vacations. Obviously, their marriage fell apart, but I didn't know it or see it." She paused, then added. "And Mom and Rick—they aren't demonstrative. Dad was."

He put the truck in park, killed the engine, and turned to her, reaching to touch her cheek with his fingers.

"You're amazing."

"I am?"

"So open."

"You, too."

He let out a disbelieving laugh.

"Open is the opposite of what I usually am. You, though–you change me."

"That's a tiny red flag right there, buddy."

"It is? Are you wearing your therapist hat now?"

"A little. I don't change you. You choose to reveal a part of yourself with me. A part that maybe other people don't deserve to see."

His head snapped back, hand dropping to hold hers.

"Not so sure about the word deserve."

"Really? What word would you use?"

"I spent more than two decades rescuing people for a living. Serving my country. Being unable to be open about much of anything. Only my team could know anything about my life."

"Were you able to talk about your emotions with them? Process experiences?"

"Sure. We were debriefed."

"Dennis." Her fingers moved to those deeply grooved, strong arms. "I'm not talking about debriefings. Those are transactional. I'm talking about processing emotion. Or trauma."

"Sometimes. The army had therapists. We went for the exact number of sessions required. Anything more was viewed as unstable."

Ana let out a ragged sigh.

"Don't blame me. I'm just the messenger."

"I am honored that you're so open with me."

"Same here, Butt Floss Lady." His hand migrated up her thigh, coming to rest on her hip. When she looked down, she couldn't help but see her enormous belly.

Little Bean added a kick for good measure.

"Can we talk about the elephant in the truck cab?"

"Go ahead."

"It's me." She patted her belly. "*I'm* the elephant."

"You are the prettiest pachyderm I've ever kissed."

"You've kissed other pachyderms?"

"Only once. At an animal sanctuary." As his words turned to a hush, he leaned over the console, his lips finding hers for the briefest of brushes before–

BEEEEEEEEP!!

Dennis jolted so hard, he hit the top of his head on the rear-view mirror, letting out a grunt and pivoting quickly to stare at the offender.

It was a woman in what looked like a perfectly maintained 1990s Ford Taurus. A very old woman with bright red hair, the color of a clown's. The corners of her mouth were turned down and she held her fist out the window.

"DENNIS LUVIEW! HOW *COULD* YOU?" she screamed.

Dennis gripped the steering wheel, ready to start the truck and peel on out of there.

"Oh, hell. It's Nadine."

"Who's Nadine?"

"Police department admin. Older than dirt. Works with my brother."

"Your brother, the police officer? The one who looks like a walking red Twizzler?"

Dennis rubbed the top of his head. "Yeah. Luke. He's actually police chief. And speak of the devil..."

Just behind Nadine, the Pepto-Bismol-colored cruiser pulled in. Ana recognized Luke from the other day, dressed in red with a black belt and shoes.

"That *is* your brother! I saw him yesterday–you look like him."

"I'm older. He's the one who looks like me," Dennis grumbled.

Nadine was struggling to get out of her car, her arm twisted in her seat belt. The difficulty seemed to fuel her anger, and when she finally extracted herself, it was with Luke's help.

Dennis climbed out of the truck, leaving Ana to wonder if she should wait for him or just jump down without a parachute. Of course, he walked around, opening her door as Nadine shouted, "Honey? You don't have to stay with him! What he did to you was criminal!"

Dennis's face went blank with fury as he reached up and effortlessly lifted her from the cab to the ground. She felt like a pillow he was lifting off a high shelf.

The man was strong.

"Nadine," Luke began, "Dennis did nothing wrong."

"He—you heard Lucinda!" She waved a phone in her hand. "I caught it *alllllll* on tape!" A smug grin turned to a grimace as she sneered at Dennis. "Showed it to everyone in town, too. You can't get away with this, you *scoundrel!*"

Luke's eye twinkled again as he looked at Dennis, then shifted into professional mode.

"You didn't stay for the rest of that argument on the common yesterday, did you, Nadine?" Luke said calmly, knowing the answer.

"There was no more! I trust Lucinda Armistead more than him!"

"Did she call you last night? Or earlier today?"

"Um." Nadine's face wobbled with uncertainty. "She—there was a message left on my recording machine."

"You mean your voicemail," Luke followed up.

Nadine waved the smartphone. "Whatever. I can't understand how to make those messages play on this silly phone!"

Luke shot Dennis a look. "Here. Hand it to me. I'll help you."

Doing as told, she gave Luke the phone, but took three steps closer to Dennis, wagging finger at the ready, two feet from his nose.

"Annabeth dodged a scoundrel with you, didn't she?"

Luke tapped her screen and said, "As much as I love watching my brother get dragged, Nadine, you're about to eat crow."

"What?"

Luke hit play.

"Nadine? This is Lucinda Armistead, calling to right a terrible wrong I caused earlier today. Dennis Luview is innocent. That baby is not his. I misunderstood and take full responsibility for maligning a perfectly good man's reputation. I am calling everyone I know in Luview to correct my mistake, and hope that you'll take my words at face value and stop talking about him in a negative light. We all know how much you love gossip-"

Nadine let out a sharp inhale of offense.

"-and especially juicy gossip. But please do not start problems at Greta's, or church, or the library, or any of your haunts. Thank you kindly."

The message ended.

"Oh dear. *Oh dear oh dear oh dear.*" Nadine's hands shook.

Luke looked at the phone before handing it back.

"She left that message about thirty minutes after the scene on the common. How long have you been spreading that video?"

Horror filled her face and her eyes darted everywhere.

"Well, one of the Forsythe boys has this popular Ticky-Tocky channel and he asked me for it, so..."

Dennis just cleared his throat as Ana tried to assess the situation. Nadine seemed to be someone of importance in the town. The admin at the police department, Dennis said? The town gossip? Whatever her importance was, Dennis and Luke were working on showing her she'd spread false information, and now she'd have to correct that.

Ana smiled and said to her, "Everyone makes mistakes, Ms..."

"Nadine. Nadine Khouri."

"Ms. Khouri."

"And you're Ana?" Her eyes went to Ana's belly.

"I am. And just to be clear, Dennis isn't this baby's biological father. I'm not hanging out with Dennis out of coercion."

"Then what are you two doing together?"

Luke grinned at her. "They're going out on their first date!"

Dennis looked like he was going to murder his brother. The police chief.

Nadine looked at Ana, who maintained composure.

"You're dating him? Now?"

"Yes."

"What about the baby's father?"

"I'm not dating him."

Nadine looked at Ana's left hand. "No ring," she said flatly.

Ana reached for Dennis's hand, threading her fingers very intentionally through his and keeping a polite smile on her face even as her bladder began singing an aria.

"Dennis, I do believe we're late for dinner." She caught Luke's eye. "Nice to meet you officially, Officer Luview."

"That's *Chief* Luview," Nadine sniffed.

"*Chief* Luview." She smiled at Luke. "I hope to get to know you better."

"My word! Are you going after him, too? And carrying another man's baby!" Nadine huffed.

"NADINE!" Both men chewed her out instantly, giving

Ana a window into how Dean Luview must have sounded when he disciplined his kids.

"What?" Defensive now, she looked more bewildered than dangerous. "I'm just confused."

"I'm married. You know that," Luke chided her.

"And I'm just sick of being the object of gossip," Dennis growled.

Ana quickly calculated the social and psychological landscape before her. Nadine was all bark and no bite, but she clearly had standing in the tiny community. If Aunt Lucinda had called her, she mattered here.

Which meant that Ana wanted to be on her good side, because she intended to be around Luview, Maine for a long time.

A very long time, if things went right with Dennis.

"Mrs. Khouri," she began. "You heard what Lucinda said about Dennis, yes?"

"Of course."

"It's all true, but it's true about another man."

"Including the..." she looked around furtively, "...the condom part?"

"Yes."

Eyes going wide, Nadine's whole countenance changed.

"And," Ana added, controlling the frame of this conversation, "I'm a bit embarrassed by all the attention. I'm trying to move on in my life. Find happiness. Prepare for single motherhood. Dennis and I have a happy past together and we're reacquainting ourselves. I'm sure you understand. You seem to be very insightful when it comes to the human condition."

Luke looked like he was about to gag.

"I most definitely am!" Nadine said, clearly susceptible to flattery. Ana wasn't being disingenuous. She could tell that the old woman wanted attention, and used gossip to get it.

Why not give her positive attention that didn't involve brokering other people's foibles?

"Then I'm sure you understand what it's like to stumble in life and work hard to get back up. Find some joy. Move forward."

"If anyone understands that, my dear, it's me." Nadine looked at Dennis. "I apologize. I came in heated and should have thought it through."

Behind her, Luke's jaw dropped open. He looked like a cartoon character.

"Now, let me move my car and stop being a nuisance!" Nadine giggled. "Have fun going out to dinner. You're having Indian?"

"Yes," Ana said. "And I'm starving!"

Grimacing, Nadine stuck out her tongue. "I can't stand that stuff. But I do like Korean!"

"Good for you!" Dennis said in a super-fake voice that made Ana want to smack him.

But it worked. Nadine pulled away, all waves.

Luke looked at her like she had just turned water into wine.

"I see why Dennis is so taken with you. You just charmed Nadine. Annabeth's mother."

"Who is Annabeth?"

Both men laughed through their noses.

"She's been hitting on me since I got home," Dennis explained, looking at her like he expected a jealous response.

"Ah."

"For you to get Nadine to like you took some skill."

"I'm a therapist," she told Luke, who shot Dennis a glare.

"You never told us that," he said in an accusing voice.

"Why would I?"

"You're going to have a field day analyzing our family," Luke told her.

"I'm off the clock in my personal life," she replied, using a well-worn phrase for moments like this.

Luke shut his eyes and rubbed his forehead, then gave her a sheepish smile.

"Sorry. What I said is like when people find out I'm a cop and say, 'Hope I haven't done anything I could get arrested for, har har.'"

"Yep, you sounded that stupid, little bro," Dennis said, deadpan. "Great job."

"Feed that meter or I'll give you a parking ticket," was all Luke could come back with. Taking him at his word, Ana walked over to the meter, which adorably accepted change, and put thirty minutes' worth in. Meters stopped charging at six.

"Bye, Luke. Go find a hot dog and some mustard and start a band."

Luke's reply was decidedly off-color. Dennis took her hand and walked them quickly toward Love You India.

"Is it always like this?" she asked.

"Intrusive? Inappropriate? The amplification of tiny details into major drama? Yes, yes, and yes."

"Okay, then."

As they approached the door to the restaurant, she smelled coriander and cumin, which wiped away the last few minutes of strangeness. The scent reminded her of Cambridge and all the great meals she'd had at Nirvana, an Indian restaurant there. But they didn't have red heart plates, or heart-shaped water glasses.

Or elephant statues with red hearts painted on the sides.

"Hello! Dennis!" A woman in black pants and a white shirt, her thick hair in a braid, met them with menus. "So good to see you."

"Hi, Davi. Two for dinner."

Davi's eyes dropped to Ana's belly. "We have a dinner buffet tonight, if you're interested."

Dennis gestured for Ana to go first, the word *buffet* looping in her head like a chant that morphed into a craving. On the way to their table, they walked past steaming dishes, all promising to taste divine.

When they sat down, she looked at Dennis, and: "Buffet," they said together.

Davi laughed. "Perfect. Something to drink?"

"Water," Ana said, and Dennis ordered water and a chai drink.

"Huh," he said, reaching across the table for her hand. "We definitely made the right choice."

"That buffet!"

"Sure. But I also realized just now that taking you to a bar probably wouldn't be much fun."

"Why?"

He looked at her waist.

"Oh! Right. I can't drink. But I play a mean game of darts."

"Don't tell Kell. He'll make us go to Bilbee's and play."

"I'd like that," she said softly, letting the reality of their attraction roll out in real time.

"Me, too."

"Next date?" she asked.

Chapter Nineteen

Dennis

A vision of the next fifty years of his life shot through him like a comet streaking to hit Earth.

Ana. Love. Baby. Marriage. Living together. Having more kids. Sharing a life here in Luview.

Or—elsewhere?

Growing old. Growing together.

Growing a life.

"You're officially invited on another date at Bilbee's. My siblings hang out there a lot. They claim a big table and harass all the other customers with terrible pool techniques and dart skills that put out eyes."

"Really?"

"Keeps the local medical center in business."

"You Luviews have some very unique abilities."

"We're special."

"I can see that."

Davi appeared with a pitcher of water and two large dinner plates. As she poured, she nodded toward the buffet.

"Fresh tray of pakoras just went out."

Ana was on her feet before Dennis could blink. As someone with a fast metabolism and a steady state of hunger, he understood wanting to eat.

But he'd never been pregnant.

No comparison.

What did it feel like, he wondered, as they selected their food, Ana *oohing* and *ahhing* over various dishes and sauces, eventually running out of room on her plate and returning to the table before he was ready. Did the baby roll around inside her like water in a balloon?

How did all that movement feel? When the baby kicked, did she get muscle spasms? Where did her organs relocate to? Her body really had changed since he met her in January.

So full.

So lush.

And so maternal.

Round in all the right places, rounder where the baby grew. A pang of sadness hit him out of nowhere as he finished spooning aloo gobi onto his rice.

He wished he'd been there from the start to watch her change. Feel her body as it shifted. Be there for her every step of the way.

By the time he returned to the booth, she was a quarter through her plate, a big grin on her face as he sat.

"I couldn't wait, I'm sorry—the food is amazing! Even better than my favorite place in Cambridge."

"You'll have to bring me there sometime."

"No way! I said this is *better*."

"Then we'll just have to come back here."

"Promise?"

"If I say it, I do it."

That made her pause, her fork in midair, her head tilting slightly.

"I've noticed."

"Good."

"We're both talking about more dates."

"We are."

"Dennis?" She set her fork down and watched him.

"Yes?"

"This is different, isn't it?"

The instinct to leap across the table and kiss her was hard to resist. He'd have to settle for holding her hand.

"Yes. It is. You feel it, too, don't you?"

"I do. I've... I've read about people like–like us. The whole just..."

"Knowing?"

"Yes."

"It feels right."

"It feels weird, too. Right and weird."

"But weird in a good way, right?"

"Weird in all the best ways."

"I wouldn't use those exact words, but yes. Same here."

"Then, in some ways, this is all just a formality," she said, letting go of his hand and picking up her fork, happily chomping away while he watched her, bewildered now.

"Formality?"

"I don't have to wonder," she said, cutting into a pakora, which she dipped in mint sauce. "We're together. And that's that."

Now he wanted to jump across the table, scoop her up in his arms, and run away to their own private island where they could hide away forever.

Instead, he picked up his fork, speared a piece of chicken, and said, "I've done it. I've actually done it."

"Done what?"

"Found someone as direct as I am."

"Maybe?"

"What do you mean, *maybe?*"

"I think I'm following your lead."

"My lead?"

"This," she said, gesturing to her pregnant belly, "is anything but normal."

"We already covered that. You don't need to keep bringing it up as if it's–"

"I know. I'm not. I'm stating a fact so I can move on to a deeper point."

Another piece of him fell for her with those words.

"You're a no-bullshit kind of guy. Very cut and dried. You see the world in black and white mostly, but in gray when needed."

"Yes."

"My entire world is gray."

"Oof."

"Right. It has to be. I'm a therapist. People aren't checkboxes. They have conflicting feelings, overlapping struggles, joys that can be sorrows at times, and they're messy. *I'm* messy. People are messy."

"Of course they are," he said, taking a bite, watching her.

"I love working with my patients. I like learning about people. Figuring out what makes them unique. Finding a way to help them see something through a different lens. I learn so much from them, too."

"You work part-time, right?"

"I do. I've had a few students leave me."

"You work with college students?"

"I work with a variety of people. Mostly older teens and women in their fifties."

"Interesting split."

"It is. But I'm not taking new patients. I'm down to only eleven now."

"Why? Because of the baby?"

"Yes. I'll take a four-month maternity leave, then go back to the office two days a week. Two of my clients want to switch to virtual, so that will make it easier."

"When do you go on maternity leave?"

"At thirty weeks."

"Isn't that early?"

"I'll likely have a c-section at thirty-two weeks."

"Whoa. You said you're at twenty-seven now?"

She nodded. He did the math, fast.

"That's only five more weeks!"

Her left hand drifted to her belly as she used the other to put more food in her mouth. She nodded again.

He reeled.

Five weeks? He had only *five more weeks* to get to know her before she had her baby? Before she had abdominal surgery and an infant to take care of?

"I guess we'll have to spend as much time together as we can before the baby's born, then," he said. "And after, of course."

She made a strange face and took a sip of water.

"What's that face for?"

"Um, well... two of those weeks are taken."

"Taken?"

"My mother scheduled a special trip for us. Our last hurrah, she calls it. We'll be in New York and D.C. Train travel. No flying for me."

"What?"

"She has tickets for every Broadway show you could imagine. Some gallery openings. Shopping trips. You know."

"Two weeks? Forty percent of what's left?"

Ana's eyes flared. "I don't turn into a pumpkin after the baby is born."

"No, no–of course not. Sorry."

She ate while he thought, trying to calm his racing brain. Her wan smile made him feel like he'd screwed up.

"Cards on the table, Ana: I want more of you. And once you have the baby, everything in your life changes. I respect that very much. Your focus will be on your son. I understand that. Your priority needs to be him. But I want to be a part of your life, too."

"I have room for both." The way she blinked, looking away, made fear spike through his spine.

"So do I."

"What do you mean?"

"Room for you and the baby."

"Have you–do you want kids?" She smiled and pointed at her stomach. "Because I'm a package deal."

"That's what I'm trying to say, Ana–"

A squeal, the kind from a small child being chased during play, ripped through the air, Davi's little boy running down the length of the booths. He couldn't have been more than four. As he laughed again, looking behind him as if being pursued, he tripped and flew through the air, arms outstretched like Superman for a split second before landing on the carpet.

And letting out a huge wail.

Ice water shot through Dennis's entire body at the same time his heart rate zoomed, the contradiction freezing him in place, the ringing in his ears so overpowering, he lost vision.

Ana turned to watch while Meera scooped the boy up and comforted him, but Dennis was worlds away.

An ocean away, with sand in his hair, his body in fire, the sound of bullets whizzing past him as if they took off pieces of his ear with each shot.

"Dennis?" Ana asked from underwater, her voice muffled and thick. Licking his lips, he felt parched, his tongue the size of a cow, his body nothing but flesh-covered air.

"Dennis," she whispered more intently, her hand going across the table to touch his. The shock of connection made him twitch, every inch of skin a raw nerve, his chest tight.

A sense of shame drove every electrical impulse that kept his body going.

Using her whole hand, she began brushing the back of his, going up his forearm, the touch making his legs tingle, shins like armies of ants, his throat an impenetrable door.

"It's okay. You're here with me. You can breathe," she told him, but could he? How? He was moving in quarter time, back in the heat across the world, the little boy's screams cut off suddenly as–

The squeeze she gave his forearm was hard, firm, the kind you administer more as medicine than as caring. Like a slap, it pulled him out of his flashback and into the present.

Barely.

Her eyes were like gemstones as he caught her gaze, his brain shrinking back from what he saw, his body in two places at once.

There and Not There.

"Take a sip of your tea," she commanded, sliding out of the booth with effort, reaching for the mug and pressing it into his open hand. The order, perfectly worded, got through the trance he was in.

He did as told.

Drinking the tepid tea fit a pattern he knew well. His fingers, arm, lips, and throat worked through muscle memory, and that was enough to help the ringing abate, the fear to crawl back into a tiny cave inside him, the shame to wash off.

Sort of.

"There you are," she said, moving into his side of the

booth, so calm, so peaceful. "How about I sit here next to you? We can be one of those annoyingly romantic couples. If my neck starts to ache, I'll go back to my original seat."

Her words were calculated, meant to soothe as much as to engage him, not just to distract him from the inner horror he was living but to rewire what he saw in his mind's eye.

It was one thing to understand PTSD intellectually, which he did–in full–and another to know how to use techniques to lessen it.

And leave the patient better equipped to reduce its grip in the future.

"Thank you," he said, hoarse now, emotion living at the base of his throat.

"You did that in January."

"Yeah."

"Happen a lot?"

"Only around small kids who get hurt."

"Want to talk about it?"

"No."

"Okay. Could you slide my plate and drink over here?"

"You don't have to sit so close." Her hip rested against his, their thighs a perfect seam.

"I want to."

"Ana."

"Dennis." She matched his tone, and something in him lifted.

"I'm never going to get away with having walls with you, am I?"

"If we do this right, you'll never need them."

A blindingly beautiful smile from her made him reach forward a few inches and kiss her cheek with a sweetness that nearly burst his heart.

"See why I was whining about only having five weeks

left?" he said as they continued to eat. Sitting next to her was weird, but it worked.

The flashback faded.

"Did it occur to you that I might feel the same way?"

"Good. Then when is our next date?"

"I chose this one, and it's not even over yet. You choose the next one."

"Fair enough. Your place. Overnight. I'll bring a bag. I'll leave Magic at home with Harriet."

"Magic?"

"My pet. I'm a foster dad to it."

"Dog?"

"Sugar glider."

"What on earth is a sugar glider?"

Oh, boy. Explaining this was going to get complicated. Fast.

"DENNIS!"

The bellowing man was none other than Jake Forsythe, aka Slicer, the guy Colleen dated exactly three times, and who nearly cut off his dick with a hedge trimmer.

And blamed Colleen's old, stupid curse for it.

"Hey, Slicer." At the mention of his nickname, Jake turned red and scowled, while Ana's eyebrows rose.

"Slicer?"

"I'll explain later."

"This the woman you knocked up on purpose and left? Sorry, ma'am," Jake added, lifting his pink Love You Cupids hat in a sign of half-way respect. "But you don't have to stay with him. Guy who does what he did to you isn't worth it."

Davi appeared at the hostess stand with a big brown bag filled with takeout, her head pinging back and forth between Jake and Dennis.

"Don't make a scene in my restaurant, Slicer. Please," she murmured.

"It's Jake," he said loudly.

Normally an even-keeled guy, Jake had a deep sense of injustice and a mouth that went along with it. The type to shoot first and read the instructions later, his heart was in the right place, but Dennis's temper was rising again.

Shouting in the middle of the dining room at Love You India wasn't helping matters.

"Can you just ignore him?" Ana asked, taking a bite and acting like nothing was happening.

"Nah. If he thinks what Nadine thought, he's right to be pissed at me. Better to correct the record."

"Then go! While you're fixing your maligned reputation, I'll hit the buffet again and get more samosa."

"I love how you have my best interests at heart." On purpose, knowing he had an audience, he gave Ana a quick peck on the lips.

She tasted like cardamom and mint.

The stroll to the hostess stand gave Dennis a chance to take some deep breaths. Still dysregulated from the flashback, he could hear a child crying, though calming down, in the back of the restaurant. Slicer's timing was awful.

"Hey, Jake," he said. "You don't know the whole story."

"Guys who treat women like shit always say that."

"And people who make wild assumptions look like the idiots they are."

"You calling me an idiot?"

"Maybe when you had that hedge trimmer accident you shaved off some brain cells along with part of your sac."

"I–"

"Dennis!" The last person he expected to chirp in his ear was his sister, Colleen. Formerly nicknamed Third Date Colleen, she'd lived under a curse in Luview for years: Every guy she dated ended up in the emergency room where she worked as a nurse.

Right after the third date.

But Jake Forsythe was unique. Claiming the curse was b.s., he'd gone on a third date with her. Shortly thereafter, he fell off a ladder while trimming hedges and nearly trimmed off his own...

Tallywhacker.

"What are *you* doing here?" Jake snarled at Colleen.

"Getting Indian food. Just like you." Colleen smiled at Davi as she reappeared with a second bag, handing it over to Colleen. "I overheard Dennis talking to our mom about eating here and had a hankering."

"Hmph."

"Jake here was just insulting me for impregnating Ana against her will, then leaving her."

A set of out-of-town diners behind them came up short, obviously eavesdropping.

"But we all know that's not true," Colleen said fiercely to Jake. "Are you spreading that old lie?"

"Old? It happened *yesterday*."

"In gossip terms, yesterday is like 2003. Didn't Lucinda call you guys?"

"Why would Lucinda call *us*?"

"She's calling everyone in town to correct the story," Colleen said impatiently. "Did you slice off part of your brain when you fell?"

"Don't you dare make fun of me for that accident. That was your fault!"

"See? Spreading more misinformation."

Underneath it all, Jake was a good guy, so Dennis had to give him more of what Ana had called the "gray" in this mess.

"Jake, I am not the baby's father."

"You're not?"

"He's not!" Ana called out from across the restaurant, turning more heads.

"Then why are you on a date with him?" Jake called back.

Apparently, they were doing this with shouting.

"Because I really like him!"

A collective *awwwwwww* sounded through the dining room.

"And you're not suffering from that—what's it called? Oslo Syndrome?"

"Stockholm Syndrome?" Ana called back.

"Yeah."

"Did you know that Stockholm Syndrome is actually not what most people think it is?" Ana said, lumbering out of the booth, carrying a piece of naan bread she munched on calmly. "People think it means you fall in love with your captors in a hostage situation because you over-identify with them. But in fact, in the bank robbery that the term is based on, one of the women—"

"Ah, geez," Jake groaned, looking at his phone. "Look at the time! I'm late. Gotta run. Glad you're all—whatever you are."

"Stay weird, Slicer!" Colleen called out. She shrugged, picked up her bag, and left quickly.

"What was all that about?" Davi asked, watching them climb into their respective cars on opposite sides of the parking lot.

"Do you really want to know?" Dennis grunted.

"No."

Ana and Dennis made their way back to the table, where they looked at their food, then each other.

"Does this happen a lot? Your siblings serially save you from people maligning your reputation?"

"No."

"Then I'm special."

"Of course you are."

"What do you have planned next for us?"

"A bookstore trip, then the hot springs."

Meera appeared with more water. "Mo closed early tonight, Dennis. Off to some Grateful Dead tribute concert in southern New Hampshire."

"Damn. Hot springs is next, then, I guess."

"Are you going to ask me to touch the water at the same time as you?"

"Of course."

"That means true love. We're magically meant for each other."

What he wanted to say was, *I don't need to touch the water to know that*, but as direct and open as they were with each other, some part of him held back.

He had to save *something* for the second date.

Her plate was full again, or perhaps this was a new plate. The two of them were silent as they ate, simply enjoying themselves, taking time as it came to them.

"I think I'm full," Ana finally declared after a huge bowl of rice pudding.

"We can stay as long as you need to be sated."

"I've discovered that if I have enough time, I can just keep eating. It's remarkable. Everything that I thought I knew about biology or my own body's lived experience has become ancient history. Little Bean is in charge now. If he wants cumin, he gets cumin."

Dennis waved for the check.

"Excellent."

"I do need a long walk. My poor calves feel like cinder blocks."

"Piggyback ride?"

"I'm not sure where I'd put my belly."

Davi appeared with the check and Ana reached for it, but Dennis had better reflexes.

"You cannot keep buying me stuff," she protested. "Candy, flowers, now dinner? Let me treat you."

"You can cover it when I come to Newburyport."

"So you were serious earlier–wait, don't even answer that. I need to stop using those qualifiers."

"Yes. You do. When do you go to New York and D.C. with your mom?"

"We leave next Friday."

"How about I come to see you Thursday?"

"Can't. I have patients."

"Then I'll have to wait until you're back from your trip," he said, their fate sealed.

"We come back on a Thursday. How about that Friday? Spend the night?"

"You can show me all the sights in Newburyport."

"I can show you the ocean, my condo, and Brie's family's cheese shop."

"It's a date."

Bill settled, they made their way out. Davi's little boy, fully recovered now, was carefully re-arranging packs of matches in a big fishbowl by the register. Dennis tried to say good-bye to Davi and Meera, but neither were visible.

The little boy waved to him and Ana.

"Over there," Dennis said, pointing to the small building where the entrance to the Love You Hot Springs was located. "Let's go where the shore's nice and easy."

"Maybe I'll wade in and soak my feet," she said as they walked along, holding hands. The sun was just starting to set, that lazy light making him slow down, breathe easier, the world aligned perfectly.

"Sounds good."

"Want to talk about it?"

"Talk about what?"

"What happened back there?"

"Slicer? Oh–it's a long story involving my sister and her curse."

"Um, that's not what I meant, but put a pin in that, because eventually I have to hear how your sister is cursed. I meant your flashback."

"I do not want to talk about it."

"No problem."

Walking in silence across the road, they let the uneasiness of that interaction loosen in the air. When they reached the entrance to the hot springs, Dennis stopped, took both her hands in his, and said, "I will. Sometime. But thank you."

"Any time."

"Hate to say it, but there will definitely be another time."

She squeezed his hands. "I hope I'm there."

Thankfully, the people at the shoreline weren't folks he recognized, a rare moment living in his hometown. Tourists loved the springs, and the weekend crowd right now was all out-of-towners. As promised, Ana slipped off her sandals and marched right into the water, gasping as the heat reached her ankles.

"Oh! This feels so good."

He wanted to make her feel good, too. Preferably in a bed, away from prying eyes.

Instead, he sat down, took off his shoes and socks, rolled up his pants, and joined her, neatly setting his shoes next to hers under the bench.

She was right. Warm and enveloping, the water hit just so, transporting him out of his head and into his body. They held hands and she looked up at him.

"Is the legend true? The one your great-great–how many greats?"

"A lot."

"Great-something-grandfather started? When two people touch the water at the same time, magic happens?"

"Actually, he said you'd find love," Dennis corrected her, pulling her into his arms, the kiss all he needed right now. Not air. Not water. Not light.

Nothing but *her*.

Their kiss sealed a deal, unspoken yet felt, one that said this was it. They'd completed the journey. Found their person.

They could rest now.

What others thought didn't matter. Other people's expectations were of no consequence. Ana was warm and sweet in his arms but tough as nails, perceptive, her life in the gray areas one that gave him shades of existence, too.

His tongue parted her lips ever so slightly, their kiss more modest than he wanted but they were in public, and even he had some semblance of decency left in him.

Not for much longer, though.

"Oh!" she breathed, pulling away. "We really should be a little more discreet."

He made a grudging sound of agreement.

"Dennis, I want to make something clear."

"Uh oh." He kept his hands on her hips, enjoying the feel.

"I can't sleep with you tonight."

He tensed up. "I wasn't expecting that."

"Wasn't expecting to be told it's off the table, or wasn't expecting to sleep with me?"

"Not sure anymore."

Her laugh made him feel like he'd lifted the world with his pinkie finger. "It's just... I'm at Auntie's house. And she made a comment about not sullying my reputation."

"She did not."

"She did! And your place sounds very full."

"I have my own house, Ana."

"And it's very public."

He couldn't argue with that.

"If you can understand, I need to focus more on Auntie

and Brie this weekend. I want to spend more time with you, but this is all... a lot."

"Of course."

"And when you come to Newburyport, we will absolutely, positively sleep together."

"I don't need a detailed plan."

She smiled and said, "It's a promise."

"You're amazing."

"So are you."

"I'm so glad we found each other yesterday, even if I did yell at you."

A deep amusement, old and friendly, infiltrated her laugh. "I'm glad we found each other in January."

"I'm never letting you go, you know."

"Good."

Chapter Twenty

Ana

Nineteen days later (but who's counting…)

Be there in fifteen, his text said, popping up just as she put the shrimp rolls in the oven. Dennis had worked an early day with his father, leaving for Newburyport a bit later than expected, but his dinner-time arrival was perfect.

Because it felt so cozy to cook him a dinner.

Like he was coming home to her.

Two weeks of travel with her mother had left her exhausted, exhilarated, happy—and frustrated.

Being conflicted the entire time, wishing she could see Dennis, made her feel like a bad daughter. Ana knew better—feelings were feelings. You couldn't control them, only your reactions to them.

Tomorrow she crossed the twenty-nine week mark, and

today's doctor appointment had been filled with joy and disappointment.

Joy because Little Bean was growing just fine. A little small, which was to be expected given her uterine problems, but everything looked good. He would survive if she gave birth now. Every day he cooked a little longer inside her safe womb was a day that mattered.

His entrance into the world was going to be fraught with concern, but it was actually happening. Ana was going to be a mother.

The vacation with Marian had involved countless conversations about her hopes and fears, though her mother preferred to focus on the pragmatic.

Including treating her to an entirely new wardrobe, some maternity and some for postpartum wear. As Little Bean grew, of course, so did Ana, and the summer dress she'd worn in Maine made her feel huge.

Everything made her feel huge.

That was reality, because she *was* huge.

For the next forty-eight hours, her life would be about nothing but Dennis. Having him overnight meant truly getting to know each other, though she felt like this relationship was happening backwards.

She wasn't nervous about spending time with him. How to fill the hours wasn't a worry.

There were, however, plenty of parts of her life he knew nothing about.

Like her home.

A simple condo, she was two houses away from the water. Harris had asked a million questions about how a part-time therapist could live there, but she'd lied to him.

Put on the spot, she'd claimed to be a renter. In retrospect, that was a huge red flag. Ana made it a practice not to lie, especially about something so personal.

With Dennis, she'd be transparent, which meant being open about money.

Her building was an old one, just off the historic market square, divided into four condos. Right out of college, she'd fallen in love with the place, knowing she wanted to stay close to Brie and her family, and to her mom. Rick had helped her navigate the process of buying, and she'd been lucky. A recession that hurt sellers had worked to her benefit.

The timing was serendipitous.

Now, it was paid off, a two-bedroom condo with a small den, big enough for her and her son.

And maybe–just maybe–a life partner.

For the last two and a half weeks she'd thought about nothing but the baby and Dennis, thinking through so many contingencies. If this worked, would he expect her to relocate to Luview? Would he be willing to move to Newburyport? Could they have both places?

Was she jumping the gun even thinking so long term?

His absence made her need to run these scenarios through her mind, as her back ached more and her legs needed more stretching, calves begging for massages she could do but that weren't nearly as good as the ones he'd given.

So many questions.

So much potential.

Transitions were hard to navigate in life. Ana had the end of a relationship, a surprise pregnancy–a medically complicated one, at that–and now, Dennis.

The biggest complication of all, in some ways.

And yet, the easiest.

Bzzz

Startled, she looked at her phone.

Here, his text read.

She pushed the button to unlock the main door, and the

sound of his steady footsteps as he came up to the second floor made butterflies launch in her stomach.

Instead of making him knock, she opened the door as he reached the top of the landing.

Carrying what looked like a five-pound bag of red foil hearts.

And wearing a smile that made her want to jump in his arms and kiss him until his smile transferred onto her face.

Instead, she took the bag of chocolate and said, "This baby will come out of me as a six-pound infant-shaped chocolate."

"Sounds like a great episode of *Black Mirror*."

"Come on in," she said, noting his small backpack. The man traveled light, but then again, it was mid-June. He wore a cotton crewneck sweater, jeans, and black hiking boots, and he looked *fine*.

"You can put your bag in the–"

Before she could finish the sentence, he cut her off with a kiss, his warmth so alluring. The embrace was a bit trickier than the last time he held her in his arms, though.

Because she was bigger.

But his mouth, oh, that mouth was the same as–no, better than–before. He tasted like coffee and smiles, plans and promises. As she breathed him in, their kiss deepened, until the oven timer interrupted.

"Oh! The shrimp rolls!" Peeling herself out of his arms, she hurried to grab an oven mitt and prevent a burned appetizer. He followed her in.

"Make yourself at home," she said as she pulled out the tray. "I'll give you the tour in a moment, or just walk around and see for yourself."

"Old building."

"It is, built in 1887. Four condos in here. Each floor has one like mine, two bedrooms and a den, and another that's a smaller one bedroom."

"This is big."

"I'm glad I got a bigger place than I needed when I bought it."

"How long have you lived here?"

"About thirteen years."

"Since college?"

"Just after undergrad."

He looked around. Ana kept her place neat and clean, more of a minimalist than most of her friends. It wasn't that clutter bothered her, more that it wasn't necessary. She preferred to have her attention drawn to pleasing sights, and that's how she arranged her home.

"Lots of sun. And you're really close to downtown and the harbor."

"That's why I love this place so much. We can walk down to the water later."

"I'd like that. What are you making? Smells amazing."

"Shrimp rolls! From a box. Just to start. Dinner is salmon and risotto, with a salad. I hope you like salmon?"

"I am the least picky eater you'll ever meet. If you cook it, I'm sure I'll love it." He sat down on her red couch, sinking in, patting the seat next to him. "Unless you need help cooking, come sit with me for a minute."

"A minute?"

"I promise I won't let you burn anything."

"I haven't started the actual cooking yet. Everything's prepped, though."

"Even better. Come here," he said, holding his hand out for hers.

She eyed her own sofa.

"I sit over there now," she explained, pointing to a wide single chair, upholstered in a taupe shade that worked well with the red sofa.

"Why?"

"Because I can't get up off the couch easily anymore," she confessed.

That made him laugh and stand up, reaching down to cradle her face in his hands before kissing her. Breaking the kiss, he said, "I'm here now. I'll help you up."

"Okay, then," she smiled, and they sat.

Maybe it was hormones. Maybe it was the two-and-a-half-week separation. Maybe it was the surreal sense that this relationship *was* real. Whatever it was, tears filled her eyes.

"I've been alone for so long," she said.

"Me, too."

"It's silly, though, because we're not! Not alone–I have Brie and her family, and my mom and Rick. You have your wonderful extended family. You even live right there at your camp with them! And yet…"

"We've both been lonely."

"Mmm hmm."

"Ana, when I'm with you, all that loneliness fades. There's a heaviness in me that I carry around but I don't feel it until it's gone. Until we met in January, I didn't know it could lift. You lift it from me."

"And you lift mine. We don't trade the heaviness, so where does it go?"

He kissed her again. "Maybe we kiss it away."

"Sounds like a lot of kissing is ahead of us."

"Better get started now."

"I thought we already started."

"Are you going to argue, or kiss?"

"I suspect we can do both, but I like kissing way more."

Sitting close, leaning towards each other, she took in the heavenly scent of her just-cooked appetizer, his aftershave, the cotton sweater that draped so nicely against his body. As the kiss went on and on, she felt it.

A lightness.

A release.

An acceptance.

All of this was real, of course. Time, though—the more time she spent in his arms, the more she soaked him in, absorbing his truth—that would create their shared timeline.

Her stomach growled.

Loudly.

"I think you have an agenda," Dennis said, stroking her cheek.

"My appetite has turned into a second libido."

His eyes flashed. "I don't know what that means, but I like it."

"Let's eat. Do you want something to drink? I could make you a caipirinha. Or I bought some beer."

"I'm not going to drink if you can't. That's not fair."

"It's fine! Doesn't bother me a bit."

"Are you trying to liquor me up so you can take advantage of me?"

Ana shot him a look. "I'm a therapist. I don't even think that way."

"Bad joke. Sorry."

"No apologies needed. But I do need a hand." Holding hers out, she made it clear Dennis was a human tugboat for her.

"Physics and pregnancy are a hilarious combination," he said, laughing and pulling her to her feet.

"Only hilarious when you're not the one stuck on your own sofa."

"I'll be your Couch 911 guy."

"You live too far away for that."

"I need to be closer, then."

"Two hours, right?"

"Drive wasn't that bad. Especially this time of year."

"I'd hate to make that trip in January."

"I have chains for my tires. No problem."

She walked into the kitchen and found a spatula, transferring the rolls onto a platter. From the fridge, she pulled out her favorite dipping sauce, a roasted cauliflower hummus she'd made earlier.

"Glasses?" he asked, pointing to the cupboards.

"On the left."

With ease, as if he lived here, Dennis removed two tall glasses and filled them with water from her fridge dispenser. She pulled out two small plates and arranged everything on the high counter, halfway through a roll before he'd even set their waters down.

"Nothing is formal here," she explained. "I hope you're hungry."

"I am."

The way he looked at her made it clear he wasn't thinking about food.

Baby Bean sure was, though. In the next three minutes, she finished half the shrimp rolls, eyeing another one but trying to be polite.

"Have more," he said generously, nudging the big plate toward her.

"I have no self-control."

"I feel the same way," he said with a wink.

Nervous energy shot through her blood, because she was going to have to tell him soon. Her visit with the doctor earlier that morning had cast a shadow over his visit.

Not yet, though. She wanted to have some fun before she had to tell him.

"Do you work from home?" he asked as he pushed the plate closer to her, wagging a shrimp roll in the air before eating it. "I'm done," he added. "The rest are yours."

"I don't," she replied, taking him at his word and dunking

another one in her hummus. "I have a small office a few blocks from here. An office share."

"Office share?"

"A group of therapists share the same office. We schedule around each other. I have Tuesdays and Wednesdays now."

"You see all your patients on those days?"

"And two virtually–I do see them from here." She paused. "I'll probably change that after the baby's born and I return to work."

"And you'll be okay?"

"Okay? What do you mean?"

"You have child care arranged? You can support yourself?"

"I'm fine."

"I'm sure you're fine, Ana. I just want to make sure you're safe and secure and well cared for."

Whoa.

"I have a question for you, first," she said, interrupting. "And I'm not trying to change the subject. But I was hoping we could go for a walk along the water before dinner." She looked outside, where the sky had turned an ominous gray.

"You live close to the beach?"

"Not really. The beaches are over on the other end of town, on Plum Island. But we're on the harbor here. Want to do that now, then we can come back and I'll cook?"

"Sounds great."

Ana grabbed her keys and dropped them in her pocket as Dennis finished off his water.

"Dishes?" he asked.

Ana looked outside and frowned. "Leave them. I'll do them when we get back. I think our window of safe weather is closing. It's supposed to rain all weekend, so this might be our only chance."

"Whatever you say. I'm at your beck and call."

Reaching for her hand, he gave her a quick kiss, then they

walked down the stairs, Ana in the lead. At the main door, she poked her head out and determined the sky was acceptable.

"You're really close to the ocean," he said, taking her hand again.

"Technically, the river. That's the Merrimack River feeding into the ocean. We're really close to the juncture of the two."

"Where are you taking me?"

"Newburyport harbor. Unless you want to go downtown?"

"I'll go wherever you want, Ms. DaSilva. This is your space. Your life. I'm just a visitor learning more about you. Show me everything."

"I don't think my feet and hips can handle everything."

He bent down, hand going to the small of her back as he kissed her earlobe.

"We'll see about that."

The flirting was killing her. She loved it. *Loved* it.

And yet...

"Is this where Brie's family has their cheese shop?"

"No. Rockport."

"She doesn't live near you?"

"Not now. We were roommates until last year, when she moved in with Martin."

"So you haven't been alone in that big condo."

"No."

"Did you and Harris live together?" The way he said her ex's name made it clear Dennis would enjoy murdering Harris with a cherry stem and an ice pick.

"Oh, hell, no. He only saw my place once."

"Really? I'm surprised. Guy like that strikes me as the sleazy type who'd try to move in quickly with a mark."

"Ugh," she said, his comment a blow to her ego.

"I'm sorry. That was a crappy thing to say."

"But true."

"Well…"

"I'm a big girl. I can handle it. In retrospect, I can see that you're right. We only dated for a few months, though."

He came to an abrupt halt. "A few months?" Disbelief came off him like a sonic boom.

"Yes."

"That's it?"

"Mmm hmm. Why?"

"I had the impression you were together for much longer."

"No. And I was close to breaking up with him when he dumped me."

"I see."

"He got past my radar. I'll give him that. But by the end of our second month together, I had seen enough red flags." Her hand went to the top of her belly. "Not fast enough, clearly."

"That means he did this to you after only a short time together?"

"Yes."

"What an immoral piece of walking excrement. I hope he rots to death in Indonesia."

"Indonesia? No. He's in Morocco."

"Not anymore."

"How do you… oh, no." Stopping short, she looked up at him, dropping his hand. "You are *not* spying on him."

"Define spying."

"Dennis!"

"I know some people who know some people who are keeping an eye on him."

"That's spying!"

"I'm making sure he never, ever hurts you again."

"You sound like my stepfather!"

"Can't wait to meet him, then."

"How, exactly, did you find Harris?"

The way his face changed as he clearly worked to find specific words to evade the question made her blood boil.

"The waterfront sure is beautiful here," he said, shading his eyes as he looked around.

"Don't you dare try to change the subject."

"I told you I could find Harris the day we ran into each other on the common."

"You didn't say you actually were going to do it!"

"After what he did to you, I asked my buddy to find someone to locate him. He left Morocco somehow and we lost track of him in Indonesia. Good riddance. As long as he never sets foot on U.S. soil again, I don't care what he does."

"And you're going to always have someone watching for him?"

"Yes."

Her breath escaped her, simultaneously relieved and horrified.

"I won't apologize for it, Ana. Won't try to justify it. This isn't a gray area. He's a threat to you and the baby. I won't stand for him having that kind of power.."

"You sound so... beastly."

"Didn't I ever tell you that's my middle name? Dennis Beastly Luview."

She couldn't help but laugh, though it came out as exasperation tinged with a weird giggle.

"Is this our first fight?" he asked, face suddenly serious. "I hate that we even have to talk about him, much less argue about him."

"This is a lot to take in. Between what Rick did, and now you..."

"What did he do?"

Yikes. She wasn't expecting to have this conversation so soon.

"Rick, well... he somehow got ahold of Harris. Convinced him to terminate his parental rights."

"I'm guessing 'convinced' means paid him off."

"Probably. I don't know. Rick wouldn't give specifics."

"So that's it? The guy has no rights when it comes to the baby?"

"It's a bit more complicated. Rick did his best. I really, really don't want to ruin our night talking about this."

"I don't feel like this is ruining anything. I respect what you're saying, though. And I'm very impressed with your stepfather."

"I'm convinced you two will be best buddies now," she groused, which made him laugh, then pull her in for a hug.

"Look. Ana. I don't want to cross your boundaries, and it sounds like I have. I spent two decades rescuing people from guys a few levels above Harris in criminal networks. They're bad news. If he pisses off someone with more power, they will come after anyone connected to him."

All the air in her body disappeared. At just that moment, the baby did a slow, tight roll, squeezing her cervix a bit.

"I didn't know that." She looked up at him, inhaling slowly. "And I'm sorry you *do* know that. That you operated in a world filled with such cruel characters."

"I don't want you living in fear. And I don't want him thinking he has any shred of power over you, or that the baby is some kind of bargaining chip. Guys like Harris are a dime a dozen, and watching them carefully is a form of insurance."

"It must cost money to have him tracked like that."

"Nope. Just favors in the brotherhood."

"Brotherhood?"

"Friends in the field."

"You are a mystery."

He tugged her toward the crosswalk, pointing to the harbor. "Let's check out the water before it gets too late."

Her stomach growled. "Apparently, my tummy agrees."

Mind swirling, she followed him until they stood at the edge of the river. If you pivoted to the far right, you could see the ocean, boats in and out of the harbor like white dots in a painting.

"This is gorgeous," he said, putting his arm around her shoulders as she leaned into him.

"Tell me more about your Army career."

He stiffened. She waited, letting the silence do its job for her.

Finally, he said softly, "My job was to help keep people safe."

"By rescuing them?"

"Yes."

"From kidnappers?"

"From situations where they weren't free to do what they wanted."

"You have confidentiality issues around what you can and cannot say."

"I most certainly do."

"Funny," she said as they watched the wake from a speed-boat, the waves lapping against a dock. "The same is true in my field. I can't talk about specifics. Ever."

"Then you understand."

"I do. But there's also a huge difference between our jobs."

"Former job, for me."

"Yes. Former job. In mine, I don't put my physical being on the line to help someone to be free."

"You use your mind."

"I do. My heart, too."

"I used all that in the field as well."

"Your flashbacks, Dennis. Those come from your missions?"

"You're just going straight for it, aren't you?"

His tone was one of marvel. Not anger.

"Isn't that what we're about? Laying it all out there?"

"You've got me there. Okay. One flashback. One incident."

"Tell me about it."

"I..." A seagull swooped down on the concrete in front of them, completely heedless of their presence. Dennis watched it, then sighed. "Can we table this?"

"Of course."

"It's like the Harris conversation. Let's not ruin our time together with it. In time, I'll talk more about it, but–"

"–not now," they said together, his hold on her tightening.

"I still can't believe this," he said, turning to her, hands on her shoulders. "How easy it is with you."

"And you. We can have conflict but we're not at odds. We're just talking it through."

"So rare," he murmured as he came in for a kiss.

Just then the seagull squawked, as if telling them to get a room.

A drop, then a second, landed on the back of her hand.

"Oh, no," she said, looking up, as the seagull took off for the water. A gray cloud appeared, and soon–more drops.

"We'll have to run for it," Dennis said. "We're only a few blocks away."

"Dennis," she gasped as they began to walk quickly back to her place. "I can't even waddle fast. Run? Hah!"

"I'll carry you."

"You absolutely will not," she insisted, waddling as fast as she could, taking him through a florist's parking lot, then into an alley, all shortcuts she'd found over the years. Neither of them seemed too bothered by the downpour, which was fairly heavy when they reached her front door.

"Ah, well," Dennis said in the foyer, running his hands through his hair. "You were right."

"Rain is fickle here, this close to the shore. You just never know."

"We'll just have a lovely night in," he said, giving her hip a love pat as they climbed the stairs.

Every bit of this date was perfect, even the conflict. Spending time with him was so natural. It seemed like he could fit into her life without a hiccup, and she hoped she could fit into his, too.

And then there was the baby.

But first things first. Like dinner.

"How can I help?" he asked as they walked in. Going straight for the dishes on the counter, he immediately started piling them in the empty sink, turning on the water.

"Um, you could put those in the dishwasher. I'll get the salmon going. The risotto and salad are already done, so dinner will be ready in fifteen minutes."

"You're a goddess."

"Just wildly overprepared."

Without being asked, Dennis wiped down the counters with a paper towel, then washed his hands.

"I'm going to ask the obvious question," she said, pulling out a skillet. "Have you lived alone your entire adult life? I know you joined the Army at eighteen, but what about a significant other?"

"Not for more than a few weeks," he answered simply. "No long-term relationships like that. You?"

"No. I never found someone I wanted to live with. Dated some people for under a year. No one ever really clicked."

"Same. In my line of work, settling down was never easy. Most of my friends have been divorced at least once, most twice. Or they never married, like me."

"How did we get to this age and never have a long-term relationship?"

"We were saving ourselves for each other."

She snorted. "Or we're impossible to live with and in for a rude awakening."

"There is nothing you can throw my way that I can't handle."

She placed both her hands on her belly and said, "I noticed."

All he did was shake his head, then ask, "Why don't I heat up the risotto?"

"It's in the glass dish in the fridge."

Ana managed the salmon, the sizzle of the pink flesh when it hit the pan a sign she had timed it just right. Rubbed with fennel seed, rosemary, and orange zest, she hoped he liked it.

As the microwave hummed, Dennis asked, "Music?"

She nodded to a Bose speaker. "You can use my phone or yours to connect. What do you like to listen to?"

"Ever heard of Radio Paradise?"

She nearly dropped her spatula.

"Heard of it? I've been a member for years!"

"Me, too," he said, turning it on using his phone. The soothing sounds of a low jazz number, infused with an African beat, filled the room. Dennis found the wall switch and turned on the dining table chandelier. "There we go. Ambiance."

"Now I want a nice Chianti." Unable to stop, she moved her hips to the beat as she cooked the salmon, smiling, heart full. Dennis came up behind her, the heat of his tall, broad body making her smile more. His hands went to her hips and he began swaying with her, nuzzling her neck.

She forgot what a good dancer he was.

"Smells good," he said.

"It's wild salmon."

"I meant you."

Ding!

The microwave forced Dennis to attend to the risotto,

leaving Ana to smile stupidly at the fish. She covered the pan and glanced at the clock, intent on checking on it in three minutes.

Dennis was stirring the rice, judging it.

He put it back in the microwave for two more minutes.

"I really like this," she announced to Dennis's back as he worked on the rice. Once he'd pressed the right buttons, he turned around to face her.

"Risotto?"

"Being domestic with you."

"Me, too."

For the next ten minutes, they worked side by side, Dennis setting the table and filling water glasses, Ana finishing with the salmon. Soon, they were seated, working their way through a delicious dinner, and Dennis complimented her cooking.

"This is amazing."

"Thank you. Do you cook?"

"I can. Limited repertoire, but one of my goals for retirement is to learn more dishes."

"What's your specialty?"

"Borani banjan."

"Never heard of it."

"It's an Afghan dish. Someone taught me how to make it."

"Someone."

"Someone I can't talk about."

"Not a love interest?"

"No."

"Ah. Gotcha. Interpreter?"

"Something like that."

"What's in this borani banjan?"

"Eggplant. Yogurt. Garlic. A bunch of vegetables like onions and chiles."

"Sounds incredible. Will you make it for me sometime?"

"I absolutely will. And you'll teach me how to make this risotto?"

"Deal."

They finished fast, and given there was no buffet, Ana's stomach would just have to be content with one course. There was always that huge bag of red foil hearts for dessert, though, and she had plenty of ice cream and cookies if Dennis wanted something more.

Or... if she did.

"Come here," he said, reaching out his hand as he stood. A classic salsa song came on and—were his hips actually moving properly?

"Don't tell me you can dance salsa!"

"I try."

"Where on earth did you learn this?" she laughed as he took her masterfully through the salsa moves, keeping it low key given her huge belly.

And her two left feet.

"*Shhhh*. Government secret."

"My taxpayer dollars were used wisely."

The song was over too soon, their bodies moving just so as he bent down for a soulful kiss, one that said it was time.

Time to move on to the bedroom.

And time for her to break it to him as gently as possible.

"Dennis?"

"Mmm?"

"I have a confession."

"Go for it."

"The second trimester is called the horny trimester."

"Oh, I like this confession! Is it? Really?"

"It is. And I went through it all alone."

"Went? You mean, it's gone?" Was he *pouting*?

"Twenty-seven weeks and beyond is the third trimester."

"So I missed it. Damn."

"You did. But that's where the confession comes in."

"I'm all ears."

Her hand dropped between his legs, bold and free, knowing he would enjoy this. "I'm pretty sure you're all something else."

His groan of pleasure made it clear she'd made the right move. "I'm literally in your hands and at your mercy, Ana. Just tell me what you want."

"I want sex, but... I have bad news." She withdrew her hand.

He frowned. "How can the words 'I want sex' and 'bad news' be in the same sentence?"

"I'm not allowed."

"Not allowed to have sex?"

"Right."

"Says who?"

"My doctor. The obstetrician."

"Oh." He frowned. "Well. That's... because of the baby?"

"Exactly. It might trigger early labor, or break my water. I'm close to thirty weeks. Everything changes now."

His somber nod was one of acceptance. Then his eyebrow arched.

"Can you orgasm?"

"Am I capable? Yes. That horny second trimester burned through loads of batteries."

"Ah, that's not what I meant. Let me rephrase, although boy, that was a fascinating window into your libido..."

Her giggles were uncontrollable.

"Has the doctor restricted you from orgasming?"

"No."

"Then we're fine!"

"We are?"

"We can be creative. I just want to be close to you. I don't need to be *in* you."

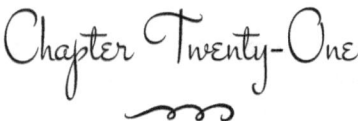

Chapter Twenty-One

Dennis

"This is the first time I've been with anyone since you, in January," she said, making him smile.

"Same here."

Her body tensed. "Really?"

"Yeah, really."

"I just assumed you moved on. Put yourself out there."

"No. I wanted *you*. When days turned into weeks, I still wanted *you*."

"Sure, but... months?"

"By the time we ran into each other, I'd resigned myself to your rejection."

"Ouch."

"Hey. Telling truths here."

"I can take it." She brushed away the hair over his eyebrows, her touch sending him deeper in love.

"I guess I'd have started dating. The pool in my hometown is pretty shallow, but..."

"Women must hit on you a lot."

"Some. I keep to myself." He wasn't about to try to explain Annabeth.

"I'm so sorry I ghosted."

"I understand why."

"I wish it were different."

"Ana, do you have any idea how much this feels like a dream?" He stroked her hair, then kissed her neck. "A dream I always knew was possible, but felt unattainable? Two decades in the field meant I could push it aside. Tell myself it wasn't time yet. Circumstances weren't right. And then I met you my first night back in the states, ready to start a new life that had nothing to do with you—until it did."

"I feel the dreamlike quality, too. Except it's firmly grounded in reality."

"Yes!" He sighed. "And that night in the alley at the hotel. Then the bar. Then my room. Waking up to an empty bed made me doubt myself."

"It did?"

"I assumed you'd be there. But you weren't. And then... you were. At the elevator."

"My panic attack was half phobia, half embarrassment."

"We made it through, though. By talking. By being who we are unabashedly. No bullshit. No games."

"That's right." She kissed the back of his hand, the brush of her lips so tantalizing. "We just are who we are. Baby included."

"I really wish I could turn back time and make it clear that I care for you regardless of the baby. Damn, that sounds wrong, because I care about the baby, too."

As if he heard Dennis's words, the little guy let out an enormous kick.

They laughed together.

"I love your body," he said, owning the words, enjoying how it felt to say them to her. She blushed, her cheeks red even in the low light, and as she looked down, her eyelashes fluttered.

"I mean it," he added. "I've never seen such a beautiful body before. You're giving life and love to your baby," he said as his hand slid along her leg, up her hip, cupping her breast as she caught her breath.

"This might be the only time to see me this way."

He paused. "Is this it for you? No more children?"

"This one is a miracle." She faltered a bit. "Are you–do you want children?"

"Do you want more?"

"I... I haven't really let myself think about that. I guess I didn't want to get my hopes up? In a perfect world, sure. I'd love more." Her shy look made something in him crack a bit. "You really want kids?"

"I do," he replied, moving his hand to her belly, splaying it as wide as possible, rubbing along the rounded curve. "You really are a goddess."

"No one has ever called me that before."

"Then every person you've ever been with is an idiot who didn't see you for who you really are."

"When you put it that way, my entire romantic life suddenly makes so much more sense."

"It's not a problem anymore." He kissed her then, both hands around her fullness, his tongue dancing with her, his body needing to be as close to her as possible. Her hands went under his sweater and shirt, crawling up his back, the touch on bare skin driving him into a frenzy.

That night in January, at the hotel, he'd had her naked for hours, sex fueled by release and change. Now, though, this was softer, gentler.

It had to be.

She needed him to be.

"I love your body, too," she said as her hands roamed his back. "You're so muscular. So big." Her finger worried a spot on his scapula. "Is that a scar?"

"Mmm hmm." His fingers played with her breast, the nipple tightening under his attentions. She shifted, her throat fluttering, and he watched her becoming aroused. "Gunshot."

"What?"

"Gunshot wound."

"Oh, my. When we slept together before, I remember feeling lots of scars on you. Wondering what they were."

"You could have asked."

"I was a bit preoccupied."

"By what?"

"Your tongue."

"Mmmmmm. My tongue would like to preoccupy you again." His hand slid over her waist, cupping her ass. Ana was a small woman, perhaps a foot shorter than he was, at least in bare feet. Her body was delicious, pregnant or not, but something about her ripeness right now was extra alluring.

As they kissed, he felt her hesitate, then pull away. Her eyes were shining as she looked up at him.

"Shall we move to my bed?"

"I would love to."

"You'll need a winch and your truck to get me off this couch."

"I think one of my arms will do."

After helping her up earlier, he knew that even pregnant, she wasn't very heavy, and the pleasure of touching her made everything so much easier.

For years, he'd wanted to want someone this much. Wanted to crave a woman's attention and focus. Wanted to lose himself in another person.

Now he had her.

And he wasn't about to let her slip away again.

He kissed her, pulling her close as he walked her backwards down the hall, Ana laughing as they did it.

"On the left. *Your* left. First door," she said. The door was open and a huge king bed beckoned, the coverlet folded back. Beautiful black-and-white photos covered the walls, most of them taken on beaches.

All of them with people laughing.

Happiness filled him like helium, lifting his heart the way he lifted her onto the bed, his mouth on her neck then kissing lower, dipping between her breasts as she reached under his sweater again, this time pulling up as if to take it off.

He obliged.

The pitter-patter of rain began on the roof, a cozy feeling that lent the room an air of privacy, of cocooning from the world. From his back, her hands moved forward to his chest as he found the hem of her dress and pulled it up, reaching behind her to unclasp her bra.

Hungry eyes met his, until she rotated to her side.

"Sorry," she said with a smile. "I can't lay on my back for too long."

"We can do whatever we need to do. Be comfortable."

"That's a noble goal."

He kissed her again, open mouthed and with purpose as his hands undressed her. Finding the strap of her thong, he slid it off, and she was naked. Gloriously, perfectly nude, her body deserved to be painted, the object of an artist's eye, preserved as an inspirational work of beauty.

"Now you," she ordered, the words making Dennis finish the job in seconds, his body bare and on the bed with her.

"I've missed you," he said, her smooth skin a contrast to his, the thick hair on his legs so different from her slim, soft calves. His hands found her breasts as he curled up next to her, Ana's hand going between his legs, finding him hard.

"Mmm," she said, stroking him until he damn near burst. Before he could come and ruin the moment, he stopped her with a kiss on her breast, then her ribs, and as he moved down her body, she let go of him.

"I want to taste you," he murmured, and he did, her thighs next to his ears, his hands on her hips, every part of being this close to her better than he remembered. His tongue wanted to take her to a place where she could relax and release, to give her so much pleasure.

She gave him so much. Giving back was all he wanted.

The way she moved against his mouth, twisted slightly onto her side, gave him a new angle to work with, and soon he saw the telltale signs of her orgasm building.

"Oh, Dennis," she whispered, her voice going tight, her hips finding a small rhythm that made him lose himself, too. As she came, he felt his soul soar. Victory came in many forms, and this was one of them.

As she ran her fingers through his hair, twitched, and sighed, he kissed her full on the mouth again, her taste lingering between them, her body going boneless.

"Creative, huh?" she said with a lopsided smile.

"That was nothing. Just wait."

"There's more?"

"We have all night, Ana. And it's been too long."

"Speaking of too long," she said, reaching for his erection. "Whatever shall I do about this?"

The way she stroked him made him shiver with desire, but it was the methodical, purposeful journey she made down to his shaft, her breasts dragging along his chest, ribs, and upper thighs, that made him want her even more.

When that warm mouth covered his tip, he inhaled sharply, certain he would come in seconds, hoping he could hold out yet wondering why he would torture himself like that. The way her tongue moved against him made him want to draw this pleasure out as much as possible, but it had also been a long time.

Too long.

One hand wrapped around him as her mouth deep-throated him, the coordination designed for maximum sensation, and damned if she wasn't a master at this. All he could think about was her naked body, those beautiful breasts, and that heavenly mouth.

And soon, he couldn't think about anything.

Ana took his orgasm full on, following him as he finished and then, to his delight, she swallowed.

He slumped against the bed, boneless, like she had been just minutes ago.

"Come here," he said, and she curled up against him. They were naked, spent, and still on top of the covers.

She peeled herself away and stood.

"Let's get under the covers." A huge yawn escaped her. "I'm ready for bed."

The clock said it was barely eight. Dennis didn't care. If going to bed early meant sleeping naked with her all night, it worked for him.

Covers and sheets rearranged, they found the right balance of skin against skin, limbs entangled, her head in the crook of his shoulder, her belly supported by a long pillow.

"Oh, Dennis. What am I going to do with you?" she said with a long sigh, laughing.

"More of that, please."

Her laughter was infectious. "Of course. But the baby's coming in a few weeks, and we're just getting started."

"So?"

"I wish–I wish I'd met you five years ago! Ten years ago! All the years ago!"

"Me, too. You're what, seven years younger?"

She nodded against his chest, yawning again.

"Obviously, it wouldn't have worked when we were eleven and eighteen, but twenty-five and thirty-two?" she said, her voice getting quieter as she spoke. He stroked her hair, his own eyes getting tired.

"We have us now. That's what counts," he said, although it sounded like a platitude.

"Yes." Another yawn. "Am I a terrible host if I fall asleep on you?"

He patted her ass. "I will give this Airbnb five stars. Great service. Owner goes above and beyond. Works endlessly to please the guests."

As they faded off to sleep, sated and happy, Dennis found himself truly relaxing for the first time in, well...

Ever.

* * *

The boy with big brown eyes begged him.

"Mama says I can't have him, but he's my friend!" The dog wiggled in the boy's arms as bullets whistled by, explosives going off all around the small market.

It happened so fast.

Sand filled his nostrils, smoke cut visibility to nothing, and worst of all, Dennis felt the bitter truth—that his entire team had been misled.

For all he knew, the kid was a plant. Could have been wearing a bomb. Same with the damn dog.

Except he knew this boy. His father was a translator. His mother cooked for him.

And the little boy begged with his whole heart.

A rope was all Dennis had to help, tying it around the dog's neck loose enough not to choke it, tight enough to give him a way to track the damn thing.

"You hide here," he said, but not in English. The words were sharp, one at a time, like bullets reluctantly discharged over his tongue. Under a broken chair, in a small alcove, he tucked the boy and the dog away just before he was hit, the bullet ricocheting off his flak vest.

A bruised liver he could survive.

Thank god for Kevlar.

Cacophony rained down on him like dirt, clods of it everywhere, as if they were being bombed with it by drones. A scream from the boy, then a flash of movement.

The dog darted down the alley.

"NO!" Dennis shouted, instantly distracted by a woman's cry for help, a baby in her arms, two doors down from the boy.

Moving in slow motion, Dennis fought to get to the woman, his hands flayed by grit and friction, his mind a blur.

And then he was midair.

When he came to, the world was nothing but a high-pitched whine and goo.

Bloody goo.

The woman with the baby screamed, her cries joining the babe in arms, and all he could think was, alive.

If I can hear, I'm alive. If they can scream, they're alive.

But then a man's hoarse shout, followed by the gut-wrenching shriek of reality's cruelty.

Dennis was face down, turned away from the man. As he pivoted on his belly, he slowly saw.

Saw too much.

Saw his failure.

Saw too much death.

Saw his–

. . .

"Dennis! *Shhh. Shhh,*" spoke the sand, the wind, the sun, all whispering in his ear at once.

"Unh!" Sitting bolt upright, he couldn't make any sense of his surroundings. Soft sheets. Smooth skin. Someone else's heat. Where the hell was he? How did he get here?

"You're safe. It's okay. Breathe," said the woman beside him, ripe and round, naked under the sheet.

And who was..?

Oh. Right.

Ana.

"Not again," he groaned, resting his elbows on his knees, hands raking his hair, pulling hard to wake himself out of the nightmare.

"You were muttering in a language I don't know," she said. "And you twitched and turned."

"How long?"

"Maybe a minute."

Lungs shouldn't shake, but somehow his did, from the inside out.

"Can't–can't–" He tried to explain but his body was in two places, two time frames, two selves, and couldn't merge.

"Just be. Let it happen. You'll be fine. You will align. Nothing that happens now can hurt you." She held his hand and locked eyes with him, saying no more.

Just breathing.

Her belly made him remember the baby, screaming in the alley.

So he closed his eyes.

And opened them right up again.

The mind's eye was an evil little bastard, bringing him intrusive images he couldn't wash away. Looking at Ana was far better.

As she inhaled, she tipped her chin up a little, then

exhaled, tipping it down. Mirroring her, he eventually forced his lungs to let air in and out in a rhythm compatible with life.

Barely.

Sweat covered his naked skin, his legs askew now, his heart hammering so hard against his ribs, he was sure they were cracked.

He let go of her hands and fell back against the pillow, staring up at the ceiling fan.

"I'm so sorry."

"For what?"

"That," he managed.

"That was a nightmare. We can't control nightmares."

"You don't need to be exposed to my shit like this."

"How often does it happen?"

"I don't know. It just does. Mostly after I see a kid get hurt."

"That's a lot."

"It is. We—we don't need to talk about this."

"Here." She reached over to her nightstand and handed him a glass of water. "Drink. It'll help."

Unable to argue, he did as told, and she was right.

It helped.

"Want to talk about it?"

"No."

"Okay."

"Yes."

"I'm here."

"I don't want to talk about it, but I do want to talk about it, but the thought of talking about it makes me *not* want to talk about it."

"I understand."

"I'm glad one of us does, because I sure don't."

"Trauma is never rational."

"Which is why I *hate* it."

"I don't know anyone who loves trauma, Dennis."

He snorted, his throat slowly relaxing from the death grip the nightmare had on it.

"It's a dream about a boy."

It hurt even to say that.

"A dream based on reality?"

"Yes."

"A real event?"

"Mmm hmmm. But the details aren't always what really happened. The themes are, though."

"Tell me more."

"It's going to sound... it's not organized."

"That's okay."

"You're not my therapist, you know."

"I'm your—what am I to you? We've never said. Girlfriend?"

"Soulmate."

"That works."

"You're my angel." He squeezed her hand.

She just smiled, sitting in the darkness with him, holding his hand.

"I couldn't save him."

"That's hard."

"I–I tried. He had a dog. His mother wouldn't let him keep it. We were fighting and he begged me to help him. Then I had to assist a woman with a baby and the dog got loose and the boy–there was an explosion. I went flying and–" He let out a grunt, nausea taking over.

"You tried but couldn't save him."

"Yeah."

"Oh, Dennis." Her arms went around him, her body curled against his side. One knee came up, tucked along his thigh, her belly heavy against his hip. "I'm here. You're here. You're not back there."

"I know that. Some part of my brain doesn't. And that part is an asshole."

"That part needs help." She looked up at him. "Is that why you retired? That incident?"

"Yeah. There's more to it, but–yes."

"Any specific triggers?"

"Well, like I said, watching a kid get hurt."

She nodded against his chest. "Like the little boy at the Indian restaurant when I was in Luview?"

"Mmm hmm. And sometimes, my niece."

"Harriet?"

"Yeah. If she gets hurt, it–it's hard. She's around the same age as the boy."

"So when we met, in the hotel alley, the boy with the cat– that's why you had a flashback?"

"Probably."

"That makes sense."

"Does it? Because nothing about this makes sense to me."

Exhaustion poured through him, sudden and harsh. Her touch, her understanding, her gentle presence kept a part of him feeling good.

The rest of him wanted to fade out.

A yawn escaped him, then another, and she caught it.

"You want to know how I knew you were special back in January?" he asked, the question rhetorical.

"Of course."

"I could sleep with you."

"We definitely slept together." She laughed. "Three times."

"Not the sex. The *sleep*. I slept so well I didn't even wake up when you snuck out. You relaxed me, Ana. Made me feel safe. That's *my* job. Making other people safe. You flipped the script on me. That's when I knew."

"Oh," she said softly, looking at him with such care. "I'm so glad I could give that to you. And that you could receive it."

"Me, too."

"Sleepy," she said, yawning again, snuggling in closer. "You make an incredible body pillow."

"A what?"

She waved vaguely toward a chair in the corner of her bedroom. "My body pillow. It helps me sleep. Positions my belly to take weight off my joints."

"I will be your human body pillow forever. Put any part of you on any part of me." Another yawn took over and soon, he was in a hazy zone, locked in her arms.

Grounded by her.

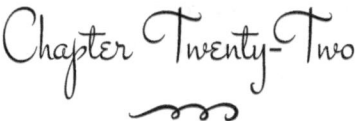

Chapter Twenty-Two

One week later

Dennis

Running late, he dictated into the phone. *Moose issue up north.*

Ana was likely waiting for him already, at the restaurant in Portland where they were having lunch. He'd rented a hotel room at a boutique inn on the water in Old Town. This would be the last week she could be away from home. She had to stay close to Boston, in case of an emergency with the baby.

Meeting halfway in Portland, with a short ferry ride and a day spent in the sun on Peaks Island, was going to be the best date ever.

You've never been late before! she texted back. *Must be a tear in the time-space continuum. Moose?*

He laughed out loud at that as he reached the outer edge of Portland, taking the exit near a Whole Foods. Unaccustomed to cities after so many months in a rural town, he re-oriented himself, waiting out the light.

Two bull moose got into a fight on Route 119. Doesn't normally happen in the summer. Stopped traffic. Big jam, all four cars had to wait for twenty minutes, he dictated.

Testosterone is a scourge, she wrote back with a wink emoji. *I just arrived at the restaurant and I'm waiting to be seated. I'll keep your place warm. Want me to order you a drink?*

Coffee, he replied.

This was a lunch date, at a famous place on the water known for their fish dishes. Then, they'd check into the hotel, followed by the ferry ride to Peaks Island. He'd already reserved a golf cart for tootling around the small island. A tour of the old munitions facility would be fascinating, then ice cream.

After they returned to the mainland, dinner at a foodie restaurant, and then a long night together, naked and intimate.

He knew the baby would arrive within the next two to three weeks. Ana wouldn't be allowed to go past thirty-four weeks because of her uterus. Dennis had to make every hour together count, because after this, they'd never be alone again.

Not for eighteen or so years.

Driving along Congress Street, his phone said he was eight minutes away now. He hoped he could grab a parking spot in a long-term lot. Another stoplight, the kind that seemed to go on longer than it should.

His phone rang. The GPS disappeared and Ana's name appeared on the screen. He answered.

"Dennis?" She was breathless and panicked. Background noise, complete with someone shouting, "I called 911! One minute!" sent his whole body into overdrive.

"Dennis! I was seated, and I needed to go to the bathroom." She started sobbing. "It's bad. Blood."

"Blood?" He hit the accelerator, the GPS back on as he used Bluetooth to talk. "What happened? Did you fall?"

"My water broke! All over the floor. And then–now there's *blood*."

His ears began to ring, every other sound dissolving, and his eyesight sharpened. The GPS told him to go straight, so he did. He had to get to her.

Now.

Ignoring a red light, he shot through it, the ringing getting louder.

Until he realized that it wasn't coming from his brain.

Red and white lights flashed behind him, an ambulance speeding. He pulled over, heart racing, Ana crying on the phone.

"It's okay. I'm on my way. I'll be there in three minutes."

"BLOOD! And it hurts. I'm in labor–I can't be in labor! What am I going to do? The baby–he can't be born like this! Dennis, I–"

Instinct made him pull right behind the speeding ambulance, a sick, cold dread hitting him as he realized that was her emergency vehicle.

That speeding ambulance must be for her.

And the baby.

"I'm coming!" Drafting behind the ambulance, ignoring the traffic, he felt his truck tires holding the road, forced to rely on other people with less-developed survival instincts to do the right thing.

"ANA! Talk to me!"

Nothing.

Silence.

That was so much worse than hearing her cry.

"Hello?"

"Who is this?"

"I'm Kurt. The manager here. The EMTs are transporting

her now. She said her name was Ana DaSilva. From Newbury-port, Mass."

"Yes. That's her name. What's happening?"

"She's unconscious. Passed out just now." The guy was huffing, like he was running. "Blood everywhere. She's pregnant."

"I know! I'm her boyfriend." The word felt weird, cold in his mouth, but it was shorthand.

"Sorry, sir. They're transporting her to the Medical Center here in Portland."

A little red compact car cut him off, forcing him to slam on his brakes, narrowly missing a fender bender. The driver gave him the middle finger.

Up ahead, the ambulance turned right and sped off, disappearing. Evidently, it wasn't hers.

"Sir?" The guy on the phone sounded alarmed. "What just happened to you?"

"What's the hospital address?"

The guy rattled it off.

"Is she—is the baby—" The question he tried to ask choked Dennis, his throat filled with fear.

"I don't know, sir. The doctors at the medical center can tell you more. The ambulance just pulled out. We'll keep her phone here for you to get wherever she's better."

Beep

Call failed.

"GOD DAMN IT!" Pulling over into a spot by a fire hydrant, he frantically punched in the address for the medical center. Unconscious? Transport? Blood?

Of all the times to be fifteen minutes late.

He was never late. She was right about that.

"BUT *NOW?*" he screamed as he squealed out of the spot, racing to follow the mile and a half route to whatever he was about to encounter.

The image of sweet Ana standing up at a restaurant and gushing blood, her panic, her terror, the way she sounded on the call–he could lose her.

He could lose them both.

Training forced him to take in a long, intense breath through his nose, making a sound like a train going through a tunnel. His lungs felt like they would burst as he inhaled to maximum physical capacity, then added two more hitched breaths for good measure.

Hold for four seconds.

Then slow release.

"Go cold," he told himself, shifting into work mode, a state of mind he'd sworn off the day he retired.

This situation demanded it. People who panicked were useless.

He didn't have the luxury of being useless right now.

As he made a right turn, his phone rang. He answered it, praying to hear Ana's voice.

Instead, it was his mom.

"Dennis! I was thinking, since you're in Portland and all, if you could stop by The Holy Donut, we'd all love two dozen of their maple bacon–"

"NOT NOW, MOM."

"Oh, my goodness. What's wrong?"

"It's Ana. She's bleeding. On my way to Maine Medical Center."

"Ana's *bleeding?*"

"Water broke at the restaurant. Blood, too."

"Oh, no! Is she with you? You're rushing her there?"

"No. Happened before I arrived. I'm trying to–"

"LUKE!" she called out.

"No, Mom. Dennis. Wrong son."

"I know who you are. Dennis, where are you, exactly? Maine Medical Center in Portland?" She went quiet again, muffled speaking in the background making it clear she was talking to Luke.

"Not yet, but almost. That's where they're taking her."

"Did you say her water broke?"

"Yes. And there was blood. And she passed out."

"They'll do an emergency c-section, then." The call went muffled again when he reached the medical center. Then his mom was back on as he pulled into the ER entrance, slammed on his brakes, and put the truck in Park by the curb.

"Dennis, we're–"

"Going in," he interrupted, ending the call.

As he climbed out, a valet shouted from a podium, "Sir, you can't just–"

But he could. And did.

Marching into the ER, he went straight to the front desk.

"Ana DaSilva. They just brought her in by ambulance. Pregnant woman, about thirty weeks. Water broke. Bleeding. Unconscious."

"Are you her next of kin?"

At the speed of light, he calculated the best answer.

The one closest to the truth.

"I'm the baby's father."

"Let me get your information," the woman said. "As soon as we know anything, I'll have someone update you."

He gave his name and phone number like he was ordering a pizza, then followed her directions, ending up in a waiting room that felt like a cage.

Bzzz

His phone had a notification on it.

You missed your reservation. It's been more than fifteen minutes. You can do this twice on our app, but after that, we have to–

If he didn't need his phone so damn much, he'd throw it through a window.

367

No information. No action plan. No role.

All Dennis could do was sit and wait.

And wait.

And beat himself up for being late.

If only he'd been there, he could have helped her. Calmed her down. Held her hand. Ridden in the ambulance with her. Given critical information to the team rescuing her.

Instead, he was stuck in traffic, and all because of two moose with machismo complexes.

"She can't die," he finally said aloud, letting the air out of him, deflation triggered.

She can't. And the baby can't die, either. They both have to survive. They have to.

When he went cold, there were no emotions. There were only goals.

But Ana made it impossible to go cold.

So right now, there were no goals.

Only feelings.

Feelings he couldn't process with her, because she was fighting for her life. Fighting for her baby's life. All in the hands of an unknown team, a surgeon who hopefully knew what he was doing.

He stood, marching back to the desk, where a busy nurse caught his eye.

"Coffee?"

She pointed to a little alcove around the corner.

"It's from a vending machine. Not great, but it has caffeine. Anything better, you need to go to the cafeteria or leave the hospital and find one of the coffee shops."

He nodded and went for easy.

Five minutes later, he was drinking what tasted like caffeinated, pulverized volcanic rock, but it gave him something to do.

Powerless, all he could do was sit.

Ana's mother and stepfather should be contacted, but he didn't have their information. Brie, too. How could he possibly–

Wait.

Lucinda.

He didn't have her information, but his mom did.

Dialing quickly, he listened as his mom's phone rang once, then went straight to voicemail.

He texted.

No reply.

"Think. Think, think, think. Who else knows Lucinda?"

Rachel.

Kell's fiancée. She was the director of development for the town of Luview and might know it.

He called her. She answered on the second ring.

"Hey, Dennis. What's going on?"

"Do you have Lucinda Armistead's number?"

"Yes. Why?"

"What is it?"

The phone went quiet; she didn't ask questions. Just did what was asked.

"There. I texted it to you as a contact." His phone vibrated from the incoming text.

"Thank you."

"What's wrong? You sound upset."

"It's Ana. I'm at the hospital in Portland. I need to reach her mother and stepfather, and Lucinda's great-niece is Ana's best friend. Look, Rachel, I have to go."

"Good luck. If I can do anything, let me know."

"You already did."

He called Lucinda, who answered immediately.

"Hello. This is Lucinda Armistead. May I ask who is calling?"

"Miss Lucinda, it's Dennis Luview."

"Dennis! What a lovely–"

"Ana's in the hospital."

"Oh!" Her voice went up in delight. "Is it time?"

"I hate to bear bad news, but she's bleeding. Unconscious."

"Oh, no! In Boston?"

"No. Here in Portland. We were meeting here for a final date before– before–"

"My goodness, Dennis. I am so, so sorry."

Composing himself, he used up a lot of grit trying not to fall apart on the phone with the wonderful old lady.

"I'm here waiting while she's in surgery. I need your help." Tears threatened then but he shoved them away. "I need to reach Brie, so she can tell Ana's mom and stepfather."

"Oh, dear boy, of course! I will call Brie now and give her your number."

"Can you read Brie's number to me, so I can call her? Just in case?"

"Yes. Let me find my book." Knowing it would take even longer to explain how she could find the number on her phone, he waited as patiently as possible.

Which was to say, not very.

"Ah! Here we have it." She read the number off to him and he typed it straight into his text section.

"Thank you, Miss Lucinda."

"Please tell Ana that I am praying for her and the baby."

Dennis closed his eyes. "I will."

"I'm praying for you as well, Dennis. May God hold you all in his grace."

All he could say was, "Thank you."

After their call ended, he stared at his text, wondering how to say this to Brie.

A call would be much better.

The call went to voicemail. Damn. Somehow it seemed

even worse to leave a message versus a text, but he didn't have much choice.

"Hi, Brie. Dennis Luview here. Ana's water broke and there was blood. We're at the Maine Medical Center in Portland. She's in surgery. I don't know the specifics, but I'm waiting here for a doctor to update me. I have no idea how to reach her mother or stepfather. Can you give them my number?" After speaking out the digits clearly, he ended with, "My apologies for leaving such a rough message."

What a Saturday. Weekends were supposed to be fun for people. Instead, he was leaving little dread bombs all over the place.

Gulping down industrial caffeine wasn't going to help him, so he sipped it slowly, mentally going through his options.

Five minutes later, he'd finished the coffee and was all out of distractions.

He could track down Brie's dad at their cheese shop in Rockport. Ana had told him that Hugh Hohenadel hated Rick, but surely he'd help connect Dennis to Marian so she could come be with her daughter.

His phone rang. Brie.

"OMIGOD WHAT IS HAPPENING?" Her breath was coming out like blunt force trauma. "Ana's having the baby *now?*"

"We were meeting at a restaurant. Her water broke, and there was blood. She was on the phone with me when she passed out. Paramedics brought her here. Now she's in surgery and I'm waiting. I'm sorry I don't know more."

"Dennis! Oh, my God! Ana!"

Murmuring in the background made it clear Brie wasn't alone. Good. No one panicking like this should be on their own.

"I'm at the cheese shop, covering my sister's shift. I can be there in—"

"Brie. *Brie.* Ana's mom and stepdad don't know. Can you contact them?"

"They don't know?"

"I don't have their numbers. Never met them."

"Did Ana—was Ana conscious long enough to call them?"

"I assume if she was, they'd have called you?"

"I don't know! Hang on." She went quiet, then: "I have a text! From Marian! Oh, hell, I ignore my phone for half an hour and *this* happens. Her text says Ana's having an emergency and they're on their way to Portland. That's all it says."

"Great." Dennis did some mental math. "They're in Gloucester, right?"

"Yes. On the ocean."

"An hour or so away."

"It's Saturday. Traffic going north is tricky in tourist season. Could be longer. Same with me. If I leave now, it could be—"

"Between me, her mom, and her stepfather, we've got it covered."

"Are you *kidding* me, Dennis? I'm coming! Shut *up!*"

The call ended.

Okay, then.

Rubbing his eyes, he let out a big yawn, the kind your body forces you into when blood needs to be moved around. As he stretched, he felt himself relax just a bit.

All the major people in Ana's life knew. She must have called or texted her mother while she was still conscious.

Everything was going to be all right.

A quick look at the clock told him he'd been here for twenty-five minutes. It felt like twenty-five years.

Four weeks ago, he was minding his own business, out on

the common for the Memorial Day celebration, dragged into it by his mom.

Now he was sitting in a hospital waiting room while the woman he loved fought for her life, and her baby's life.

A month. One short month changed *everything*.

And now one short hour could, too.

Restless as hell, he stood and began pacing. No one else was in the little waiting area, so he found a rhythm, walking the perimeter of the room, trying to zone out.

Failing.

He went to the front desk again, waiting behind someone who wanted their parking validated. Finally, it was his turn.

"Is there any information on a patient named Ana DaSilva?"

"Have you been waiting here the entire time?" The desk clerk was a young woman with long, straight hair, the color of honey, with blue and pink streaks in it. She couldn't have been more than twenty.

"Yes."

A sad, sympathetic shrug was all he got as she fiddled with her eye glasses. "Then you haven't missed any updates. I'm sorry. I don't have control over any of this."

His phone rang. The number was new to him, but it had a Massachusetts area code.

"Hello?"

"Is this Dennis Luview?"

"Yes."

"This is Marian DaSilva Gianetti. Ana's mother."

"Hello! Sorry to meet under these circumstances."

"Do you know anything more? We're stuck in this hideous traffic at the New Hampshire border." She let out a teary huff.

"I'm sorry. I don't."

"Please tell me everything you *do* know."

"We were meeting for lunch at a restaurant on the wharf.

She called me to tell me her water broke, and she was bleeding. Someone had called 911. She was scared. Then a restaurant manager came on the phone and said she'd passed out and they were taking her to Maine Medical Center. Now I'm just waiting here."

"Oh, Lord."

"She called you?"

"She texted. It said, *Water broke. Bleeding. Going to Maine Medical Center in Portland.* That was it, that's all I knew until I called you. Brie gave me your number. She said you called Lucinda to get hers."

"I'm trying to be sure Ana has all the support she needs."

"Thank you so much, Dennis. Ana has been talking about you lately, and I knew we'd eventually meet, but I didn't think it would be in a waiting room. Did they say—is she—is the baby..?"

"No news at all."

"Ugh."

"Tell me about it. I'm here, though. I'll make sure she knows you're on your way if she wakes up before you arrive."

"Thank you. See you when we get there."

The call ended.

Knowing Ana had so many people who loved her made him happy.

The adrenaline faded out of his body and the caffeine did absolutely nothing to help, his limbs feeling like concrete. After protracted missions, he always crashed, and this was an area of concern.

Brie, Marian, Rick—they were all on their way.

He had to stay sharp.

And the doctors would come out at any moment with news, news that could go either way. More than two ways. So many possibilities, some of them horrifying to contemplate.

"Dennis Luview? For Ana DaSilva?"

Startled, he turned to find a petite woman staring at him, wearing scrubs and a surgical cap.

"Yes?"

"I'm Maren Horchance, one of the attendings in obstetrics. I'm here to give you an update. Your baby is now in the NICU."

"He's okay?"

"He's being monitored. We're not sure yet, but he's breathing on his own, which is always good."

"And Ana?"

"She's still in surgery. You're the father, correct?"

"Yes."

"Are you Ana's next of kin?"

"Ah, no, her mother is."

Dr. Horchance gave him a short nod. "I'll have more information for you when I know more. For now, just know that your son is alive and we're doing the best we can for him."

"Thank you."

Your baby. Your son.

The words ricocheted in his head, bouncing around until they turned into a ringing he wanted to shut off. The lie made sense because it gave him access to information, but the more he thought about it, the less of a falsehood it was.

He wanted to be this baby's father.

If Ana would let him.

Reaching for his phone, he tried to call Marian back. The call went straight to voicemail, so he composed a short text. Same deal with Brie—both of them must be either on the phone or stuck in cellular dead zones on the highway. He texted Brie as well, then closed his eyes and took a deep breath.

Jumping to his feet, he went to the information desk.

"Excuse me," he said to the attendant. "If a baby is in the NICU, can I visit?"

"Are you a parent?"

He nodded. "I'm the father."

"I'd have to check." She held up one finger. "Hold on. What's the name?"

"DaSilva."

If he couldn't be with Ana, he could be with the baby, which he knew with all his heart would make her happy.

As the attendant spoke on the phone, a burst of activity came from behind him.

"DENNIS!"

He turned around to find his mother and Luke, still in his red uniform.

"What the hell are you doing here?" he nearly shouted.

Deanna grabbed him in a fierce hug and he softened into her, grateful for his mother's love but flabbergasted she had made it to Portland in—what? Forty-five minutes? It was an eighty-mile drive.

"I called Lester at the Bethel airport. He found a helicopter tour guy willing to help out," Luke began to explain as Deanna fluffed her absolutely destroyed hair.

"You took a *helicopter* here?"

"Hardest part was getting here from the Portland airport. What's the update?"

"Baby's born. In the NICU. Ana's mother and stepdad are stuck in Saturday traffic from Mass. Same with her best friend."

"But they're all on their way?" Deanna asked, half hugging him.

"They are."

"Have you seen the baby?"

Just then, the attendant interrupted.

"Sir? Mr. Luview?"

"Yes?"

"You can't go into the NICU to see your son just yet, but soon."

Luke and Deanna's jaws dropped.

Before either of them said something stupid, Dennis replied, "Thank you. I can't wait."

Then he pulled them back to the small waiting room where he'd been earlier.

"'Your *son?*" Deanna asked.

"It was the only way to get information about Ana."

"Oh, sweetie," she said, hugging him again. "This is a lot. Any word on her?"

"No. And it's killing me."

Luke gave him a sympathetic look and asked, "That's your truck out there, isn't it? Parked by the curb?"

"Yep."

Luke held out his hand. "Give me the keys. I'll take care of it."

Dennis handed them over like a robot, unable to feel gratitude. Eventually, he would, but right now, he was a mess. Normally in complete command of his emotions for maximum efficiency, he was falling apart in pieces.

"Come here," Deanna said, urging him to sit. "Have you eaten?"

"I had coffee. We were about to have lunch when this happened."

"I'll get Luke to run out and grab us something. It could be a long wait."

"Why? Why would it be a long wait? She's had the baby. What else could they need to do to her that would take so long?"

"Honey," Deanna said, holding his hand. "I'm so sorry. It's hard when you're helpless in the face of someone you love so much being in crisis."

"No shit."

"I've never seen you like this."

"I've never *been* like this!"

His mom smiled. "You know, Denny, when you up and joined the Army, you broke my heart. I was happy that you were doing what you wanted to do, but you chose a life I would never, ever have chosen for any of my kids. I assumed you'd meet someone, get married, have kids, and all of it very, very far away from me. In my imagination, Dean and I would be on planes whenever we could to see your family, and the only way we'd have a relationship with your kids would be long distance."

"You imagined all that?"

"I did. But then it never happened. You didn't have long-term partners. No one we ever met, at least. No kids. You just... didn't. And I was so sad for you."

"Sad?"

"I wanted you to find love. To give and receive it. To feel in the marrow of your bones what it's like to be bonded to another soul, so deeply connected to them that you'd do anything for them." She patted his hand. "And now I see it in you. Took you longer than most, but you found it."

"I did. And so help me, Mom, if something bad happens to her–"

"Mr. Luview?" A doctor in scrubs appeared.

"Yes?"

He was tall, thin as a rail, and had kind brown eyes framed by long black lashes. "We can take you to see Paolo now."

"He–she named him?"

"Ms. DaSilva has been conscious enough to tell us her wishes. She identified you as the baby's father and gave us Paolo's name."

"She did?" He and Deanna exchanged glances.

"Are you ready to meet your son? You won't be able to touch him yet, but you can come to the NICU and see him."

"What about Ana?"

"I'm from the NICU, so I don't know."

Deanna grabbed his arm. "I'll be here in case there are updates."

"But her mom and stepdad are coming. And her best friend, Brie."

"I can spot a frantic mother and friend, Dennis. Go! When Ana is awake, she'll be comforted that you were with the baby. He needs someone who loves him to be with him."

"Right." Dennis pulled himself up straight. "Let's go."

The doctor smiled. "Congratulations. First child?"

Dennis just blinked as they strode toward the elevator.

"That's one way to put it."

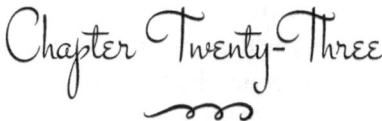

Chapter Twenty-Three

Ana

Grief stole her soul, then joy gave it right back.

Her baby was alive. Whole. Would be fine.

She was alive, would heal, could raise her perfect son.

But she'd lost the ability to give *this* man what he wanted.

More children.

"Oh, Ana," her mother said, holding her hand, rubbing her thumb joint over and over like it was a worry stone. "I'm so sorry."

"How's Paolo?"

"Dennis is with him. You told the hospital staff he was the father?"

"It seemed easier. And it meant Paolo wouldn't be— wouldn't be alone," she said, sobs taking over her words. Crying made her belly hurt, but this pain was worse than the absence of her baby or the surgical cut.

This was about losing so much more.

Like her uterus.

"You lost so much blood," her mother said softly. "The doctor said it was touch and go after they removed Paolo. The uterine rupture we were worried about happened, and was made worse by your condition."

"It hurt so much, Mom."

"I'll bet." She squeezed her hand. "We're just so thankful you're alive, Paolo is alive, and so far, so good. You're both healthy."

"I know I should be grateful. I *am* grateful," she whispered. "But..." Gesturing toward the pitcher on her tray, she asked for water.

Marian gave it to her. A few small sips from a straw felt good.

"I want to see Paolo."

"Dennis is with him. He's in the NICU. He's so tiny!" Her mom held up her phone. Dennis was texting pictures in a group chat with Marian, Ana, Brie, and Lucinda.

Ana's tears flowed freely. Her nipples tingled, a strange ache that made her cry harder.

"I want my baby." She shifted in bed, her legs like rubber bands.

"You can't walk yet, sweetie. The surgery and the anesthesia and the IV—"

"I want to hold him! Why can't I go in a wheelchair?"

Marian surprised her by crying, too, holding Ana's hand and pressing it to her face.

"I wish I could fix this for you. I do. But you're okay, and so is the baby. All I can do is tell you I love you, Ana. I was so scared we might lose you."

"I love you too, Mama." Using her old name for her mother tipped Marian into sobs, the two of them crying, Marian from relief.

Ana from grief.

After lots of tissues and a bit of time, Marian looked at her phone.

"Rick says he's talking to Dennis–he's back in the waiting room. He wants to see you."

"I want to see him, but Mom, how do I tell him?"

"He'll understand."

"I–"

"That man loves you, Ana. I don't know how you two found each other, but I've never met a man so driven. And Rick likes him! Do you know how rare that is? Rick hates everyone!"

Even Ana had to laugh at that, though it hurt her incision.

"Can I tell Rick to send Dennis up? He says I can go to the NICU and see Paolo now."

"Go. I'm fine."

"You're not fine."

"I'm–go. It's okay." Nothing was really okay, but this would have to do.

Marian leaned down and gave Ana the sweetest of kisses on her forehead. As she left the room, Dennis entered. Marian looked back and blew her another kiss.

"Hey, there," he said as he walked in, holding his phone toward her, showing a photo. "You made a beautiful baby. Here."

A tiny, red-faced cherub was in an incubator, a few electrodes on his body and a little oxygen tube near his nose.

"Is he–is he okay?"

"Three pounds, thirteen ounces. Not bad for just over thirty weeks. They say he needs to be in the NICU for a bit, maybe another two or three weeks. But so far, his lungs are good. They let me touch him, but not hold him."

Her nipples felt like someone attached electric wires to them, her eyes filling with tears.

"I want to hold him!"

"Soon, Ana," Dennis said, reaching for her as she cried. "Just a few more hours and we can find a way for you to see him. The nurse said something about expressing breastmilk, and something about... kangaroo care, I think? But the doctors are amazed he's as healthy as he is. You did a wonderful job, Ana. I'm so proud of you."

He leaned in to kiss her, but the peck on her cheek felt alien.

"Thanks." She didn't feel strong or worthy of praise.

She felt like a failure.

"My mom and brother are here, getting to know your mom and Rick. Brie is texting me, too. She's stuck behind some kind of accident near the Saco exit. But all the people who love you are pulling for you and Paolo." His eyes were so tender, so kind. "And thank you for saying I'm his father. It made such a difference to me."

"I hope you don't mind. I tried my best to make it easy for everyone. I texted my mother and told the EMTs your name."

"You've been through so much. But the worst is over. Now we do everything possible to help you recover and give Paolo the best possible chance."

Ana squeezed her eyes shut, awash in emotion.

"Dennis. There's something I have to tell you. Did Mom mention to you why my surgery took so long?"

"She said you wanted to explain something to me. What's going on?"

She let out a long sigh. "I–the bleeding. The reason it happened was uterine rupture."

"I gathered that."

"They couldn't stop it. The bleeding, I mean. And they had to–had to do a complete removal of my–of my uterus."

He stopped short, the look on his face so painful that Ana turned away, staring out the window and sobbing. Her body rose and fell, the stitches pulling.

"I can't have your baby," she said through sobs, shaking so hard, her tears making it look like she was living through an earthquake.

Which was emotionally true.

"Ana. *Ana*."

She stayed turned away from him.

"You're breaking my heart. I can't handle seeing you in this kind of pain."

He moved around the bed. She closed her eyes, tears pooling at the bridge of her nose and dropping at a steady rate onto the sheet.

"Look at me." When she did, she saw his exhaustion. His worry. The last few hours had taken its toll on him, too.

And now this. The end of an imagined future.

He pointed to the door. "Paolo."

"What about him?"

"You already *had* my baby, as far as I'm concerned. I want to be *that* baby's father, if you'll let me."

"It's not the same."

"Yes. It is. It is if we say it is. I love you. I know the world thinks it's too fast, but I don't. On my timeline, it's taken far, far too long. I love you, Ana. I love Paolo, even though we've barely met, and only through a window and with one finger touch."

She laughed through her tears, the sniffle at the end one of disbelief.

And hope.

He squeezed her hand, those beautiful eyes focused on her like she was nothing but love.

"If you'll have me, I'm all in. One hundred percent."

"I don't think you know how to live any other way, Dennis."

"I don't know how to *love* any other way."

"It's easy to say all of this now, at the height of emotions and trauma. I know how this works. You feel this way in the moment, but–"

"Don't tell me how I feel. I know what I want. I want you. I want Paolo. I want us to be a family. Together."

"You said–the last time we were together, at my place, you said you wanted more children."

"So did you."

"I said if I could have them."

"Right."

"But Dennis, I *can't* have more. I'm so lucky I was even able to have Paolo."

"And I'm lucky to have you. So lucky. Both of you."

"Dennis…"

"I need you to hear me, Ana. *Really* hear me. Not with your ears, with your heart. You may be all about the gray areas, the undefined, but I'm not. This is black and white for me. I love you. I love Paolo. I want to be his father. Your hysterectomy only concerns me because it causes you so much pain. Everything else we can figure out, because I love you so much that the sheer force of my love will carry us."

She turned back to him, his eyes shining with… tears?

"Telling the EMTs you were the father came so naturally."

"Good!"

"And it's what I want," she confessed. "I wish I could go back in time and make you his biological father. But I can't."

"This is close enough, Ana. Just say yes."

"Yes!"

His kiss was sweet, not too hard, not too polite. Exhaustion and overwhelm swirled all around her, but so did love.

So much love.

"I love you, Ana. I knew it the second I saw you on the common in your gorgeous sundress dress. I love Paolo, and I knew it the second I saw him in the NICU."

"I love you, too."

Another kiss.

Then a knock on the door made them turn.

It was Brie, holding an enormous bouquet of flowers with three giant mylar balloons attached, openly crying.

She put the bouquet on a table, then plunked down a big bag of red foil chocolate hearts, which made Ana start laughing, Dennis joining in.

"Is there room for the honorary aunt in this lovefest?" she asked as she made her way to Ana's bed, arms outstretched, smelling like lavender and cheese.

There was.

Because there was always room for more love.

Epilogue

Ana

"I have climbed the outsides of seven-story buildings. Parachuted into rain forests. Taken on six assailants with my bare hands and won," he whispered to a deeply amused Ana over the baby's head. "None of that prepared me for this."

He pointed to Paolo, then touched his back.

"My back is killing me," he grumbled.

"The sling makes him fall asleep."

"Shhhh," he said as softly as possible, Paolo's little eyelids losing their fight with gravity. Watching her big, strapping partner sway with her son's breath made her smile even more, a hopeful lightness filling her chest.

Colic turned out to be the bane of their existence.

Dennis's cottage was adorable and quiet, so silent compared to her condo in Newburyport. For the last two months, since Paolo had come home from the hospital and they'd settled in, Dennis had come to her.

This was their first foray north, and other than a two-hour car ride filled with fifteen minutes of full-throated screaming at the end, it had been fine.

Frustrating, but fine.

Because Paolo wouldn't sleep.

And if he didn't sleep, Dennis and Ana had no time alone. Time they desperately needed, with an emphasis on the frustrated part.

The *horny*, frustrated part.

At this point, she'd settle for a quickie against a wall, which was how they'd had sex the last time, back at her place. Being physically intimate had proven to be a journey through rough terrain as she healed from her surgery and juggled a colicky NICU baby.

Now, as her little boy developed chubby thighs, and Dennis soothed him to sleep, she began to see a smoother road ahead.

A smoother, hopefully orgasmic road.

Dennis's hand went in the air, waving at her, then pointing to the portable crib in the corner of his living room. She nodded with an enthusiastic thumbs' up, her body going warm and wet on the spot.

It was happening.

They were finally – *finally!* – about to have a nice, long time for sex.

Baby nap gods be willing.

Recovering from the emergency c-section and losing so much blood had been harder than expected, and Ana still wasn't back to her full functioning self. Dennis split his time between working with his father and in Newburyport, sleeping over at her place three nights a week. Brie took one night and her mother took three during those first two months, but now she had the baby on more of a schedule, breastfeeding was going fine, and she needed less help.

But not less of Dennis.

Dennis's cottage was adorable, if rough. He'd shown it to her in plenty of Facetime videos, but this was the first time she'd been in it. The kitchen was lovely, renovated with lumber from the trees on site, with all-new appliances. All of the walls in the second bedroom were torn down to stubs, and the bathroom shower didn't work, so he'd been using his parents' bathroom as he remodeled.

The bones were there. Strong, good bones. Once he was done with the work, it was going to be beautiful.

And now there was talk of adding an addition.

Tiptoeing into the kitchen, she poured a small coffee for herself, cooling it with a splash of milk, drinking it faster than she did before having a baby. Everything had to be done quickly, while she had a chance.

Including sex.

Babies were sneaky that way. Just when you thought they were down for a nice, hour-long nap, they tricked you and woke up, instantly destroying your plans.

Movement caught her eye and she turned to see her big, muscular boyfriend coming out of the living room, arms raised in victory, big biceps bulging with triumph as he shook his fists high. Grinning madly, he swooped in for a kiss as she swallowed fast.

"I have defeated the colic. The sexfest can commence."

"Last time we tried, he woke up within seven minutes."

"It's been so long I only need three." He began kissing her neck, hands cupping her breasts, pushing against her with a knee between her legs.

"Three?"

"Two if you stop looking at me like that. So judgey." His hand went between her legs, her pulse migrating to where his fingertips played.

"Dennis."

"I want you so much."

"*Dennis.*"

"Mmm?"

She plucked the infant carrier still strapped around his midsection. "This is not sexy."

"What if I use it to tie you up?"

She gave him a hard stare.

"I doubt," he said as he unclicked the various fasteners and tossed it onto a kitchen chair, "the next Magic Mike movie includes that in one of their dance routines."

Before she could reply, his mouth was on hers and he was leaning her back on the dining table, a long farmhouse slab of wood with an unfinished edge, gorgeous in its natural state.

And perfect for a little mid-afternoon delight.

He unbuckled his belt, unzipped himself and she pulled off her panties, thrilled to be wearing a skirt. It only took a few seconds but he was in her, her legs wrapped around him, the gentle but obvious tug of her c-section scar not so much painful as reminding her it existed.

"Oh, you're so warm. So wet. So good," he groaned against her neck, each thrust making her orgasm grow, the need to have him in her almost feral. Only in the last few weeks had her body began to resemble anything she could call "normal" for her, and her sex drive had decided to roar back just this week.

Her fingers dug into his back, gripping hard, as he thrust again and her head hit something on the dining table. Not caring, she pushed back against him, shifting the angle slightly so that oh–

"Oh! Oh!" she cried out as he groaned her name, pushing hard inside her until her head hit the thing again and –

CRASH!

"No!" he hissed, hard and fierce, looking over her head. "Sugar bowl! Broken."

"Keep going!" she hissed back, but it was too late.

"WAHHHHHHHHHHHH!"

His hips moved one more time inside her, but she was already struggling to sit up, nipples tingling, and not from the sex.

"Damn," he grunted as he pulled out. "So close."

She stood, straightening her skirt, as a sudden rap on the door made them both leap out of their skin.

"Denny? Ana? You okay? I heard something crash in there."

His mom.

Dennis closed his eyes and looked like he was expending every ounce of energy to avoid committing murder.

"You get the door. I'll get the baby."

"I'll carry my blue balls out to the wood shed in a sac," he muttered.

"Just think of it as edging," she whispered, giving his ass a love pat.

"That does not help," he replied through gritted teeth.

"I'll get Paolo back to sleep and you get Deanna to leave."

"One of those is easier than the other," he said in a resigned tone that told Ana her job was going to be the simpler one.

As she reached the port-a-crib and picked up a red-faced Paolo, reaching under her shirt to help him latch on, Dennis opened the door to his mother.

And Ana realized this was it.

This was life.

And it was more than she ever could have dreamed of.

THE END

Bonus Epilogue

Dennis

"And here he is as a three year old, learning to ice skate," his mom said, pointing to an old, slightly fuzzy picture. "He was so fast it was hard to get a clear shot!"

Ana sat on one side of his mother, Dennis on the other, as his dad stood behind the couch, drinking coffee and looking through the old albums. Paolo nursed in Ana's arms. It was the day after Christmas, and Ana's mother and stepfather were on their way for a two-night visit, staying in the rustic guest cottage Kell had been working on with Moore.

Thankfully, the snow was cooperating, the roads clear enough for Ana's family to get through.

"Three?" Ana gave him a skeptical look. "The only reason to teach a kid that young is hockey."

"Dennis was a defender for the Luview High School team!"

"No way," Ana said looking over his mother's lap at him. "You've never said a word!"

"You never asked me to play."

She stuck out her tongue at him. "I have rubber bands that masquerade as ankles."

"You'll do fine." He looked at the baby. "We can get him in a learn-to-skate program when he's three, too."

"Hockey is so brutal!" Ana hissed, instantly earning bewildered glares from all three Luviews.

"What?" Deanna blurted out.

"Uh, I mean, that would be wonderful for Paolo to learn such a fine skill so young," she backtracked.

"Dennis was scouted his junior year. Could have gone through junior league and who knows," Dean said, giving Dennis a well-worn look that said Dean wanted to have known. Wanted a son who played professional hockey.

Wanted to be the father of the next Cale Makar.

"Dad," Dennis grumbled. "You say that all the time, but it's not true."

"It is true! Those Canadian scouts weren't kidding. They hounded us for a while, especially after that Hat Trick against – "

As he argued, his mom continued turning pages, Ana making appreciative sounds. The scent of his dad's coffee made Dennis want some, too, so he went into the kitchen, Dean on his heels.

"You know Luview had a kid make it to the junior leagues in Croatia? Couple years ago. Might get recruited by the NHL."

"That's nice, Dad." Dennis poured from the half-full pot.

"You nervous?" Dean asked.

"About what?"

"Her parents."

"Should I be? I've met them plenty of times."

"It's different when they come and stay overnight. Everything changes. Gets more serious."

"We're already serious. This is just about making sure you

and mom get along with Marian and Rick." Dennis shot Dean one of his father's winks. "You're the one who should be nervous."

"Oh, hell. No one told it to me like that," Dean replied, pretending to be alarmed. "Maybe I should have at least showered. Brushed my teeth."

Ana made the strangest sound from the other room, instantly activating Dennis's protective radar.

"What's wrong?" he said as he hurried in, holding his coffee. Ana and Deanna looked at each other in shock.

"No!" Deanna said.

"Yes!" Ana pressed her index finger into the scrapbook, tapping it repeatedly, her long ponytail brushing against the page.

"Impossible!"

"It's right there, Deanna!" Ana looked at him, her jaw dropped. "Dennis! We met when we were kids!"

"What?"

She was pointing to a newspaper clipping from the Boston Globe, the paper faded under the clear plastic wrap on the page. The little girl in the picture always cracked him up, her eyes crossed, tongue sticking out as he accidentally dumped chocolate hearts from the tray on her laughing father.

"What do you mean, we met? That's a picture of me working at Love You Chocolate. My first year working there. I was fourteen."

"That's you?" Ana shouted. "Deanna said you're the person in the heart costume, standing right behind me and my father."

"You and your *father*? Ana, what are you talking about?"

Deanna rose, holding the book so she could read it.

"Gloucester, Mass. businessman and his seven-year-old daughter visit Love You Chocolate in 'Love You' Maine for a sweet taste of western Maine fun."

Dennis damn near dropped his coffee.

"That picture is famous around here! It's hanging in Lucinda's store!" Dean said, moving behind Deanna, looking over his shoulder, eyes bouncing from Ana to the book.

"I know! We have a copy in my scrapbooks at home. My father wouldn't give them our names, so they printed that as the caption."

"Hold on," Dennis said slowly. "You're telling me that twenty-right years ago, we *met*?"

"Photographic evidence is clear, Den," his dad declared. "You two really are meant for each other."

"Auntie must have known all along!" Ana said, breathless.

"I don't think so," Deanna mused. "When it all happened back then, everyone was in a tizzy. But that was a long time ago. Most people have forgotten that was Dennis. And the only place that displays that clipping is Love You Chocolate."

"That was the one and only time I've ever worn one of those stupid costumes, too. You have any idea how much teasing I got at school after that?" Dennis groused.

"Is that when you soured on the town?" Deanna asked, suddenly serious. "Because of a bunch of teasing?"

"Maybe." He refrained from saying anything else by drinking more coffee.

"My father loved that photo. Thought it was hilarious. I'll bet he shook your hand that day. He was so gregarious, and loved meeting new people." Ana's mouth began to quiver as she looked at all three of them, then the baby. "He would have been so happy that I found you. You would have all loved him."

Dennis set his coffee down and moved to the couch, wrapping his arm around her shoulders, hugging her.

"I have wished I could have met him since we got together, and now it turns out I did. I might not remember him, but I like to think that there's a reason for all this."

Paolo's eyes fluttered as he finished nursing, his splayed hand reaching up. Dennis gave him a pinkie finger to hold.

The kid hung on for dear life.

"Fate," Dennis whispered in her ear. "Lucinda said she just knew when she met Donald. Dad and Mom tell me all the time they just knew."

"It feels so easy now. With you. Like it really is fate." She let out a sniffle, then a small laugh. "Maybe I need to believe in magic more."

"Speaking of," Dean said as they all heard Harriet shriek outside. "Looks like Magic escaped from Harriet again."

Dennis groaned. "Am I going to have to go out there and get him out from the flower box?"

Dean chuckled. "She's a good little pet owner. Let her figure it out."

"Some grandpa you are!" Deanna chided him. "She's ten!"

"When I was ten I was chopping a half cord of wood alone in the woods behind the house!" Dennis complained.

Ana squeezed his arm. "And it shows."

"You're welcome," Dean said to her with a wink.

As they all laughed, another sound caught Dennis's attention, this one sending joy through his blood. Ana moved the baby into an upright position and as she did, he giggled, a joyous sound like laughter being set loose from a bottle.

"Oh, my goodness!" Ana cried out. "He's giggling! He's so happy!"

Radiant smile across his face, Dennis's son laughed some more, the whole crew enthralled.

Something in Dennis relaxed a bit more, his heart full.

Maybe – just maybe – living in the 'love-liest' town on earth wasn't so bad after all.

Heart costumes and all.

What's Next?

The "Love You, Maine" series featuring the four Luview family siblings is now completed (600,000 words! Whew!), but don't you worry — we're not even CLOSE to being done with the world of Luview, Maine.

When I started this series, my goal was to create a small town devoted to love, where the very fabric of everyone's existence was focused on the *business* of love, as well as creating love in a community full of acceptance and affirmation.

Though I'm writing about a small town in western Maine, this is a big world, with more series coming. Next up:

The Love You Handymen series, featuring the Forsythe family, who run Love You Hand(y) Jobs, Inc.

Get ready for a different viewpoint of Love You, Maine, from the perspective of a rough-and-tumble family. While they're quite different from the Luviews, they're no less charming, dealing with second chance love, enemies-to-lovers relationships, and so much more.

Why a handyman series?

Because their hands fix *everything*. ;)

Stay tuned for upcoming titles LOVE YOU WOOD

GUY, LOVE YOU FIRE GUY, and LOVE YOU PLOW GUY.

Hop on my newsletter mailing list at jkentauthor.com/newsletter to make sure you get an email from me when the new books launch!

And thank you so much for reading my world set in the "love-list" town on Earth. I hope it's been as much fun to read as it is to write. <3

About the Author

New York Times and *USA Today* bestselling author Julia Kent writes romantic comedy with an edge. Since 2013, she has sold more than 2 million books, with 4 New York Times bestsellers and more than 21 appearances on the USA Today bestseller list. Her books have been translated into French, Italian, and German, with more titles releasing in the future.

From billionaires to BBWs to new adult rock stars, Julia finds a sensual, goofy joy in every contemporary romance she writes. Unlike Shannon from *Shopping for a Billionaire*, she did not meet her husband after dropping her phone in a men's room toilet (and he isn't a billionaire in a rom com).

She lives in New England with her husband and children in a household where everyone but Julia lacks the gene to change empty toilet paper rolls.

Join her newsletter at http://www.jkentauthor.com

Also by Julia Kent

Fluffy

Perky

Feisty

Hasty

In Your Dreams

Her Billionaires

It's Complicated

Completely Complicated

It's Always Complicated

Eternally Complicated

Random Acts of Crazy

Random Acts of Trust

Random Acts of Fantasy

Random Acts of Hope

Randomly Acts of Yes

Random Acts of Love

Random Acts of LA

Random Acts of Christmas

Random Acts of Vegas

Random Acts of New Year

Random Acts of Baby

Maliciously Obedient

Suspiciously Obedient

Deliciously Obedient

Christmasly Obedient

Our Options Have Changed (with Elisa Reed)

Thank You For Holding (with Elisa Reed)